HIGH PRAISE FOR SHIRL HENKE

Deep as the Rivers

"You can always trust Shirl Henke to give you a great read!"
—*Romantic Times*

"*Deep as the Rivers* . . . is historical romance at its best."
—*Affaire de Coeur*

Bride of Fortune

"Delicious, exciting, innovative and colorful!"
—*Affaire de Coeur*

"Shirl Henke always delivers a top-notch romance, and *Bride of Fortune* is Shirl at her best." —*Romantic Times*

"Shirl Henke weaves a spell as rich with details as the splendid era she portrays. Mysterious, sensual, heart-wrenching, with an ending that will leave you breathless, *Bride of Fortune* has it all!" —*The Literary Times*

More . . .

Deep As The Rivers

SHIRL HENKE

St. Martin's Paperbacks

DEEP AS THE RIVERS

Copyright © 1997 by Shirl Henke.

Photo of author by Ocasio.

ISBN: 0-312-96011-5

Printed in the United States of America

St. Martin's Paperbacks edition/March 1997

10 9 8 7 6 5 4 3 2 1

For Carmine V. DelliQuadri, Jr., D.O.
who's mighty handy with a gun or a knife!

The Missouri was a river to make strong men
weep and rich men poor.
—Richard Edward Oglesby

Even God dare not cross the Mississippi.
—Time-Life *The Trailblazers*

Deep As The Rivers

∽ *Chapter 1* ∽

Colonel Samuel Sheridan Shelby finished off the dregs of his brandy and peered at himself in the Girondole looking glass hanging over the mantel. It felt odd to be in uniform again. He ran his fingers through long, shaggy black hair. It wanted barbering. Tish would be upset, saying he looked more like a backwoods ruffian than an officer of the United States Army, but since returning from his mission this morning, he had little time for the niceties of civilization. He had spent the afternoon meeting with President Madison and his secretary of war, William Eustis. Shelby rubbed his eyes tiredly and blinked, girding himself for the ugly scene to come.

"Perhaps if we'd had children, things might have been better," he mused aloud, taking a sip of brandy as he paced across the Aubusson carpet that graced the drawing room of his Washington home.

Letitia had conceived within the first months of their marriage but lost the babe shortly thereafter. Now Samuel strongly suspected she had taken an abortifacient to rid herself of the unwanted burden. As soon as President Jefferson had sent word to him about the miscarriage, he had rushed home from his assignment in Canada to find her holding court from her bedchamber.

Richard Bullock had been at her side, of course. Her stepbrother had glared at him hostilely, as if getting a child on his own wife made Samuel responsible for the miscarriage. Letitia had looked amazingly well in spite of the ordeal, with silver gilt ringlets artfully coiled about her shoulders and the blush of excited laughter staining her ivory cheeks. All traces of merriment had been instantly erased as she reached out to him with a theatrical sob while her huge amber eyes filled with tears.

When Richard had ushered the other callers from the room, she had clung to Samuel saying that she could not bear the pain and the loss, that she never wanted to carry another child beneath her heart. At the time he had ascribed her outburst to the ordeal she'd just suffered, but as the months stretched into years, Tish had kept her resolve. He'd found the sponges and the vial of pungent liquid in which she soaked them and knew she employed them to prevent conception.

After several years of marriage, Samuel became grateful that he had never succeeded in giving her a baby. A child would only be a pawn she could use to manipulate him, a victim of its parents' stark enmity.

Tish was at her dressmakers, being outfitted for the ball at Senator Downey's tonight. She never missed a Washington gala, with or without him. Richard was always her escort in her husband's absence. Because they had been raised as brother and sister, no one remarked on it. *Tish would never do anything to cause gossip.* Grimly, he anticipated her rage when he confronted her.

As he had ridden through the sweltering humidity of the swampy Florida backcountry, he had mulled over what to do about the shambles of his life, as Elkhanah Shelby had done a generation earlier. But his father had been blessed enough to have his impossible French wife quietly leave him and return to Paris. Would that Tish might give up so easily. Samuel knew she never would. There would be tears and temper tantrums, threats and thrown hairbrushes. He laughed mirthlessly, thinking of how he had believed he could avoid the volatile temper of his mother by choosing a gently reared daughter of the Virginia aristocracy for a wife. Letitia Annabelle Soames had seemed so demure and malleable when they met.

Sighing for past mistakes would avail nothing. Neither would getting coshed, he thought with disgust, firmly replacing the stopper on the crystal brandy decanter. Bleakly he looked down at the faceted crystal glittering in his hand. Waterford, imported by Tish's father all the way from Ireland. Much of the beautifully appointed mahogany furniture had been shipped from the workshop of Duncan Phyfe in New York. The whole lavish house had been bought and paid for with Soames money.

"God save me from rich women," he muttered as the clatter of horses' hooves sounded in the courtyard outside: Tish returning from her dressmaker, with Richard carrying her finery in a tower of beribboned boxes. Their laughter echoed from the foyer where a tall case clock struck the hour. Then he heard Tobias say, "Mastah Samuel's returned, mistress. He's in the parlor."

After a flurry of leave-taking from Richard, Tish opened the door and swept into the room. No one had perfected the art of the grand entry more impressively than Letitia Soames Shelby, not even the incomparable Dolley Madison. Tish's amber eyes flashed as they glided over him from head to foot and back. She stood poised just inside the door with one small beringed hand at her slender white throat. Pale golden curls were piled high on her head, peeping out from the brim of the ruby silk bonnet which matched her day gown of rich velvet trimmed with jet buttons.

"I . . . I didn't expect you for several weeks, Samuel darling," she said coolly as she took rapid inventory of his dress uniform and unattended hair while deftly removing her bonnet and fluffing her own gleaming curls.

"The situation in British Florida heated up unexpectedly. I had to report to the president."

"Will there be war then?" she inquired, swishing over to press her lips to his, then tilting her head up to gaze measuringly at his expression.

He looked down at her with a cynical gleam in his eyes. "You don't give a damn if the United States goes to war against Britain—or Napoleon's whole bloody army."

"No, but I do see the opportunities for a colonel to become a general if he applies for the right duty assignment during the conflict and distinguishes himself," she said, brushing a speck of lint from the shoulder of his uniform with wifely propriety.

He removed her hand firmly. "We've had this conversation a thousand times, Tish. It avails us nothing." His voice was level and cold.

She snatched her hand away and stamped her foot. "Only because you're too stubborn to see the future! Don't you realize with a few military honors to your credit my father could pass along his senate seat to you—even place you in the White House? Your family name and mine combined are unbeatable—Virginia's finest, far better than that paltry Madison's with his Philadelphia Quaker for a wife. She's a nobody."

"That 'nobody' is the most brilliant hostess and beloved lady in the nation. You'll never supplant her," Samuel said sharply.

"Only because you insist on skulking around out of uniform like a common criminal, doing the dirty work for Jefferson and Madison while they get all the glory!"

"There's little enough glory in being president and more than enough grief. I serve my country best doing what I've become good at, which is not a topic open for further debate, Tish."

Sensing his tightly leashed anger and seeing the darkening glitter in his eyes, Tish decided to change tactics. She swayed closer to him, lowering her lashes and nuzzling her lips against his throat as she embraced him. "Don't let us quarrel on your first night home, darling. I'm every so sorry I was cross." She brushed her full breasts against his chest, then turned quickly away and began to unfasten the long row of jet buttons on her gown, revealing the milky white smoothness of her skin. "Lock the parlor door, Samuel," she said in a husky voice. "We have not done this in far, far too long."

"No. It's no good, Tish." He turned away from her and stared out the floor-length window at the stark outlines of the "wilderness capital" as European wags had dubbed the District of Columbia. Rows of two- and three-story brick houses were scattered helter-skelter across the tidal basin swampland, sitting between tangles of elderberry bushes and quack grass. Tree stumps stood up in bare clusters like ugly gashes, raw and new as the city itself.

Tish came up soundlessly behind him and looked at the silhouette of the Senate and House of Congress which dominated the north shore of the Potomac. The pale buff stone building that housed the president was visible from the opposite side of their house. She could picture the White House in her mind's eye as she slipped her dress from her shoulders and let it fall to the carpet. "I've been thinking of you, Samuel . . . missing you, darling." Her voice wheedled as she tugged playfully at his arm, turning him to face her. She wore a French lace corset that pushed her large breasts up to overflow across the top in bounteous splendor. Their rigid nipples were visible through the sheer pink silk of her camisole.

He stood in amazement as she reached up and began to unfasten the buttons on his uniform. "You're incredible, you know, really incredible. The day I left for Florida you were screaming like a fishwife that you hoped the Seminoles would cut my throat or the British would stand me against a wall and shoot me. You've banned me from your bed for nearly two years, and now you try to seduce me as if nothing at all were amiss. Such a loving wife." He tsked in mock irony.

"No matter what else is between us, you always liked it well enough in bed, Samuel," she said with a pout, undeterred.

"So I did, Tish," he replied with a self-deprecating chuckle. "But a man has to stop thinking with what's between his legs sooner or later."

"Don't be vulgar, Samuel," she snapped back, suddenly reverting to the role of haughty Virginia belle, a pose difficult to maintain while standing half-dressed in front of the parlor window.

"We have to talk, my dear . . . seriously. I suggest you slip back into that fetching little frock and have a seat. I'll pour us a drink. I think before this is done we'll both need it."

Olivia St. Etienne reclined against the plush maroon velvet upholstery of the carriage, listening to its wheels roll rhythmically along the dirt roads of the capital toward the Phelps mansion, which was located several miles south of the city high on the Potomac bluffs. Uncle Emory's voice droned on about all the eligible men who would be at the Phelps ball, ticking off their property holdings, social connections, political influence, even now and again mentioning whether or not they were young or handsome.

"I say, my dear, are you attending me?" Emory Wescott asked with a hint of irritation roughening his voice.

"Certainly, Uncle," she replied dutifully even though she was not and he was not really her uncle, but rather her guardian, a wealthy patron who had befriended her parents.

"I was explaining that Royal Burton will be at the Phelps gathering tonight. He's one of the wealthiest merchants in Boston, a good solid Federalist. And he's just past his year's mourning for his dear wife, Credelia. A fine figure of a man."

"I shall endeavor to be most gracious to Mr. Burton, Uncle," Olivia said, smoothing the folds of her new emerald silk gown.

Emory snorted roughly. "Gracious, is it? And that's all— cool and gracious and damned off-putting. You have the most accursedly proper way of handling yourself—a hoyden at the racetrack, but all the proper lady when you're around suitors."

"I don't mean to be ungrateful, Uncle Emory. You know how much I appreciate your taking me in when my parents died. I don't know what I should've done if not for you."

"But you don't choose to wed any of the eligibles I present to you—even the cream of the nation's capital here."

"Is that why you insisted I accompany you to Washington again?" Some imp made her add, "Or was it perhaps because of the big race at The Elms this weekend?"

"No use trying to change the subject at hand. Gypsy Lady will win with or without you," Emory said snappishly as the curricle pulled into the circular driveway of the Phelps mansion.

Rayburn Phelps was the richest planter in Virginia. If his neighbors had suffered under the late trade embargo, he apparently was quite unaffected by any financial reverses. It was rumored in some circles in Washington that he had secret ties to the British and was able to smuggle his contraband cotton under the protection of the Royal Navy. Olivia had always wondered if her guardian and Phelps had any business dealings, but she did not know. In fact, she knew very little about how Emory Wescott made his money, other than by wagering on horses, which although lucrative, could hardly account for his considerable fortune.

A servant assisted Emory down from the curricle and he adjusted his satin waistcoat over his thickening middle as Olivia alighted. With a thatch of iron gray hair and a meticulously barbered beard, he was an imposing figure of a man. But his most arresting feature was the chilly gray gaze with which he assessed people. Turning it on Olivia, he inspected her with a swift glance of approval before he offered his arm. They strolled sedately across the flagstone walk and ascended the impressive marble steps to the huge front porch with twenty-foot-tall wooden pillars dwarfing its occupants.

"You'll be receiving a good deal of attention tonight—not only from Royal Burton. Look around, fill up your dance card and evaluate all the eligible men in the room. I daresay one I'd approve should take your fancy."

"I shall dance every dance and flirt outrageously, Uncle Emory," Olivia said, trying to generate some enthusiasm although she felt none.

"See that you dance. As to the flirting, have a care for your reputation," he intoned sternly.

Emory Wescott wanted her married off. She hated being a burden to a busy man who had spent his life traveling the length and breadth of North America pursuing his interests without the encumbrance of a young female of marriageable age. But she could not bear the thought of marrying someone simply to escape the unpleasant circumstances under which she presently lived.

Marriage should be for love and laughter, for the joyous companionship her parents had shared, not merely a soulless financial arrangement. But her guardian had been generous in spite of his brusque, chilly manner, outfitting her as handsomely as any pampered debutante in Philadelphia or Boston. She had tried to repay that generosity by working with his horses. However, his dearest wish was to arrange an advantageous match with a man who was not only wealthy but politically influential.

General Phelps, who still clung to his old army rank a generation after retirement, stood with his tall gaunt wife, Maude, at the head of the receiving line. Olivia and her guardian stepped into the ballroom after giving their cloaks to servants in the front foyer. The room, like all of the house, reflected the Phelpses' love of formal display. Two huge crystal chandeliers filled with hundreds of fine spermaceti candles illuminated its vast proportions. The puncheon floor, made of ash and waxed to a brilliant luster, reflected and magnified the light.

An orchestra composed of slaves played Mozart from a raised dais in the back of the room and various other household servants scurried through the crowd of laughing guests, serving delicate pastries along with wine and spirits. Rows of shield-backed chairs were placed at discreet intervals along the walls and in the alcoves screened by huge Egyptian urns filled with palms and ornamental trees.

Olivia and Emory wended their way through the receiving line making polite conversation with their host and hostess and various other acquaintances among the guests. It has been Olivia's observation that Emory Wescott had many acquaintances but no friends. She had often wondered how the spartan New Englander and her profligate French father had ever become so close. Perhaps that unusual bond explained why he had undertaken her guardianship.

As soon as they stepped onto the ballroom's polished floor Royal Burton materialized out of the crowd. "I say, Emory, is this the enchanting young ward you spoke of?" he inquired in a nasal New England twang that grated on Olivia's ears.

Used to the graceful cadence of her native French and the lilt of Italian that she had grown up with, Olivia found aristocratic British English and the modulated smoothness of Virginia Tidewater accents to be pleasant. But the harsh speech of Kaintucks and Yankees was decidedly the opposite. Burton looked as unprepossessing as his accent. He was cadaverously thin with a shallow pockmarked face. She supposed he did have his own teeth and a fine head of heavy light brown hair, neatly clubbed with a black satin ribbon.

She smiled and curtsied as her guardian performed introductions. Just then the orchestra struck up a sweeping waltz and Burton took her hand, drawing her onto the floor. He was a surprisingly graceful dancer in spite of his gangly appearance, but he held her closer than was appropriate and his breath reeked of whiskey when he leaned down to speak.

"You were born in France, Mademoiselle St. Etienne. Yet you have scarcely a trace of the accent."

"My parents became émigrés as soon as the revolution began." She omitted the small detail of their elopement and her mother's disinheritance. "I grew up traveling from country to country. Much of my childhood was spent in various Italian states, then England. We came to America when I was fourteen, so you see, learning foreign languages has become second nature to me."

He chuckled. "Quite an experienced traveler for one of such tender years. You spoke of parents yet Emory Wescott is your guardian."

She suspected he was probing in the hope of gaining an admission about how much she owed her guardian. "My parents were killed when the carriage they were riding in overturned. I was left completely alone in the world but for my father's friend Monsieur Wescott."

"And you are most suitably grateful for his kindness, are you not?" he purred.

She stiffened and would have frozen in midstep but the music ended. "My feelings for Uncle Emory do not concern you, Monsieur Burton," she said frostily, making a slight curtsy and spinning away in the press of the crowd.

That blackmailing old cur! She did not care if he were as rich as the Emperor Napoleon. He was manipulative and sly and his breath reeked. She would not be bought like some piece of merchandise to be an old man's trophy. Surely there was someone young and handsome, filled with charm and laughter who could win her heart as *Père* had won *Maman's*. She vowed to begin her search in earnest tonight before her guardian forced the issue with someone as unpleasant as Royal Burton. *If only I could trust my own judgment.*

She had adored her frivolous, thrill seeking parents and they in turn had quite outrageously indulged her. Olivia knew her mother had perhaps chosen unwisely in Julian St. Etienne. Indeed, when they arrived in New Orleans, her own brother Charles had turned them away, just as the rest of her family in France had done when they wed. Although Olivia's father was a gambler and a wastrel, he was sunny and charming, utterly devoted to his two *belles filles* as he called them. Their life had been one of feast or famine, high living one week, sneaking out of a hotel's back door the next when *Père's* luck at the gaming tables deserted him.

Olivia had loved the adventure. She would probably be smitten with someone just as unsuitable and reckless as her father. Perhaps that was why she had resisted the idea of marriage thus far. She looked around the room, quickly inventorying the young men who returned her perusal with favor. Olivia had never wanted for male attention since she turned fourteen. She smiled at a towheaded young naval officer who blushed furiously as he returned her gaze.

Samuel Shelby was in a foul humor as he handed his cloak to the butler and strode across the foyer. He detested Rayburn Phelps almost as much as he loathed the endless rounds of glittering social events that every politically ambitious man in the capital had to attend. And every woman. Tish adored the whirl of parties. Tonight she was no doubt dancing and flirting at Senator Downey's ball, escorted by her lapdog Richard.

Samuel was at the Phelpses' gala to meet Don Luis de Onís y Gonzalez, the man the Spanish government in exile had appointed ambassador to the United States three years earlier. Onís had indicated to Shelby that his government might be amenable to financing a filibustering expedition in Louisiana Territory. Since the Spanish loyalists were decidedly short of cash at present, it was Samuel's job to learn if British sterling stood behind the offer. Also to get the names of any agents who were engaged in subverting American territorial interests on the frontier.

His eyes searched the room, looking for the Spaniard's slim imperious figure, always resplendent in satin cutaway coat and old-fashioned knee breeches and hose. Just as they alighted on Onís, they skimmed past a flash of brilliant fire red, a woman's hair. Intrigued in spite of his preoccupation, Samuel found himself returning to study the lady in the exquisite gown of emerald silk. It was cut in the latest fashion, high-waisted with a low, rounded neckline that revealed the slight swell of creamy breasts and gentle undulation of slim hips and long legs. The soft whispery sheerness of the fabric emphasized her slender figure to perfection. She was tall for a female, a bit out of fashion in an era that prized flamboyant voluptuousness—but the flaming glow of that heavy hair was flamboyant enough in itself. Again, not the fashionable thing. Dark hair like Dolley's was all the rage now or his wife's fair blondness. But that striking mane glowed beneath the chandeliers like living flame, wild and vibrant in contrast to the deep richness of her dark green dress. She drew admiring glances from men and envious glares from women around the room as her musical laughter floated on the warm air, soft as a serenade.

Samuel observed her from the side, wondering if she would turn around so that he might see her face more fully. In profile, it was intriguing. She had a piquant nose and high cheekbones. Arched dark red eyebrows rose above deep-set eyes with thick lashes. Her chin was pugnaciously stubborn. All in all, she was unconventionally enchanting. Just as he struggled to break contact and wend his way on to the Spanish ambassador, she looked up.

Olivia had spent the past hour dancing until her head whirled with dizziness and her feet ached in the pointy toed satin slippers. When she cried off any further exertions no less than half a dozen men brought her champagne from the refreshment tables. She bantered flirtatiously with them trying vainly to have fun and forget her guardian's desire to marry her off to some stodgy older man. But her coterie of youthful admirers with their puppy dog adoration quickly grew tiresome just as it always had in the past. She felt bored and restless, needing—no expecting—something to happen, although she had not the slightest idea what.

Then it began, a prickling along the back of her neck, running up and down her spine. Someone was watching her from across the room. A man. It had to be a man and not just any man. Why did she know that in her bones? Unable to register what was being said to her, Olivia took a sip from her champagne glass and looked in the direction where she felt his presence.

Bright green eyes collided with stormy blue ones. And held.

It seemed like an eternity but could only have been seconds. Samuel stared into a pair of slightly slanted, exotic cat eyes. That, combined with her cheekbones gave her face a wild gypsy look. She boldly returned his perusal. There was bemusement mixed with determination in her expression. She had a compelling face in spite of its youthfulness. He decided she must be no more than eighteen or twenty. *God deliver me from missish young virgins! Haven't I learned anything since I met Tish?* Chastising himself for the uncharacteristic lapse into romantic fancy, he broke eye contact and strode angrily across the floor in the opposite direction to attend to business.

Olivia met the stranger's dark blue eyes and felt the breath suddenly drain from her. She could have drowned in those hypnotic eyes, cold and restless like the storm tossed Atlantic. He was tall, over six feet, lean and hawkish looking with shoulder-length shaggy hair more often seen on the St. Louis riverfront than in polite Virginia society. Night black and gleaming like a raven's wing, it was thick and coarse. Her fingers curled at her sides as if she could feel them combing through it. One black eyebrow arched sardonically as he studied her with unabashed sexual speculation. His beautifully sculpted lips smiled, dissolving the cynical harshness from his perfect features. Never in her life had she seen a man so striking, so polished, yet so reckless, whose face seemed to combine boyish charm with potent danger. He wore the uniform of colonel in the American Army, but somehow she intuited it was not his normal mode of dress. How did she know that? Was this how *Maman* felt the first time she laid eyes on *Père*?

Before she could consider further, his smile slipped and his face once more took on a hard-edged remoteness. He turned from her and strode across the room. Heat tinged her cheeks red as her hair, yet she could not help but follow his lithe pantherish steps as he moved gracefully through the press of people. She should be angry. She had certainly been humiliated. After all, he had initiated the heated exchange, smiled lasciviously at her, then scowled and stalked rudely away as if she'd turned from a fairy into a troll before his eyes.

Yet Olivia was only puzzled and for some utterly inexplicable reason, hurt.

∾ *Chapter 2* ∾

Dolley Madison's only son, Payne, was a grave disappointment to her. Perhaps that was why she had taken to mothering Samuel ever since he had begun working as a special agent for his father's old friend Tom Jefferson. Jemmy Madison's sparkling wife had been the official hostess at all presidential functions as well as social arbiter of the nation's capital even before her husband assumed office. There was not a man from eighteen to eighty who was immune to her charms, Shelby thought ruefully as he watched her working her way determinedly toward him, graciously smiling and chatting with the guests at her famous Wednesday afternoon salon. Josephine Bonaparte herself had never presided over more brilliant gatherings, nor possessed more aplomb than the irrepressible Dolley.

"There you are at last, Samuel. I vow, I worry myself half to death every time you leave Washington on one of those dangerous assignments. A soldier's life is so uncertain," she said, giving him a fond hug, then holding him at arm's length for a motherly inspection. At forty-three, the president's lady was an imposingly handsome woman with dark hair as yet untouched by gray, clear blue eyes and a porcelain pale ivory complexion. Fashionably dressed in a fawn-colored muslin gown and matching turban with ostrich feathers sticking rakishly from its top, she was taller than her diminutive husband but still had to look up to meet Shelby's eyes.

"As you can see, Dolley, I'm none the worse for my last duty, not even a scratch," he replied with a slashing white smile.

"You certainly do look unscathed—not to mention indecently handsome. I vow all the unmarried young belles have been aflutter since your return to Washington—and not a few of the married ones as well," she added with a wry chuckle.

"You must regale me with all the latest gossip," he said, taking her arm and tucking it around his elbow with a courtly flourish.

"La, where shall I begin?" she replied gaily, leading him through the crowd toward a set of doors, chattering on about inconsequential social matters. As soon as they slipped undetected into the deserted hallway, her expression instantly sobered. "I expect you have some news of last night?"

"Not much," Samuel responded dryly. "Ambassador Onís was not quite his garrulous self, to say the least. His British friends in Canada have given him some sobering news. They expect an American declaration of war."

Her Irish blue eyes flashed. "A self-fulfilling prophecy, I fear, although Jemmy still hopes to avert the conflict."

"The War Hawks in Congress are pressing him hard, I know. That's why I brought the filibuster from British Florida to talk with the president. Has the new secretary of state returned yet? He should hear what Allenworthy has to say. The whole southern border is a powder keg, not to mention what's simmering on the Mississippi."

"Mr. Monroe has just arrived and he will be at your rendezvous. Do you have the directions?" she asked.

Shelby took a slip of paper from his jacket and handed it to her. "Allenworthy refuses to come into Washington. He'll be waiting at this location. I'm sorry for the inconvenience for the president and Monroe."

Her eyes danced. "I rather think Jemmy enjoys the intrigue of it. Secret meetings and all." Her expression sobered as she placed one pale, plump hand on his sleeve. "How is Tish, Samuel?"

Shelby smiled grimly recalling yesterday's confrontation. Pulling his mind away from it, he answered Dolley. "Our marriage has become a hellish nightmare. The situation won't ever change. I've finally admitted that to myself."

Dolley Madison watched the proud and lonely young man as he walked across the small sitting room in which they were sequesterd to stare out the window. His back was stiff, his expression stern, revealing so little of the awful pain bottled inside him. He had been hurt so often by women it was small wonder he trusted so few. She counted herself fortunate to be one he genuinely respected. "This may sound scandalous, Samuel, but Tish was simply not the woman for you. Perhaps . . ."

A pair of slanted cat green eyes framed by a fiery halo of curls flashed into his mind but he dismissed it, shaking his head. "No, after this ill-fated 'romantic' venture, I'm not at all disposed to believe that there exists one special woman for me—unless of course you'd consider leaving the president and running away with me?" he teased, deliberately lightening the somber tone of their conversation.

"I'm old enough to be your mother, you young flatterer," she admonished, then could have bitten her tongue. Samuel's mother, a flighty spoiled Frenchwoman had deserted his father when Samuel was a boy, taking his beloved older sister with her back to Paris. Although sister and brother had finally been reunited, their father had died of a broken heart because of the defection. "Samuel, I didn't mean—"

"Tut, Dolley, I only wish you could've been my mother." He raised her hand for a kiss, eliciting a tremulous smile.

"And I do wish you could've been my son," she replied as their eyes met and held in understanding for a moment before he changed the subject.

"I'm going to sell the plantation, Dolley. I've never felt at home there since Father died."

"Elkhanah would understand, Samuel," she replied gently. "You've been rootless these past years in spite of owning it."

"I plan to set down some new roots in the West. To start over again in St. Louis."

"St. Louis? Isn't that where your sister and her husband have established a trading house?"

"No detail escapes you. Yes, Santiago travels up from Santa Fe every year to trade with the Americans. Now that their youngest is old enough to travel, Liza has taken to coming with him. I haven't seen them since my namesake's baptism three years ago."

"I can imagine how you look forward to being reunited with your sister, but, Samuel dear . . ." her voice trailed off worriedly, "about your brother-in-law . . ."

He smiled. "Don't fret, Dolley. We've made our peace. Santiago Quinn is a good man, and he makes Liza happy. Along the way he has become quite an entrepreneur. He's making wagonloads of money but needs a partner he can trust. I'm going to buy a share of their business and help run their American warehouse."

"Why, that is marvelous!" She clapped her hands together. "This will be a whole new beginning for you, even though Jemmy and I shall miss you terribly."

"I'll not be resigning my commission for some time, not with a war on the horizon."

"Always duty before all else, Samuel," she said gravely. "Jemmy shall be glad of it, but I don't want you to sacrifice your happiness."

A tap on the sitting room door interrupted before he could reply. "That will be Toby warning me that I'm missed in the salon," she said, patting his hand affectionately. "I'll give the directions to Jemmy as soon as the guests depart. He and Mr. Monroe should be able to meet you and your filibuster by midafternoon."

"You'd best go first. I'll slip back into the crowd in a bit. After all, we couldn't have gossip about the president's lady now, could we?"

"Flatterer," she called out affectionately as she sailed from the room.

Warm afternoon sunlight touched Samuel's face as he rode back toward the city. The meeting with Jemmy Madison and his newly appointed secretary of state, James Monroe, had gone well. Fiercely ambitious, Monroe was in many ways the opposite of the frail, scholarly and retiring little president, but like his chief, the secretary of state possessed a keen analytical mind.

They had questioned Allenworthy and gained enough information to substantiate their worst fears about impending trouble with Spanish and British officials along the republic's borders. Land hungry American settlers were eagerly planning to expand those borders in all directions—not that America's European rivals were themselves innocent of provocation. Samuel had shared with his superiors the contents of his sister's letters.

Liza was still addicted to intrigue, no matter that she now presided over a brood of children. Long before he had become a presidential agent, his sister had worked secretly for Tom Jefferson. She had been his finest agent and was still a loyal American citizen, no matter that she resided most of each year in Spanish territory. Liza had a genius for ferreting out information. When rumors about British activity among the Osage reached St. Louis, she began making discreet inquiries.

Smiling grimly, Samuel could well imagine her arrogant Spanish husband's reaction to her efforts. She had unearthed enough information to convince the president to investigate. War against Great Britain and her ally Spain seemed almost inevitable now. The external threat along the eastern seaboard and around the Gulf was bad enough without having America's enemies inciting the various Indian tribes along the Mississippi Valley to attack from within. No nation could hope to win a two-fronted war. Colonel Shelby's assignment was to see that the United States was not forced to fight one.

The air was redolent with a hint of spring. Samuel looked around the low marshy countryside, still sere and brown from winter's cold. Tall patches of marsh grass grew in thick clumps off to the east side of the wide rutted road. Two gulls circled in the distance and the bare branches of a willow tree rustled softly in the brisk breeze.

By the time he reached St. Louis the weather should be breaking. The thought heartened him, as did the fact that he would be leaving Tish and her whole family behind. He threw back his head and took a deep breath of air. The slight movement saved his life as a bullet whistled a fraction of an inch from his temple.

Years of conditioning took over as he responded with pure reflexive action. He swung low to the right side of his mount, but before he could turn the horse and kick it into a gallop, another shot rang out. His horse stumbled to his knees. Samuel kicked free of the stirrups and threw himself away from the dying animal. He landed hard, thrown onto his right shoulder, striking his head a glancing blow against the cold rocky earth. The gelding nearly fell on top of him as it convulsed in its death throes, then lay still. A third shot grazed his cheek before he could flatten himself behind the fallen horse. Quickly he studied the terrain, trying to locate better cover. There was a dense copse of pampas grass in a slight swale to the east of the road. His eyes swept the rest of his surroundings, searching for a way to cover his retreat even as his hands pried desperately at the stock of his Bartlett flintlock, which was wedged firmly in its scabbard beneath the dead horse.

No help there, and his Martial Pistols were not accurate enough at the range from which the assassin fired. Mercifully there seemed only to be one man, but he was damnably proficient at reloading and firing. Cocking a pistol, Samuel futilely returned a shot where he saw faint movement in the brush. Cursing, he pulled out the second pistol.

Quiet. For several moments Shelby heard nothing. Then another shot rang out, this time burning through his jacket sleeve and slicing a furrow across his left bicep. The killer had circled around to his left. Soon Shelby would be without cover. He surveyed the clearing in which he lay and decided his only chance was to make a run for the tall grass at the opposite end from which the last shot had come. If only his foe had not again circled back, waiting for him to do precisely that.

Shelby shook his throbbing head to clear it, ignoring the raw burn of his arm. Just as he tensed his muscles, preparing to make the deadly dash, the drumming of hoofbeats broke the deceptively bucolic quiet. A faint rattling of harness grew louder as the tempo of the hoofbeats accelerated. A vehicle was coming around the bend in the road, the galloping horses headed straight for him.

The driver, hidden in the shadowy interior of the small phaeton, slowed the team as they neared Samuel's position. A high, clear voice yelled out, "Jump aboard!" as the wheels narrowly missed the fallen horse.

Samuel tumbled onto the seat, sprawling half on the floor of the small carriage as another shot rang out, whizzing past his head. The driver whipped the well-matched team of bays into a gallop with a sudden lurch. Dazed, he hung on to the side of the phaeton and struggled into the seat. Another shot whistled harmlessly over the top of the carriage as they hurtled toward the capital.

"You're bleeding all over Uncle Emory's new velvet upholstery," a soft feminine voice said in lightly accented English.

"So, we meet again," Samuel replied, arching one black eyebrow at his rescuer.

"We never *met* in the first place," Olivia said sharply, recalling the cool way he had cut her, turning his back and stalking across the ballroom floor.

"We've not been introduced, no." He could see that she was piqued at his dismissal last night. The spoiled little cat wasn't used to having men ignore her. "Given that a beautiful young lady has just saved my life, the very least I must do is offer my name. Colonel Samuel Sheridan Shelby, at your service, my dear." He grinned as her cheeks pinkened at the suggestive tone of his voice.

"I am not your 'dear,' " she snapped, giving the reins a

sharp slap although the horses were already galloping. "Use my scarf to bind up your arm. I can't have you passing out and falling beneath the carriage wheels before we make good our escape."

He pulled a heavy woolen scarf from her neck and wrapped the cloth securely around his throbbing arm. The roadside moved by them in a blur. When the phaeton took a curve on two wheels, then righted itself with a swaying bounce, he cautioned. "Careful or you'll overturn us."

"I've driven some of the finest and the worst carriages ever made as fast as they can go and I've never overturned one yet, 'my dear,' " Olivia replied smugly.

"Beautiful and modest, too," Shelby said dryly, his eyes assessing her delicate profile with amusement. Damn but she was a stubborn beauty with her chin jutting pugnaciously and her pink lips pursed in concentration. He was forced to admit that she handled the reins with considerable expertise. "Am I not to receive the favor of your name, at least? After all, according to custom, when one person saves another's life, it belongs to the rescuer from that day forward."

"I've never heard of such a custom," she said, curious in spite of herself. She pulled on the reins and slowed the lathered team to a trot.

"Tis a common belief among certain of the Indians of the Far West."

"You've been west?" she asked, turning to look him full in the face for the first time. A slight bruise had begun to discolor his left temple and his face was smeared with dust and sweat in spite of the chilly air. For all that, he was still so devastatingly beautiful and disturbingly male, that her breath caught in her throat. Then he smiled, and Olivia was lost. The brilliance of that smile outshone all the candles on the biggest chandelier in the White House.

"Yes, I've been west. I've spent some time among the various tribes on the Great Plains, even those living in the vast mountain ranges that crossect the continent."

"You sound as if you've traveled with Lewis and Clark," she said, her eyes alight with curiosity.

Samuel realized he had already revealed more of his background than he normally ever did to a strange female, no matter how beautiful or plucky she might be. "No, I was not privileged to make that journey. I've had other assignments across the Mississippi. You still have not told me your name.

I know you're French." He cocked his head, studying her with blue eyes so piercing that she looked away.

Olivia could feel his gaze on her and knew her body was responding most unsuitably, making her face an unbecoming shade of pink that clashed with her hair. *Merde!* Why did he have to fluster her so? "I'm Olivia Patrice St. Etienne. Also, it would seem, at *your* service for this afternoon's work." There, dare him directly! If only she could muster the nerve to return his stare. Olivia forced herself to meet those penetrating dark blue eyes, which at the mention of her surname seemed to grow an infinitesimal bit wintry. Then he smiled again and she was not certain if she had imagined it.

"Charmed, Mademoiselle St. Etienne."

"How did you know I was French?" she blurted out, curious about his reaction—or her imagining of his reaction—to her name.

"Although your English is fluent, there is a faint trace of an accent," he hedged. He had no desire whatsoever to discuss his mother with the beauteous Mademoiselle St. Etienne.

"Have you some aversion to my countrymen, Monsieur Colonel?"

"Certainly not to the lovely young lady who has just saved my life," he replied gallantly.

Olivia recognized evasion when she heard it, having been raised by Julian St. Etienne, a luckless gambler who had been more expert in his choice of words than his choice of cards. She chose a frontal assault to test how much Samuel would reveal—or conceal. "Why was someone trying to kill you back there? Do you know who it was?"

Samuel shrugged. "I have no idea. Probably a simple robbery. My horse was quite valuable."

"But of course! Precisely why the assassin shot it out from under you, so he could lug it off to the meat market," she responded scornfully, meeting his eyes with a dare.

"Maybe it was an unlucky shot," he said smoothly. "His first shot nearly took off my head. I was turning the horse suddenly, trying to reach cover when it went down. Lucky for me the brigand was something amiss as a marksman."

"He was not all that bad a marksman or you would not be dripping blood like that," she replied with asperity. The woolen scarf was soaked dark red now in vivid contrast to the colonel's face which was growing decidedly pale beneath his sun bronzed tan.

"Don't worry. I won't pitch over the side and spook your horses," he said in grim amusement. "I've suffered far worse. It's just a scratch."

"That *scratch* is bleeding profusely," she countered. "How can you remain so calm while your lifeblood just seeps away?"

"Practice." He swore beneath his breath. Between the burning nuisance of his arm and the throbbing misery of his skull all he wanted was to lie down, preferably on some surface not bouncing wildly up and down.

Olivia reined in the team as they neared a farmhouse situated on the outskirts of the capital. There was a well by the roadside with a bucket beside it. "Maybe you'd better clean up your wounds. We must stop the bleeding before you ruin the upholstery. We could see if the people here have some fresh bandages. If not," she fluffed her voluminous skirts and added boldly, "I can always use one of my petticoats."

He grinned at her cheerful voice, noting that she turned a bit green around the gills when she looked at his blood-soaked arm. "Now you must promise not to faint and fall beneath the horses' hooves," he teased.

Olivia gave an indelicate snort as she jumped from the phaeton, scanning the farmhouse for signs of occupancy. A mangy old yellow dog eyed them suspiciously from the rickety porch and bared his gums in a toothless growl. "No one seems to be about," she said with a sigh, turning back to Samuel who by now had climbed out of the carriage.

He walked determinedly to the well and lowered the bucket, then cranked it back up with his uninjured arm. Lifting the moldy oak container, he leaned forward and poured it over his head, then let it drop by its rope once more into the depths below with a splash.

Olivia watched as he shook his head to clear it and combed his finger through his glossy black hair. Brilliant droplets of water sprayed around him in a rainbow arc of color. She felt her heartbeat accelerate when she observed a fine sheen of droplets forming on his face and rolling slowly over his boldly masculine jaw and down his throat to vanish beneath the collar of his uniform. This was not wise, not wise at all. Other than the fact he was devastatingly handsome and charming, what did she really know about Colonel

Shelby? He seemed to be involved in some mysterious intrigue and people most certainly were trying to kill him. She was altogether too attracted to this stranger.

"Damn. I lost my hat when I fell. It was brand-new. This whole uniform is ruined," he grumbled, inspecting his bloody, torn and dirt smeared clothing.

"You . . . you had better see about that wound, else more than your uniform will be ruined," she said, moistening her suddenly dry lips with the tip of her tongue.

"Not out here," he replied distractedly as he pulled up the bucket and unfastened it from its rope. "It's a bit cool now that the sun's setting . . . and it's too exposed."

After a quick glance back down the road, she watched him stride toward the front door of the log cabin. "What if no one is at home?"

He turned at the uncertainty in her voice and raised one eyebrow. "Then we just go in. I don't plan to rob them, just use the shelter long enough to change this dressing . . . that is if the offer of your petticoat still stands good?" He waited, watching her to see what she would do.

She walked up to him as if taking the dare, but then as he turned to open the door she said, "It really isn't proper for us to be alone . . . indoors, that is."

Samuel threw back his head and laughed heartily. "You are a caution, *ma petite*. It is a bit late for the proprieties now. First you come thundering wildly to my rescue out of nowhere, alone and unchaperoned. Then you drive like a London hackney and nearly kill us both on the road. Now you suddenly turn vaporing belle."

Olivia felt like stomping her foot at his mocking laughter. "For a man who owes me his life, you are very rude, Monsieur Colonel." Anger thickened her accent.

Samuel noticed the shift in cadence as well as the blaze of emerald fire in her eyes. "My apologies, mademoiselle . . . but you still have not explained why you were driving alone in the middle of nowhere," he could not resist adding as he turned and entered the obviously deserted house. The hound on the porch raised its head once, then thought better of the exertion of further protest and instead slunk inside the shelter of the cabin behind Shelby.

Olivia stood alone in the yard for a moment. The impulse to dash to the phaeton and take off leaving the arrogant colonel stranded was tempting. But he was injured, and she was more attracted to him than she had ever been to a man before in her life. *Fool*, she berated herself.

Chapter 3

Olivia reluctantly followed him into the dark interior of the cabin and watched as he unwrapped the soaked scarf from his upper arm. In spite of a slight wince of pain, his hands remained steady. Then he began to unbutton the heavy uniform jacket. As he slipped it easily off his good arm and began to work it carefully free of the injured one, Olivia stood rooted to the floor of the deserted cabin. The sheer white lawn shirt beneath his jacket stretched across his broad shoulders and clung lovingly to every inch of his lean, muscular torso. Then he started to remove the shirt, too!

"What are you doing?" Her voice cracked on the last word.

"If I'm going to wrap this wound to stop the bleeding, I first have to bare the skin," he replied reasonably, continuing to pull the ruined shirt off.

She had thought his chest and shoulders were revealed through the sheer lawn covering. Now she could see how mistaken that assumption had been! Darkly bronzed skin rippled with sleek muscles as he tossed his shirt onto the crude wooden bench beside the table. A heavy pelt of black hair covered his chest, then tapered into an enticing vee that arrowed down to disappear beneath the belt buckle at his narrow waist. Her eyes would have strayed scandalously lower but a bitten back groan distracted her.

Samuel cursed as he tried to flex his injured arm. "The bleeding's grown worse. If I don't get it stopped, I might pass out and bleed to death before you can summon help. I'm afraid I'm going to need those petticoats."

"M-my p-petticoats," she stammered, then instantly felt like a fool.

"You're not going to faint now that the shooting's done, are you?" His voice was light but a sheen of perspiration glistened on his forehead in spite of the chilly evening air. "I'd search around here for some cloth for bandages but somehow I suspect that any to be found in here would blood-poison a possum," he added wryly as Olivia came out of her trance.

His whole arm was soaked with blood and here she had been gawking at his naked chest as if she had never seen one before! Well, come to think of it, she *had* never seen a grown man's bare chest before. With clumsy fingers she began to tear at the top layer of her petticoats but the heavy linen would not give.

"Here, allow me," he said with mock gallantry as he knelt in front of her and reached for the snowy slip with his uninjured hand. In the other one a wicked looking knife gleamed. He sliced through the hem of the undergarment, then let her tear it until she had a little over a yard of cloth with which to wrap his arm.

"Tear another piece about the same length," he commanded as he lowered his injured arm into the bucket of cool water he had placed on the table. A small hiss of pain escaped his clenched jaw but he made no further sound as he bathed the injury until the water ran red between his fingers.

Olivia stood holding the makeshift bandages, feeling utterly useless and somewhat queasy as she watched. An ugly furrow marred the perfection of his upper arm, slicing in a nasty angle across his bicep. She swallowed and moved closer as he raised his arm out of the water. "I'll wrap it," she said.

He held out his arm and let her cover it with the linen. He could feel the tremors that wracked her body vibrating through her hands as she worked. "Pull it tight so the bleeding stops. Aargh! Yes," he rasped as he pressed the end of the linen against the wound to hold it in place.

"I'm hurting you!" she gasped, dropping the bandage.

"No! I mean yes, but it can't be helped. Just get the damn thing wrapped around my arm and tie it off good and tight." He began to wrap the bandage himself. Suddenly Olivia's fingers, soft and cool, brushed his hand as she once more took over the task, pulling on the wrapping the way he had instructed her.

As they worked, their hands continued to touch each other. Her skin felt silken and she smelled of jasmine. He watched her bite her lower lip in concentration as she tied off the bandage. Her mouth was soft, pale pink, utterly kissable. And he was utterly insane. He was still a married man and he knew nothing about her except that she was young,

French and spoiled. That should have been enough to deter him but somehow it was not. Her hair had come loose from its pins during the wild carriage ride and a fat bouncy curl of pure flame brushed against the sensitive inside of his wrist.

Without thinking Samuel cupped his hand around the back of her slender neck and lowered his face to hers as he drew her against him. "Such good work deserves a reward," he murmured as his mouth tasted the soft pink lips that had beckoned him.

Olivia felt herself melting toward the hardness and heat of his chest. Her palms pressed against the crisp hair and her fingers kneaded in it as her lips tilted upward to meet his descending mouth. The kiss was fierce and hungry yet oddly delicate and exploratory at the same time. His lips brushed, then pressed hers and his tongue lightly rimmed the edges of her mouth until she emitted a tiny gasp of delight, allowing him entry to taste the virgin territory within.

She'd had the adulation of legions of lovesick young swains but she had never been kissed like this. Olivia could feel the pounding of his heartbeat against her palms and the answering acceleration of her own wayward heart. The exotic texture of crisp chest hair delighted her questing fingers but it was her mouth that felt the full drugging persuasion of Samuel's sensual coaxing. The tip of his tongue dipped and glided inside her lips, then danced a duel with her tongue and retreated only to plunge in for another jolting foray. She heard a low mewling sound like a lost kitten crying, without realizing that it was her own voice.

She was pliant and willing yet there was an inexplicable sense of surprise and wonder in her responses that did not befit a belle of her apparent experience. Yet the hunger that he felt left no time for further consideration or caution. It had been far, far too long since he had lain with a woman. As the enmity between him and Tish had grown, their physical hunger for each other had waned. Two years ago he had quit her bed when he learned that she had visited a notorious abortist in Maryland. Sickened and desolate, he had never touched her since. When his physical needs became unbearable he betrayed his marriage vows with carefully chosen professionals. The encounters always left him with such bitter, sordid regrets that he seldom succumbed. Instead he buried himself in his dangerous work.

His compelling attraction to Olivia St. Etienne was utter

madness. She was obviously from a good family, gently reared with the expectation of a proper marriage even if she did behave irresponsibly. There was no place for such a female in his life. Then why was he drawn to her with such an inexplicable longing? His hand, deft and sure, had found the small sweet enticement of her breast, cupping it through the soft linen of her jacket. When he rubbed his thumb against the hard bud of her nipple she cried out against his mouth and pressed closer to him in the mindless desire they shared. His fingers tangled in her thick, lustrous hair and he twined the curls around his fists like scarlet ribbons.

If he did not stop at once he would take her here in this filthy deserted cabin on the rough plank floor, rutting like the cur dog that lay quietly in the corner of the crude bare room watching them. This was insanity born of simple deprivation. Surely it couldn't be anything more. With an oath he pulled away, supporting the breathless, dazed girl by holding her shoulders. He could feel a shudder of surprise rippling through her. She raised her head and their eyes met. Hers were wide and dazed, turned the deep green of a tree shrouded forest pool.

The pull of her mute entreaty frightened him with its intensity. Without words she asked him why he had ended the passionate interlude. Without thinking he replied, "I've wanted to do that since the first moment I laid eyes on you. Don't deny that you wanted it, too," he added, stung by her wounded expression and his own guilt.

Shame washed over her in waves. Feeling her face flame, she raised her hands and pressed them to her cheeks, backing away from him. Dear merciful lord, what had she almost done—allowed him to do? "No, I am scarcely in a position to deny anything." Her voice was hoarse, soft as if coming from a great distance. She could still feel his heat, the virile magnetic presence that held her in thrall. His eyes pierced to her very soul. She felt naked as he was, defenseless.

Samuel could feel her vulnerability and the pain of it hit him like a slap. He turned to pick up his discarded clothing. The shirt was a blood soaked mess which he quickly abandoned, attempting instead to slip his injured arm through the sleeve of the heavy uniform jacket.

Olivia watched him struggle with the stiff coat, then stepped closer and pulled the blood caked sleeve straight, helping him ease it over his bandaged arm. He shrugged the other arm into the uniform, then began to button it. She stepped back yet their gazes locked and held. When Samuel had completed the task, his arms dropped to his sides.

He continued to study her with those unnerving blue eyes. "I'm truly sorry," he said stiffly. "You saved my life and I behaved abominably."

"You dared nothing I did not allow," she replied with candor, meeting his gaze unflinchingly.

"There is something between us, Mademoiselle St. Etienne, something quite remarkable . . . . disturbing . . . and dangerous," he said, groping for a way to express his tumultuous emotions without revealing too much.

She smiled wistfully. "Yes, I believe you are right." Then appearing thoughtful she added, "Since I've already been as bold as any hussy, I may as well be even bolder. Don't you think after all that has happened, you might call me Olivia?" Her bones melted when his face, so harsh and austere a moment earlier, split into a heart stopping smile.

Olivia. How classically lovely. It fit her perfectly. "Hussy you are not. Bold you definitely are. My name is Samuel, Olivia." The sound of her name rolled off his tongue like song. Damn, he was bewitched! "We had better return to the city before you are missed by your family."

She returned his earlier smile. He was clever at extracting information without revealing himself. "I have only my guardian, Samuel. Emory Wescott, a St. Louis merchant who is currently in the capital to attend to business matters."

"St. Louis?" he questioned, caught off guard.

Olivia picked up on the surprised note in his voice and turned to him as they approached the phaeton. "Yes, that is where we reside, unless Uncle Emory takes me traveling with him."

"Even a guardian so remiss as to allow his charge to go careening about the countryside unescorted will be upset if she's at not home by dark," he ventured as he helped her into the carriage.

"Not tonight he won't. He is yet in Maryland . . . collecting some bills owed him," she said with a mysterious smile. "As long as I present myself all packed and ready to sail for home on Friday he will not note my absence. Anyway, 'tis I who must see you home since I am the driver and you are the passenger. Now, let's hurry so *I* get *you* home by dark."

A smile hovered about his lips. "Such solicitude for my reputation! How can I refuse so generous an offer?"

Dusk had settled over the city with a glittering cloak of frost when Olivia's phaeton pulled up in front of the elegant three-story Georgian brick house that had been Senator Worthington Soames' wedding gift to his beloved "Tisha-Belle." Samuel hated the looming monstrosity.

Olivia eyed it with amazement. "Your house is as grand as any I've seen, even in London," she murmured, wondering how Samuel could afford it on a colonel's pay.

He could see the questions looming: Mercenary speculation? Or mere curiosity? As the daughter of French émigrés she had grown up living with the grating reality of champagne taste and gin swill income. Although it had always bothered him to admit the house and its lavish furnishings were a gift, he especially did not want to confess such to Olivia St. Etienne. Nor in their long and earnest conversation on the ride into the capital had he confessed that he was married. *But what if he were free?* Free to do what? Become involved with a wild young French hoyden who drew him like a wet hound to a warm fire?

"It's just a house. I don't even own it," he replied dismissively, raising her hand for a chaste salute. Somehow once he had pressed his lips to the jasmine scented silk of her skin, he could not release her.

Olivia's fingers curled around his wrist while their eyes communicated in eloquent silence. He surprised himself by saying, "I'll be posted to St. Louis within the month. Perhaps we'll meet again."

Her smile was dazzling. "St. Louis is not so large a city that you could hide from me. I shall delight in tracking you down!"

Letitia Soames Shelby stood behind a Brussels lace curtain at an upstairs window watching Samuel and Olivia say their farewell. Her eyes narrowed to pale golden slits as the sound of their laughter drifted up to her. "Such tendresse. Who is the red-haired tart?"

Her companion peered out in the gloom and swore as Olivia's flame-colored hair danced in the light from the torch held by a servant who had come out to greet Samuel. "That's the rig that rescued him! An expensive lightweight phaeton with those superb matched bays."

Tish turned to face him with a scornful expression hardening her patrician features, robbing them of the doll-like beauty that always turned heads. "You mean to say you were foiled by a little slut—probably one of Samuel's light-skirts?" she asked incredulously. Anger blazed in her eyes. She smoothed a hand over the arc of her hip, which was amply revealed through her sheer mull gown of pale blue.

Richard Bullock watched her move across the room, as aware as she of every inch of her voluptuous flesh. She always had her "at-home" dresses made up from virtually translucent fabrics which she wore only for him in the privacy of her apartments. He wet his dry lips and stared enraptured as she waited for his reply.

"I don't know who the chit is, but the way she was driving her phaeton on the Post Oak Road she is one hell of a horsewoman," he said defensively, watching Letitia toy restlessly with one long silver gilt curl that hung enticingly across her cleavage.

People often remarked that they looked like sister and brother, for Richard, too, possessed the same pale hair and gold eyes. They were in fact only bound by marriage. Worthington Soames was widowed shortly after Letitia's twelfth birthday. He had remarried a widow with an eight-year-old boy in the hope that she would give him his own son to claim his senatorial seat and carry on the prestigious Soames name. Richard and Tish were stepsister and brother, raised together with every advantage.

When the new Mrs. Soames failed to provide the requisite heir before passing to her reward, the senator had turned his ambitions to his beloved daughter. Whatever "Tisha-Belle" wanted, she received, including Captain Samuel Sheridan Shelby, who was now proving to be a grave mistake. One she planned to remedy with Richard's help.

"Forget the worthless little nobody driving that carriage. Tell me why you failed to kill Samuel."

"I had him pinned down. Bloodied the bastard, too. He had nowhere to run until that carriage came flying around the curve in the road. I tell you, Tish, no one knows about that deserted old road except Shelby. I have no idea how she happened on us before I could finish him."

"You apparently bloodied him right enough," she said, slightly mollified as she thought of the blackened stain on her husband's left sleeve.

"We can hope he'll take the red poisoning from it and die," Bullock said lightly, watching her pose for him before the cheval glass in her dressing room. No one knew he was admitted to her private quarters except for Tish's personal maid, a slave girl who had been raised with her on her father's tidewater plantation.

"We cannot leave his death to chance," she rebuked sharply.

"Don't be angry, my pet. You know I can abide anything but your displeasure," Bullock wheedled, gliding across the carpet toward her. He was whipcord thin and slight of stature yet a deadly swordsman, swift and cunning in duels, always ruthless when crossed—except for his stepsister who dared say or do anything she wished to him.

Tish studied his intense narrow face with its sharply chiseled almost feminine features, then reached out and pressed her heavy milk white breasts against the perfumed satin of his waistcoat. He kissed her savagely, his thin fingers digging painfully into her heavy golden hair as his mouth ground over hers. She rocked her hips against his pelvis and chuckled low in the back of her throat when she felt his erection pressing into her belly. Then she broke away abruptly, turning back to the mirror. He stepped up beside her and they gazed into its silvery surface, two perfect golden figures.

His lips nipped and bit at her neck, leaving small angry red marks that stung. She liked him to hurt her when he made love to her. A low ragged moan tore from her throat, exciting him past endurance, but when he reached up and began to tear the fragile muslin of her low-cut bodice, she stopped him.

"No, not now," she said breathlessly. "You know how dangerous it is with him in the house. He might walk in on us and kill you."

Richard scoffed. "He hasn't set foot in your quarters for two years."

"But he's been shot. It's my duty as his wife to attend him," she said mockingly, feeling him stiffen when she said the words "his wife."

How Richard hated being reminded that Tish had shared another's bed. She had seduced him when she was seventeen and he a stripling lad of thirteen, teaching him well, turning his boyhood adoration into something far more intense and binding. She had learned at a tender age how to use sex not only for her own pleasure, but as a weapon. It always worked with Richard. But not with Samuel.

Samuel. She recalled the electric thrill she had felt the first time she had seen him, so tall and dashing in his captain's uniform, so dark and rugged, the veriest opposite of pale, effeminate Richard. But her husband had become a bitter disappointment outside the marriage bed. The confrontation between the two of them yesterday afternoon replayed itself in her mind once more. She and Richard had been to her dressmakers to pick up her gown for the gala last night. Samuel had just returned home after months of absence, off on another odious secret mission.

They had another of their endless arguments about the same old thing—his utter disregard for his political future. She had actually abased herself by undressing and trying to seduce him—only to be rejected with cool indifference! That was when she knew a momentous change in their lives was about to occur.

A tremor of genuine alarm had shivered down her spine when he said, "We have to talk, my dear . . . seriously. I suggest you slip back into that fetching little frock and have a seat. I'll pour us a drink. I think before this is done we'll both need it."

His voice had been calm and his expression glacial as he handed her a goblet with over an inch of brandy in it. She had always been so sure of her plans, so sure of her husband. Brave, honorable Samuel, a dashing soldier. Perfect presidential material with some direction and polishing—which she and her father would supply. She had moistened her lips nervously, trying to read what lay behind the grim lines etching his face. "Don't say you've found a Spanish senorita in the wilds of Florida—or some English pensioner's daughter," she said with forced lightness.

After taking a sip of his brandy he sighed deeply and began, "While I was hacking my way through miasmic swamps I did have a great deal of time to think. We're on a collision course, Tish. I married a sweet girl who I thought would make a good soldier's wife—"

"But that's not fair! I *would* make a splendid soldier's wife—if you were a soldier instead of some sort of agent provocateur skulking around the borders in disguise."

"I'm afraid that's the way I can best serve my country.

There will be war soon, possibly against Napoleon, probably against Britain and her ally Spain—the latter two happen to occupy our northern, southern and western borders. No matter the lack of glory in it, that's where I can do the most good."

She had sensed something was seriously amiss, something even all of Worthington Soames' money and influence could not fix. *Surely he couldn't have found out about Richard and me! There's no way—I was so careful* . . . Her thoughts had whirled frantically until his voice interrupted them.

"No use sugaring the medicine, is there, Tish." His next words dropped like stones in the silent room as he said, "I'm asking Tom Jefferson to handle a petition for divorce."

The shock of his plans to divorce her had rocked Tish to the very core of her being. Her life would be over, finished, done. She would be utterly disgraced, a social pariah, without hope of ever achieving the overweening ambition upon which her father had nurtured her. That was when she had decided Samuel must die.

"I could kill him right now, in his own bedroom," Richard whispered against her neck, interrupting her troubling reverie.

"No, his man Toby is no doubt with him. We have to think, to plan something. Now that this first attempt has failed so miserably, he'll be on his guard. Samuel hasn't survived all these years as a presidential agent by chance. He is a very dangerous opponent."

"Ah, but so am I, my pet . . . so am I," Richard murmured softly.

❦ *Chapter 4* ❦

The courier lay sprawled on the muddy red earth, the rifle ball in his chest leaving a slow trickle of blood to pool around his body. It had been a clean, efficient kill in spite of the difficulty of the shot—the rider had been traveling at full gallop.

Richard Bullock rummaged quickly through the leather pouch tied behind his saddle, strewing the contents carelessly on the road while he kept an ear alert for sounds of any approaching travelers. It would be a waste to have to kill anyone else simply to silence them. He disliked waste.

Then his eyes fastened on the document he sought and he smiled serenely as he slipped it inside his jacket. This would give Tish the time she needed, the time he needed to complete his task. Samuel Shelby's divorce request would not reach his old friend Tom Jefferson before the colonel began his long and dangerous journey to the Far West.

Tish had been smiling and that always worried Samuel. He had expected tears and pleas if not outright threats to bring down the wrath of almighty Senator Soames on his head. Instead she had been reserved and cool, almost insolently amused as she watched him instruct Toby to pack his few belongings in trunks and send them to a storage warehouse owned by an old friend at the mouth of the Potomac.

"What damnable game is she playing now?" he muttered aloud as he tied the bulging saddlebags to his packhorse. As he completed the task, his wife's malicious yellow eyes faded from his memory, replaced by a pair of mesmerizing emerald ones, slanted and sensuous, framed by a piquantly lovely face. "Forget her, you damned fool," he chided himself. "Think of your mission."

The journey ahead of him would be a long one, but he relished the prospect. First he would ride through the pristine rugged beauty of the Appalachian Mountains across the length of Pennsylvania to the frontier river town of Pittsburgh where he would begin a long water passage by flatboat down the tortuous Ohio River, then travel overland through the dangerous wilds of Indiana Territory to St. Louis which lay across the wide and mighty Mississippi.

Ever since his first journey all the way to Santa Fe back in 1806 Shelby had been obsessed with the Far West. As the only city centrally located on the one-thousand-mile length of the mightiest river on the North American continent, St. Louis was indeed the gateway to all the riches that lay in the uncharted wilderness beyond. The epic expedition of Meriwether Lewis and William Clark to the Pacific and back to St. Louis had only scratched the surface. Samuel knew the future of the United States lay inevitably over the western horizon and his blood quickened just thinking of the freedom and the excitement of playing a part in building the future.

In truth, he was also eager to see his sister again. Liza seemed happy enough with her Spaniard, Santiago Quinn. Shelby was still amazed that she was content to live under a Spanish flag in the largely unsettled province of New Mexico, especially considering that she, too, had worked as a presidential agent, risking her life for the United States. But she staunchly maintained that the American flag would fly over Santa Fe in their lifetime. Perhaps she was right, although right now he was more interested in what was going on in the Mississippi Valley than in distant New Mexico.

Liza and Santiago should be in St. Louis by the time he arrived. Every year the Spaniard took a trade caravan from Santa Fe to St. Louis and back, even though the Spanish provincial authority forbade trade with the Americans. But the border between the Louisiana Purchase and Imperial Spain's possessions stretched thousands of miles and there were only a small handful of troops to patrol it.

Quinn's trading ventures were making a tidy profit. Samuel was going to buy into the expanding business. His sister and brother-in-law had been urging him to join the company every time he visited with them. Well, he had truly burned his bridges in Washington now. With Jefferson's considerable influence in the Virginia legislature, his divorce should be granted by year's end.

Thoughts of Olivia St. Etienne again surfaced. Tish hated the wilderness but Olivia had spent years on the Mississippi. She was waiting for him right now in St. Louis. The thought appealed and alarmed at the same time. The last thing he needed to do was jump from the frying pan into the fire.

Marriage to Letitia Annabelle Soames should have taught him something.

She had been young, lovely and biddable. The demure Virginia belle he courted had changed dramatically into a shrewish bitch who killed the child growing within her body. Perhaps it was for the best. Tish would have made a truly terrible mother.

What kind of mother would Olivia be? He quashed the dangerous thought at once and swung up on the big rangy blue roan he had selected from the stock remaining on his plantation. Along with the divorce petition, he had asked his father's old friend Tom to arrange the sale of the estate and disposition of its furnishings. Tish would receive a share of the profits and the rest would go to purchase his share in the Quinn's trading company. He fully expected his wealthy wife to sneer at the paltry settlement, but it was all he could offer.

Was Olivia rich? She had been elegantly attired at the ball and drove an expensive rig, but that was all provided by her guardian. She had described a childhood of feast and famine, living high when the cards went her father's way, sneaking out of hotel back doors when luck deserted him. That sort of existence could give a woman a real hunger for life's pretty baubles.

Why did his mind continually keep turning back to the little French chit? A smile grudgingly spread across his face. He would see her again when he reached St. Louis. Why not anticipate the inevitable and stop fighting it? He was hardly the green youth he had been when he met Tish. He'd take Olivia St. Etienne's measure, perhaps even enjoy her delectable little body and get her out of his system. But he would certainly never marry again—her or any other woman.

That night he stopped at a rugged way station, really little more than a long, crudely built log fort in the wilds of the Maryland interior. The accommodations were primitive, but it would be his last chance to sleep in a bed with a roof over his head until he reached Pittsburgh. After a passable meal of fried pork and biscuits in the main room, he made his way upstairs to the small narrow cell he had rented for the night. After depositing his pack beside the spartan pallet, he surveyed the lumpy mattress, hoping he would not roll on his left arm in the night. It was healing nicely, but the bullet had cut deep enough to require over half a dozen stitches. The doctor had removed them last week but the muscle was still tender.

A rap on the sash interrupted his settling in. He shoved aside the heavy leather curtain that served as a door and saw the sloe-eyed little barmaid standing with a tall stein of foaming ale pressed against her ample cleavage. She was a robust German girl with the dark hair and complexion of a Swabian.

"I bring you somesing cool to drink . . . and maybe somesing else warm, ya?" She licked her lips slyly and swished her coarse cotton skirts in an obvious invitation.

Fleetingly he considered it, then immediately thought better. True, he had been celibate far too long, but she smelled of pork grease and garlic and her teeth were already beginning to rot although she could be no more than twenty. "I thank you for the most generous offer, but I'm exhausted from the day's ride and I have to get an early start in the morning," he replied, fishing in his breeches for a coin to appease her.

"You will at least drink the ale, ya?" she asked earnestly. "It vill help vit sleep."

He took the stein and handed her the coin, noting with distaste that she had dirt encrusted beneath her broken nails as she slipped her payment down the front of her low-cut bodice and swished away.

After depositing the stein beside his pallet, he sat down and began to tug off a boot, noting the snores and lustier noises issuing from the other cubicles up and down the long hallway. Taking an experimental sip of the ale, he decided it might indeed help him sleep. He turned his attention to the other boot which was slick with mud. Cursing the lack of a bootjack, he grinned wryly. In the wilderness there would be no such amenities. He had better get used to roughing it. As he yanked the second boot free, it slipped from his hands, knocking over the stein of ale sitting on the floor. The rough-hewn split log floor thirstily soaked up the liquid.

No use cursing his own clumsiness. Samuel stood up and padded in his stocking feet to the crude wooden stand where a pitcher of clean water and a chipped basin stood. He washed quickly, then slipped beneath the quilts and fell into a fitful slumber, dreaming of cat green eyes and flaming red curls.

Several hours later the scrape of the stiff leather door

cover being pushed aside awakened him. Shelby's dangerous career had taught him to sleep lightly, even when he was exhausted, and never to go to bed without a weapon by his side.

The room was shadowed with only a few feeble rays of moonlight peeking through the cracks in the log wall. Samuel groped quietly with his right hand, searching for the pistol on the floor. Just as his fingers found it, he saw the icy gleam of a knife as it arced downward toward his throat.

Before he could grasp the gun, Shelby had to twist his head to avoid the blade's deadly slice. His hand swept up to block his assailant's wrist. He came up from the pallet and smashed into the other man, who had knelt at his side. They rolled across the floor, thrashing and punching. His foe was smaller but incredibly strong and agile as a weasel. Samuel held the deadly blade at bay with one hand around his assailant's wrist while he punched into the man's chest with the other.

Shelby was rewarded by a grunt of pain, but before he could follow through with another blow he felt a searing agony in his injured arm. His enemy had dug his fingers into the bicep and tore at the tender healing flesh, almost causing him to lose his purchase on the other man's wrist. Gritting his teeth, Samuel held on, smashing the knife wielding hand onto the hard log floor. The assassin lost his grip on the weapon and it skittered across the uneven boards landing in the opposite corner of the room.

Samuel tried to carry through with another punch but the other man twisted free and rolled to his feet, ferret quick, then vanished through the leather curtain. Seizing the gun he had been unable to use in the scuffle, Samuel ran after his quarry but the hallway was deserted. By the time he scrambled down the narrow stairs and ran through the empty taproom to the front door which stood ajar, all he could see was a dim figure on horseback disappearing into the forest.

Giving chase in the middle of the night over wooded, hilly terrain would certainly be dangerous and probably useless. By morning the killer could be halfway back to Washington. His arm throbbed wickedly and he could feel the faint dampness where some of the scab had been torn off. Best he clean the injury and wrap it before he ended up fevered and unable to travel.

As he trudged back upstairs, Samuel turned over in his

mind who the devil his rather persistent assassin could be. He was certain the man tonight was the same one who attacked him on the Post Oak Road several weeks ago. How else could he have known to attack the injured arm? As a presidential agent traveling all across the continent, Shelby had made many enemies. Perhaps one of the filibusters he had convinced Allenworthy to betray had found out about his role in foiling their schemes. Dozens of possibilities flashed into his mind including a thought about Tish and Richard, but he dismissed it as ridiculous. As devoted to her as her stepbrother was, she held no hold over him which would impel him to risk his life sneaking around backwoods inns with knives!

"Another failure! The man has more lives than a cat or you have the luck of a blind beggar to let him get away again." Tish slammed her glass down on the pier table and paced furiously across her sitting room. It was late afternoon and she had just returned from a tea for the wives of high-ranking army officers.

As she stormed past him, Richard stood stiffly in the bedroom door, his eyes narrowed and face flushed a dull red. "All the luck was with him. Apparently he decided not to partake of the drugged ale. The minute I entered the room he was on me. Damned lucky for both of us he wasn't able to recognize me. In that case he might have returned with a few questions for you, my pet." He steepled his slender fingers thoughtfully and placed them below his chin. "I shall have to take ship to New Orleans, then go upriver to St. Louis. At least with the divorce petition destroyed, I will have plenty of time in which to plan his demise. They say God would not dare to cross the Mississippi." A chilling smile touched his narrow lips. "Who knows what violent end will befall the colonel on such a dangerous journey?"

Tish unfastened the long rows of tiny pearl buttons down the front of her suit jacket and shrugged it off, then slipped the hook on the waistband of the matching skirt of pale chocolate silk and let it slip into a soft pile on the floor. Beneath it she wore a minimum of undergarments and knew Richard was watching her hungrily.

She should deny him as punishment for his failure, but seeing him in buckskin breeches, smelling of musk and horse excited her. Richard was normally so meticulous about his appearance, perfumed and dressed like a dandy. This way he seemed raw and vital. *More like Samuel,* a voice inside her mind taunted. *Damn you, Samuel! What will I do about you now?*

Another thought had been niggling at the back of her consciousness since Richard reported his second failure to kill her husband. Reaching for a violet satin dressing robe, she donned it letting its heavy sensuous folds cover her flesh as she belted it at her waist. "I've decided on a new strategy, Richard darling. As you've said, we have plenty of time now that the messy matter of divorce has been dealt with."

"What sort of strategy?" His voice was ragged, his eyes tiger yellow, hungrily glued to her voluptuous body.

It was Tish's turn to smile now, beckoning him to come to her by raising her arms so the robe gaped open to reveal her turgid nipples through the sheer beige lace of her low-cut chemise. "You've ridden long and hard, my poor darling," she cooed.

"Not half so hard as I'll ride now," he ground out, seizing a fistful of her silvery hair and yanking the pins from it as he pulled her against him for a brief, brutal kiss. He bit Tish's lip none too gently, turned her to face the bed, and then guided her to a kneeling position upon it. Flipping up the dressing robe and ripping away her undergarments, Richard bared her lush rounded buttocks. As he struggled to rid himself of the buckskin trousers, he alternately kissed and nipped the delectable flesh as Tish groaned and wriggled in anticipation. When he succeeded in working the trousers down his thighs, he drove into her. The blonde moaned and her upper body collapsed on the bed.

Richard thrust slowly, savagely. "And now for that ride." Suddenly, he slapped Tish's rump a stinging blow with the flat of his hand. She shrieked. He crooned as if speaking to a wayward mount. "Now, pet, a rider must use a touch of the crop to put his mare through her paces." He laughed as Tish moaned, but thrust her hips into him. "And sometimes," he continued the violent pumping of his own hips, "a touch of the spur helps as well." He reached between her legs to pinch the tender flesh of her inner thigh. Tish buried her face in the rumpled bedclothes to muffle her whimpering moans of pain . . . and pleasure.

* * *

Spring came early to St. Louis in 1811. Although March had just begun, buds grew fat on the cottonwoods and willows stood tall and thick along the riverbanks. Warm winds blowing from across the vast western prairies smelled sweet with the greening of grass. A hint of spring wildflowers wafted across the high-ceilinged room whose wide glass-paned doors had been thrown open to let in the fresh air.

Soon Santiago Quinn's men back in Santa Fe would begin preparation for their long journey to St. Louis, but he had wintered in the American city this past year with his wife, Elise. Or Liza as her stubborn American brother insisted on calling her.

Quinn looked across the crowded ballroom of the Chouteau mansion, watching his wife charm a circle of male admirers, cleverly extracting information from them as Samuel observed in silent amusement. The whole reason the Quinns were here in this press of people, dressed to the nines in uncomfortable clothing instead of home enjoying the warm beautiful evening with their children, was to aid his brother-in-law.

As respected members of St. Louis society, even if they only resided in the city a few months a year, the Quinns could give Samuel an introduction to all the socially prominent citizens. And hopefully a lead on the British agent who had been stirring up dissension among the local Indian tribes. The mysterious Englishman had a sympathizer high up in the social hierarchy of the city, someone who had given him information about St. Louis's defenses.

Santiago smiled as Elise and Samuel made their way across the polished walnut floor. They were two of a kind. *Spies.* Once the idea had appalled him, but that was when his wife had still been actively engaged in the dangerous profession. Now she had retired to raise their children, leaving Samuel to chase villains threatening the security of the fragile American republic.

Quinn's dark auburn eyebrows arched sardonically as he raised a crystal goblet of champagne and saluted his wife. She smiled serenely as they exchanged glances. Samuel felt the subtle chemistry between them charge the air like summer lightning. Santiago Quinn, son of an Irish mercenary and a Spanish noblewoman, had always been a bit of an enigma to Shelby but the russet-haired rogue made Liza happy. In the final analysis, that was all Samuel really cared about. Although if he were to resign his commission after the impending war and join in the Santa Fe trade, it was best that he and his brother-in-law come to understand each other better.

"As always, Liza had everyone eating out of the palm of her hand," he said to Santiago. "Postmaster Easton and Mr. Charles, the editor of the *Gazette*, had very definite opinions about the danger of having Indians live so near the city."

"Somehow I never thought a leading citizen such as James Rogers a menace. And I can't imagine his white wife scalping anyone," Santiago replied, his eyes hooded as he studied Shelby.

"Jamie Rogers is a Shawnee and they've lived peacefully with Missouri settlers for a generation and have become completely 'civilized,' " Elise interjected, knowing her husband was merely baiting her brother.

"Not at all like his fellow Shawnee to the north, Tecumseh," Shelby replied with equanimity. Quinn was heir to an old Spanish title which he spurned, preferring the unlikely appellation given him the length of the Santa Fe Trail— White Apache. He had spent his youth living among the Lipan Apaches and trusted no white government, not even his wife's.

"Yes, Tecumseh is hostile now, but he was not always. Your government's broken promises and land-greedy settlers drove him to hate the United States," Santiago replied.

"I'll grant that he had justification, but I suspect there was also just a bit of encouragement for his anti-American sentiments from our British neighbors to the north," Shelby replied dryly, not wanting to be drawn into an argument.

Elise grew thoughtful as she weighed the evidence that there would soon be war not only at sea, but here on America's frontier as well. "I'm certain that young War Hawk William Henry Harrison is eager to deal with all the northern tribes who ally with Britain."

"That's his problem. Mine is trying to find out who's supplying whiskey and weapons to the Indians in the Missouri and Mississippi valleys. If all the tribes in the region ally with Britain, these rivers will run red with blood. Manuel Lisa seems to think a Scot called the Red Head could be the agitator," Shelby said, studying Quinn's reaction.

"Robert Dickson is a British agent, but I've never heard that he comes as far south as this. He pretty much keeps to

Prairie du Chien and environs," Santiago replied. "I know the Osage have had no dealings with him. So does Lisa. After all, he's been appointed a special agent by Washington, just to keep them in line."

"And so he has—he and our most gracious host's brother Pierre," Elise said, looking across the room at the elegant and ever genial Auguste Chouteau.

"The Osage are the most powerful tribe in the region. If they desert us, the Sauks, Foxes, Sioux and Kaws will certainly follow suit," Shelby replied with a worried frown. "Since your traders travel through their territory, you should be concerned."

"So should you after investing your life savings in my trading company," Santiago said with an arrogant grin.

"The Osage nations have been our most loyal friends," Elise interjected. Her husband was especially friendly with those Indians. "Chief Pawhuska pledged himself loyal to the American government," she added as if that settled the matter.

But for Shelby, it didn't. "He's getting older now. What about the young hotheads I've been hearing about—Bad Temper and Man Whipper?" His eyes moved from his sister to Santiago.

Quinn shrugged. "Keep your settlers off their land and don't let any of the white men start taking potshots at Indian women picking berries. Then tribal leadership will be able to keep peace."

Shelby looked dubious as Elise continued to oil the waters between them.

Across the room, Olivia St. Etienne gnawed her lip as she watched the beautiful raven-haired woman place her hand proprietarily on Samuel Shelby's arm. She recognized the other tall man engaged in conversation with them, Santiago Quinn, a trader from Santa Fe who was in partnership with a fellow Spaniard, Manuel Lisa, one of St. Louis's leading merchants. But she had never seen the stunning female before. Whatever her relationship with the handsome colonel, it was obvious they were on very friendly terms!

Olivia had waited impatiently for weeks, watching every time the crude long rafts ferried travelers across the turbulent Mississippi, hoping Samuel would be aboard. Finally she had all but despaired, thinking he had perhaps only teased a lovestruck girl with promises to see her again.

Last week she had abandoned haunting the hill overlooking the landing at the bottom of Market Street. The riverfront was rough, filled with odoriferous fur warehouses and loud taverns inhabited by foul-mouthed Kaintucks, bold French voyageurs, and even painted red Indians. Of course, no one recognized her for she wore a disguise in such a neighborhood, but it was nevertheless a foolhardy place for a woman alone. She had believed her watch in vain. Perhaps it still was.

"You are wondering who the handsome young American is, are you not?" a gravelly voice whispered in French with a conspiratorial chuckle.

Olivia turned from her shockingly unladylike perusal of Samuel to confront the social arbiter and first lady of the city, Madame Chouteau, Auguste's mother. The elderly woman's small black eyes sat surrounded by crinkling skin darkened by the hot Missouri sun. All her long life Madame had been an avid gardener and beekeeper, a wealthy woman unafraid to do unconventional things. "I know who he is," Olivia confessed. "Colonel Shelby and I met while I was in Washington with my guardian."

A broad smile pursed Madam's lips, stretching the thin skin until it was drawn tight, revealing several missing teeth. Her shrewd eyes took on a speculative gleam. "Ah, then it is the woman with Count Aranda you wish to know about!"

Madame Chouteau used Santiago Quinn's Spanish title. The Santa Fe trader was mysterious and much whispered about in St. Louis, but Olivia was not interested in him. "Is she Spanish then?"

"No. She is American as is her brother, although her French is flawless as your own. She is Elise Quinn, Aranda's wife. . . . the colonel's sister."

"His sister." Olivia tried to tamp down the delight in her voice but knew she failed when Madame's raspy chuckle tickled her ear.

"True, his sister. The colonel is a fine figure of a man, young, strong and quite devilishly handsome. I found him most charming." A sly smile played about the old lady's mouth as she regarded Olivia, then Samuel.

Madame Chouteau had always been a bold and self-possessed woman. Married off at fifteen to a man three times her age, she had found him so uncongenial that she did the unheard of in eighteenth-century New Orleans society. She took their young son Auguste and returned to the convent where she had been raised, although she did not languish there long. She fell in love with a dashing young adventurer named Pierre Laclede, the founder of St. Louis. Madame lived openly with him as his wife, for there was no divorce recognized among French Creoles. She had borne Laclede four children and followed him upriver to settle the raw frontier at the confluence of the Missouri and Mississippi rivers.

Upon learning the older woman's background, Olivia had immediately felt a kinship with her. They both lived unconventional lives. "How long has he been in the city? I had hoped . . . " her voice faded away as she realized she might well be making a fool of herself over a man who cared nothing for her.

Madame Chouteau was swift to reassure her. "I am given to understand he only arrived yesterday. I think in light of your previous acquaintance that you should welcome him to our city," she said, giving Olivia a gentle shove toward Samuel, who had just excused himself from Elise and Santiago.

Well, why not? The worst he could do was cut her cold as he had done at the Phelps gala back in Washington. Summoning her courage, Olivia walked straight across the crowded room toward him. As if by magic the laughing chattering guests seemed to melt away, clearing a path between them until he turned and saw her. At once those stormy blue eyes lit with recognition, but he stood stock-still in the center of the floor, watching her with an unnervingly magnetic smile on his lips.

Did he welcome her or scorn her impulsive boldness? There was only one way to find out. Olivia's chin raised another notch as she sailed across the glassy floor with her heart ready to fly from her chest. Could Samuel hear it beat?

Chapter 5

Samuel watched her make her way across the floor toward him. Her bold walk held none of the sly, subtle nuances of the belle but rather was incredibly self-confident and forthright. Whatever she might be, Olivia St. Etienne was nothing like his soon-to-be ex-wife. Tish's vapid blond beauty paled by comparison to the fiery freshness of the young Frenchwoman.

His eyes were not the only ones fastened upon her as she approached. Not a man in the room was immune. She was a vision of spring in pure yellow, a difficult color for many women. The vibrant sheer muslin whispered around her slender curves and set off her lightly sun kissed complexion. In contrast her hair, piled in bouncing curls atop her head, seemed as dark and bright as living flames. Her only adornments were the tiny pearls woven artfully through her coiffure, and embroidered across the neckline of her gown. The effect was exquisite yet virginal.

He desired her with a schoolboy intensity that appalled him. His eyes swept up the long-legged contours of her delectable body, past the set of that determined little chin to pause for an instant at the lushness of her slightly parted lips, then moved on to her exotically slanted cat's eyes. The senator had given Tish an emerald necklace and earrings. The heavy deep green stones had overpowered her pallor, but he could envision them caressing Olivia's sun kissed throat, dripping from her tiny ears, matching the dark fires in those incredible eyes. He could imagine her wearing the emeralds and nothing else. *Stop it! Fool.* What was it about this chit that so affected his lusty fancies?

As she approached him, Olivia watched those stormy blue eyes assess her with frank male appetite, but he made no attempt to meet her halfway. Rather, he stood arrogantly in the center of the floor, tall and splendid looking in the perfectly fitted blue uniform, waiting for her. Did he find her as beautiful as the sophisticated women he must have known in Washington? Could he see how she wore her heart on her sleeve? Before courage deserted her, she stopped directly in front of him and smiled, praying her voice would not crack.

"We meet once again, Monsieur Colonel. I warned you I would track you down."

A small smile touched his generous mouth. "And you proved yourself an able huntress, but I thought we'd agreed to dispense with titles, Olivia."

Just then the musicians resumed playing. Without thinking she raised her right hand and asked, "Would you do a lady the honor of dancing with her, Samuel?"

His smile was a dazzling white slash now as he took her hand and swept his other arm around her waist, pulling her closer to him than was strictly proper, even in such a scandalous new dance as the waltz. They glided across the polished walnut floor to the lilt of violin strings, a striking couple moving with grace and verve.

"You are an exceptional dancer, Samuel," Olivia murmured, positive he could feel the frantic tattoo of her heart keeping rhythm with the music.

"As are you. St. Louis is quite a surprise. No one back east would have imagined waltzing in the wilderness."

"Last year a dance master from New Orleans set out an advertisement to teach the waltz and other of the latest dances from Europe. We're not so backward as you Easterners believe," she replied gaily, giddy with the magic of being held in his arms and whirled around the dance floor.

"Not backward at all but quite unconventionally forward," he could not resist teasing.

She felt the blush begin at her throat and rise to the roots of her hair. "Do you find me too forward?" she asked, then instantly wished she could call back the impulsive question when an enigmatic expression passed fleetingly across his face.

Then he smiled again. "And here I thought it was only American women who are so earnest and outspoken."

"I am American—or at least, I am becoming American. I have lived in this country since I was fifteen, a mere slip of a girl."

"And that, of course, was ages ago," he replied gravely.

"At times it seems that way," she said, thinking of her parents' laughing faces, now gone forever.

He looked down at the thick dark red brushes of her lashes that shielded her intense emerald eyes. What made her so suddenly pensive? The French were ever mercurial in temperament. "And do you never repine for your old home?"

Olivia looked up, aware of a subtle shift in his tone. "I miss *Maman* and *Père* terribly, but if you mean France . . ." She shrugged. "The Terror began when I was only a babe. I remember little about any of it and care less. We traveled from country to country throughout my childhood. 'Twas a marvelous adventure but as I grew older I longed for a real home."

"And is this home—St. Louis, a raw frontier town inhabited by fur traders, Creoles and Spaniards, surrounded by Indians?"

She could hear the doubt in his voice, see it in his faintly cynical expression. "I like St. Louis well enough. Someday it will be a great city and all the Louisiana country will become part of the United States."

"You sound just like my sister," he said, suddenly struck by the insight. In spite of their different coloring and backgrounds, Olivia reminded him of Liza.

"She is most beautiful. I confess I was taken with a fit of jealousy when I first saw you with her."

He raised one eyebrow sardonically. "Were you now?"

She blushed again. "For some reason my mouth outruns my brain when I'm around you. A most singular occurrence. It seldom afflicts me otherwise."

"I, too, must confess a certain . . . impulsive train of thought when I'm with you." He stared into wide green eyes, as dark and fathomless as the waters of the Florida glades. Just as mysterious. And just as dangerous.

Olivia stared up at his harshly beautiful face, wondering what went on behind those piercing eyes, now storm tossed to a steely gray. Just then the music stopped. They stood facing each other, still touching, oblivious of those around them quitting the floor. "You sound as if you are angry with me because of this . . . impulse, yet it is you who have come a thousand miles to my city."

"Point well taken," Samuel replied, shaking his head ruefully to break the spell. He offered her his arm and they strolled through the crowd.

"Why are you here? I do not think it is because you have followed my siren call through the wilderness," she added dryly. The question seemed all too natural to Olivia. She waited, wondering if he would answer since he had been so evasive about himself until now.

"Cat's eyes and cat's curiosity. Careful, puss, lest it get you in trouble, too," he said, ushering her through a door which opened onto Madame Chouteau's gardens.

"Am I in danger then?" she asked as they walked into the soft gold light cast from lanterns suspended overhead in the trees growing around the side of the mansion.

"In more ways than one," he murmured, feeling the cool silkiness of her skin where his hand pressed lightly against her back. The delicate fragrance of redbud and daffodils scented the night air combined with the pungent moisture of fog that drifted up from the river after dusk. Yet he smelled nothing but the perfume in her hair and wanted nothing more than to spill its fiery splendor around her bare shoulders and bury his face in it.

The terrace was sparsely populated by strollers since the early spring evening had begun to turn cool. Then, too, proper young ladies did not wander unattended into the darkness with their dance partners. Olivia was acutely aware of the man walking beside her who guided her with the lightest touch as if she were his creature, utterly malleable, eager to do his bidding. That incredible and troubling kiss in the deserted Virginia cabin had haunted her dreams. She could still feel the heat and hardness of his body, taste his mouth, smell the male scent of him, as if he had marked her for all time with just that one brief encounter.

"I should not be out here with you," she finally said as the glow of lantern light faded and only the sliver of a new moon cast its silvery light on them.

"No, you probably should not," Samuel said, guiding her farther away from the house into the cool isolation of the yard. A large stone wall, ten feet high, surrounded the grounds. When they could go no farther, he stopped, uncertain of what he would do next.

Olivia stood surrounded by shrubbery, her head and shoulders dappled by the shadows of a redbud tree which had just begun to blossom. She faced him and did not move. A slight tremor shook her slender figure as a breeze arose, but she did not tremble from the cold. A dark pervasive heat infused her being.

Samuel saw the tiny shudder, heard the soft expectant catch of her breath and he was lost. Uttering an oath he gathered her into his arms, pulling her against him as he stepped behind the redbud. When his mouth swooped down to hers, she gave a small incoherent cry and flung her arms around his neck.

From the opposite end of the yard a figure stood in deep shadows watching the young couple kiss with such fierce ardor. The embrace continued for several moments as Shelby slanted his lips against hers, shifting and deepening his caresses while Olivia molded herself to him, clinging and whimpering in acquiescence.

When Shelby backed against the cold stone wall, he seemed to regain his senses and broke off the wildly passionate kiss, holding her at arm's length, then touching her face tenderly with his hand. They exchanged a few murmured words as she repaired her dishabille. He offered her his arm and escorted her back to the bright lights and music coming from the house.

Emory Wescott moved out of the shadows, his cold gray eyes narrowed in calculation. Then a slow smile insinuated itself across his fleshy face.

Emory and Olivia rode up to the bluffs north of the city as the sun rose in dazzling splendor across the wide expanse of the Missouri River rushing below them. A wide open rolling stretch of grassland had been made into a racetrack where all the citizens of St. Louis congregated, from rough river rats to wealthy businessmen.

"Yer awfully quiet this morning, gel. Not feeling quite the thing? Did you drink too much of old Auguste's French wine last night?" Emory studied her with hooded eyes.

"Of course not," she replied more waspishly than she intended, then softened her voice assuringly, "I sipped only one glass of champagne. Never fear, I shall do fine this morning."

"Only see that you do," he admonished, squinting ahead at the gathering crowd as he reined in the carriage horses beside a thicket of sumac growing near the side of the road.

When the phaeton came to a halt, Olivia seized a small carpetbag from the floor and gracefully climbed down. "The usual place after?" she asked. He nodded peremptorily as he snapped the reins and the vehicle lurched forward. Uncle Emory was really a terrible driver, she thought as she turned toward a narrow path snaking through the dense undergrowth, carefully holding the skirt of her stiff twill morning suit away from the scratchy weeds.

As she walked through the undergrowth, Olivia's mind returned again and again to the preceding night at the Chouteaus' soiree, or more precisely, to the interlude with Samuel Shelby in the garden. He had kissed her with such savage intensity and yet such sweetness. She had dared to hope that he planned to court her. She had melted into him, lost in that strange new maelstrom of desire to which he had introduced her back in that deserted cabin months ago. Touching her lips with her fingertips she could still feel the passion bruised tingling, remember the heat and the wild beating of her heart—before he crushed it once more by breaking away from her.

"This is insane, Olivia," he had said raggedly, holding her at arm's length.

If not for his support, Olivia knew she would have fallen to the ground and quite ruined her expensive new gown. She could not look at him for a moment, but then he had taken her chin in his palm and raised her face so she had to meet those troubling blue eyes. A blush had stained her cheeks and her heart was still beating like a mad thing.

"Once more I must apologize for manhandling you," he had said ruefully as he gently tucked an errant curl back into place.

Anger fueled her boldness. "That's it, then. Another apology, nothing else?"

"What would you have of me, Olivia? We've only met twice and both circumstances were only a bit less than scandalous. I'm here on assignment at Fort Bellefontaine and have yet to report to the post commander."

He had seemed uncomfortable at that juncture and his loss of cool control gave her courage. She stepped closer and began to smooth her bodice as she spoke. "And once you begin your duties . . . what then? Surely the army cannot take twenty-fours a day of your time. The fort is scarcely an hour's ride from my guardian's house."

His smile had melted her bones then. "I really don't know what to make of you, Olivia. You're like no other woman I've ever met."

"At least that is a start. Perhaps you'll find me full of even more surprises . . . and I you . . ." She had let the last sentence hang in the air, a question unanswered, perhaps unanswerable, as they walked sedately back to the house.

Would he call on her? In the clear light of day, Olivia realized he had made no promise. She would simply have to wait and see what happened.

At the opposite end of the river bluff a lone rider made his way uphill toward the deserted racetrack for a secret rendezvous. Reining in his rangy dun gelding, Stuart Pardee surveyed the open meadow from the cover of a dense patch of scrub oak growing on the hillside. His rawboned hands held the reins loosely as he slouched in the saddle. Tall and gauntly thin, his body gave the impression that its various parts did not fit together as a unified whole, misleading the casual observer to think him clumsy and ineffectual. He was anything but. Pale, colorless eyes, set deep in his pockmarked face, scanned the horizon with predatory efficiency. Running one big hand over his thatch of heavy tan hair, he caught sight of his target. A slow smile slashed his wide mouth revealing a set of large yellow teeth. Pardee kicked the dun into a canter, skirting the edge of the woods, headed toward their usual meeting place.

The small black phaeton pulled up in front of the rider. "You racing today?" Emory Wescott inquired, noting the light saddle on Pardee's mount.

"Thought I might try my luck. The track'll be slow from last night's rain," Pardee replied in the heavy Yorkshire accent he had never lost in spite of emigrating to Canada at the tender age of fourteen. He leaned forward resting his forearm across the saddle horn and spit a wad of blackened tobacco juice near one polished carriage wheel. "The whiskey here yet?"

"It takes a while. Smuggling sixty barrels up the Mississippi without attracting notice isn't easy," Wescott replied tightly.

"Thought the bloke had a hidden compartment in the bottom of his keelboat," Pardee said.

Although the morning air was clear and cool, Wescott felt a fine beading of perspiration forming on his forehead. "There are such matters as bad weather, changing channels in the river, hostile Southern tribes, all manner of things to cause delay."

"Hell with your bloody delays. I need that shipment before I head upriver. The Osage will be breaking winter camp in a few weeks. It's easier to deal with them before they scatter to the west for the spring hunt."

"You might easier convince the young malcontents to ally with the British once they are out of the villages and away from the old men."

"You don't know a bloody thing about savages, Wescott. They don't work that way. I plan to speak before their tribal elders and the two great chiefs. If I can win them over, it'll mean more than five thousand Big and Little Osage breaking their treaty with the Americans and joining His Majesty's government."

"There's another matter you'd better consider as well. My contacts in the capital advise me a presidential agent from Washington just arrived in St. Louis." Wescott watched with self-importance as the arrogant Englishman digested that unsettling bit of information.

"Who is he?"

"Name's Shelby. A colonel in the army, ostensibly assigned to the Bellefontaine Cantonment. His real mission is to find you."

Pardee's pale eyes flashed with scornful amusement. "And *you,* I dare say. It'll be easy enough to kill him," he added, enjoying watching Wescott's face redden.

"No." The flat pronouncement surprised the Englishman. Pleased to have his undivided attention, Wescott elaborated. "Shelby will be a deal more useful to us alive . . . if we can learn what he is about and keep one step ahead of him and those bungling Republicans in Madison's administration."

"How are you going to accomplish that?"

Pardee's interest was piqued and Wescott relished the sense of power it gave him. Smiling in satisfaction, he replied, "I have my plans, Stuart, I have my plans, never you fear. Only remember that I have served your king quite effectively and will continue to do so after the war comes. I am on Britain's side."

Pardee laughed mirthlessly. "You ain't on nobody's side but yer own, my good man. You'd sell yer own sister—or that fire-haired ward of yours—if the price was right. You just remember I hold your gold until you bring me the whiskey. I'll keep an eye on your soldier boy, too, never fear." He started to ride past the carriage, then reined in right beside the cab and leaned over the dun's neck, patting him.

"Wouldn't want to make a little wager on who wins today's race, would you . . . say the price of that shipment?"

"My horses are one business. Trade with you is another. I make it a policy never to mix the two," Wescott answered stiffly. Damn, he hated the way the English bastard made him sweat! It would serve Pardee right if he switched sides and turned him in to Shelby. Then, again, he might get an early installment on that British gold. "On second consideration, perhaps we might arrange a small wager . . ."

Eyes hooded, Pardee again slouched over his saddle. "How much?"

The crowd that gathered on the bluffs for the race reflected the motley composition of the city below. Barrel-chested, banty-legged French-Canadian voyageurs in ragged buckskins drank and laughed animatedly. A fair-haired, pale-skinned Kaintuck towered over them, with his Pennsylvania long rifle slung loosely in the crook of his arm as he lobbed a noisome wad of tobacco onto the muddy earth. Two sharp Yankee lawyers sweating in black suits stood gawking, looking dull as crows. A gaggle of jovial, florid-faced German merchants and Italian wine growers with dancing dark eyes loudly exchanged bets on the local favorites. Swarthy Spaniards and elegant Creole families held themselves aloof from half-naked Osage, Kickapoo and Sioux Indians who wandered about. A handful of slaves stood deferentially in the background as their owners made wagers. Ladies fanned themselves against the rising warmth of the day and exchanged gossip about the previous night's social event.

A babble of French, Spanish, English and a smattering of Indian dialects all intermixed in accents crude and cultivated. On a race day, the cream of St. Louis society mingled with the roughest elements from the riverfront and the wildest denizens of the backcountry. Samuel surveyed the crowd from the vantage point of his big roan stallion.

Elise Shelby Quinn sat beside him on a dainty white mare. Her violet eyes were fixed on her husband as she recalled the first time she had seen Santiago Quinn race at this very track six years earlier. How splendidly their lives had turned out after that. And how tragically unhappy her brother's personal life had become. Elise had instinctively disliked Letitia Soames from the moment she had met the Virginia belle, but by then Samuel had already wed her. Over the past four years she had read between the lines of his none too infrequent letters. Now that they were together she had observed firsthand his dissatisfaction with his marriage. It did not take her skill as a former presidential agent to know that her brother was unhappy, yet Elise had been shocked and saddened when he told her about the divorce. What must he have endured to be forced into such a drastic decision?

She longed to give comfort but was loath to pry. "Samuel, I know how I felt when you asked me about Edouard . . ." she began tentatively, "and I'll understand if you don't wish to talk about it, but I thought perhaps since I survived the failure of a disastrous first marriage, I might be a good listener."

"I guess it was rather a bombshell yesterday, wasn't it?" he replied. "I didn't mean to spring it on you, but I've been preoccupied with this assignment. Tish and my life back east are behind me now . . ."

Elise watched a haunted expression pass fleetingly across his face, then vanish, replaced by the smiling cynical harshness that had become second nature to him in the past four years. "Oh, Samuel, what has become of the earnest young idealist you used to be? You had such faith in life, such joy in it."

"Did I? It seems so long ago, I don't remember," he said absently.

"I remember a brave and foolhardy younger brother who risked his life to free me from Edouard."

"Be happy, Liza. At least one member of the Shelby clan deserves a good marriage. Lord knows Elkhanah never had one and neither have I."

"Father's case was different. He and *Maman* had been wed for sixteen years with two children when she left him. You've yet to see your thirtieth year and have no children with Tish."

"No, she never 'burdened' me with children," he said bitterly. "She didn't want the encumbrance. Being *enceinte* would've interfered with her political ambitions."

Elise blanched as she watched his jaw clench. The roan shied nervously when his hands inadvertently tightened on the reins. She reached out and placed her hand on his. "I remember how bleak things once appeared for me. Someday this will change for you, too. There will be a woman—"

"No, Liza, at least not the way you mean. I'll never marry again." There was a flat finality in his voice.

"I said the same thing once, and I did not even bother with a divorce. Only wait and see what life has in store, little brother."

A smile softened his features as he turned toward her. "As I've often reminded you since we were children, Liza, I may be younger than you but I am *not* smaller."

She returned his smile, then caught sight of Emory Wescott. "That odious New England merchant seems intent on making his way up the hill to us." Dressed in expensive black wool worsted, he looked formidable, even afoot. "I wonder what he wants."

"We'll find out shortly. Why do you dislike him?" Samuel eyed her curiously, always trusting her keen insights.

"Call it feminine intuition or my credence to some vague rumors about how he makes his living."

"I thought he was a trader in mercantile goods between here and the Eastern seaboard."

"He is that and also dabbles in breeding and racing horses, but none of his ventures seem sufficient to explain his wealth."

"How do the rumors explain it?" Shelby's interest was piqued, not only because of his mission but also because of Wescott's ward. The thought annoyed him.

"I heard it mentioned that he was originally from Maine and the New England states are in the British hip pocket when it comes to trade. I haven't lived here long enough to learn anything more. I merely dislike him . . . because I dislike him."

Samuel stroked his jaw consideringly. "He might actually be my link to the Englishman, that agent stirring up the tribes in the area." Abruptly he shifted his focus, asking, "Do you know anything about his ward, the French girl?"

In spite of the casual way he asked the question, Elise picked up the subtle nuance of change in his voice. "That striking young redhead? No, but she's quite breathtaking. I seem to recall that you danced with her last evening." Elise turned her attention from the puffing Wescott back to Samuel.

"She was rather bold about approaching me. Asked me to dance, as a matter of fact." His face actually reddened an imperceptible bit beneath his tan, something he knew his sister would note. He would not arm her for matchmaking by explaining his earlier encounters with Olivia St. Etienne.

"I've not had the opportunity to meet her yet but I'm certain I will once we get settled in our house here. The children are a bit homesick but I think a few months a year out of New Mexico won't hurt them."

"You want them reared under the American flag, don't deny it," Samuel only half teased.

Elise sniffed dismissively. "Here comes Mr. Wescott. Shall I inquire after your redhead or will you?"

"She's not *my* redhead, only a pretty bit of fluff with whom I shared a dance." *Liar.*

"Good morning to you, Mrs. Quinn, Colonel," Emory Wescott said as they walked their horses down the long incline toward him.

"I don't believe I've had the pleasure of an introduction," Samuel said as he dismounted and then assisted his sister from her mare.

"Samuel, this is Mr. Emory Wescott, one of St. Louis's leading merchants. Mr. Wescott, my brother, Samuel Sheridan Shelby." As Elise made introductions, the two men shook hands and took each other's measure. Wescott was barrel-chested and powerfully built but going to fat around the middle, still a formidable man in a free-for-all, Shelby guessed, meeting those cold gray eyes and reading utter ruthlessness in their icy depths.

Superficially Wescott was all joviality. "I am a merchant, but today I'm wearing my horse trader's hat, so to speak. Admired that blue roan of yours as soon as I spotted it from across the track. Looks to be a fast 'un. Unusual color, too. How much would you take for him?"

"He isn't for sale. I just crossed half the continent with him. A soldier needs a reliable mount."

"I'd give you five hundred in gold for him."

In spite of Wescott's offer, which was generous in the extreme, Samuel knew that their encounter was not about a horse. What was Wescott after? Had he perhaps found out about his relationship with Olivia? *Not likely, else he would've come after me with a shotgun and a preacher.* Still there was something about Emory Wescott that did not ring true. Liza had felt it at once and he agreed with her intuition.

"The offer is generous, but I'm afraid I must decline," he said with a shrug. When the New Englander nodded in acceptance, Samuel knew he was little bothered by the refusal.

Wescott turned to Elise and said, "I understand your husband's blood bay is running today. Now there's another horse I'd dearly love to own—or his sire."

"Red Hand and True Blood are my husband's finest horses. He'll never part with either, as he's already told you."

"I have a fine sorrel running this morning. Fast young mare, Gypsy Lady."

"Is that boy riding for you again?" Elise asked. "He's quite a horseman. Even my husband, who learned to ride among the Apaches, says he's remarkable."

"And the lad's small frame makes him damned hard to beat on that fleet little mare. Care to make a wager on your brother-in-law's horse, Colonel Shelby?"

"How could I refuse, especially since I'm going into business with him?" Samuel watched Wescott's reaction to that piece of news which was not generally known as yet.

"Are you now?" Wescott nodded, only superficially interested. "I still want the roan and my sorrel is prime horseflesh. What if we wager them? If Red Hand finishes ahead of Gypsy Lady, I forfeit her, but if Gypsy beats the bay, you forfeit your roan." He waited, hands across his brocade waistcoat, rocking back on the heels of his expensive Hessian boots.

Cocky bastard. "Does Gypsy Lady always win?" he asked his sister.

She shrugged. "She's never been beaten, but she's never run against Red Hand either."

Samuel turned back to the older man. "How can I be disloyal to my sister?"

Elise interjected, "Samuel, don't risk your new mount."

Brother and sister exchanged brief glances, enough for her to understand what he was about. She made no further protest when he said, "You have your wager, Mr. Wescott."

∽ *Chapter 6* ∽

"Look, Samuel, the contestants are getting ready. Let's move closer so we can watch the start," Elise said as nearly a dozen horsemen lined up behind a marker sunk into the mud.

"The rain last night really made a mess of the course," Samuel said as they wended their way down the hillside and into the crowd where Wescott had disappeared when he left them.

"You'll get used to Missouri weather. It's ever changeable. If you don't like it, only wait for a moment," Elise said, dimpling.

"It'll be a slow track today. That should work to the advantage of a big strong brute like Red Hand."

"You mean you hope so, else you lose your stallion," she replied with a cheeky grin, but then her expression turned serious. "You want to know what he's really after, don't you?"

"He didn't simply want my horse."

"Maybe he saw you dancing with his ward last night and wanted to see if you're a proper suitor."

Samuel gave her a baleful look. "I'm no woman's suitor, Liza. Just remember that." He began to scan the crowd for Wescott. "Keep your ears attuned for British accents," he murmured as they wended their way through a babel of languages all being spoken at once.

"I've heard several already but I'm sure none of them is your quarry," she replied.

"I didn't think it would be easy," Samuel replied glumly. "Best I watch who our friend Wescott approaches."

"Samuel, I'd like to get a better view of the race, away from the crowd. See that stand of oaks?"

He followed her finger across the wide plain to a timbered area. "You mean around those sink ponds?"

"Yes. The racecourse turns there and I know a cut through where we can see the riders coming around the bend into the homestretch. That's where Santiago will let Red Hand go, after the others are winded."

He grinned at her. "You mean you hope he will."

She kneed her mare ahead, calling over her shoulder, "You mean he'd better or you'll be walking home!"

As they made their way through the crowd, Samuel sized up the horses and riders at the starting line. They were a motley group, as international as the city itself. A dandified Creole gentleman from New Orleans sat a smart looking chestnut mare. Next to him a buckskin clad Kaintuck struggled to keep a piebald with rolling eyes under control. Santiago Quinn's blood bay was to Samuel's way of thinking the finest looking piece of horseflesh in the race, but a gaunt, rawboned man's tough, rangy dun looked as if it might be a stayer on such a long course over muddy ground.

Then he saw Wescott talking to the youth who was riding his entry. The sorrel was long-legged and sleek, obviously from excellent bloodlines. The fine arch of her neck indicated some Arabian in her ancestry. If he won the horse, what the hell would he do with her? A grin tugged at his mouth as he considered for what price he'd sell Gypsy Lady back to Emory Wescott.

"What are you thinking?" Elise asked.

"How much Wescott would be willing to pay to keep his sorrel."

"Don't be too cocky. Remember Santiago told me that Wescott's mare hasn't lost a race since that boy started riding her."

Shelby studied the youth who was slight but held his mount's reins with complete self-assurance. His features were obscured by the brim of his slouch hat beneath which he wore a bright green bandanna tied in the fashion of a black field hand, but his coloring was too light even for a quarter blood. Something nagged at Samuel as his eyes swept over the youth, but then the boy was swallowed up in the crowd.

Elise led the way to the vantage point she had chosen, about a mile across the meadow. The bluffs above the Missouri River were, for the most part, flat with a few gently rolling hills, but pockmarked in this vicinity by small ponds, caused by a collapse in the ceilings of the limestone caves that ran throughout the area. Some of the pools were seventy feet deep and all were surrounded by dense vegetation just now beginning to turn green with the warm kiss of spring.

When they neared the stand of timber around the sink pond, the shot signaling the start of the race rang out. They turned to watch the horses take off on the arduous three-mile course. A small black took an early lead but the nattily dressed youth riding him was pushing him too hard for his lead to last. As they expected, Quinn held Red Hand back, letting the others churn through the mud. By the time they swung past the wide-open stretch of the track that arced around the grassy meadow, Wescott's sorrel and the big dun were neck and neck.

When they neared the southern edge of the sink pond, Elise said indignantly, "Look how the dun is crowding the sorrel. That rider ought to be disqualified."

"You know these races don't have rules, Liza," Samuel replied, watching the skill with which the boy was avoiding the jostling tactics of the larger rider. But when the big man began to use his coiled rawhide whip trying to unseat the youth as they went into the turn, Samuel cursed and rode toward them.

The two horses were dangerously close to the steep muddy embankment of the sink pond and the dun's rider was trying to force Gypsy Lady down into the water. For a moment it looked as if the game kid would outdistance his tormentor but then the mare's hind foot slid in the mud, throwing her off stride and the dun caught up again with a mighty lunge.

The big man raised his whip for another punishing blow that would surely send the sleek mare and her rider plunging down the steep brushy incline headlong into icy water of unknown depth. Samuel came bursting through the grass from the opposite side to intersect the dun. Seizing the rider's whip he tore it from the man's grasp, in the process almost unseating him. The big man turned in his saddle with a snarled oath as the other contestants began to fly past them and onto the homestretch. While he and Shelby struggled over the whip, the boy attempted to guide the mare away from the lip of the pond but the ground was covered with slick green mud and the horse could find no purchase.

Samuel heard the combined screams of horse and rider as Gypsy Lady slid, on her haunches, toward the water. Halfway down the mare's progress was broken by a thick oak sapling. The impact sent her rider tumbling out of the saddle and down the slope toward the pond.

Forgetting the dun's rider, Shelby leaped from his stallion's back and began scrambling down the bank. His opponent viciously kicked his horse into a gallop, overtaking the pack, and then slamming his way through the horses ahead of him until he was approaching Quinn's bay which was just taking the lead.

Wescott's jockey hit the water with a splash and a blood-curdling screech with Shelby a moment behind. Despite the warm spring morning, the water was cold. He had to pull the boy out before he was immobilized and sank. The youth flailed ineffectually as Samuel slid to the water's edge, grasping a sapling to keep from ending up in the icy drink himself.

"Calm down, dammit! Grab my hand," Samuel yelled, bracing himself at the water's edge and struggling to get traction as he reached for the small thrashing figure. He succeeded in grasping the youth's wrist as the boy splashed toward the bank. The thought flashed through his mind that the youth's arm was incredibly slim to control a racehorse over such a rough frontier track.

Samuel pulled on that arm and reached for the boy's leather belt, all the while blinking water from his eyes. Just before his vision cleared, his palm came in contact with something full and soft and quite unmistakable beneath the voluminous folds of wet shirt. A breast—a woman's breast! The nipple was hardened and distended by contact with the icy water. It was outlined brazenly beneath the wet cloth that clung like second skin to her body.

He blinked again and focused his eyes. "You!"

Olivia cringed as he let out a thunderous oath and impaled her with his saber sharp blue glare. She tried vainly to gain her footing on the slippery rocks at the water's edge. It was no use. His grip on her arm tightened as he reacted, jerking her forward so she lost her balance. With a loud smack she landed full-length against the hard warm wall of his body, knocking them both down onto the muddy bank. He growled another particularly vile expletive as a big wad of mud-smeared dark red hair plopped onto his face.

Spitting it out of his mouth and yanking it away from his eyes, he glared at her incredulously. "You do have the damnedest ways of running into a man that I've ever seen, Miss St. Etienne."

Struggling vainly to wad her wet hair back beneath the bandanna which had slipped off, she replied breathlessly, "Oh, dear, we're back to surnames again. Does that mean you no longer consider us friends?"

He pushed up with both elbows braced in the mire behind him and looked up at her with a sardonic lift of his eyebrows. "Considering our rather compromising position at the moment, some people might think we're a hell of a lot closer than friends!"

She was straddling his lower body, her buttocks pressed against his fly so that her slightest movement ground her pelvis against him in an exceedingly improper manner and an even more improper location. "Ooh!" Olivia tried to wiggle off him as his eyes raked her with a sudden blaze of lust.

Lord above but she was beautiful. He had seen her bedecked in embossed muslin when he danced with her in the Chouteaus' ballroom, but soaked to the skin, muddy and filthy, clad in boy's clothes, she was even more bewitching. The baggy tan trousers and oversized gray homespun shirt had now metamorphosed into second skin, clinging to every inch of sweet saucy curves. Amazing that a woman so slim could have such magnificently flared hips and rounded buttocks and such high pert breasts. His palm still burned from touching one, feeling the hard nubby point of its nipple. Samuel felt himself growing hard as she wriggled to escape him, slipping and sliding in the muck.

Quickly, lest she see the effect she had on him, he rolled up and rested his forearms on his bent knees. "That bastard on the dun could've broken your neck!"

"He's not the first one to try. As you can see, I'm still intact."

There was more than one way to take that remark. He scarcely had time for the cynical thought to surface before she rushed on.

"I've raced Uncle Emory's fastest horses on tracks from here to the East Coast. I hardly ever lose—wouldn't have today if Gypsy hadn't lost her footing before I could slip past that miserable dun."

Samuel stared in dumbfounded amazement, watching those pretty little haunches work as she clambered up to where her mare stood patiently waiting. She boasted as arrogantly as a swaggering sixteen-year-old boy. "You're actually proud of sneaking around dressed in britches," he accused.

Olivia turned back to him stiffly. "Why shouldn't I be? I've won a fortune for Wescott Stables. I learned to ride as a small girl. The duke of San Giorno himself gave me my first pony when I was four years old," she said, soothing the frightened mare. "As to the disguise"—she shrugged—"it's not my fault men are so insecure they're afraid to let a woman compete."

"Afraid?" he echoed, bristling.

"Afraid," she pronounced smugly. "I've never lost once at the St. Louis track in our three years of racing."

He ground out, "Well, you have now. What kind of guardian would allow his ward to take such risks for money?" As the breeze picked up, she began to shiver harder. Before Olivia could answer his accusatory remark, Samuel jackknifed up and seized her by one grimy little hand. "Come on, let's get you wrapped up in my bedroll blanket before you take a lung fever."

Olivia felt herself being pulled up the steep slippery slope behind Samuel. "Wait"—she tried to jerk free—"I have to get Lady—"

She never got to finish the sentence. The earth simply seemed to move beneath her feet. When she went down, her arm was nearly yanked from its socket. Her fall created a chain reaction, the abrupt yank throwing Samuel off balance, causing him to lose his footing.

In a blur he went down on top of her and they rolled halfway to the bottom of the incline again, arms and legs entwined, fortunately coming to rest against the mushy softness of a large rotted log. Her small wet body trembled beneath his big warm one as she looked up into his eyes.

"Your concern for keeping me warm is most admirable, Monsieur Colonel, but do you think this is quite proper?" she teased, unable to keep a straight face. The devilish lights dancing in those green eyes gave way to laughter bubbling up inside her.

Shelby looked down into her face and shook his head, then threw it back with a loud rumble of laughter. "You *are* the most damnable female I've ever met, Olivia."

His mouth hovered over hers. A small smudge of mud

brushed against one side of her lower lip. He felt an urge to lick it clean and taste the soft pink skin of that mouth.

Olivia smiled up at him, forgetting her earlier pique, even forgetting the cold misery of her drenched clothes. She had never felt so warm, so safe, so protected in her entire life. She willed him to kiss her.

Samuel lowered his mouth. The tip of his tongue snaked out to flick away the tiny daub of mud, then his lips brushed hers. Before he could deepen the caress a loud halloo echoed across the meadow. The race was over and someone had come in search of them.

"I think we had better find that blanket for you," he said thickly as he stood up and helped her to her feet. "Let's not retrace our path through that mudslide." He led her in a diagonal line up the slope using rocky and brushy ground to gain purchase until they crested the rise a few yards behind where his roan stood grazing peacefully.

Samuel quickly untied the blanket and wrapped her in it. As she stood shivering, he climbed back down the hill and led Gypsy Lady up.

Olivia was relieved that her mount seemed unharmed. "Oh, Gypsy, you good girl. Thank heaven you're all right," she exclaimed as she knelt to examine the mare's forelegs.

Samuel looked across the meadow to where a group of people approached them. Upon seeing Olivia's long red hair, several of the men exclaimed in anger and a loud buzzing spread through the crowd as its mood grew more ugly. Lyman Simms, the track proprietor, had a black scowl creasing his forehead so deeply it looked as if he had been hit with an ax. A tight-lipped Emory Wescott drove his phaeton just behind, followed by several highly scandalized Creole gentlemen, including one race participant, who until that last turn, had been soundly outridden by a slip of a girl. The only ones who looked happy to see Samuel and Olivia were the smiling Quinns. Santiago must have won.

"Just what the hell is going on here, Miss Olivia?" Simms asked, although he could plainly see for himself.

"Looks like Ollie is a lady," one Kaintuck said with a raucous laugh, to which his companion jibed, "Dressed in britches, she shore ain't no lady."

"After such an affront, Monsieur Wescott and his jockey should be banned from all future horse racing in Louisiana Territory," Georges Jadot said spitefully.

Several other men chorused agreement, but Simms's voice rose above the cacophony. "I wouldn't have believed it if I didn't see it for myself," he said, turning red-faced away from Olivia, who struggled to hold the blanket around her shoulders. "You know I ought to bar you from racing here again, Emory."

"Now, Lyman, the girl's a natural jockey. You've seen her ride dozens of times in the past years and she's never lost a race."

"She's a female. It ain't fittin' and I will not have it on my track," Simms said stubbornly.

"The hell with what's fitting. Can't you *gentlemen* see the lady's half-frozen?" Samuel interrupted angrily.

"Yes, certainly, certainly," Wescott replied. "I shall see to my ward, Colonel. As to our wager, I'd like the opportunity to make you an offer for the mare."

"Uncle Emory, you bet Gypsy Lady!" Olivia exclaimed, horrified.

"If *you* hadn't lost, I'd still have Gypsy, and I would've won that splendid blue roan," Wescott said testily, then turned unctuously back to Shelby. "About the mare—"

"I'll be at Quinn's warehouse tomorrow. We can settle up there," Samuel replied, wanting nothing more than to get out of the wind and into some clean, dry clothes. Olivia looked as if she could use the same, but the stubborn little chit had stomped over to the mare and swung up into the saddle as nimbly as a stableboy. She looked down at her guardian, still furious over the bet, then shifted her gaze to Samuel and smiled as if daring him to challenge her right to the horse. He turned away from Wescott and walked over to her. Even muddy she was delectable. "Get home and into a hot bath, urchin," he whispered.

"You could use one, too," she said with a husky laugh. "Now we're almost even. I saved your life. Maybe you saved mine—if I still don't take lung fever and die."

Samuel stood watching her ride away, bemused. He did not see the calculating look in Emory Wescott's eyes. Elise Quinn did and it troubled her.

"Emory was sure the big loser today," Santiago said as they strolled into the front parlor of their new house, flushed with his success at the race. Although nowhere as grand as the Chouteaus' home, it was tightly constructed of stone with two-foot-thick walls to hold the merciless summer sun at bay, two-stories high with six bedrooms to accommodate their growing family and frequent visitors.

"I really wanted to get my hands on that bastard who rode the dun. He could've killed Olivia," Samuel said.

"He knew better than to stick around after everyone found out that boy he rode into the sink pond was really Wescott's ward," Elise said, chewing on her bottom lip pensively.

"What would make a responsible man risk his reputation by allowing a woman to race his horses?" Santiago asked.

"What respectable woman would agree to do it?" Samuel asked.

"She's certainly proven herself capable in past races," Elise responded, feeling the need to defend her sex against male prejudices. "We women aren't the frail helpless creatures you men would like us to be," she added sweetly. "Remember it was you, dear husband, who gave me my first lesson in riding astride."

"Not in men's clothes," Santiago replied.

"Not at first, but I wore them, anyway," she countered.

Quinn sighed and Shelby laughed, both knowing it was useless to argue further. With a nod of her head, Elise swept from the room, headed upstairs to check on the children. A rap on the front door brought Santiago to his feet. He opened it to one of Postmaster Easton's young riders, Nathaniel Everett.

The boy nodded politely and swallowed, his prominent Adam's apple bobbing nervously. "Mr. Easton thought you'd want to have this as soon as possible, Colonel," the boy said, holding up a black-edged envelope for Samuel.

A strange sense of foreboding gripped him as he felt the weight of heavy velum paper in his hands. As he slowly tore open the envelope, Santiago thanked the messenger and saw him out the door.

The words on the page danced before Samuel's eyes as he read the terse message from Worthington Soames with disbelief and a disquieting elation:

Dear Samuel,

It is my tragic duty to inform you that your wife is dead. Letitia and Richard were enroute to the Miller plantation when the boat on which they were traveling ran aground and sank in the swollen spring current . . .

Samuel scanned the rest of the letter, fastening on the senator's signature at the bottom of the page. *He must be prostrate with grief.*

But you're not, some demon of conscience taunted, for along with the thought about his father-in-law came another one, utterly unbidden—Olivia St. Etienne returning his passionate embrace in Chouteau's garden.

God above, what sort of monster am I that I feel relief and think of another woman when I learn that my own wife is dead? But then the somber voice of reason reminded him that it was Tish's relentless ambition that had killed his finer feelings for her just as she'd killed the child they'd created. Had he sunk to her level then, so cold and ruthless that he could see only his own advantage in another's tragedy?

Feeling his brother-in-law's hand on his shoulder, Samuel turned, breaking free of the melancholy, self-examination as Santiago said, "Bad news, I take it." Quinn poured two shots of whiskey while Samuel reread the letter. He offered Shelby a glass and waited patiently.

"Yes and no." He combed his fingers through his hair and cursed. "Which is a hell of a thing to say. Yes, it's bad. Tish is dead. Drowned in a boating accident while she and Richard were enroute to the Miller plantation on the James River. Poor devil, he's probably beside himself with grief because he wasn't able to save her."

Quinn watched Shelby down the whiskey in one clean gulp, then pour a refill. "She was a self-centered, destructive woman. I've known a number just like her. In fact, only luck favored me in escaping marriage to one. There's no need for false grief."

"It seems a bit callous to feel relieved, though, doesn't it?" Samuel replied acerbically. "One of the first images that flashed into my mind when I read Tish was dead was of a red-haired hoyden." He muttered an oath of self-loathing.

"Don't punish yourself because you can't mourn Tish and the end of a loveless marriage," Santiago said.

Samuel, deep in thought, seemed not to hear him.

Emory Wescott was pleased. Not inordinately, completely pleased, for he had lost a steady source of income from the girl's racing, not to mention the embarrassment of having her unmasked. She was in disgrace now, a liability, certainly not to be welcomed in polite society. But he had a use for her which pleased him all the same. He leaned back in the seat of his town carriage enjoying the warm morning sunshine as he drove across Main Street toward Quinn's big new warehouse.

That fool Pardee had been the cause of it all, but at least he had been officially disqualified in the race so Wescott need not pay him the substantial wager they had made. As to Gypsy Lady, well, after his offer, that lust besotted young fool Shelby might actually pay *him* for the mare! He chuckled in a self-congratulatory manner. It was really so beautifully simple. Losing the bet yesterday only gave him the excuse to state his offer so precipitously without raising the canny spy's suspicions.

The carriage pulled up in front of a large stone building and the stench of curing pelts wafted out the door. Pelts, especially prime beaver, were the currency of the Mississippi Valley, more widely used than coins or paper money, both of which were exceedingly rare in the wilderness. Much was settled by barter in the West. Emory Wescott thought of the barter in which he was about to engage and smiled.

Chapter 7

Samuel squinted at the spidery writing in the ledger, columns and columns of lists, everything from fox furs to flints, raccoon skins to ribbons. Quinn's clerks labored with incredible diligence, inventorying all the varied goods transferred in and out of the burgeoning warehouse. "Do you actually read and keep track of all the entries?" he asked Santiago as they strolled through the crowded outer office.

Quinn laughed. "Hardly, but I do spot-check for significant discrepancies." They walked out of the clerks room back into the cavernous brick warehouse. Passing by boxes, crates and barrels filled with Eastern goods and bales of peltries from the vastness of the West, Quinn opened another door and ushered Shelby into his private office, then closed the door.

Santiago picked up a sheaf of papers on the large oak desk, then took his seat behind it. After scanning them, he handed the documents to Shelby.

Samuel took the papers, then seated himself on a soft leather chair in the small but opulently furnished room. The walls were lined with books, mostly Spanish, some French, all expensively bound with cordovan leather and embossed in gold leaf, part of his inheritance from the Aranda estate. Samuel spoke both languages fluently and was impressed by the breadth of interest indicated by the selections. Santiago Quinn was a man of many parts.

"That is the partnership agreement I had drawn up," Quinn said. "See if it suits you. I've already purchased shares in Manuel Lisa's spring expedition up to the headwaters of the Missouri."

Samuel looked up at Santiago. "Up the Missouri, you say? How soon? It would provide good cover for me if I went along with Lisa as an investor."

Quinn grinned. "Actually he's getting ready to leave any day now."

Shelby asked, "Would he balk at my going along—in an unofficial capacity, of course?"

Quinn nodded. "Manuel would love having an American officer along."

"Good. How soon can we make the arrangements?"

"I'll handle it. I have some other matters to discuss with Manuel anyway. You look over that agreement and sign it while I'm gone," Santiago said, shoving back his chair. Just as he stood up, a discreet rap sounded on the door. "Come in, Labidoux," he said, expecting his chief clerk. Emory Wescott stood in the doorway which Labidoux held open.

Quinn quirked one reddish eyebrow in surprise. "To what do I owe the honor of your visit, Mr. Wescott? Perhaps to propose a rematch?"

Wescott's face reddened slightly but he clamped down on the impulse to use his heavy silver-handled walking stick to cane the arrogant Spaniard. "No, as a matter of fact, I've come to see Colonel Shelby regarding my wager with him."

Samuel had almost forgotten the fleet mare he'd won, although her rider had never been out of his thoughts. Quinn excused himself, allowing the two men the use of his office to settle their affairs.

"You mentioned yesterday that you're going into the Santa Fe trade with your brother-in-law," Wescott said as the two men shook hands.

A frisson of repugnance coursed through Shelby when he felt the older man's peculiarly fleshy but firm grip. He offered Wescott a chair and took one across from him. Liza was right. Something about Emory Wescott made him distinctly uneasy, too. "I've bought a modest share in Santiago's company. After I retire from the army I plan to settle here in St. Louis."

"Do you now," Wescott said smoothly. "And how soon, may I ask, until you resign your commission?"

As his gaze swept casually past Wescott to the door left partially ajar by Santiago, warning signals went off in Shelby's brain. *The bastard is playing with me. What does he want?* Could Wescott know about his mission? He had been in Washington when Samuel returned from Florida to report on British activities. That was where he first met Olivia as well. A coincidence? "I'll not resign my commission immediately," he replied vaguely, then shifted the conversation to the matter at hand. "About the wager, if you'd like to keep the mare for your ward, I'll understand."

Wescott waved his hand dismissively and smiled. "It is rather about Olivia that I've come to talk."

Samuel studied the florid man's smug expression with a prickle of alarm. *So, this is about your beauteous ward.* "Oh, what about Mademoiselle St. Etienne? I trust she is recovered from her unfortunate accident yesterday?"

"Yes, quite fully recovered. It's come to my attention that you have . . . shall we say, a certain tendresse for her." Wescott let the words drop, gauging Shelby's reaction.

"I was happy to come to her rescue during the race," Samuel said cautiously. Wescott emitted a sharp bark of laughter that grated on Shelby's nerves.

"Did you also come to her rescue at the Chouteaus' ball? Come now, Colonel, I saw the two of you in the garden and you scarcely acted like strangers."

How much had Olivia told the canny old devil? Did Wescott know about that Virginia backroad? Hell, had he been behind the shooting and her timely rescue? Samuel smiled disarmingly and shrugged. "We'd met briefly in Washington several months ago. Your ward is a most remarkable woman, Mr. Wescott. I will confess to a certain mutual attraction, but if you plan to force me into doing the honorable thing, I'm afraid—"

"Oh, I know you're already wed to Senator Soames' daughter. I could scarcely expect you to marry Olivia."

"Really. You'll pardon my curiosity, but is there some other reason you've taken such an interest in my personal life, Mr. Wescott?" Now he was certain Wescott had a hidden agenda of some sort.

Rather too casually the older man shrugged. "No particular interest, Colonel. I know about your wife because Worthington Soames is an old friend of mine," he said self-importantly.

"Are you going to call me out for my reprehensible behavior then?" Shelby asked, highly dubious such was Wescott's intent. But what was he up to?

"That would be most dangerous for a man of my age. I've heard rumors about your lethal skills on the field of honor. Several years ago you dispatched a French diplomat who was accounted to be a far more deadly swordsman that I ever was. No, rather I'm proposing a simple business exchange. Each of us has something the other wants. You now own my most valuable young racer, Gypsy Lady. I, on the other hand, have possession of another *jeune fille,* Olivia. Might I suggest an exchange?"

Samuel felt all the blood drain from his face. Then a furious surge of anger replaced the shock. "Let me get this straight. You're offering your ward to me as a mistress—in exchange for a horse? Damnation, *I* should call *you* out!" Why the hell was he defending the chit? She was probably in on this whole accursed charade!

"Please, Colonel, I really have no desire to visit the dueling fields on Bloody Island," Wescott replied calmly. Business negotiations had always been his forte. "Admit it. You're taken with the chit and she's made it abundantly clear to both of us that she returns your ardor."

"She's from a good family, titled before the revolution in France, or so she told me. I can scarcely believe the spoiled Mademoiselle St. Etienne would accept being my paramour," Samuel said cynically, still horrified with himself for actually considering the obscene proposition.

Admit it. You want her even if she's a British agent.

"After yesterday's scandal, do you think any of the good families in St. Louis will allow their sons to court her?" Wescott asked.

"She raced with your approval. And made a hell of a lot of money for you doing it. You're to blame for sullying her reputation."

"I allowed the girl to race to keep her from other, er, more willful diversions, if you take my meaning. Her parents were libertines, quite hot-blooded, those French, eh?"

It was all Samuel could do not to smash his fist in Wescott's jowly bulldog face. Instead he sat very still, willing himself to remain calm as his guts clenched with sick fury. Damn her, the bewitching little minx, teasing and tantalizing as a courtesan one minute, then as doe-eyed and vulnerable as a green virgin the next. He hated to believe Wescott's nasty insinuations, but they were far from groundless. She was used to having men make fools of themselves over her and she certainly had allowed him to make exceedingly improper advances on several occasions. She ran around the countryside unchaperoned, even dressed as a male and hung around racetracks, scarcely the sort of thing a proper society belle would do.

It was idiocy to get mixed up with her and her unsavory guardian. He was a fool to desire her now that Wescott had confirmed his suspicions about her morals. Samuel cursed silently, hating himself for what he was about to do.

"I may well live to regret this, but you're right. I am taken with her and she does seem to return my regard. If the lady is willing . . ." He shrugged. "Send her to this address tonight and you may keep your horse." He stood up and stepped over to the desk where he scribbled a street number on a slip of paper, then handed it to Wescott as the older man arose.

"Very good, Colonel. I'll give Olivia your regards."

Pointedly Samuel did not offer to shake hands on their unsavory bargain about which he was already having second thoughts. Ever the consummate spy, he casually leaned against the desk and folded his arms across his chest, crossing one booted foot over the other. As Wescott reached the open door, he could not resist a mocking taunt, "Oh, Emory, your intelligence regarding my personal life is sadly in arrears. My first wife is dead." He smiled nastily at the look of surprise and greed written across Wescott's face. "But I do not have the slightest intention of ever making that mistake again."

"Just so you take her off my hands any which way it suits you. The chit's altogether too headstrong for me to trouble myself with any longer," Wescott said sourly as he stormed out the door.

Shelby walked over and closed it firmly. Neither man saw the small figure huddled behind the bales of beaver peltries stacked against the wall next to the office door. Once the coast was clear, Olivia stood up on wobbly legs, testing to see if they would support her.

Nausea churned inside her like boiling acid. She blinked back the stupid girlish indulgence of tears. There was no time for that now. She had to think, to plan. To escape! Furtively she held her dainty gold muslin skirts away from the smelly furs which surrounded her. Her eyes and chest burned, although she knew it was not from their acrid aroma.

What a nightmare this was! Sold by her own guardian and Samuel actually bought her like a slave on the auction block—in exchange for a racehorse! Numbly she realized why Uncle Emory had not been more upset with her for losing the race and having her disguise uncovered. He had been plotting this all along.

She had believed the day so bright with promise only a

few hours ago. After overhearing her guardian tell the housekeeper that he was going down to the mercantile district, she had impulsively decided to follow him so she could "accidentally" run into Samuel while shopping at the Quinn warehouse. Olivia knew Emory intended to settle his debt with the colonel there and she wanted desperately to look her best for the handsome young officer after the debacle yesterday. She had spent an hour fussing with her hair and selecting one of her prettiest new day gowns to impress him.

How could he? The question hammered at her over and over again as she slipped from the busy establishment out into the dust and noise of Main Street. She hailed her servant Obie, who waited patiently with the small rig in the shade of a two-story building across the way. Settling into the padded seat she squeezed her eyes closed and tried to think, but all she could do was replay over and over again the ugly scene she had overheard in that office.

Even though she had always feared that she was a burden to him and a disappointment when she refused his attempts at arranging an advantageous marriage, the depth of her guardian's perfidy shocked her. After the debacle yesterday her reputation in St. Louis was in shambles. No surprise that he should want to rid himself of a reminder of his own blunder in allowing a mere female to triumph on such sacrosanct male turf. Well, she could survive Emory Wescott's treachery.

It was Samuel Shelby's she could never forgive.

He had lied to her from the first time they met. That splendid house in Washington he claimed not to own he shared with his wife. He had been married and never told her. He led her on to hope that he might court her once he arrived in St. Louis. Fool that she was, she had melted like molasses in the sun beneath his touch. Her cheeks burned with shame as she remembered how she had flung herself against his hard body, kissing him back with every bit as much fervor as he had shown in kissing her.

No wonder he thought he could buy you for his plaything!

But the final insult had been his cold announcement to Wescott that he was widowed and never intended to wed again. What utter contempt he must feel for her and for all women. He would use their bodies with delicious skill, but he cared nothing for their finer feelings. He had taught her the pleasures of passion and now he had taught her the pain of betrayal.

"We'll just see, Samuel Shelby, if you ever get the chance to learn the truth about me!"

Samuel sat in front of the table with a brandy glass in one hand, watching the flames on a branch of candles flicker as they burned down. The hour was growing late. She would arrive soon. He sipped the fine old cognac and glanced around the room, wondering what she would think of it. He had leased the small house on Plum Street from an elderly widow who was returning to live with her family in Kaskaskia. The house was made of timber, cut in the French style, the split logs placed vertically with the flat side facing inward. Puncheon floors gleamed with beeswax polish and the walls were whitewashed. The second-story attic, set with two dormer windows, extended over the wide front porch. The rooms were spacious with large glass-paned windows, but the entire house was comprised of only a parlor, dining room and kitchen with the sleeping quarters in the finished attic upstairs. It was cozy and quiet but hardly possessed the elegance of Monsieur Chouteau's grand mansion or even that of the Quinn's big rambling home.

His thoughts centered on the bed upstairs which he had purchased after renting the place. Madam Soulard's small narrow canopied bed would never have accommodated a man of his size. Instead he replaced it with a big feather stuffed mattress set on a specially constructed frame six feet wide by seven feet long. Samuel could see Olivia, slender and vibrant, sitting in the middle of that big soft bed with her pale golden skin gleaming by candlelight and that mass of brilliant coppery hair falling around her shoulders, over her breasts as she opened her arms to welcome him.

Hell, he was rock hard and aching just thinking about her. Best to slow down and think of something else or he'd tear off her clothes and ravish her the moment she walked in the door, never mind the bed upstairs! He sipped more brandy and considered the incredible twists of fate that had taken Tish from his life and brought Olivia to him.

Tish had been treacherous and manipulative. It was unlikely that the St. Etienne girl would be any different if her guardian was to be believed. But was he? This was the tangle that Samuel had been loathe to face all day as he waited for her to arrive. Should he have trusted the word of a knave like Wescott? A man so base and unprincipled as to sell a woman entrusted into his care was scarcely a reliable witness to her virtue—or lack thereof. Could he possibly trick an innocent girl into coming here, confidently expecting a lecherous soldier to use her, even against her will? Damn it!

He could still see her expression, so wide-eyed and vulnerable that day in Virginia and again after the fierce kiss they had shared in the Chouteaus' garden. There had been an innocence to her, an utterly unpracticed shyness in her passionate responses. Was Wescott lying? Was Olivia a virgin given away by a selfish man who could no longer exploit her skills at the racetrack?

Of course she willingly participated in that dangerous charade and even boasted to him of it. At the Chouteau soiree she had pursued him with the startling boldness of a woman of the world. The only thing about which he remained certain was that she was beautiful and that he was inexplicably attracted to her to the point of near obsession.

But what if she *was* innocent, forced out of Wescott's home into his bed against her will? "I'll have to keep a cool head and learn the truth when she arrives. Then we can decide what to do if she has been the victim," he murmured, praying he could maintain enough self-control to carry through the vow once she walked in the door. The problem was that the desire he felt certainly seemed to be mutual. If she was innocent and yet melted into his arms as she had done in the past, Samuel did not know what he would do. But he knew one thing he would never do: marry her.

Taking the responsibility of a mistress was encumbrance enough. Never again another wife. Even if he could trust a woman enough to want to build a life and have children with her, his work was too dangerous. Soon there would be war. He owed his first allegiance to Jemmy Madison, at least for the duration of the conflict.

Thoughts of the impending war again brought Samuel to consider Emory Wescott and his possible motives for placing Olivia in his life. They could both be working for the British. An unsettling thought indeed, but still one he would do well to consider and carefully question Mademoiselle St. Etienne about when she arrived.

Samuel glanced up at the Seth Thomas clock on the mantel. Midnight. Past time that she should be here. He rose and walked over to the front door to look outside. The night still held the brisk chill of early spring but the sky was ablaze with stars. The street was utterly silent in the isolated area where the house was situated. Good folks were asleep. Where the hell was Olivia?

Baptiste Lacroix was drunk. However, his three-day binge was not the problem. The condition of his companion, Sylvestre Robard, was. Sylvestre was dead. Baptiste sat staring disconsolately at the other French Canadian trapper who had unfortunately incurred the wrath of a great "Boston" keelboatman.

Behind the waterfront tavern called Le Coq Rouge, Baptiste lay sprawled against the rough stone wall staring at Sylvestre's body which reposed in the gutter. It was rather the worse for its encounter with Bullfrog Gentry. One ear was chewed off and his jaw broken, but the coupe de grace was the gouged out eyeball dangling across Robard's cheek.

"*Mon ami,* what am I to do now, eh?" Baptiste groused to the corpse in a slurred voice. "I have contracted you to Monsieur Lisa and you had to go and die on me. I must find another to sign on in your place or forfeit the bounty. And, *sacre bleu,* Marie will skin me slick if I have no coin for return passage to New Orleans."

He held his head in both hands to still the pounding in his skull and tried to think. Perhaps the dawn would bring an answer. Already faint rays of pale blue and lavender streaked the flat Illinois prairie on the opposite bank of the vast rolling river. He crawled over to Sylvestre and struggled to hoist the slighter man's remains on his shoulder, then stood up and began to make his way toward a copse of bushes a quarter mile down the bank. The least he could do was lay Robards out where drunken "Bostons" could not spit in his poor mangled face or teamsters run over the body.

Olivia made her way slowly along the riverfront, heading toward the mountainous piles of pelts deposited on the wharf at the bottom of Market Street. In the dim dawn light the boats clustered along the river's edge looked like a low brushy forest in winter, the keelboat masts sticking up like so many dead trees. Numerous smaller craft, crude flatboats and graceful bark canoes, bobbed gently on the current as if signaling their readiness to embark up- or downriver from the central locus of the city.

Many of those boats were headed downriver to New Orleans where her mother's brother, Charles Durand, resided. When first they landed in America he had turned them away just as all *Maman's* family in France had done, disowning her for her forbidden marriage. *Père* had spit on the banquette in front of the Durand mansion, saying he would never again beg from any man. At the time Olivia had been filled with pride for his boldness, but now she must return as a supplicant once more.

Pride was a luxury she could no longer afford. Uncle Charles must surely take her in, for the alternative was unthinkable. Samuel Shelby's blinding white smile and magical lips flashed into her mind's eye but she would never again experience his fiercely possessive kisses or bask in the radiance of his smile—that traitor's smile. No, she would never come to his bed, a shamefully purchased plaything to be discarded when he tired of her.

The difficulty lay in making her way downriver. A woman alone could not travel with rough boatmen and she had no money for passage anyway. She seriously considered stealing some from Emory Wescott's office but in spite of his perfidious attempt to barter her to Samuel, he had taken her in and provided handsomely for her with no obligation to do so. Anyway, if she took his money he might be vindictive enough to set the law on her, in which case Uncle Charles would certainly think her cut from the same cloth as her gambler father.

If only there was a good family heading downriver from whom she could beg asylum—or at the least a job as a nursemaid or servant in return for passage. But she knew of no such family traveling at this time, and time was her enemy for her guardian would have his agents out searching for her in a few short hours. Not that any decent family would shelter her or even hire her now that she had disgraced herself at the racetrack. Everyone would turn her away, possibly even forcibly restrain her until they could fob her off onto her guardian for his tender disposition.

She had no one to rely upon but herself. But if Julian St. Etienne's daughter had inherited nothing else from her father, she had his keen instincts for survival to see her through.

She had employed the disguise she had used with such success for the past several years. Hidden in the bottom of her wardrobe had been several pairs of the baggy britches and voluminous homespun shirts which she had worn to race the Wescott horses. She had returned home after leaving Quinn's warehouse yesterday and made ready for her escape. Pretending civility to her "uncle" had been difficult, but she had succeeded. Then before he could broach his odious news, she had pleaded a headache and sequestered herself in her room. By the time he discovered her absence at the dinner hour, Olivia had been gone for hours and a scruffy boy named Ollie arrived on the riverfront.

But St. Louis after dark was a dangerous place, even for a boy. The taverns belched forth smoke and liquor fumes that seemed all the thicker for the drunken French songs and coarse Anglo-Saxon oaths that also spewed out into the narrow streets. She found a root cellar behind a deserted cabin on Second Street and went to ground for the night. Dawn found her approaching the welter of boats and boatmen at the bottom of Market Street where she hoped to sign on as a crewman on a flatboat laden with peltries bound for New Orleans.

Moving the unwieldy boats was hard labor requiring brawny men. A skinny, smooth-cheeked boy like Ollie quickly encountered jeering rejection. After half a dozen false starts, she had become desperate, seeing in every hard-eyed riverman an agent sent by her guardian to penetrate her disguise and drag her back to Samuel. She was growing frantic when an argument between a swarthy Spaniard and a volatile Frenchman caught her attention. She edged closer to listen.

"You promised me a man for the journey, Baptiste. Without him I will not pay you," the Spaniard said in heavily accented English.

"But, Monsieur Lisa, I must return to New Orleans else my Marie, she will kill me," the French voyageur pleaded.

Olivia observed their argument, recalling her guardian's mention of Manuel Lisa, a mysterious Spaniard from New Orleans who had begun to make money and enemies in the St. Louis fur trade. Taking courage in hand, she approached the disconsolate Baptiste after the beetle-browed, dark-eyed Lisa had dismissed him.

"I couldn't help overhearing your argument with the

Spaniard," she said in French, rubbing her dirt smeared hands on her pants, then hooking her thumbs arrogantly in her belt.

"Yes, and what of it?" Lacroix asked, too wretchedly intent on his hangover to pay attention to the scruffy urchin.

"I need that job—I am experienced. I've worked the boats from New Orleans all the way up to the forts on the Missouri," she lied.

"You look awfully young—and scrawny to have poled a keelboat."

Dredging up every bit of information she had gleaned from her guardian's river trade, she boasted, "I have cordelled through icy water shoulder deep and climbed on logjams. I was the one the men sent to shinny up the trees when we had to winch a keelboat past an embarras blocking the main channel of the Missouri. Why floating down to New Orleans will be child's play for me."

Baptiste's bloodshot hazel eyes lit with interest. The boy mistakenly thought Lisa was headed to New Orleans, not up the Missouri, but he did seem to know about the river. Hell, Lisa had a big crew already. This little one could chop wood and haul water when they camped. "You come with me but let me do all the talking, eh?"

An hour later Baptiste Lacroix had purchased passage aboard a keelboat headed to New Orleans to meet his virago wife. Ollie, against Manuel Lisa's better judgment, had signed on as cabin boy and cook's helper. Neither Lisa nor the "boy" had any idea "he" was headed in the opposite direction from his desired destination.

Chapter 8

Jeremiah, the Wescott butler, bowed deferentially as he ushered the tall army officer into his master's dining room. Bright light poured in the bay windows at Emory Wescott's back as the sun rose that morning. He sat at a Sheraton table while the remains of a hearty breakfast were removed by a kitchen wench.

"Good day, Colonel Shelby. I rather assumed you'd be around, although I confess I thought it would be a bit later. May I offer you coffee? Perhaps some of Sallie's maple cured ham and biscuits?"

"What you may offer me is Olivia." Shelby's voice was low and deadly, his anger tightly leashed beneath an icy mask. He had waited until two before finally abandoning his vigil in the front parlor to ride through the streets of St. Louis, tracing Olivia's route from his house to Wescott's, fearful of foul play. Finding not a trace of the girl, he had returned home to finish off the bottle of brandy, assuming she had reneged on the deal. He was not in good humor.

"I'm afraid I must disappoint you, Colonel. Olivia is not available," Wescott replied with a bitter twist of his lips. "The flighty chit took off sometime yesterday afternoon from what I can gather from her maid. Spoiled little baggage," he muttered angrily into the delicate cup he sipped from.

"She ran away? From me?" Samuel struggled to keep the horror from his voice. Were his fears about her being an innocent pawn true?

Wescott scoffed in disgust. "Of course not. In fact, I had no opportunity to even discuss our arrangement with her. The damned gel just lit out, but not to worry, she's done it before," he lied smoothly.

"You mean she just rides off—dressed like a boy—to attend races without your permission?" Samuel asked incredulously. Surely no woman would dare . . . but then he had an insistent feeling Olivia St. Etienne would dare a great deal.

"She'll be back, none the worse for it, perhaps a bit chastened. Probably she's at some horserace down in Kaskaskia or New Madrid. Gypsy Lady's missing, as well." Once Wescott had discovered that Olivia had fled early last evening, he'd taken the precaution of removing the mare to a safe hiding place. She had left everything behind but those clothes she rode in. Already he had his men combing the riverfront for a scruffy boy who wore a bandanna tied around his hair, covered by an oversized felt hat.

"I'm leaving on a trading venture for my brother-in-law and expect to be upriver for several months. I trust that will be adequate time in which to recover your *chastened* ward," Samuel said sardonically.

"She'll be waiting for you, Colonel, never fear," Wescott replied.

Shelby arched one eyebrow and studied the crafty older man seated at the table. His jowly face was expressionless except for the feral watchfulness barely evident in those hooded gray eyes. "Just what game do you play, Mr. Wescott, I wonder?" Without waiting for a reply, Shelby turned and walked from the room.

Lisa's big keelboat was eighty feet long with a cabin box large enough for a man to stand upright in it, this despite the false bottom floor in which the dearest of their trade goods were concealed. The trader had the new boat made to his precise specifications with a two-foot-wide runway along each side of the cabin box on which the polemen could walk back and forth at their laborious task, propelling the boat against the big river's powerful if sluggish flow. Specially rigged with a heavy mast and square mainsail, the boat could take advantage of favorable winds when available. At the top of the mast a heavy cordelle rope was fastened to use when the crew was forced to pull the boat from shore. A heavy swivel gun perched ominously on the bow to repel boarders in the event of any encounter with either hostile Indians or river pirates.

Almost two dozen men were milling around Lisa's boat, which was tied up fifteen miles above the small French village of St. Charles. The trading party had set out from St. Louis the preceding day but had been forced, as was often the case, to delay while drunken stragglers among the crew trickled into camp. Having paid their final farewell to the amenities of civilization by swilling rotgut whiskey, most of the men were penitent enough to allow Lisa's second in command to round them up and bring them to fulfill their contracted obligations. Samuel Shelby had been assigned the unenviable task of collecting the unrepentant.

Lisa's expedition provided him with the perfect cover to head up the Missouri into Osage country. In addition, the shrewd trader was well-known among the Big and Little Osage bands and would quickly learn of any rumors regarding the Englishman as they traded and gossiped with the Indians enroute. All Shelby had to do in return for his passage was to round up the drunken *engagés* and hunt for game.

The former chore he completed after breaking one trapper's nose and loosening several teeth of another. He nursed a bruised left fist from punching Jean Lebeck and a sore jaw from Billy Walgren's roundhouse swing. Of course the clumsy blow would never have landed had not the colonel been occupied at the time breaking a cane chair over Hiram Skeeter's head. When the dust cleared after his brawl with the three drunken rivermen, he had become something of an instant folk hero around the St. Charles countryside. Eight sullen men, reeking of stale whiskey and all but bleeding through their eyeballs, stumbled listlessly into camp to the jovial catcalls of their fellows.

"All present and accounted for," Shelby said as he swung down from his horse.

Lisa nodded. "I see Santiago Quinn did not exaggerate your skills," he said in Spanish. His shrewd dark eyes assessed the tall Anglo from beneath beetled black brows. Manuel Lisa was slight of stature but deceptively strong. He was dressed in typical rivermen's garb, greasy buckskin breeches and a laced buckskin tunic. His belt held a wicked looking skinning knife and a brace of pistols. From his piratical appearance, no one would mistake him for one of St. Louis's leading businessmen. He grinned, revealing two missing teeth and one prominent gold one. "Come, have some coffee and we will talk."

After pouring steaming inky coffee into tin cups, the two men walked between several campfires that crackled brightly in the spring twilight. They quickly left the raucous babble of laughing, cursing Frenchmen and Americans behind. "How many days until we reach the first Osage village?"

Samuel asked in Spanish, a language he had been fluent in since childhood.

Lisa shrugged. "With good weather, ten days, two weeks, but I do not know if your Englishman will be at the first camp we encounter. Already the Indians have begun leaving the big winter settlement where the Osage River runs into the Missouri, heading onto the plains for the spring hunt."

"They trap most of their beaver before the hunt. I'd think British traders would arrive before the Osage scatter," Shelby speculated.

"British traders, yes, but this particular man who brings whiskey and weapons, promising the return of their ancestral hunting lands when the great king across the ocean defeats the Americans—of this one I do not know."

"You told Santiago you thought it might be Robert Dickson from Prairie du Chien."

"Last winter I believed so, but having heard the rumors my men brought back as they traveled downriver from Fort Raymond this spring, I no longer think it is him."

"If only we had a name, or even a description of the bastard," Shelby said in frustration.

Lisa grinned. "To an Osage, all white men fall into two categories, the Heavy Eyebrows or the Long Knives. As a Spaniard I am one of the former, you the latter, as are all Englishmen from Canada. Not much to go on, I fear."

"Once I pick up his trail in an encampment, I'll follow it until I find him."

Observing the steely determination in Shelby's hard blue eyes, Lisa said, "Tread lightly, my friend, with the Little Ones. The Osage have been allied with the Americans for a long time, but they demand proper respect, ceremony and dignity—things the British excel at. You cannot barge in waving an American flag and drag away this English agent, no matter if he is trespassing on soil your government has purchased from Napoleon. Before there was a United States or even a France, there was an Osage nation hunting and farming along the Mississippi."

Samuel raised an eyebrow sardonically. "You sound like my brother-in-law."

"We are both Spanish, yes, but we are men without a country now, belonging neither to the Old World nor your United States. Perhaps that is why we deal so well with the Indians. We understand dispossession."

Shelby sighed thoughtfully. "Tom Jefferson believes that one day the United States will stretch across this continent. That means Spain and Britain will be forced to give way. So will all the hundreds of tribes of Indians, I'm afraid."

They walked back to the campfire in melancholy silence.

Lisa's crew was up with the dawn, raucously breaking camp in preparation for the long journey upriver. The French Canadian trappers who made up the majority of the company laughed and exchanged bawdy jibes while their Anglo counterparts worked grudgingly, for the most part in dour silence. Everyone was hungover, but it seemed to burden the Gallic spirit less. Several Indian women married to trappers, stoically hefted huge packs with camp gear, more inured to such labors than most Eastern men.

Shelby sat clutching a cup of steaming coffee in a crude pewter cup, watching all the flurry around him. He would travel aboard Lisa's big boat along with another man, hired as a hunter. Seth Walton also planned to keep a diary, recording the marvels of their journey along the banks of the Missouri. Walton and Shelby would not be required to participate in the backbreaking labor of propelling the massive keelboat upriver. They had only to make forays along the banks to bring down deer, bison and other game for the stew pots of the squaws.

In the event the party was attacked, Shelby would assume command of the men. But for now, having little to do while the final loading took place, he strolled about the camp, assessing the men and their weapons. The majority carried ancient muskets but a few were better armed with long rifles, mostly the Americans. All were seasoned veterans of the wilderness, sun and wind blasted, unshaven men with tough stringy muscles and an incredible ability to endure hardship. The pungent stench of unwashed bodies and greasy buckskins wafted on the chill morning air, not so bad in the open but cloying at close quarters aboard the boat. Fortunately the *engagés* would spend much of their time on shore or in the water pulling the boat upstream with brute strength.

It took hardy men to earn their livelihood that way. Samuel's eyes assessed the crew, then lighted on one slight figure, a slip of a boy, beardless and thin. He looked far too young and green to handle his share of the chores. Then Lisa yelled for him to secure the foodstuff for the cabin box and bring them aboard. The youth was a cabin boy of sorts. Sam-

uel shrugged and started to turn away, then paused to watch
the boy struggle with the awkward bundles of clattering cook
pots and bulky bedding. There was something naggingly familiar about the way the grim urchin moved. He started to
walk closer but a couple of voyageurs carrying a long canoe
blocked his path. By the time they passed, the boy was clam-
bering aboard the keelboat. Samuel shrugged and forgot
about him, returning instead to gather up his small cache of
belongings.

The youth kept rather mysteriously to himself over the
next several days, fetching and carrying for Lisa and keeping
the dark, musty quarters of the cabin box in order. It seemed
to Shelby that the boy avoided him, for whenever he entered
the big cabin the youth would find some way to engage himself at the opposite end of the long boat. He spoke only in
French, which was hardly unusual for a St. Louis inhabitant.
Shelby would have assumed he merely felt uncomfortable
around an American military officer and preferred the company of his compatriots, but the boy also stayed clear of the
boisterous French-Canadian rivermen as well.

The journey was uneventful for the first several days. The
crew rose with the dawn each morning and poled the boat
until it became too dark to move it in the treacherous waters
at nightfall. Everyone was so bone weary by the time camp
was made, they consumed their supper of mush and tallow,
then quickly fell into the dreamless slumber of exhaustion.
Shelby posted guards in two-hour shifts, taking responsibility for security as long as he remained with the party.

On the fourth night he debated ordering the boy to take a
turn at watch with the others. Lisa said he had found the
youth asleep, scrunched into a corner between two wooden
crates that afternoon. He was only fourteen or fifteen years
old. Instead, Samuel assigned a hatchet-faced American the
first watch, then went in search of the boy, Ollie Moreau. By
the time this journey was over, he would be a lot tougher, or
he'd be dead.

Shelby walked around the half-dozen campfires scattered
on the sandy bar at the river's edge where they had moored
up for the night. The beach was perhaps thirty feet wide
with the Missouri glistening blackly to the north as it ran its
relentless course down into the Mississippi. On the land side
a steep limestone bluff stretched high overhead, choked with

scrub pines that cast jagged shadows which moved with the night wind.

Moreau was nowhere around. Shelby stopped to ask several groups of men but no one had seen him. "He isn't aboard the boat. Where the hell has the fool boy wandered off to?" he muttered to himself just as Seth Walton came striding into the circle of firelight. "You seen the Moreau boy?" Samuel asked.

Walton scratched his stubbly chin. "No, can't say as I have but I passed some of the men walking toward that next island. There's a narrow channel between it and the bank. I figger they'll cross it and do a little private celebrating with a jug they don't plan on sharing."

"Thanks, Seth. Maybe he's with them," Shelby said, striding into the darkness with his Bartlett flintlock clutched angrily in his hand. *If he is, he'll soon wish he weren't.* Sneaking off in the wilderness to get drunk was a foolhardy danger, not to mention against the rules agreed upon by all the men of the company.

Samuel headed upriver, following the gradual rise of the bank into a dense brushy stand of hickory and sycamore. A thick blanket of meadow grass had sprung up, covering the earth knee-high in places where it had not been trampled by deer to make their beds. He followed an old, well-worn Indian trail that twisted along the river, all the while keeping alert for any signs of movement.

The night was cool and the wind had stilled to a slight breeze. The fecund musty smell of river and earth filled his nostrils as he paused to gaze at the sky overhead. Ever since his first journey west in 1803, Samuel Shelby always experienced a physical thrill when he saw that big sky, an endless vault of blinding blue by day and star studded brilliance by night. The heady sense of freedom he felt was tempered by a feeling of insignificance in the face of all the untamed vastness spread before him. A three-quarter moon hung low on the horizon, casting silvery light around a long bare stretch of sandbar in the middle of a narrow sluggish neck of the river.

Such islands were always temporary, an old river rat had once told him when he first traversed the Mississippi. The great river changed course, often overnight, erasing all traces of land as if the hand of God had simply smoothed them back from whence they came. Then the power of the water would again disgorge another island up into its channel at another place, in another time. The deeper channel was on the opposite side and the narrow water between this bank and the island was easily fordable. Through the dense brushy cover Shelby could see the orange flicker of a low campfire and several shadowy figures gathered around it. He began to descend the embankment.

Once he neared the water's edge he could hear the unmistakable sounds of a scuffle. Two men were holding a third down on the ground while another knelt over him, tearing at his clothes. Although Shelby could not see his face, he was certain the thin small figure kicking and writhing in the sand was Ollie Moreau. The boy fought fiercely yet made no attempt to cry out. Shelby had seen that before, a youth too ashamed to ask for help from his fellows, enduring a painful violation in frantic, desperate silence. That grown men could ease their lust with a boy had always appalled and sickened him. He checked the pistols in his belt, then raised his rifle and began wading across the shallow water toward the island.

The men were too intent on lust to hear the sounds of splashing but when he pulled back the hammer of the rifle, the distinct metallic click caused one of them to look up at the shadow looming fifteen feet away. Before the riverman could do more than loose his hold on the boy, Shelby's voice cut through the sounds of hoarse panting.

"There are squaws happy enough to accommodate you back at camp—unless you have an unnatural taste for buggering your own sex," Shelby said with withering contempt.

One of the men, a short, fat Frenchman, released his hold and tumbled backward onto the sand, scooting frantically away. The second fellow lost his grip on his captive's arm when Moreau jackknifed up, twisting free as the third culprit glared unrepentantly at the tall American. "Ain't never been thet hard up fer my pleasurin'. This here's no boy."

One big hairy hand jerked aside the voluminous folds of the torn shirt shrouding his prisoner. A pair of pearly white breasts with impudently pointed pale pink tips peeped out through a tangled veil of long dark hair that had come unfastened in the struggle.

Samuel felt poleaxed when Olivia St. Etienne's blazing emerald eyes met his. He expected terror or gratitude, but instead her expression was one of searing hatred. She shook off her tormentor's hands and wrapped the shirt over her nakedness, all the while glaring defiantly at Shelby.

"You! How the hell did you end up here?"

"You ain't sayin' she's yore woman, air ye, Colonel?" the other American asked while the little Frenchman cursed fluently as he scrambled away in the darkness.

"In a manner of speaking, yes," Samuel said with a sardonic laugh.

"I am most certainly not!" Olivia seethed, gritting out each word.

"Oh, then you'd prefer these gentlemen?" Shelby countered with an almost courtly flourish.

Before she could respond, the ringleader, a big burly fellow with shaggy gray hair and rotted teeth bellowed, "I found her out 'n took her. By Gawd, she's mine!"

"I think we'll let Manuel Lisa decide the matter," Shelby replied, leveling the rifle directly at the contender's midsection. "Of course, I'll tell him you dragged her off a mile from camp along with a jug of his whiskey . . . that is whiskey from Señor Lisa's private cabin, isn't it?"

Some of the belligerence evaporated as the burly American stood up. "Now let's not go 'n do somethin' plumb foolish, Colonel. We kin share 'n share alike. The whiskey 'n the woman. We caught her fair 'n square. No respectable woman'd be out here alone. She's nothin' but a camp whore."

Olivia spit a startlingly explicit French expletive she'd learned from the voyageurs and lunged, placing a well-aimed kick between the man's legs. He toppled back onto the sand with a string of curses.

"Pick up your slightly castrated friend and take him back to camp before I give her a skinning knife and let her finish the operation. Leave the whiskey," Shelby commanded.

The younger man helped his companion to stand up, then slung one arm across his shoulders and half dragged him into the river shallows without uttering another word.

Samuel lowered the rifle as the silence thickened between him and Olivia. Finally he asked, "Why the hell did you do such a wild, irresponsible thing? Did you think this would be another adventure like racing Wescott's horses?"

She stood facing him, her booted feet spread defiantly, small fists clenched at her sides with the nails cutting into her palms. "At least it was of my own choosing. Anything is better than being sold like one of Wescott's horses! How could you do it? I trusted you and you betrayed me. You told me you weren't married when all the time—"

"I never told you a thing about my marital status," Samuel shot back. Guilt reddened his face but in the dim firelight she could not see it.

"You deceived me!" she cried. "I thought you were—" She stopped short, horrified. *I thought you were the man of my dreams, the man who loved me.* Instead she accused, "I thought you were a gentleman. All you are is a vile immoral piece of offal! Scum! Bastard! Son of a—"

"Cease fire! I think you've made your point, Mademoiselle St. Etienne. I take it you somehow learned of your guardian's provisions for you and they didn't exactly meet with your approval," he said dryly.

"No, they did not," she snapped. "You would have taken my virtue without a single qualm."

He looked at her with disgust. "Your *virtue*," he emphasized the word disdainfully, "it seems to me, was already quite thoroughly compromised long before you ever met me."

"That's a monstrous lie!" she yelled, ready to lambaste him with her fist.

"Is it? You couldn't bear the idea of being my mistress, so instead you decided to take up with a whole crew of randy rivermen. Am I to assume these charming fellows were more to your liking than I? How could you be so stupid as to travel up the Missouri into the wilderness with them and not expect to have them rip you to pieces?" He could feel his simmering temper rising out of control, realizing what could have happened to her had he not been there.

"I did not intend to go upriver. I planned to go to my uncle Charles in New Orleans," she replied stiffly.

"Well, for someone who's lived several years on the Mississippi, you sure have a lousy sense of direction."

"I was desperate and it was dark the morning we left. Monsieur Lisa let me sleep in the cabin box the night before. I did not realize we were headed northwest until we camped that night. By then I could scarcely lodge a protest," she replied with withering sarcasm. "It was too late to do anything about it. You left me no choice."

"Me?" he asked incredulously. "I didn't sell you—your guardian did and apparently with good reason." He felt guilty. Damn, why should *he* feel guilty because of this hare-brained hoyden!

"So, that made it all right for you to buy me—for a damned horse!" That sounded pitiful to her own ears. At once she added, "It so happens I'm worth a hell of a lot more than that horse and I'm going to find a man who appreciates that fact."

He snorted in derision. "Well, it damn well won't be me now, will it? On reconsideration, I'd prefer to 'ride' the horse. Not only does she have a sweeter disposition, she does not bellow or curse."

He had almost told her that he would not have forced her to become his mistress, that he didn't believe all Wescott had told him, but just looking at her, feeling the raw sexual energy she exuded, having her throw down the gauntlet so blatantly made him realize he'd been a fool. She was spoiled and wild, just like the reckless French aristocracy from which she had sprung, living only for their own self-gratification, for the pleasures of the moment. Oh, yes, and she had experienced pleasure and given it. He could see that in the lushly sensuous pout of her full lips, the wicked slant of those exotic gypsy eyes, the bold way she stood with her feet planted apart, hands on the sweet curves of her hips, near-naked breasts thrust outward just begging for a man's caress.

"How the hell did I not recognize you for the past four days? How did any man in the party ever for an instant think you were a boy?" The question asked itself before he could stop himself from blurting it out. Then another thought hit him with a crash. "Or did someone know? Do you have a lover here—someone who appreciates your worth?" he asked, lacing the last words with scorn, although he immediately dismissed the idea as foolish.

"I will not dignify such an insult with an answer." Let him believe that she had a lover. At least he would keep his distance then, she assured herself. But the pain of the accusation cut far more deeply than she would ever have imagined that it could. Why had she become smitten with so unworthy a man? *Fool.*

Samuel slapped at a mosquito that was drawing a banquet from his neck. "It's past time we got back to camp before Lisa has to send Walton out with a search party looking for us."

"I'm not going anywhere with you." Her eyes narrowed and she backed away a step as he approached her.

"You're going to do precisely what I say, when I say. From here on, you will consider yourself *my* woman whether you want to be or not."

"I'll never belong to you!"

"You already do. I just took you from those three men. Once the rest of the crew learns there's a white woman in camp they'll cut each other's throats to claim you. The best we can do to prevent chaos is to pretend that you're mine."

"What if I did have another lover in camp?" Stung, she could not resist taunting him.

He raised one eyebrow and looked down at her. "To date he's done a miserable job as your protector. I just fired him, my pet. Come along, but first I'd cover those breasts again if I were you."

He turned his back to kick out the fire, arrogantly assured that she would follow him to camp like some mindless lackey. Olivia's eyes scanned the bare sandy islet searching for a weapon with which to bash out his brains. Other than the small brittle pieces of driftwood littering the sand, there was nothing—but the whiskey jug left by her attackers. Half-full and made of heavy crockery, it would do handily. She seized it and raised it up to deliver the coup de grace.

Samuel sensed more than saw her faint shadow move up behind him and whirled in the nick of time, blocking her blow with his forearm. With an oath he wrested the jug from her and tossed it into the river while holding one of her slender wrists.

Olivia kicked and clawed at him but he was more agile than the luckless trapper had been. Neatly avoiding her flying feet, he pulled her against him with bone jarring force and held her with arms pinned at her sides as she screamed curses at him, recalling every insult to his ancestry and description of his sexual practices that she had overheard among the rough rivermen.

"Be still, you damned hellcat. Do you want to bring the whole camp down on us? If they come to watch, I guarantee that I can give them quite a show."

His voice was a threatening growl. He would actually do it, the miserable cur! She gritted her teeth, unable to control her rage, especially while he was holding her pressed against him. She could feel every inch of his hard chest, flat belly and long lean legs, even that most mysterious and threatening male part that seemed to have grown alarmingly since their struggle began. "No! I won't let you—"

"See if you can stop me," he snarled. Tossing her up over his shoulder, he began slogging through the water back to the riverbank.

His boots were soaked, his feet half-frozen by river water, he was chewed alive by mosquitoes and now the damned hellion was clawing at his back. He gave her sumptuously rounded derriere a hard swat to silence her, then cursed at that part of his own anatomy which ached most of all. Keeping her with him was going to be worse than Apache torture, but what other choice did he have? And how could he complete his mission with the responsibility for this impossible female on his back, now quite literally? Grimly he decided he would worry about that when he picked up the Englishman's trail.

Chapter 9

When they neared the crackling campfires and scattered tents where the rivermen slept, Samuel slipped the seething but quiet Olivia from his shoulder and deposited her on the ground. She stood glaring at him, her jaw mutinously clenched and her entire body rigid with fury.

"Are you going to behave or do you plan to create another scene calling even more unwanted attention to yourself?" he asked almost conversationally.

"The most unwanted attention I've suffered in my life has come from you," she hissed.

"No doubt. Now, tuck all that hair back under your hat and pull that damned shirt together," he ordered, brushing aside her outburst as his eyes swept over her body. How the hell could he or any other man have ever believed she was a boy!

She continued to pierce him with hate-filled eyes as she rearranged her torn shirt, carefully overlapping the front which had gaped open even more in her uncomfortable ride across his shoulder. Then she stood stock-still, daring him to touch her again. "What do you think you are going to do with me?"

He smiled nastily and slipped an evil-looking knife from the sheath at his belt. "Right now, if you don't follow my orders I'm going to give you a haircut, a partial scalping, as it were."

"You wouldn't dare!" she squeaked as one hand reflexively reached up to clutch a long strand of fiery hair.

"Try me," he said. With lightning speed he seized a fistful of the thick curls spread across her shoulders and raised the knife.

"All right! I'll put it up," she yelped, pulling desperately away from him until her scalp prickled.

He released the silky strands and watched as she braided it hastily and wadded it beneath the battered cap. "That's better. Even if the men know you're female, it's best the rest of them don't see all that bright red hair. It might prove an irresistible lure for them—not to mention how any Indians in the vicinity would fancy it—quite a trophy on some buck's scalp pole."

She paled. *That* thought had never occurred to her but she still resented his high-handed orders and threats. She resented *him.* "There. Does that satisfy you, Colonel, sir?" she sassed, making a mock salute that somehow dripped with contempt.

"You make a damn poor excuse for a soldier or a worker, but since you hired on to be a cabin boy, I suppose you'll do to tend to some camp chores for me while we're forced to travel together."

"I already have my assigned chores, gathering firewood and hauling cooking water for Monsieur Lisa."

"That was while everyone still thought you *were* a boy. From now on you'll be under my protection. I'll explain to Manuel. He'll be angry, but he's already told me you weren't pulling your weight so I don't expect he'll think you're much of a loss."

"I was too pulling my weight! I worked until my hands were blistered and my back ached," she retorted, stung by that Spanish oaf's lack of appreciation. Never in her life had she struggled so hard as she had loading the cargo on the boat and doing the endless fetching and carrying. Unconsciously she rubbed one hand with the other. Once they had been soft and white; now they were hideously reddened with the nails broken. She had been reduced to utter misery and it was all this lying, arrogant lout's fault! "What do you plan to do—use me as your squaw? If so, I warn you, once you've abused me, you'd better never plan to sleep again."

There was something lethal in her speech, impassioned and foolish as it was, that made him take notice. In spite of himself he admired her grit. But she was spoiled and selfish and had put them both in terrible danger, not to mention jeopardizing his mission. Swallowing his anger he said evenly, "I find I no longer have a taste for you, even though I'm sure the rest of the men might not be so fastidious. You're filthy and disheveled . . . and you smell. No, to be precise, you stink. However, we're stuck together for the time being and you should be damn grateful that I'm willing to take responsibility for your safety."

"I never asked for your protection. I don't want it. Just leave me alone!" She could feel the sudden surge of tears beginning to sting beneath her eyelids and was horrified. After all she had endured, his cold rejection was simply too much to bear. She turned and tried to slip past him back to the camp, but he caught hold of her arm and pulled her up against his body.

"You brainless little idiot. Has no one in your entire spoiled life ever made you understand the word *no?*"

"You certainly will not," she snapped back, shoving at him.

He let her go with a snarled oath and she stumbled backward. "All right, run into camp. See how far you get before several of the men grab you and push you to the ground in front of the fire. They'll rip off your clothes and then they'll take turns at you, one after another until—"

"No!" She put her hands over her ears, shaking her head as the horror of her brush with rape replayed in her mind. She could feel the bruises the rivermen's big callused hands had inflicted on her arms and legs, smell the whiskey on their breath, their rotted teeth and the feral stink of their lust. She shivered in revulsion and then straightened up defiantly, forcing herself to assume a calm facade. "You've made your point. Better the devil I know than those I don't. Consider me under your protection, Monsieur Colonel," she said with scathing sarcasm.

"How gracious of you to consent, Mademoiselle St. Etienne," he replied dryly, relieved that she had at last seen reason enough to do as he demanded. Perhaps they could get through the men without his having to engage in mortal combat with half a dozen of them for her favors—favors he would not avail himself of no matter that he burned with wanting her.

Cursing his ill luck and even worse taste in women, he strode toward the camp with Olivia following respectfully behind him.

Olivia awakened to a gust of icy air as the blanket she had been huddling beneath was ripped from her body and tossed across a pile of lashed together crates inside the long, narrow cabin box of Lisa's keelboat. River damp instantly penetrated the thin shirt and trousers in which she slept. She looked up into Samuel Shelby's scowling face. In the dim light she could see the darkening shadow of beard stubble on his jaw. He was out of uniform today, dressed in a pair of soft well-worn buckskins that hugged his thighs scandalously. A loose brown cotton shirt, as yet unlaced hung open revealing a good deal of his bare chest. He looked like a river pirate.

"Get up and make some coffee while I'm gone. Manuel just spotted some deer drinking at the water's edge a hundred yards upstream. I'm going after one."

She sat up, rubbing her aching back. "The men have already made coffee. Go get your own," she replied in a surly voice. She had always hated rising early and was scarcely at her best in the mornings.

"I don't want that brackish swill. I've always made my own." He gestured to a battered pot and sack of coffee beans lying beside one of his opened packs.

"Then make it now. I'm certain my humble efforts wouldn't please you," she replied saccharinely.

He finished fastening his shirt, then tucked it into the buckskin breeches. "If everyone in the party is to believe you're under my protection, you'd better start performing some simple female chores around here."

"I don't do simple female chores. I was hired as Señor Lisa's cabin boy."

"That was before everyone learned you aren't a boy. I discussed the situation with Manuel after you went to sleep last night. You were performing your work so poorly he was going to set you off at the first outpost. We're damn lucky he hasn't put us both afoot on the riverbank and left us to walk all the way back to St. Louis. He's agreed that your services will be rendered to me for the duration of the journey—as long as I can keep the rest of the men from causing trouble."

Your services. She bristled up like an angry porcupine. "I am not at *your service* that way!"

He smiled sardonically, without a trace of humor in his eyes. "If you recall, I've already declined those services, mademoiselle. I would suggest that you perform the camp chores I assign you and wait on me like a good little girl."

"I am not a little girl."

"You're certainly not good either, except at causing trouble."

The overweening arrogance of the man! "I refuse to be your lackey," she said, standing up to face him. Just then the boat took a sudden lurch as a large driftwood log struck the bow. She lost her balance and toppled forward against his chest.

As Samuel caught her in his arms, her breasts brushed against him with their tantalizing softness. "I don't keep useless pets," he gritted out, setting her away from him and struggling to bring his body under control. "You will work for me in exchange for your passage and keep, or by God I'll turn you over to the three charming fellows who accosted you last night." He slung his shot pouch around his neck and fastened his powder horn at his hip, then seized his rifle and stalked out of the dimly lit cabin.

Olivia sat back against a crate filled with strouding and wrapped her arms around her chest, feeling heartily sorry for herself. How could she ever have been so naive as to be attracted by that crude, ill-mannered lout? He was so unprincipled he might well hold to his threat and give her to the men who had tried to rape her.

He doesn't even want you that way.

She shook her head to banish the nagging thought. "Damn him, I'll make him coffee. I'll make him coffee he'll never forget!"

She slipped on her boots, then stomped outside the cabin. Morning fog hung chill and dank across the wide river. The sun was a dim molten ball barely lighting the eastern horizon yet the men were all up and about, packing their gear and preparing to shove off. Several campfires blazed cheerily on the sandy beach. She considered grinding the beans on the small sharp-bladed grinder Lisa kept on deck, then decided not to bother. Instead she climbed over the side of the big keelboat, clutching the pot and sack of beans in one hand while she negotiated the crude unsteady plank to the bank.

The water that lapped up onto the sand was murky with mud that had washed downstream with the spring thawing, but the Missouri, or Big Muddy, was always silty. She knelt at water's edge and sloshed a generous amount of the gritty liquid into the pot, then looked at it. Deciding it was still too clear, she reached down into the muck and scooped up a handful of the rich river bottom and added it to the pot.

"That should give it body," she muttered, adding a fistful of the whole beans. "There, that should do it. Nice and crunchy. Food and drink all in one, and if his colonelship doesn't like it this way, he can strain it through one of Señor Lisa's socks, for all I care."

She walked over to the nearest fire and slammed the pot down in the middle of the hot coals to boil. An iron pot of unappetizing hominy sat bubbling evilly on the opposite side. Her stomach growled. She was starving but since the fare of the boatmen was mostly comprised of pork fat, wee-vily hard biscuits and mush, she had eaten little since the journey's beginning. One of the squaws dished up a tin plate of the hominy and offered it to her. Olivia accepted, noting as she dug in with a none too clean spoon, that the woman was studying her with curious eyes.

Word had spread that she was a woman masquerading as a boy . . . and now belonged to Samuel Shelby. *And he didn't even have to buy me. I stupidly let myself be dropped into his lap.* She raised her head, proudly ignoring the murmuring and stares, then dug into the sticky grayish lump on her plate, thinking with relish of how much Samuel was going to enjoy his morning coffee when he returned.

Shelby sat motionless watching the fat buck drinking at the water's edge. As he waited patiently for the deer to move into a better positon for the shot, he thought of Olivia St. Etienne. What the hell was he going to do with her? He knew he had been hard on her, perhaps even too hard, but she had the most irrationally infuriating effect on him.

In hindsight, he realized making the obscene arrangement with Wescott had probably been a mistake. He should have refused. If the girl had really been her guardian's innocent victim, she could have come to him for asylum. Now he would never know if that had been the unlikely truth. Of course, there were still several other far less appealing possi-bilities. She could be the wildly immoral hoyden Wescott hinted at, a social embarrassment he wanted to rid himself of, or even more sinister, she could be in league with her guardian to infiltrate Samuel's mission and report to the British about his work.

If the latter were true, he was in a real quandary for he had to pick up the Englishman's trail and strike out into the Osage villages in pursuit of him. He could scarcely take a white woman with him, especially a citified French belle like Olivia. There seemed to be no answer. He rubbed his eyes, then steadied his rifle in the fork of a cottonwood. The deer drew nearer, lowering its head to drink once again. Shelby sighted and fired.

When he dragged the buck into camp, Olivia was

crouched at a campfire tending the coffeepot. Good. At least
she was willing to obey orders. One of the squaws came over
to him and inspected his kill. Seth Walton was still out, farther afield in search of game and was not expected to catch
up to the boat for a day or two. The woman was delighted
with the first fresh meat they'd had in several days. She
called for another of the squaws to help her with the butchering.

Samuel strode over to the fire where Olivia sat watching
him with an unreadable expression on her face. She looked
younger yet oddly sensuous in the morning light. Ignoring
the ache in his loins that had become a constant companion
ever since he'd first laid eyes on Olivia St. Etienne, he knelt
down beside her and picked up a tin cup. Smiling, he
reached across for the pot and poured himself a cupful.

Olivia resentfully watched as he used the heavy leather
mitt rather than burn his hand on the molten handle as she
had foolishly done when she tested the horrendous brew. As
he raised the cup to his mouth her burned hand was forgotten
and a slow smile spread across her face. "How is it?" she
inquired sweetly.

Samuel spit out a mouthful of silty vile-tasting brown
water, causing the campfire flames to sputter. He threw the
cup to the ground as a fit of coughing seized him. Something
had lodged in his throat! He blinked his eyes rapidly and
coughed harder, trying to dislodge the lump. When he finally
succeeded, he stared at the ground in amazement. A clump
of burned whole coffee beans! He picked up the pot and
dumped its contents onto the fire, watching as a goodly portion of his supply of high-grade coffee beans bounced into
the flames while the muddy coffee water extinguished them.

He looked at her in bald amazement. "Either you are too
incredibly stupid to know that coffee beans should be ground
before being boiled, or else you deliberately set out to choke
and poison me. I hope for your sake that it was stupidity."

His voice was conversationally soft but she could read the
blazing fury darkening his eyes. A small tic at his left temple
further warned her that she had gone too far with her act of
defiance. Olivia scanned the camp looking for help, knowing
none was available. If she cried out, God only knew how
many of the rough dangerous men might join in Samuel's
sport. She'd best take her chances with him.

"I am not stupid," she said, deliberately enunciating each syllable. "Do your worst."

Olivia sat bolt-upright, eyes blazing and chin high, glaring at him as if he were the one who might be mentally deficient. Only her small hands, balled into fists, gave away her fear. In spite of his anger, once again he could not help admiring her gall, but he could not let such gross insubordination pass without punishment. Life in the wilderness was chancy and dangerous at best and greenhorn lives often hung on their willingness to obey the orders of those more experienced.

He considered turning her across his knee and paddling that delectable little rump, but decided it would be dangerous to tempt fate with two dozen women hungry rivermen looking on. When the two squaws dragged the deer carcass to a clearing near their fire and set to work with skinning knives, he was struck by an inspiration. With an evil smile wreathing his face he said, "Walks Fast and Wind Scent need some help with that deer and it's apparent that you need to learn how to cook. Come with me."

He stood up, motioning for her to follow. When she was slow to respond, he reached down and seized one slender wrist, yanking her up. "Don't push me any further. Lisa's more than ready to get rid of you. I don't think you have the survival skills to last an hour alone in this wilderness," he added with just enough menace in his voice to convince her that he might be serious.

Olivia stumbled as he pulled her behind him. She jerked away but continued to follow his lead until they came to where the women were working. She gagged at the grisly sight before her. The deer lay on the hard-packed sandy earth, with blood seeping from a small hole on the upper side of its head just below the ear. A wide chocolate eye stared sightlessly up at the morning sky. One squaw held onto the carcass while the other plied a sharp blade, splitting its belly from front to back. Gooey red entrails, steaming with warmth, started to ooze out of the opening.

"Good kill. Clean inside. No bloody shot-up," Walks Fast said in serviceable English, beaming at Samuel. She was Osage, plump and toothless and of indeterminate age, married to an American trapper named McElroy.

"I've brought my woman to learn how to clean and prepare meat. Put her to work. She is eager to help."

Wind Scent, a comely young Sioux currently living with

a Frenchman, looked disdainfully at Olivia. "She has many summers not to know such a simple thing."

Samuel felt Olivia stiffen in affront and grinned to himself. "She is swift to learn new things, aren't you, Livy?"

Olivia gritted her teeth, hating the mock endearment. So this was woman's work out in the wilderness. She had never needed to worry about such unpleasant realities, for her life in St. Louis had been smoothed by servants. Olivia had never so much as made her own tea, only poured it for guests at Emory Wescott's elegant social gatherings. Both Indian women were staring at her, the older one curious and the younger one hostile. She would show them. She would show that smirking, odious colonel, too.

"Oh, give me a knife. I'll clean the damn deer," she said with a lot more bravado than she felt as she knelt down alongside the two women.

"No knife. Use hands," the ever practical Walks Fast said.

"She knows better than to trust you with anything sharp." Samuel chuckled, looking on with his arms crossed over his chest, highly amused.

Olivia gaped at the older woman as if she had lost her mind. "What do you mean, use my hands?" Her voice broke on the question.

"Pull out gut, liver." Walks Fast finished widening the opening in the cavity, then raised the deer's ribs with one hand while illustrating with her other hand how to root through the gore inside, working various organs out. Those and a portion of intestine would end up in the stew. Her companion wielded a knife expertly, cutting the treats free of the visceral membranes holding them.

The fetid warm stench emanating from inside the deer wafted on the heavy fog laden air, hitting Olivia with the first deep breath she took when she leaned forward over the carcass. She tried to focus her eyes but her vision was becoming increasingly blurry. The earth seemed to have begun spinning. In front of her Walks Fast extracted the greatest prize, a great purplish black clump of gelatinous slime, which she elevated in triumph.

"Liver, still warm," she pronounced with satisfaction offering it to Samuel as the hunter's due.

Several drops of blood spattered on Olivia's hand as she watched the seemingly pulsating lump with horrified fascination. The Indian woman's arms were stained up to the elbow with gore.

Samuel quickly realized his tactical error. He had been so delighted watching the haughty French belle being brought down several notches that he had forgotten the old Indian ritual, now enjoined by the white trappers and hunters, but one he had never had the stomach to enjoy. A ring of men had gathered around them, all eyeing the delicacy enviously. Before he could bluff his way out of the quandary, Olivia solved his dilemma by creating a diversion.

She fought the hot dizzying surges as she watched Samuel eye the raw dripping liver being offered to him. Sacred Blood, was he going to *eat* it? When she raised one hand up to rub across her suddenly dry mouth, the coppery smell and taste of blood assaulted her. She stared in horror at her own blood spattered hand and knew she'd smeared it across her face. Without further warning her stomach revolted.

Samuel caught her as she turned away from the deer and emptied her breakfast of coffee and hominy onto the moccasins of one of the French trappers who jumped back with a startled oath. Olivia wretched until nothing more would come up as Samuel held her head, careful to keep her fat plait of hair away from her face as she was wracked with spasm after spasm of dry heaves.

Around them the men burst into raucous laughter, jeering loudly at Shelby, saddled with such a useless female, masquerading in men's britches but possessing the stomach of a five-year-old girl.

"*Mon ami,* I pity you, cooking and cleaning for such a helpless one."

"What does she do when you stick *her, hein?*"

"Trade her in fer a good squaw, Colonel. They know how ta stick 'n be stuck, both!"

Amid advice and catcalls, Samuel scooped Olivia up and carried her back to the water's edge while Manuel Lisa sat in judgement over who got the liver and other delicacies, taking the first portion for himself. Finding a soft place in the sand, Shelby dropped her unceremoniously by the water's edge. They were screened by a copse of dry winter grass, newly greening up, which lent an aura of seclusion as they faced each other.

She landed with a solid thunk, her pride actually injured a great deal more than her rump. Indignantly she sat up and tried to speak but was utterly humiliated when she could get out no more than a raspy squeak. Her whole mouth and throat were parched and sour from her earlier exertions.

"Drink some water and clean yourself up. Lisa will have the boat loaded and ready to shove off by the time the women finish dressing the deer," he said not unkindly.

With that he was gone, leaving her alone in her misery, discarded like a piece of driftwood washed up on the riverbank. Olivia had never felt more wretched or alone in her life. The thought of spending months in the ghastly wilderness surrounded by savages red and white, worked to exhaustion, fed nothing but greasy tallow, salted meat and starchy tasteless hominy brought tears to her eyes. But crying never solved anything. Hadn't she learned that when her parents died?

If only Samuel had turned out to be the charming suitor that she had first imagined, she would have been willing to endure the rigors of a journey all the way up the Missouri. "But my prince has turned into a toad," she muttered disconsolately.

Well, the way he treated her these days, at least she was in no danger of catching warts. With that small consolation, Olivia made her rude toilette by the riverbank, then scrambled back toward the boat when she heard Manuel Lisa call out the order to shove off.

Over the next several days Olivia and Samuel fell into a routine, spending little time together. During the days he took an occasional turn poling but mostly he was ashore, scouring the rolling hills beyond the river bluffs where the woodlands teemed with game. She did manual chores, fetching and carrying while the big keelboat was propelled upstream, assisting with cooking and cleaning up when they camped. Her hands were reddened by cuts and blisters and her skin was itchy and miserable from sleeping on scratchy strouding and the grimy irritant of ground-in dirt. She longed for a tub of clean hot water and a bar of scented soap with an intensity she once would have only expended wishing for an Arabian horse or a diamond necklace.

The men pitched crude little tents ashore each night and slept on the ground. Mercifully Olivia and Samuel had their own cramped cots aboard Lisa's boat, although her narrow spot between several crates was barely large enough to accommodate her.

Bone weary, she slept through the cacophony of male snoring as Manuel Lisa and Seth Walton sawed in harmony far into the night. At least she was spared the indignity of having to share a tent with Samuel Shelby.

Nonetheless, she had to admit that traveling up the river was an adventure. The chief means of propulsion was by poling. The men pushed fifteen-foot-long oak poles deep into the muddy bottom, using sheer brute strength to lever the boat forward as they walked back along the elevated narrow planks that ran from bow to stern on each side of the eighty-foot craft. Often with the hot spring sun beating down on them, the sweaty rivermen would remove their shirts and work bare-chested. At first scandalized, Olivia quickly became inured to the partial nudity, until Samuel began taking his turns.

She sat huddled in one corner, by the door of the cabin box, watching the rippling play of muscles across his broad back as he plied the unwieldy pole with surprising grace. Rivulets of sweat trickled down his sun darkened skin, which gleamed in the reflected light. What would his hot satiny flesh feel like—taste like. Unconsciously she found herself putting her fingertips to her lips, as if attempting to answer the illicit question. Ashamed of such unladylike musing, she looked away, watching the river bluffs rise to the east.

Great limestone cliffs lined both sides of the river for miles at a stretch. Eons of wind, water and blistering heat had scoured and sculpted the stone into fantastical shapes, bowed out in places, hollowed inward in others. Caves and pinnacles of silvery white were studded with the deep green verdancy of hardy pines that grew with nothing but tiny crevices for purchase. The river stretched endlessly, over a mile wide yet mostly shallow except for a few narrow channels around the chains of islands strung along it. Some were overgrown with hardy stands of cedar and willow but many were simply ephemeral sandbars. When the wind picked up, it would blow the stinging particles in thick swirls, enveloping everything in its path. The Indians called the Missouri the Smoky River when this happened.

All manner of flotsam washed downstream with water from the spring thaws in the mountains. Once Olivia saw what looked like a cluster of boulders floating toward them. Panicked at the thought of having the boat pulverized into kindling by the weight, she screamed a warning, much to the amusement of the men. The floating stones were pumice, a coarse, light substance that could remain above water for short distances but was no threat to their safety.

Uprooted by the swirling current, whole trees floated by as well. Unlike the pumice stones, the trees were a danger. Often entire stretches of the bank washed away, carrying clumps of grasses, brush and densely tangled small trees which would eventually form barricades across narrow necks in the twisty river. The first time Olivia saw one she thought it was merely some sort of island they must get around.

Lisa ordered the men to pull to the bank. "Why don't we just pole around the island?" she asked Samuel, who was studying the mass with a worried expression. At first she wondered if he would bother to answer her, but then he did.

"See how the island bobs and moves with the current? It isn't solid land. It's an embarras. The sudden pileup of all that wood and grass has made the current around it much too swift and treacherous to pole past."

"Then how will we get by it?" she asked, daring to hope they might be forced to turn back to St. Louis.

"I imagine Lisa will use the cordelle ropes and let the men pull us through, but it will certainly slow us down. Stay right here unless I call you," he instructed, then left to confer with the cluster of men at the opposite end of the boat.

The passage past the embarras was a nightmare. Lisa's men were forced to wade into the rushing icy water, often shoulder-deep, with the cordelle ropes attached to their waists. They struggled to throw the ropes across low-lying tree limbs, sometimes resorting to climbing the trees. Then they attached pulleys so they could winch the boat upriver, agonizing foot by agonizing foot. Olivia watched Samuel's dark head as he swam against the buffeting current with a rope in his hands. Once he gained solid footing a few feet ahead near the bank he stood up in waist-high water and searched for someplace to fasten the rope for leverage.

She watched horror-struck as her gaze traveled across the embarras where a mass of the roots jutted upward, securely embedded in the thicket. "No!" The word slipped out as she hunched at the bow of the boat, but no one heard her over the roaring of the river and the babel of curses. She closed her eyes in thankfulness when he decided not to swim to his

target but instead attached a wicked looking grappling hook
to the end of the rope and began whirling it in the air until
he was able to wrap it around the roots and pull it tight.
Several more men joined him to pull on the rope from the
side of the boat.

On the bankside to the left a large cottonwood towered
high above and one limb jutted out over the rushing current.
A young French-Canadian *engagé* took another cordelle
rope and scrambled up the tree nimble as a squirrel. He
crawled out onto the limb and secured the rope and pulley
but suddenly an ominous cracking noise rose sharply over
the din of the river and the limb snapped, tossing the youth
into the boiling water below.

Samuel saw him fall and quickly kicked off after him.
Dazed and semiconscious, Cousteau quickly floated downriver but Shelby's swift powerful strokes cleanly cut through
the water. He seized the lad by his sodden shirt. In minutes
they were on the riverbank. Lisa yelled for Raoul Santandar,
a Spaniard from New Orleans, to examine the injured fellow
whose arm had been broken. Santandar was the nearest thing
they had to a company physician. Setting the arm would
have to wait while the dangerous operation of moving the
boat past the embarras continued.

Several times the ropes slipped or gave way and the boat
crashed against the sinking edges of the embarras, sustaining
no major damage but sweeping two men who were poling
into the water. The first quickly bobbed up, then swam
ashore but the second was a poor swimmer and floundered,
trying to climb back aboard the boat near the stern. He was
helped back up by two of his fellows as Olivia watched from
her vantage point.

From shore Samuel saw her move away from the secure
position by the front of the cabin box where he had instructed her to remain. Damnation, a city bred female was a
burdensome liability in the wilderness! "Get back inside the
cabin where you'll be safe," he yelled at her.

Olivia either could not or would not hear as she watched
the men pull their sodden comrade to safety. Never in her
life, not even in the thick of a close horserace, had she seen
so much excitement. For a brief time the adventure made her
forget her own troubling and uncertain future.

Once the polers were back at their work, she scampered
along the narrow end of the deck. The heavy mast high

above her groaned beneath the bright afternoon sky as the ropes attached to it pulled it against the fierce current. She stepped over to where the rudder man held the sweep steady, guiding the boat that was now powered by human muscle and blood.

Suddenly the boat hit a sawyer, a submerged tree whose branches had been mired in the river bottom, leaving the massive trunk and roots to bob up without warning, smashing into any craft luckless enough to run afoul of it. The sawyer was big enough to capsize the boat. Only the men pulling the cordelle ropes with all their strength held it steady as the long craft eased by the clawing grasp of the tree's roots.

But the bone-jarring impact caused one casualty. Olivia, made even more careless by her excitement, was catapulted overboard with a loud splash. And she could not swim a stroke!

∽ *Chapter 10* ∽

Water closed in over her head like a coffin lid. Murky blackness, icy cold and fast moving, surrounded her as she thrashed frantically, trying to propel herself upward to breathe, to scream for help. What if no one saw her fall? What if they continued upriver without stopping, leaving her to a watery grave in the wilderness? No, she refused to accept such a horrible, lonely death.

Her hands and feet scraped the muddy bottom, restoring her sense of direction and allowing her a firm base from which to push off. She kicked upward with all her strength, clawing her way to the surface. The instant her face felt the cold fresh wind she sucked a great gulp of air into her lungs and screamed with all her might, "Samuel!" Then she was pulled beneath the swift rushing water once more.

Blackness closed in again. The relentless force of the current buffeted her as if she were no more than a hollow stick of driftwood. She thrashed and floundered, growing more hysterical each second her burning lungs were without oxygen. Suddenly a powerful band of steellike strength and hardness encircled her waist, squeezing out what little breath she had left. Olivia kicked and flailed more desperately as she was lifted.

The bright light of day broke over her again and a hoarse voice muttered near her ear, "Stop struggling or by God I'll drop you back for the fishes to eat!"

Now she could feel the warmth and solidity of his body as he held onto her, treading water while he tried to subdue her hysteria. "Samuel! You heard me," she choked out, wrapping her arms around his neck as she coughed up wet sandy bile. It felt like she had swallowed half the Missouri River.

When Samuel had seen her tumble overboard and vanish into the roiling water, his heart had stopped beating for a moment before he collected himself and plunged from the embarras where he was working into the swiftly moving current. Thank God she had been able to come up once and cry out to him, else he might have dived repeatedly in vain, for the water was far too muddy and filled with bracken from the spring thaw to locate one slender woman without some clue as to what direction the undertow had taken her.

The fear that she was lost had squeezed his chest, almost paralyzing him. Her fiery head breaking the surface with his name on her lips had propelled him through the freezing water like a frantic otter. As soon as he made contact with her kicking, thrashing body he had seized hold of her with the strength born of desperation and some other even stronger emotion which he was loathe to name. All he felt now, he convinced himself, was fury. "Move around to my back and hold tight while I swim to shore," he commanded. When she complied, he made for the bank with fast, sure strokes, feeling the soft allure of her supple body pressing against him as she held on for dear life.

Olivia could feel the tense anger that radiated from his body with each stroke. When they reached the shallows he hauled her up against him and half carried, half dragged her up the bank to a grassy spot where he pulled her down and knelt by her side.

Positioning her on all fours, he instructed, "Hang your head over and get out the rest of that water." Samuel pounded on her back until her coughing yielded several violent regurgitations of brackish water and lumps of river bottom.

She raised her head after the last choking gasp, intending to thank him for saving her life but before she could utter a word his facial expression silenced her.

"Of all the stump stupid stunts you've ever pulled, this is the best yet! Don't you have the brains of a possum? I told you to stay in the cabin box at the bow. What the hell were you doing hanging over the stern? You're goddamn lucky you didn't crack your skull on the sweep. But on second thought, that couldn't have hurt one bit. You haven't a brain inside the damn thing!"

"Are . . . you . . . quite finished?" she choked out, still struggling to get enough air into her aching lungs. Her throat was raw and her voice so hoarse that she was certain she must have swallowed enough twigs and leaves to build a vulture's nest.

"Mademoiselle St. Etienne, I haven't even begun. If you ever again disobey my orders, I will take down those raggedy britches and show you how the buffalo hunters tan a hide."

"Over my dead body!" she shrieked back.

"It damn nearly *was* your dead body," he snapped with a furious oath. "Given your propensity for plunging into ponds and rivers, why the hell did you learn to race horses bareback yet neglect to learn something as elementary as swimming?"

"A lady would have to bare her arms and legs to swim, but not to ride astride—unless she was Lady Godiva," she said with all the disdain of a duchess.

"Well, you goddamned might as well be Lady Godiva, swaggering around without undergarments, showing off your breasts and hips in boys shirts and britches!" She had straightened up defiantly, with her back arched provocatively. Her high upthrust breasts with pointy nipples were outlined clearly through the soaked shirt that was plastered to her body. Her hair fell in a shining wet curtain around her shoulders, framing her face. Those exotic green eyes were darkened with mutinous rage. He wanted to kiss her . . . or kill her. Right now one would serve as well as the other.

Before he did something exceedingly stupid, he stood up and stomped off to rejoin the men. "The squaws have started a fire up ahead a half mile where we'll camp tonight. Walk up and dry yourself out before you take a chill. I'll see you get some dry clothes from the boat."

Olivia sat back on her haunches, too stunned and furious to reply until he was gone. "I guess I don't have any more brains than a possum, thinking I was ever in love with you, Samuel Shelby," she muttered, struggling to haul herself to her feet. Then she began to walk in squishy misery toward the promised warmth of that fire.

Some secret part of her hoped that Samuel would bring her dry clothes from the boat but he did not. Instead a gnarled old *engagé* brought them, then stared at her with lascivious little black eyes, as if he could imagine her stripping herself naked to put on the dry clothes. Damn Shelby anyway! Sure as she went into the bushes to change, one or more of the men would spy on her and her "protector" was nowhere around to stop them. She decided it would be best to wait until the boat was brought up and use the privacy of the cabin box to don the dry clothes.

Huddling in front of the fire, Olivia was grateful that the

sun was warm and her upper body was almost dry. Only her boots remained soggy and cold. She took them off and toasted her feet in front of the flames, while the heat of the fire dried the soaked leather.

Samuel was one of the last of the men to come into camp that evening. He approached her, his mouth a grim slash across his taut face. She decided he was still angry about the river incident and decided to coolly ignore him.

"You're still in those damn damp clothes," he accused, throwing the heavy bundle he had been carrying onto the ground in front of her.

"I could scarcely change with Jaques looking on so avidly, now could I?" she replied without looking up. "Or would you rather I did and he charge admission so half the men could watch and then ravish me as you so graphically described the other day?" She stared sullenly at the heavy canvas bundle lying at her feet but asked nothing about it.

"Were you not so self-absorbed, you might have noticed that the men are far too exhausted either for a peep show or a ravishment. And two of them were badly injured on that embarras today. Lisa doesn't want them sleeping on the cold ground in tents. So we're evicted from the cabin box."

Her head flew up in consternation at his dispassionate announcement. "You—you mean we're to sleep out in the open—together?"

"Unless there's someone else here whose company you'd prefer to share." He gestured around the camp with a mock flourish, taking in the motley assortment of crude, evil-smelling *engagés* slumped around the fires. "That lover you boasted of, perhaps?" he taunted.

She suppressed a shudder of revulsion, hating the arrogant, knowing smirk on his face. The thought of sharing a bedroll with him frightened her—or at least that's what she told herself the strange little shivers running up and down her spine and the flush staining her cheeks meant.

But he doesn't want you. Olivia ignored the cruel reminder ringing in her ears. Lifting her chin proudly, she swallowed for courage and looked him squarely in the eye. "I suppose you leave me no choice."

"No, I don't, but at least your delicate sensibilities will be spared sleeping in the open. Can you put up this tent while I'm gone?" He kicked the heavy canvas mass with the toe of his boot.

"Me?" she asked in consternation. Then catching the beginnings on his face of what had become that all-too-familiar look of disgust, she shrugged.

"Of course." But she could not resist asking, "And where will you be?"

"I'll be helping Lisa and Santandar set a broken arm and stitch up a foot-long rip in a man's thigh. Have you had experience as a nurse? Maybe you could employ your fine embroidery hand to sew up human flesh and skin."

The mere thought of it made her stomach pitch sourly. She paled but gritted her teeth. "I said I would put up the damn tent." At least they would have shelter from the prying eyes of lascivious *engagés* when she and Samuel slept in separate bedrolls side by side.

Samuel headed back to the boat without another word. Olivia set doggedly to work unpacking the cumbersome piece of canvas and a tangle of ropes and short sturdy oak poles. She had seen the men rig their small rude shelters in the evenings, but never really paid much attention to how they did it. By now most of the tents were up. A few of the men were still working on theirs. She surreptitiously watched one wiry little Canadian drive the two lead poles into the hard clay soil with effortless ease, then toss the canvas covering over them and secure the outer perimeter to shorter stakes already set in the ground using stout rope ties. It seemed straightforward enough.

First she had to select a site. After making a visual sweep of the area, she settled on the far southwestern edge of the campgrounds in a shallow open swale. That should provide a modicum of sound proofing from the noisy snoring she had put up with in the cabin box ever since this hellish journey began.

It took her until dusk to unsnarl the ropes and lay out the canvas, which was far more awkward and heavy than she had ever imagined, even after dragging it across the clearing. Mercifully, a gruff old French Canadian had taken pity on her struggles and carried it the rest of the way as several others heckled him about messing with the Long Knife's woman, as they had dubbed her. She had dismissed him with thanks, afraid of the ugly scene with Samuel if he were to return and find her alone with one of the men.

Her next chore was to drive in the smaller stakes and lead poles, a feat far easier observed than emulated. Finally, after hitting her own fingers with the crude wooden mallet until she was certain several digits would rot off in the night, she had all the poles in place, although several were a bit wobbly. By now it was nearly full dark and she was working by the dim flicker of firelight. She decided the poles were secured well enough.

Standing up she spread the big canvas tent and pulled one end across a lead pole, then threw the other end of the stiff cloth over the opposite pole. She began tying off the sides, working her way around the perimeter. The center of the tent sagged so much she could not stretch the canvas to reach the last of them. She released the edge of the cloth and crawled inside the low enclosure, emitting a fierce oath. If she remained in this heathen wilderness much longer, she would have the vocabulary and manners of a river rat!

Olivia blinked her eyes at the stygian darkness inside the tent, then groped her way to the center and began to raise the sagging middle of the canvas and pull it toward the left lead pole. Suddenly the right pole wrenched free from its shallow mooring and toppled forward, striking her across the back. She jumped away with a loud yelp of pain, pushing against the canvas, which in turn caused the rest of the short pegs anchoring its edge to pull out of the ground. The whole tent enveloped her in an oily, smelly cocoon. The more she thrashed, the more the stiff greasy canvas seemed intent on swallowing her. She was suffocating. Letting out a loud shriek, she tried to flatten herself to the ground and slither out from under but could make no headway. Finally in desperation she rolled onto her back, kicking and screaming like a child having a tantrum.

That was how Samuel found her. Wrestling the canvas off the thrashing, cursing woman, he added a few succinct oaths of his own as he dragged her to her feet. "You are like a bear cub! Trouble follows you everywhere."

"It's not my fault I'm not strong enough to drive wooden stakes into this stone hard clay! I am a woman, not a woodsman!"

"Then you should've stayed in St. Louis," he snapped all too acutely aware of her gender. He had to lie in a small tent and sleep beside her tonight without touching her. Damning the excretal fates that had saddled him with Olivia St. Etienne's nubile presence, he took a breath and counted silently to ten.

"If I'd stayed in St. Louis, you'd have despoiled me of my virtue, then sauntered off into this wilderness without a backward glance!"

He raised one black eyebrow sardonically. "Your only virtue, madamoiselle, as far as I can detect, is that you can survive the most incredible blunders and never stop whining."

Whining! How could she ever have thought this priggish self-righteous lout was charming? Her fingers curved into claws and she raised her right hand. Before she could wipe the arrogant expression off his handsome face, he seized her wrist and held it fast.

"Don't even think it," he purred, then flung the offending hand away from him as if it were an adder ready to bite. "I'm heartily sick of Walk Fast's mushy strong stews, so I've brought a chunk of venison haunch to roast over a fire. I suppose it's too much to hope that you can build a fire to cook it while I set up the tent."

It was not a question. Olivia did not dignify it with an answer, just waited for him to issue more preemptory orders.

"Take the meat over to Liguest's fire. He's finished cooking. Break off some willow sticks to skewer the meat. You've seen it done." He handed her a small knife from his pack with which to cut up the juicy chunk of venison.

Taking the weapon from him with a surly jerk, she asked sweetly, "Aren't you afraid I'll use it to slit your throat while you sleep?"

"You haven't the humanity to be so compassionate," he replied dryly, turning his attention to the crumpled mess of their tent.

Once she had stomped off with the venison and the knife, Samuel set to work. He realized immediately that pounding the heavy poles into the unyielding earth would be an impossible task for a pampered city woman, not that he held much hope she would prove a decent cook either. What the hell was he going to do with her?

Seth Walton had come in tonight saying he had talked with an Osage scout that afternoon. They would reach the first of the Osage winter encampments in a couple of days. He planned to leave Lisa's party at the confluence of the Missouri and Osage rivers to search for the Englishman moving among the Indians. He had to find someone to protect Olivia and see that she was returned to St. Louis or perhaps even

see her downriver if the story about an uncle in New Orleans
was to be believed.

Somehow the thought of sending her all the way to New
Orleans and never seeing her again did not sit well with him.
"I really am crazy," he muttered to himself as he worked.
The idea of her waiting for him in the house he had rented
in St. Louis held a strong appeal. His mind's eye pictured
her at the front door dressed in a soft muslin gown and
smelling of jasmine, with all that bright hair falling down
her back, smiling and welcoming him with open arms.

He decided eating Walks Fast's greasy mush must have
softened his brains. Olivia would never wait with a smile of
welcome for him. She had made that abundantly clear. And
he had learned enough about her to recant his bad bargain
with her guardian, no matter how much he desired her. The
only sensible thing to do was to provide her with a safe escort and money enough to reach her uncle in New Orleans—or whoever it was there to whom she had tried to run.
With that resolution made, he decided to talk to Manuel
Lisa tonight about taking the girl under his protection. Once
they reached the first of the trading outposts at Council
Bluffs, Lisa could find someone trustworthy to accompany
her downriver. Samuel finished setting up their tent, then
went in search of the Spaniard.

Olivia sat huddled miserably in front of the fire. Her
clothes had dried but were crisp with mud that abraded her
skin in itchy misery. She looked at the sticks hung over the
fire, roasting two fat chunks of venison. Juice dripped into
the flames, making a sputtering noise and giving off a heavenly aroma. Her mouth watered when she inhaled.

Perhaps if she were quick she could slip away from the
fire with her clean clothes and find one of those small
streams feeding into the river where she could bathe and
change. Samuel had been right when he said the men were
too exhausted tonight to pay her any mind. She eyed the
meat again. It was still quite rare. Plenty of time. She would
only be gone a few minutes. Perhaps she could find Samuel
and tell him to tend to the cooking while she changed. After
all, *he* was the one who had accused her of smelling bad! A
quick search around the fire revealed that he was missing.
Damn the man, he was as reliable as an egg-sucking dog in
a chicken coop!

Olivia took her clean clothes and set out, watching to be

certain she was not followed. No one paid her the slightest attention. The moon had risen and cast clear silvery light across the river, which glowed like a living thing, now shimmering with metallic beauty, utterly different than the boiling brown torrent it was by harsh daylight. She found a small spring of icy cold water spilling from a limestone formation a few hundred feet from the edge of camp. Colonel Shelby would be furious at her for disobeying his high and mighty orders but she didn't give a fig. After all, she still had the knife with which to protect herself.

Quickly she pulled the board-stiff shirt off and sponged cold water over her freezing upper body, then used a strip of toweling she'd hoarded to dry off. After repeating the process with her lower body, she was shivering as she slipped into the clean clothes. Sacred blood, she was heartily sick of wearing shapeless rough boy's britches and homespun shirts. Once she had reveled in the freedom of movement and loved to flaunt convention when she was Ollie, the jockey who raced her guardian's horses. But then she could return to being Olivia and wear silks and jewels and bask in male admiration.

Now she was forced to admit there was only one man whose admiration she wished. And he had made it plain he could no longer abide the sight of her—just because she was not Mrs. Daniel Boone! Of course, she was also forced to admit she had gone to great lengths to spurn his ardent overtures when she ran away from him in St. Louis. But what choice did he leave her? He had broken her heart, treating her like some dockside slattern who could be bought, then discarded.

What would become of them here in this awful wilderness? He seemed to thrive on its discomforts and dangers while she was a wretched misfit totally out of her element. She had prided herself on being a tough survivor after being left alone in the world when her parents died. "I will not give up. He desired me once. If I can make him want me that way again . . . perhaps I can wring an honest proposal of marriage out of him." Then to salve her own pride she added, "Of course, that doesn't mean I have to accept it!"

Feeling better she approached Liguest's fire. He had retired and was passed out on his bedroll with a jug of "panther piss" clutched to his chest, snoring loudly. Just like a man, Olivia thought. Lisa had apparently rewarded his crew

for their extraordinary labors that day by issuing them
enough whiskey to get them all drunk.

She walked past him and knelt by the coals, searching in
the dim flickering light for the two chunks of venison. The
sticks on which she had spitted them were nowhere in sight.
Had some greedy *engagé* stolen her meat? Then she caught
a whiff of it—the blackened, smoldering lumps lying to one
side of the coals.

Horrified, Olivia pulled the knife from her belt and poked
at the suspicious substance which was giving off an acrid
charred stench. Impaling one chunk on the blade, she raised
it up to examine it. No doubt, it was the venison, now burned
beyond recognition. "But how?" she wailed.

Samuel picked that very moment to walk up behind her.
Smelling the burned meat he stepped past her and kicked at
the coals. "I told you to cut willow sticks. You used the
branches from one of those old sycamores, didn't you?" he
accused, taking the chunk of venison and the knife from her.

"Willows. Sycamores. They're all trees to me. I didn't
know it made any difference," she replied defensively.

"The sycamore's low branches are mostly dead, dry. They
burn up within half an hour. The willow twigs are green.
They don't," he explained as if to a child. "Why didn't you
fish the meat out with the knife when it fell into the fire?"

"I only left for a few minutes to change my clothes.
You're the one who accused me of being smelly," she
huffed, then instantly hoped that didn't sound as if she were
trying to please the insufferable wretch.

"Like the child you are, you should be sent to bed without
supper," he gritted out.

"Why not starve me? You've done everything else." Her
stomach picked that inappropriate moment to growl loudly.

"Not *everything* else," he replied evenly, then threw down
the ruined venison in disgust. "If you hurry you can still get
a couple of bowls of Walks Fast's stew before she dumps it
out. Bring them to the tent." He turned around and started
to walk away.

"I'm not your slave. Samuel," she snapped. "Get your
own bowl of stew."

He turned on his heel and glared glacially at her. "If I do,
then I will sleep alone in my *own* tent. Do I make myself
perfectly clear, Olivia?"

She clenched her teeth and stomped off for the two bowls of stew.

They ate by the dying coals of a small fire Samuel had built outside their tent. He could feel her eyes on him when she thought he was not aware of it. *Probably thinking of sleeping with me in that small tent,* he chuckled to himself mirthlessly. Hell, he was just as unhappy about it as she was but for completely different reasons. No matter that she made him so furious he wanted to choke the life from her, he still desired her. Just thinking about lying beside her made him iron hard. He shifted uncomfortably on the cold earth while his senses ran wild, smelling her delicate female musk, knowing all he would have to do in the night was to reach out and bury his hands in that thick fiery hair—or bury his body inside her hot sweet sheath. . . .

Stop it, he thought to himself. With a disgusted oath he tossed his spoon into the half-empty bowl and flung it none too gently on the ground, then stood up. "How that squaw can take perfectly decent venison and make it taste like rancid crow I'll never know."

"Neither will I. My guardian always employed excellent cooks." Some insane impulse made her bait him, but the moment the words spilled forth he fixed her with a stony glare that indicated just how contemptible the remark was.

"On the Missouri people learn to cook for themselves . . . or they go hungry."

"Or, if they're men, they can buy a woman to do it for them." Would she ever learn to think before she spoke? Olivia felt the blush to the roots of her hair and was grateful for the darkness as she shoved away her bowl of mostly uneaten stew.

"A good squaw is worth half a dozen fine horses. I only paid one for you." He waited a beat, then added, "I should've kept the horse."

Samuel turned away and headed toward the tent. He reached down to pull open the end flap just as Olivia's stew bowl flew over his head, splattering him with several greasy chunks of meat that bounced away like rubber balls, leaving a sticky spray of gravy and vegetables behind. He straightened up and brushed the goo from his buckskin shirt, all the while cursing with fluid inventiveness. Then he raised his arms and pulled the shirt over his head in one fluid motion.

Tossing it to Olivia he said in a low deadly voice, "That will be washed and ready for me to wear by tomorrow night."

Olivia sat silently as he disappeared inside the tent. Her mouth had gone dry when she watched the dim firelight cast shadows across the bronzed beauty of his bare torso. She remembered how hard that furry chest had felt when he pressed her breasts against it and kissed her and how powerful his arms were when they had seized her in the water and pulled her tightly to his body. To her utter mortification, tears welled up in her eyes and a lump as hard as Walks Fast's biscuits seemed to close down her throat.

I still want him to want me . . . and he doesn't . . . not even as a leman. All they seemed to do was strike sparks off each other. Everything she said and did antagonized him more, whether she intended it or not. What was wrong with her anyway? She had never mooned over any man before, not even the most ardent admirers she'd garnered in Washington. Perhaps it was because she was so alone now, aware of her guardian's perfidy, stranded in the wilderness with a band of rough, dirty, dangerous men. Samuel was the only one to whom she could turn.

But he does not want you.

"Well, I don't want him either," she whispered to herself. But she knew she lied.

Samuel heard her creep into the tent a good while later. He had been unable to sleep in spite of aching exhaustion. All he could do was lie awake and think of the maddening miss outside. He had almost gotten up to go in search of her, fearing she had run into some new sort of trouble. When she climbed into her bedroll beside him, he rolled over with a muttered oath, turning his back to her.

Olivia lay with her arms pressed against her sides, staring into the inky blackness, aware of how small the tent was . . . and how large the man beside her was. His vital male presence seemed to fill the confining space. He exuded an unnerving hostility that made it difficult for her to lie passively beside him, but she was afraid to move, afraid that if she tried to roll over and turn her back that she might brush against him in the dark, or worse yet, sob aloud and humiliate herself.

I can't go on this way. It would be another two months until they reached Lisa's outpost on the Upper Missouri. Two more months of taking his curt orders and enduring his foul temper or icy disdain when she failed to perform her chores satisfactorily. Back in St. Louis she had believed naively that the worst thing that could happen was to become Samuel Shelby's mistress. Now she knew that it was far worse to have him so utterly disgusted with her that he would not even touch her.

As she lay in the dark contemplating every cruel and scornful word he had spoken to her on this trip, her tears fell like silent rain, rolling over her cheeks and soaking into the scratchy wool blanket beneath her head. Several times she almost did the unthinkable. She almost reached out to him, throwing her arms around his broad shoulders and clinging to him, begging him not to be angry, not to hate her. Each time she squelched the desperate impulse with greater difficulty until finally the truth became clear to her.

She was in love with Samuel Shelby, a man who believed she was without morals, a harlot for sale to the highest bidder, exchanged by her guardian for the price of his favorite racehorse. After the confidences she had shared with him in Washington and the way he had kissed her in Chouteau's garden, Olivia could not understand how he could have accepted Emory Wescott's lies.

The bitter fact remained that he had believed every nasty insinuation, thinking that because she disguised herself in boy's clothes to race horses that she was not fit to bear his name. Not that he ever planned to bestow that singular honor on any female, lady or otherwise, again. He had admitted as much in that ghastly conversation with her guardian. *He* had been a married man when he flirted with her and kissed her until she was dazed and helpless on that Virginia backroad. He had been the aggressor, she the innocent. Life was so unfair.

She finally did roll over and curl up in a small fetal ball. There had to be a way to escape this horrible quandary. If she could only return to St. Louis, she might this time be able to obtain passage on a boat bound for New Orleans. She would begin all over again and let the devil take Colonel Samuel Shelby. Surely retracing the past weeks' journey back down the river could not be that difficult. In spite of Samuel's dire warnings, there had been no Indians sighted, not even so much as a dangerous wild animal. But then she remembered the wide, swift-moving streams that had fed into the Missouri, easily bypassed aboard the big keelboat, not so easily traversed afoot by a woman who could not even swim. If only she had a horse she might make it, but there were no horses. On that dismal note she finally fell asleep.

The temperature dipped low and the small fire outside their tent burned out. Still deep in sleep, Olivia felt the chill and moved instinctively toward the warmth emanating from Samuel, who had rolled nearer as he tossed and turned in the night.

He felt the slight tickle of long hair as it brushed against his face, then the soft insinuating presence of her hand as it glided across his chest beneath the heavy woolen blanket. He normally slept naked when he had the comforts of a bed, but here in this dangerous wilderness he had grown used to sleeping partially clothed, yet even in his exhausted slumber he could feel her fingertips touching his bare chest. Then the distinct curves of a female body pressed against his side, a most delightfully female body. He was dreaming.

The fire-haired seductress stretched out her arms beckoning, enticing. She was swathed in a loosely belted robe of a translucent gauzelike material. Samuel could see right through it, and his erection ached. His hand traced the indentation of her tiny waist and the enticing firmness of a perfectly molded breast. He cupped his palm around the small globe and felt the nipple tighten into a nubby point. Samuel came into her outstretched arms. His mouth dropped down, instinctively making contact with hers, pressing against the soft allure of her lips, demanding entrance to taste of her. She moaned softly and obliged, letting her arms glide up and around his shoulders, holding onto him as he savaged her with the hungry kiss.

Still half-asleep, Olivia was warm now, in fact she was on fire. A deep keening pain stretched outward from low in her belly, tingling in her breasts, aching in her nether parts as she wriggled and arched her hips restlessly. Something, someone was pressing her against the bedroll, moving over her, touching her body in the most intimate, incredible ways. When his lips claimed hers she was catapulted back to that incredible encounter in the cabin when Samuel had first kissed her.

Samuel.

She knew his hunger and she knew his heat. Every nuance of his body had been imprinted on her in their few brief encounters. Drugged by sleep and desire, she gave in to the lure of his body and let her instincts and his hands guide her. She felt him pull her shirt open and fondle her breasts. Shocking little spikes of pleasure radiated from the crests as he cupped and teased them. She clung to him, returning his kiss, letting her fingers trace the hard satiny contours of his shoulders and back, then dig into the thick night black hair of his head. She was drowning in a whirlpool of exquisite new sensations and she never wanted to awaken and have it end.

Samuel tried to pull the gauze robe from his temptress. He reached down to free it and encountered a tight waistband. When his hands slid lower they felt the coarse flat seams of a pair of men's pants! He reached in front of her and felt the fly, tightly buttoned. Britches? Where was the transparent wrap? Where was his seductress?

Olivia!

Shock awakened him like a bucket of icy river water. They were in the tent and she had tried to seduce him, the damnable little she-cat! Randy fool that he was, he had almost succumbed. Muttering an obscenity, he climbed off her as if she were a scorpion.

"I suppose you concluded you'd catch more flies with honey than vinegar," he said scathingly. "It almost worked. You should've taken off the damned britches yourself. Then I might have plunged right into your warm welcome."

Olivia blinked her eyes in the darkness, feeling the cool air as it touched her bare breasts where before Samuel's warm body had cocooned her. He had moved abruptly away from her, awakening her and leaving her chilled. Awareness of what had transpired flooded her mind with horror! She must have crawled closer to him seeking warmth and he believed she had tried to seduce him!

"If I wanted to seduce you—which I certainly do not—I would have taken off my britches—which I obviously did not," she said in a rush as she pulled her shirt back together and groped for her own blanket, pulling it up and huddling beneath it, grateful that the darkness hid them both. She succeeded only partially in stifling a sob. "Don't blame me for your lust."

His only reply was a series of snarled curses and the loud rustling of his bedroll when he settled himself back into it, as far from her as he could get and still remain within the shelter of the crowded tent.

When Olivia awakened in the morning, Samuel was gone. The small tent seemed somehow larger and very empty as she stared at the flat grassy space where his bedroll had been. How had he managed to pack it up and leave without awakening her? She could hear the boisterous curses of the men, the clank of cook pots and rustle of tents being pulled down.

As remembrance of the disastrous encounter returned in the merciless light of morning, she sat up and put her head on her knees, hugging them in abject misery. What must he think of her now? How could she face him after what they almost did? She huddled there for several minutes until she heard footsteps approaching. Then a man cleared his throat and called out to her.

"Mademoiselle St. Etienne. It is Manuel Lisa and I must talk with you."

Chapter 11

"**W**hat do you mean, he's gone!" Olivia croaked, staring at Manuel Lisa's swarthy countenance with an expression of horror and disbelief on her face.

"Señorita St. Etienne, I try to explain to you," Lisa said in his halting, heavily accented English, spreading his hands in a placating gesture. "The colonel, he must travel to the Big Osage. Their village, it is a day's journey up the Osage River, not far."

"Then he'll rejoin us in a couple of days?" she asked suspiciously, not liking the way the barrel-chested little Spaniard refused to meet her eyes.

Lisa shrugged. "If all goes as he hopes, it is possible . . . but if he must go farther into Osage country, *quien sabe?* That is why he gives me this." He handed her a letter signed by Samuel.

Olivia perused it quickly. "It's a letter of credit . . . to keep me at his house in St. Louis." The amount was most generous—a thousand dollars, which she could draw upon from the Quinn Mercantile where the colonel had deposited his money. She blushed darkly, knowing the shrewd Spaniard had drawn his own conclusions about her relationship with Samuel. She was under his protection but not affianced. *In effect, his whore.* And last night she had almost become so in fact.

"I will return you to St. Louis as soon as I deposit my cargo at the forts. I must attend my business affairs. Then the journey downstream will take twelve to fourteen days, no more."

"But how much longer to get upstream to the forts on the upper Missouri?" she asked, noting he had deliberately omitted that rather vital detail.

Lisa sighed. "With a good wind to fill the sails we will gain five to ten days," he replied, using the fingers of his right hand to give visual punctuation to his remarks.

"How long for the entire trip, Señor Lisa?"

"Perhaps two months. But fear nothing. I have given my

word to your colonel. I, Manuel Lisa, will keep you safe. I have promised," he said with finality, nodding his head as if that settled the matter.

Olivia could see that arguments or cajolery would avail her nothing. Perhaps tears? Unlikely. This was a seasoned veteran of decades on the rivers who had his life savings tied up in this trading venture. He would not jeopardize it for one stowaway female, even if she managed to weep a bucket of tears! "When do we leave, Señor Lisa?" she asked with diplomatic meekness.

After two more days of gathering information and smuggling food into her bedroll, Olivia was ready to strike out. If "*her* colonel" could walk up the Osage River, she, by damn, could walk down the Missouri. After all, they had only come a little over a week upriver from the last settlement at St. Charles. Here and there along the way they had passed isolated farms and a few small riverfront outposts. Thankfully she had squelched her first impulse to tear Samuel's letter of credit into a dozen tiny bits and throw them in Lisa's face. For once prudence—or was it a growing sense of self-preservation—led her to curb her temper and hold onto the letter. She hoped to trade it for a horse and enough food to see her back to St. Louis.

I will not endure another two or three months in this hellish wilderness just because of Samuel Shelby. After all, it was his fault that she had been forced to flee St. Louis in the first place. Never mind that she had mistakenly headed in the wrong direction; she was going to correct that mishap this very night. As soon as everyone was asleep in their tents, she would slip from the boat where Lisa had insisted she spend the past several nights since Samuel's treacherous desertion.

The bedroll was heavy, the scratchy strouding stuffed with hard biscuits and several pouches of greasy pemmican. Olivia supposed if she got hungry enough she could stomach the rancid stuff. There was a full moon and the sentry was posted at the stern of the boat. She could crawl over the bow and wade very carefully through the shallows undetected. Once on the bank, there was a brake of tall willow shoots to hide her. The only trick would be managing not to drop the unwieldy pack or the knife she had filched from a crate in the cabin box. It was a poor weapon, but even if she stole a rifle, she had not the slightest idea of how to load or fire it, so she had decided it was a heavy encumbrance not worth carrying.

Slipping off in the moonlight was not nearly so easy to accomplish as she had hoped. Bright light bathed the deck but the river shallows were shrouded in shadows cast by overhanging cottonwood limbs. The swift movement of the river did cover any noise she might make. When her feet touched the water a tiny hiss of misery escaped her lips. She knew it would be cold on her bare feet, but it was best to keep her boots with her gear, dry in her arms, not wet on her feet.

The water was only knee-high near the shore and the bow of the boat was moored firmly into the soft sandy bank. But treacherous small rocks, some lichen coated and slippery, others sharp as razors, were scattered along the riverbed. She bit her lip to keep from crying out as she made her way, one agonizing step at a time, to freedom. Balancing the bedroll was even more difficult than she had imagined. Several times she came within a gnat's breath of dropping it in the water when she slipped or jerked back her foot from a sharp rock. By the time she reached the cover of the brake, her legs were going numb from the cold.

At least I won't feel how bad my feet hurt, she thought with grim humor as she carefully wended her way through the bracken to dry ground. The nearest campfire with tents scattered around it was only thirty feet away, but the flames had died to pale orange coals and the sound of loud snores vied with the croaking of bullfrogs on the still night air. She walked silently down the muddy beach until the fires were out of sight, then climbed to the top of the embankment about fifteen feet higher up.

Under the cover of scrub pines and cottonwoods, she could look down on the boat and the camp as she sat on the ground and pulled the dry boots over her cold and aching feet. Rough and miserable as her life with the rivermen had been, it was still one of relative safety. Once she left them, she would be completely alone in a strange and hostile wilderness. Could she attempt it—*should* she attempt it?

Ahead lay unknown dangers, but here lay another two to three months of unremitting drudgery and shame. Here was where Samuel Shelby had deserted her, turning her over to Manual Lisa as he would any other nonessential possession he might value only enough to make minimal arrangements for its "storage." She turned her back on the comfort of the fires and began to walk inland, steering a course around the camp and then back to the riverbank downstream from where the boat was moored.

"In a week I'll be back in civilization, on a boat bound for New Orleans," she promised herself.

It took two days for Olivia to admit she was lost. The first night she had made her way through the inky blackness of the woods with only small strips of moonlight to help her find her way back to the river. Now she was becoming increasingly certain that it had been the wrong river, not a narrow channel of the mighty Missouri, but only the last one of three small tributaries they had crossed the day before her escape. She must have followed it for a dozen miles headed vaguely northwest instead of southeast. The sun never seemed to be in the right position and the river seemed too narrow and clean-running to be the Missouri.

The situation was hopeless. She was miles from another human being. Not even a savage red Indian had shown his face. Her feet were blistered and her arms and legs scratched raw from thrashing her way through the dense underbrush that overgrew the bank of the river. After walking all night and most of yesterday with only brief stops to eat and drink, she had collapsed in exhaustion last night, rolling up in her blanket and lying on the dank, moist earth, listening to the eerie night sounds of the woodlands. Snorting, rattling and clucking noises emanated from the water while even more ominous screeches and howls echoed through the forest and across the open grassy meadows.

But Olivia had been too exhausted to remain awake for long. Clutching her knife in her fist, she quickly passed out, only to awaken with bright sunlight streaming in her face. Doggedly she had started out again that second morning after choking down one of the hard biscuits smeared with a bit of Walks Fast's greasy pemmican. By midmorning she could definitely see that the river was narrowing far too much. At this rate it would soon be little more than a trickle. She finally admitted she was following the wrong river.

Reasoning that it ran at a right angle to the Missouri, she decided to ford it and then angle in a southwesterly direction back toward the big river. A dangerous course to follow but her only hope if she were ever to make her food last until she reached some sort of white settlement. After once more removing her boots, she very carefully stepped into the cold rushing water, feeling her way along the bottom, praying there would be no sudden drop-off. The water reached her waist at its highest point before she climbed out on the opposite bank.

Teeth chattering, she scrambled up and found a cluster of boulders set amid some scrub pines. The sun had warmed the rocks and they felt delightful to her wet clammy skin as she reclined against one. She remained motionless for several minutes until the sleep of exhaustion claimed her again.

Olivia awakened to the sounds of soft snorting and odd sounding squeals. She blinked her eyes at the dazzling azure canopy overhead. It must be noon. Her clothes had dried in the spring heat. She sat up to orient herself and to search for the source of the sounds she had heard. Her eyes swept the rocky stretch of clearing around the edge of the stream. There, only a dozen feet or so from her, amid the boulders, two very small black furry creatures rolled and jumped clumsily around each other in fierce play.

"How sweet!" Olivia was not exactly certain what they were, but they were cute and cuddly, almost like fat puppies. She slid from the rock quietly and knelt to coax them to come to her, eager for the comfort of something warm and furry and alive to hold.

"Come here, come, come," she called in a soft musical voice. They stopped playing and observed her through liquid black eyes, wary and curious at the same time. She moved forward a step with her hand out but they retreated. Then remembering the pemmican in her pack, she pulled it down and opened it, taking out one of the rawhide parfleches. Scooping out a handful, she again extended her arm, offering the treat to them.

They sniffed the air and approached slowly. Just as she was almost close enough to feed them, an earsplitting growl rent the placid noontime air. A great black bear came running in a swift yet ponderous rhythm along the edge of the riverbank, headed directly toward Olivia.

Bear cubs. They were bear cubs! Holy Mother! Olivia remembered hearing stories about how fierce and dangerous she-bears could be. She turned to run, almost tripping over the pack in her desperate haste. Her boots lay uselessly on top of the boulder. She would have to run barefooted through the thick woods. With a sob, she clawed her way over the rocks, hearing the thudding of the bear's paws on the ground, closer and closer. She screamed for help even though she knew it was useless. The hot fetid breath of the bear seemed to scorch her back but she was too terrified to turn around to see how close the creature was. Alone in the wilderness, she would be torn to shreds and die without a trace or any remembrance.

"*Maman! Père!* Samuel! Someone help me!" She crashed through a stand of dry grass and snagged her shirt on the prickers of a berry bush. Her lungs were exploding with fire, her eyes hazing over with sweat pouring into them. As she stumbled and started to go down, she yanked the knife from her belt and clutched it in one small white fist. She would not let herself be devoured without a fight. *This is the end.* She turned to face her death. The first words of an act of contrition formed on her lips as the bear reared up to deliver the killing blow. Still holding fast to the knife she braced herself for the cruel bloody fate awaiting her, determined to inflict some small injury on her killer.

Suddenly a deep masculine voice boomed in a thick Appalachian twang, "Missy, don't hurt thet bar!"

Olivia looked up at the biggest man she had ever seen, a towering giant brandishing a blazing torch. He stepped across her small crouching body as if she were no more than a pebble on the riverbank.

"Yee-haw! Now git back to them younguns o' yourn. Damn, if yew ain't the plumb ugliest mother critter ever turned out o' the' woodshop o' creation!" he bellowed at the bear.

Her rescuer placed himself between her and her attacker, poking a glowing, smoking faggot toward the animal's sensitive nose. He advanced toward the bear brandishing the crude torch and yelling curses all the while.

The woodsman must have been six and a half feet tall with so much matted grizzled hair on his head and face that he nearly resembled a bear himself. His clothes were all of buckskin, elaborately fringed and beaded and he carried an arsenal of weapons on his person, including an enormous curved hunting knife the size of a scimitar strapped on one hip. A powder horn and shot pouch hung suspended from his shoulders and he clutched a mountain rifle in his right hand.

"Shoot! For God's sake, shoot," Olivia shrieked in English as the bear reared up, swatting ineffectually at the torch, which was burning down almost to the great meaty fist that clutched it.

Suddenly the bear dropped back on all four feet and wheeled around clumsily, then lumbered away, heading back in the direction of her cubs. Olivia sat staring at the big black bear's retreat, numb with disbelief, while her giant rescuer threw his makeshift torch to the ground and stomped out the flames. Then he turned back and extended one massive arm. His callused hand seemed larger than the bear's paw. It enveloped Olivia's arm as he pulled her to her feet.

"Yew all right, gal?" the giant queried. Solemn brown eyes swept from her tangled hair down to her muddy bare feet and back.

"*Oui*—yes, I'm all right," she answered, amazed to be alive after so terrifying a brush with death. She felt the trembling begin then, from the soles of her feet traveling all the way up her body until her heart felt like it would burst and her head reeled with dizziness. "No, I'm not all right at all," she murmured as her knees turned to jelly.

"Yew look plumb peeked ta me," the big man said, squinting at her uncertainly. "Course, I have thet affect on lots o' folks. Reckon I ain't much better lookin' than an ole buff'lo bull in full spring molt. Thet's why I purty much keep ta myself in these here woods. I'm Micajah Johnstone, missy." He made an awkward bow, touching in an old-fashioned courtly way, then set aside his rifle and steadied her by taking hold of her arm and leaning her against the trunk of a big oak tree.

Olivia looked down at the rifle and asked, "Why didn't you just shoot the bear instead of risking your life with that torch?"

"Naw, I couldn't do thet. Hit wuz a she-bar. Yew saw her young'uns. They'd die without her. Sides, I knowed I cud skeer her. I have me a camp jist upriver. Grabbed a stick out o' th' fire when I heered the ruckus. Bar's 'n all wild critters is afeared o' fire. Come on ta my camp. I expect yew cud use some coffee 'n grub."

As he helped her stand, he asked, "Whut's yore name, missy?"

"Olivia St. Etienne, Monsieur Johnstone. Thank you for saving my life. I am most grateful . . . and most hungry."

He guffawed loudly. "I got me a big pot o' stew simmerin' 'n coffee a boilin' away. Should all be ready by now."

Hot food sounded like heaven. Olivia's mouth was watering before they ever reached the campsite, which was situated in a small clearing not far from where she had forded the river. A fire crackled merrily below a small iron kettle that was suspended above it on an iron bar. The coffeepot nestled in the coals near the edge of the fire pit. Nearby a large buckskin gelding grazed peacefully, secured only by a braided hackamore. A heavy travois was leaning against the trunk of a towering sycamore tree at the edge of the clearing.

Olivia sank down on a soft pile of buffalo robes and looked around. This must be a trapper's camp, although she saw none of the small willow frames on which beavermen stretched and cured the hides of their catch. The only evidence of any hunting, besides the bedroll, was one deer, hanging suspended head down from the limb of a cottonwood. It had been gutted and the body was held gaping obscenely open by a series of wooden sticks wedged across the interior.

Micajah started to pour coffee into a big tin mug, then remembered that he had drunk from it before. Surreptitiously, he rubbed the rim with his greasy buckskin sleeve before filling it with the steaming black liquid. He offered it to the girl who sat enveloped in the mountain of his bedroll.

Olivia accepted it eagerly and watched as he ladled rich brown gravy, filled with chunks of meat, onions and other vegetables into a bowl. It smelled heavenly. She took a sip of coffee and found it was strong but not at all the inky bitter stuff the squaws and rivermen made. A small smile touched her lips as she recalled the hideous muddy bean mess she had made for Samuel.

"Good to see yew lookin' a bit more pert, Miz St. E'tane," he said, handing her the bowl of stew.

"You make much better coffee than I ever could." She set down the cup and accepted the bowl with thanks, then dug in with the spoon.

"Ain't nothin' ta makin' coffee 'ceptin' ta throw in a fist full o' grounds fer a couple cups o' water."

"But you do have to grind the beans . . . and use water, not mud." At his puzzled look she gave him a quick description of how she had performed the task and elicited a hearty thigh slapping laugh from him.

"Thet feller whut drunk hit must've been plumb pole-axed."

She had been the one nearly poleaxed, but Olivia did not bring that up. "This is really delicious stew." She took another big mouthful and closed her eyes with pleasure at the rich spicy flavor. "Is it venison?" she asked, looking over at the deer carcass hanging on the tree.

"Naw. I only jest kilt the deer 'n bled hit out. This here stew's been simmerin' since't early mornin' when I lucked on thet skunk."

"Skunk!" She dropped the spoon with a clatter and stared at him. Surely he could not mean . . .

"Hit's a pure delicacy." He pronounced delicacy "deli-kay-cee," with great relish. "Sweetest tastin' meat a feller ever snagged a tooth inta—thet is, if'n he gits th' critter afore hit kin waggle hits tail. I got this'un clean. Alls yew got ta do is cut thet leetle sac out real careful like so's hit don't spill onta th' meat," he explained carefully.

Oliver was torn between hunger pangs and the delicious aroma of the stew on one hand and the idea of eating vermin like a skunk on the other. Hunger won out and she dug in again. It *did* taste sweet.

Micajah watched her eat ravenously in spite of her initial aversion to the highly uncivilized treat. The little gal had grit. When she had fallen with that bear hot on her heels, she had been clutching a puny little knife in her fist ready to fight gamely to the last.

"Yew must be a city gal. What 'er yew doin' all alone here dressed like a tadpole?" he asked, studying her soft pale complexion and the scruffy boy's clothes she wore.

"I was running away . . . from a man who betrayed me . . . no, actually from two men who betrayed me," she added, taking a deep breath and looking into Micajah's warm brown eyes. His face looked "used" by life, like a well-worn buffalo hide blanket, sun and wind blasted and just a bit greasy. Long dark hair and a full bushy beard were liberally sprinkled with gray but his big rawboned frame remained erect and powerful, although she judged him to be well past fifty.

For all the intimidation of his physical appearance there was an odd gentleness about the man. In her whole life Olivia had never had anyone to really confide in besides her parents. Micajah Johnstone looked to be a good listener. Before she realized, she was telling him the whole sad and star crossed tale of her parents' deaths, her guardian's treachery and, most painfully, Samuel's betrayal and desertion.

He scratched his head when she had finished. "Sounds ta me like yew ain't got no real kinfolk anywhere 'ceptin' mebee thet uncle down in New Orleens 'n he's probably no account, him turnin' away yore ma and all. Way I figger hit, any man thet'd deny his own sister ain't no better 'n a he cat on th' prowl. Worse. Animals only do whut comes nat'ral but the good Lord gave humans a mite more ta live up ta. Not thet they do very often," he added in a peculiar melancholy tone of voice.

"Is that why you live alone here in the wilderness?" Olivia asked. For some reason she felt a strange kinship with Micajah Johnstone, as if they had both been betrayed by life.

He looked at her with surprise. "Yore real keen fer bein' so young. Yep, reckon I come here ta find peace. Nature is harsh but hit's fair. Rules make sense. With people . . ." His voice faded as he stared at the fire.

"Do you have a family?" She knew he must have, to react so strongly when she told him about Uncle Charles rejecting *Maman*.

"I did once't. Back in th' Carolina mountains. My woman, Mariah, she wuz a good'un. We had us a small farm. I did some smithin' when crops wuz bad. We had one daughter, no sons. She pined real bad on thet, until Waylon come ta live with us. Her sister's boy. His ma died when he was a tadpole. Pa was a no 'count who run off 'n left him. We raised him like our own. He wuz sorta sickly when he was leetle. Mebbee thet's why he got so wild later on, drinkin' 'n raisin' hell with th' gals in town until he got hisself in a passel o' trouble. Plumb broke my Mariah's heart when he got hisself kilt fer stealin' a horse."

"What happened to your daughter?" she asked hesitantly.

Micajah sighed. "She always wanted ta get clear o' th' hills. Hated bein' pore. She up 'n run off with a planter from Virginney when she was fifteen. Her ma had th' preacher write her ta see how she was doin'. She sent back one letter, sayin' her new husband didn't want no truck with hill folk. Never heerd a word from her after thet even though Mariah kept sendin' letters, but hit didn't do no good. Mariah took sick and died. After she wuz gone I decided ta move across th' Cumberland." He grinned at Olivia, letting the harshness of the past fade. "Hell, alls I had ta do ta leave Carolina wuz pack up my horse, call th' dawg, spit on th' fire 'n' lite out."

Olivia had believed that her life had been one of great adversity in recent years, but she felt humbled in the face of Micajah Johnstone's suffering and his courage. "You traveled all the way from Carolina, crossed the Appalachians, then through Kentucky before you even reached the Mississippi?"

"Aw, shucks, I been a lot farther west n' this. Took a leetle trip with a feller named Coulter a couply years back. Went up in th' biggest danged mountains anywheres. They's so tall they like ta scraped th' clouds clean outta th' sky. Seen a salt ocean and water 'n mud boilin' up outta th' ground like they wuz shot from a cannon. Place smelled like Ole Scratch hisself wuz livin there. Thet's when I decided ta hightail hit back ta th' Missouri country."

Olivia had heard secondhand the incredible descriptions of Coulter's Hell, the boiling mud pits and geysers he claimed to have seen out west. Few in St. Louis believed him but watching Micajah's eyes, the girl knew that he spoke the truth even though the route of Lewis and Clark did not encounter such natural wonders. "You've sure been a lot of places. Isn't that what they call 'seeing the elephant'?"

Micajah's sides heaved with laughter. "Missy, I not only *seen* the elephant, I done shot him, skinned him 'n et him."

She felt a burble of laughter building up inside her. "Oh, and what did he taste like?"

He paused for a moment and considered, scratching his great woolly head and studying her with merry brown eyes. Finally he replied, "Wrinkled."

They both laughed.

"Seems ta me yew seen yore share o' th' world, too—all them fancy Uropeen places. Paris 'n suchlike. I cain't even think whut hit must be like ta cross a salt ocean."

"For a long while I wanted to go back, but that was before my parents died."

"'N now?" he prompted.

Oliver shook her head. "No, there's nothing there for me anymore. I'm an American now, just like you. Are you a trapper?" she asked, looking at the big deer hanging from the tree.

"Naw, I only kill fer meat. Them fancy gents across th'

ocean don't need beaver hats so all fired bad that men here should take ever' pelt betwixt th' Mississip 'n th' western ocean. Killin' a critter jest fer hits hide is purely a waste, ta my way o' thinkin'."

"If you don't trap and you don't farm, then how do you make a living in this wilderness?" She was frankly intrigued with his philosophy.

He chuckled good-naturedly. "Oh, I do a leetle o' this 'n a leetle o' thet. Got me a comfortable cabin farther up th' Gasconade. I farm some corn 'n a few greens fer th' pot. Got fruit 'n nuts growin' on trees, fish in th' river 'n all the deer, bar, buff'lo 'n other game I need fer meat 'n hides. Tracked this here critter fer miles." He gestured to the buck.

She dimpled, her eyes alight with mischief as she said, "But you don't believe in killing bears."

"Never kill any female whut's breedin' 'er got young'uns. Thet's purely wrong unless hit's in self-defense. I done kilt bar when they wuz no way round hit. Good sweet meat 'n warm bed robes."

"I'm glad this time the bear got to keep her hide and I got to keep mine," she said with a laugh.

He looked at her empty bowl. "Yew still hungry? I got more."

"No, thank you, Monsieur Johnstone, but it was delicious."

"Even if'n hit wuz skunk?"

"Even if it was skunk," she averred.

"I'd be obliged if'n yew'd call me by my Christian name, Miz St. E'tane. Onliest one whut ever called me mister wuz ole Judge Braddock when he fined me ten dollars for runnin' a still back in Claxton County."

"Please call me Olivia. Do you have a still at your cabin on the Gasconade? I've heard mountain men make some fiercely powerful whiskey."

"Naw, mine's flatland whiskey, jist strong 'nough to make a man right frisky, yessir. Smooth as a lady's silk stockin', too, but I don't make much 'n I never trade hit to th' Injuns. Plumb ruins 'em." He scratched his head. "Course, hit plumb ruins lots of white men, too."

"That's why you only make what you can drink yourself," she said.

"Yep, 'n a wee bit more, jist in case I git visitors. A feller's got ta be hospitable, doncha know?"

"Well, you've certainly been hospitable to me even without the whiskey."

He hesitated a moment, then looked her in the eyes and asked, "Whut yew figger ta do now thet yew got yoreself so far from home?"

A strange faraway look came into her eyes. "Home," she said softly. "I'm not sure I ever really had one. My parents were aristocratic gypsies, if you can imagine that. I've spent my life traveling from country to country. The longest time I've ever spent in one place was the past three years with Emory Wescott." She shuddered. "I certainly have no wish to go back there."

"I cud take yew back ta St. Louie, but if'n I did, how'd yew figger ta get ta New Orleens?"

She brightened. "I have a letter of credit from—well, never mind, I just have the credit and I can exchange it for passage on a steamer downriver." Suddenly a thought struck her. "Oh, it's in my bedroll. I left it at the river when the bear chased me. Everything I have in the world is in that pack."

"Don't go a gettin' all het up. We kin go back 'n fetch yore fixins soon's thet mama bar takes her youngun's off. Let me finish cleanin' out thet deer. The way should be clear by then."

He stood up and walked over to the carcass, then began removing the sticks inside the body cavity.

Olivia swallowed the bile rising in her throat and watched. At least the entrails had already been disposed of and she was far enough away not to smell the meat. She was surprised to find that she was curious in spite of the gristly nature of the task. Somehow when Micajah explained his philosophy about killing game only to provide for his basic needs, it made the gory task less repulsive. She had watched rivermen shoot wildlife from a moving flatboat just for target practice, or for the pure fun of killing, and it had sickened her.

Thoughts of how he had reacted to the deer Samuel had brought in for the squaws to clean came to mind. She squelched them and asked Micajah, "Why do you have those sticks holding the body open like that?"

"Got ta let hit git th' air so's hit starts ta cure and don't go bad." As he explained the various nuances of the butchering, he worked with a long, wickedly gleaming blade, carefully scraping out and cleaning the body cavity of the deer, tossing the offal into the grass some distance from the camp—for the possums and raccoons to scavenge, he explained.

As soon as he had completed his task, he washed his hands down at the edge of the river and then they retraced their path back to the place where Olivia had forded. When they reached the boulders, she shrieked in horror and dashed over to where the remains of her pack lay scattered across the ground. The blanket was in pieces, her clothes had been tossed hither and yon as if by a tornado. The worst of the damage was to the leather pouch in which the sacks of pemmican were stored, along with her few personal belongings. A tiny miniature of her parents lay unharmed in the dirt. She seized it with a sob, clutching it as she searched through the debris for the letter of credit. All that remained were a few badly shredded pieces of paper. She picked them up and tried to put them back together, but they had been water stained until the ink ran and several sections were missing.

Olivia knelt on the hard rocky ground, staring at her only means of passage out of the wilderness. Destroyed, utterly useless.

Micajah looked around, shaking his head. "Thet bear was lookin' fer th' pemmican sacks. See where she tore inta 'em? I'm afeerd she pretty much tore up ever'thin' else jist lookin' fer vittles."

"I'm trapped. Without that letter of credit, there's no way for me to buy passage to New Orleans." She blinked back tears. "I have nowhere to go."

Micajah Johnstone hesitated awkwardly for several minutes as he watched the silvery droplets coarse silently down her cheeks. Shifting from one foot to the other, he cleared his throat and said, "Yew got grit, gal. I cud tell thet when yew faced up ta th' bar. I expect yew cud make a pretty considerable o' a woodsman . . . if'n yew wuz a mind ta. If'n yew want ta, yore plumb welcome ta come with me." He raised his hands quickly as she looked up. "I don't mean as my squaw 'er nothing like thet neither. When my Mariah up 'n died thet part o' my life wuz done. Our daughter, Jo-Beth, looked a leetle like yew, only her hair wuz darker red like her ma's. Sometimes I miss her . . ." His voice trailed off as he watched Olivia and waited for her to reply.

She smiled slowly and stood, looking up into the big

man's face. "So you expect I could be a woodsman—as good as Mr. Daniel Boone?" *I'll show you, Samuel Shelby, see if I don't!*

Micajah grinned. "Hell, yes, gal, as good as ole Dan'l hisself. Course now, tho' I dislike ta brag, he warn't ne'er as good as me."

Olivia threw back her head and laughed.

Chapter 12

"**W**hite Hair says he has touched the feather. He will not betray the Americans," Man Whipper said in disgust, wiping rivulets of sweat from his hairless brow with the back of his forearm. The autumn sun beat down blisteringly hot on the open grassland, causing the air to shimmer before their faces as they sat in a circle.

Stuart Pardee studied the young Osage warrior patiently. He had been searching for months for the small group of young renegades led by Man Whipper. His earlier attempts to bring his whiskey to the big villages on the Osage River had failed. That damnable presidential agent Shelby had beaten him to the council and convinced them to remain loyal to their treaty with the Americans. The Englishman had narrowly missed killing the bloody bastard and fully planned to finish the job as soon as circumstances permitted.

The summer had not been a total waste though. He had experienced far more success in his dealings with the Osages' ancient enemies the Sauks and Foxes to the east. After securing their allegiance for the British, he had moved north and received assurances from the Sioux and the Rees that they would also support the father king, although they were too distant geographically to matter much. Now his most difficult task faced him, getting the most powerful of the Missouri River nations to fall in line.

His pale gray eyes penetrated the youth's arrogant armor of self-assurance like two sharpened war lances. "And are you afraid of this old man White Hair?"

Bad Temper, apparently second-in-command of the band, bristled and clutched the hatchet at his waist but Man Whipper only tossed his long scalplock over his shoulder and laughed disdainfully. "The Englishman must be a fool. He knows nothing of the council of the Little Old Men. White Hair is too strong with them to challenge openly—unless the English score a great victory in the east." He turned to Pardee, raising the naked skin of his shaven eyebrows. "Have you such victory?"

"Soon there will be. Already the word spreads from the north to the south, far away as the place where the Father of Waters empties itself out into the great ocean," Pardee said, gesturing dramatically. "Your brothers of the great Shawnee Nation move among all the tribes that live along the great river and far to the east of it. The Muskogee and the Seminoles, the Cherokee and the Choctaw, all listen to our father king's friend Tecumseh. The chief of the Shawnee speaks of a vast confederacy stretching from the Great Lakes of the north to the ocean of the south. If all these tribes follow Tecumseh into war against the Americans, will the Osage be the only ones to sit beside their fires like women?"

"Your tongue is brave here, but would you speak thus in front of our council of elders?" Bad Temper dared.

Pardee narrowed his eyes. "Try me."

Man Whipper considered as he took a desultory puff from the long clay pipe the three had been smoking, the tobacco a gift from the Englishman. He wanted to gain ascendancy in the tribal leadership by becoming war chief, but the position was nominally hereditary and appointed by the tribal council called the Little Old Men. Although not born into the line of chiefs, he might persuade the council to give him the position if he could impress them—and defeat Pawhuska, old White Hair, his bitter enemy. Perhaps the canny Englishman was just the ally he needed.

"When all the scattered bands return to the great village on the river to harvest their crops and prepare for winter, I will get you a hearing before the council, if you will speak loudly and offer enough presents to convince them of your father king's generosity."

"Only give my father king the opportunity, Man Whipper. He can be most generous," Pardee replied, "most generous indeed."

With that he produced a bottle of whiskey and handed it to Bad Temper, who uncorked it and took a deep swallow. *Yes, only give my father king—and me—the chance . . .*

The autumn sun beat down on Olivia's back as she dug potatoes from their small garden. It had been an unseasonably warm fall and the winter promised to be mild, which was good for the harvest and the hunt. She had already pulled carrots and selected several choice ears of young corn for the pot. Now all their evening meal lacked would be a fistful of wild onion that she would gather down in the woods. Smiling as a light breeze cooled the sweat trickling down her temple, she sat back on her heels and looked around the small beautiful valley that had become her home over the past months.

Micajah's cabin was situated near the banks of the Gasconade, a twisting crystal clear river that snaked through beautiful rolling woodlands and into the foothills of a small mountain range to the south. The dwelling was made of cedar logs snugly chinked with mud and straw to keep the winter winds at bay. A simple one-story square of small dimensions, it had a flat roof made of poles interwoven with tough field grasses and covered with more of the claylike mud mixture that filled the walls, forming a waterproof barrier to summer rain and winter snow. Two windows and a door were the only openings to admit light, but the door stood wide-open and the greased parchment window coverings were neatly rolled up during warm weather.

Two crude flower boxes were attached to the sills, filled with a bright profusion of black-eyed Susan, butterfly weed and bergamot. Olivia could still remember her amazement when she saw the fierce looking mountain man pointing with such pride to the flower garden he had planted alongside rows of corn, beans, potatoes and other vegetables. He also grew herbs for cooking: thyme, parsley, sage and rosemary. Micajah was a man of many parts, who continually amazed her with the apparent contradiction between his fierce outer appearance and his gentle inner being.

"Only a fool 'ed live on biled meat without no greens. I seen dozens o' men die o' th' grippe from eatin' nothin' but meat. A man needs pone 'n honey, too. Thet's why I grow corn an' keep a eye out fer a good bee tree whenever th' honey supply gets low."

"What about the spices and the flowers?" she had teased.

"Herbs make cookin' taste better. My Mariah, she always grew 'em. She loved flowers, too. Said they wuz a aid ta digestion. I carried th' seeds with me all th' ways from Carolina. I like th' smell o' flowers around th' windeys when I look out," he had added unabashed.

He was a dear man, patient and sensitive, with a lusty sense of humor. And he played a fierce fiddle to boot. Humming one of his Carolina mountain tunes, she carried her vegetables down to the water's edge, stopping along the trail to pluck a few wild onions. He had taught her how to ferret out the bounty of nature, wild fruits, nuts and berries, as well as roots and tubers that were tasty in the stew pot, and what poisonous plants to avoid, such as the pretty grapelike berries of the nightshade vine.

Her first attempts to cook in the big granite fireplace in the cabin had been near disasters, but after suffering cuts and blisters and eating hard dry corn pone and rubbery venison, she was learning to simmer a tender roast in the Dutch oven and bake up light, crisp corn pone in a heavy iron skillet. She could even dry venison and buffalo jerky and pound it together with suet and berries to make tasty pemmican far superior to the greasy gray stuff Walks Fast had prepared.

The city girl was learning all the skills necessary to survive in the wilderness. She could skin out a buffalo, scrape the hide clean with an iron adz, then rub brains and ashes into the skin to cure and soften it. The first time she followed Micajah's guidance and dug her hands into the squishy gray mass, working it into the buffalo hide, she remembered the queasy spoiled girl who had vomited when Samuel had ordered her to help the squaws clean a deer. She had vowed never again to let the sight or smell of blood affect her so.

Micajah took her hunting small game, teaching her how to patiently set a snare. She had mastered dressing plump wild rabbits for the pot as well as squirrels and turkeys, although her marksmanship was only now getting good enough for her to bring down wild game with a clean shot. She had learned to track prey through the woods and each day her aim grew better as she continued to practice on targets that Micajah devised. They killed only what they needed to eat, although Micajah had explained they would salt down an extra supply of big game to see them through the winter months. She was eager to go on the hunt, which they would undertake within the week.

Olivia washed the vegetables at the edge of the stream, then headed back to the cabin. A few yards from the front door a cooking pot hung on an iron spit suspended across a low bank of coals which glowed brightly in the afternoon sun. In warm weather they cooked outdoors to keep the cabin cooler for sleeping. She knelt at the side of the fire and removed the lid of the ancient iron pot. The rich succulent aroma of venison and rosemary wafted up. She stirred the thick stew, then quickly pared the clean vegetables and added them to it. While it simmered over the next several hours, she worked on cutting a carefully cured deer hide to make herself a warm winter coat.

"For a woman who never even learned to thread a needle while she was growing up, I'm not doing too badly," she murmured to herself as she patiently plied the big steel needle through the tough leather the way Micajah had instructed her.

Around noontime she heard the sound of voices echoing down the valley and stood up with an anticipatory smile of welcome on her face.

"Umm, mm, somethin' smells powerful good, Lil' Sparky," Micajah called out from across the clearing. He had given her the affectionate nickname not only because of her fiery hair but also because of her sometimes equally fiery temperament. He emerged from a dense stand of cottonwoods that grew up the side of the hill. A huge dirty white hound with a badly chewed right ear bounded past Micajah and raced to greet her, tail wagging as he let out a long, high-pitched howl.

"Dirt Devil, you old rascal you," she said, reaching out to envelop him in a fierce hug as he nearly knocked her sprawling onto the ground. His liquid brown eyes filled with adoration and a big grayish tongue snaked out and slurped her with kisses.

Laughing heartily, she wrestled affectionately with the big dog, remembering how frightened of him she had been the first time she set eyes on his gristled mangy old hide as he stood bristling, guarding the cabin door. It had not taken her more than an hour to win him from baring his yellow fangs to rolling on his back for scratches. Micajah had pronounced it nothing less than a full-blown miracle since the old hound had been abused as a pup, before he rescued him from a couple of drunken trappers. Dirt Devil had hated every other human he had ever come into contact with—until Olivia. Quickly they had become boon companions. She fed the hound choice tidbits and lay in front of the fire in the evenings scratching his belly and singing to him as Micajah played the fiddle.

"I brung us company," Micajah said, as he neared the roughhousing pair. A tall, lithe Osage man walked beside him.

"Iron Kite, welcome," Olivia said, rising and bowing respectfully to the fierce looking warrior. As was the custom of his people, he plucked all his facial hair and shaved his head except for the long scalp lock at the crown, which hung down his back adorned with feathers and shells. His lean, muscular body was a dark copper-bronze color, naked except for a breechclout, and covered with elaborate blue tattoos depicting his exploits in battle. His ears were pierced and the lobes greatly elongated by the weight of bone and glass bead earrings. Several heavy beaded necklaces hugged his throat. Iron Kite carried himself in barbaric splendor.

Once she would have gone faint at the sight of such an awesome savage, but since coming to live with Micajah Johnstone, she had learned to deal with many of the local tribes, especially the dominant Osage. Micajah was friendly with all the Indians and traded fine steel hatchets, knives and other survival tools made by the whites in exchange for whatever took his fancy, or what he could trade to the white rivermen: fine buckskin vests worked with porcupine quills, beaded moccasins, clay pottery and watertight rush baskets.

Iron Kite returned her greeting gravely, nodding to the "boy-daughter" of the Great Bear, as Johnstone was known among his people. She was dressed in buckskin leggings and a short cotton tunic similar to those her adopted father wore, and she hunted and lived as a Long Knife in the wilderness. He did not understand such a way for a female, but he had learned to accept her because of his respect for Great Bear. They conversed in a polyglot of English, Spanish and Osage.

"It is good to see you again. Are you prepared for the fall hunt with all your butchering tools sharpened?" Iron Kite asked with the hint of a smile dancing in his eyes. He knew the "boy-daughter" was going to hunt with Great Bear, not sit with the squaws until the killing was done.

Olivia smiled, calmly ladling up two big bowls of stew and handing one to their guest.

"Great Bear and I bring our sharp tools . . . and our sharp eyes to hunt the buffalo," she replied.

Micajah slapped his thigh and guffawed. "I done tole yew my Lil' Sparky's got grit. Yew shouldda seen her th' first time I put a carbine in her hands 'n tole her she wuz gonna learn ta shoot." Micajah took his bowl of stew and squatted down in the shade of the big cottonwood beside the house next to Iron Kite to continue his story. Contrary to Osage custom, Olivia served herself at once and went to eat with the men.

As Micajah was warming up to the story about her first encounter with a rifle last spring, she could still remember it as if it were yesterday. She relived it as he described it to their guest.

Micajah had insisted that she carry the unloaded rifle every time she left the cabin. "Git yew used ta th' heft o' hit," he had said. She had practiced lining up the sights and squeezing the trigger. For days he drilled her, until she had "killed" scores of rocks, saplings, soaring hawks and scampering squirrels. At last he pronounced her ready to actually load and fire the .69 caliber dragoon flintlock carbine.

Under the big man's careful scrutiny, she began just as he had taught her to do. She finished priming the pan and then stood ready. Micajah nodded his approval. "Touch slow, but yew'll pick up speed with practice. Now, thet's yore mark." He pointed at an oak about seventy-five yards away where he had shaved off a knot on the trunk, forming a white blaze a little larger than one of his hamlike fists.

Olivia started to cock the hammer. "Hold thar, Sparky. Lookee. Whenever yew git th' chance, use a rest. Jist lean yore left shoulder agin' thet dogwood yore standin' next ta. Hit'll help steady the barrel. Thet's fine. Now let 'er rip."

As she had practiced a hundred times, Olivia cocked the rifle, brought it to her shoulder, took a breath, and exhaled partially, lining up the sights on the blaze. The trick was, her mentor had taught her, to do everything in one smooth motion. As soon as the sights "found" the target, squeeze, not pull, the trigger. The rifle cracked loudly, belching forth a cloud of smoke. Prepared for neither the deafening report nor the choking smoke—not to mention the kick of the rifle butt against her shoulder—Olivia dropped the weapon.

Her shocked glance flew to Micajah, who was staring at the distant oak while scratching his chin hidden beneath the dense undergrowth of whiskers. "Well now, yew missed yore mark. Hit the tree, though, seen the bark fly." He turned his attention to the rifle at Olivia's feet. "Cain't be throwin' down yore piece after ever' shot, Sparky. Makes reloadin' powerful slow." He walked closer, towing the flint that had been dislodged from the flash pan. "Kindey hard on th' piece, too."

Olivia pretended to be looking down at the weapon as she

chewed her lip, blinking back tears of humiliation. "All right, Sparky," the big man said patiently, "put thet carbine back together and load 'er up agin. I'll see whar yore ball hit."

As he walked slowly toward the target, Olivia refixed the flash pan flint and prepared the rifle for another shot. She was ready when Micajah returned. His fingers were once again buried in his whiskers, searching for his skin, and he was smiling. "Reckon my eyes ain't so good's they used ta' be. Did a mite better'n jist hit th' tree, Sparky. Yore ball's only a whisker below th' mark, but dead center. I knowed fellers couldn't do thet good after a lifetime. Yew jist might shine at this bidness." Olivia flushed with sheer joy. "All right, now, try 'er agin."

She raised the rifle smoothly and confidently aimed. This time she missed the entire tree! She looked in astonishment at Micajah, who threw back his head with a roar of laughter. After a moment, Olivia could not help but join in.

"Okay, gal, load 'er up agin n' try ta remember yew ain't Miz Dan'l Boone yet. Don't be gittin' too cocky."

Then Micajah's voice brought her back to the present as he said, "Iron Kite here tells me he seen a pretty smart scatter 'o buff'lo where th' Osage runs inta th' Big Muddy."

"That close! I expected we'd have to travel all the way to the plains where the Kaws hunt," she replied, excited at the prospect of seeing and participating in her first buffalo hunt.

"The last hunt of the year will begin as soon as the crops are gathered. In one moon," Iron Kite gestured holding up his index finger dramatically, "we will rendezvous at the place of the two rivers. Then the Osage men shall perhaps take a lesson in hunting from the Great Bear's boy-daughter, Ember Woman."

"You do me great honor to allow me to ride with such mighty hunters as the Osage. I will do my utmost to prove worthy," she replied gravely.

Olivia knew the warrior had offered a fine bride price for her, which Micajah had very politely turned down, explaining that she already had a husband, a Long Knife who had entrusted her to the Great Bear's care while he was away soldiering for the Americans. Although the idea struck painfully close to her memories of Samuel, Olivia agreed that it was the best solution to a ticklish situation for as long as she remained with him in the wilderness.

After the hunt they would return to prepare for winter by salting down meat, making more pemmican and drying the vegetables and fruits they had harvested. Although the snowy season in the Missouri woodlands was not unduly harsh compared to the fierce icy blasts on the upper reaches of the great rivers, it was still best to respect Mother Nature by preparing in case snows were deep, game scarce or in the worst case, if one of them became ill or injured.

Once spring arrived, Micajah would make his annual journey to St. Louis for the few simple necessities he bartered for with the city merchants. Olivia pondered what she would do when they returned to what used to be her home. Now and again, Micajah broached the subject of Samuel, speculating about whether he might be stationed at Fort Bellafontaine.

The canny old mountain man knew she still had feelings for the unprincipled rogue. Perhaps he even considered dragging the colonel at gunpoint to wed her. The very idea made Olivia shudder. Always she remained cool and noncommittal about Shelby since that first foolish unburdening she had made to Micajah when he had rescued her from the bear last spring. How she wished she could call back her teary confession about thinking the young colonel was the man of her dreams! Such dreams were the stuff of which ashes were made, she thought ruefully, pushing all her fears about the future from her mind. Right now she would enjoy her new life, exhilarated by a newfound sense of self-sufficiency and freedom, the likes of which she had never imagined when confined by city streets.

Come spring she would decide what direction her life would take. The one course she knew it would not follow was that which went anywhere near Colonel Samuel Sheridan Shelby.

Samuel's summer and fall had proven not nearly so productive or enjoyable as had Olivia's. After leaving Lisa's party, he had spent weeks trekking from one small Osage camp to the next, smoking the ceremonial pipe with the elders and explaining about the coming war between the Americans and the English from across the ocean.

He had beaten the English agent to White Hair's band, but at many other encampments it seemed the Englishman, stirring up discontent with his weapons and his whiskey, was always one step ahead of him. Samuel was very careful to make clear that the Englishman's king lived far across the ocean and had no permanent interest in the Osage, nor could he protect them from their enemies, while the American president would continue to be a presence along the Missouri. It was with the American government that the Osage must treat and it was the Americans who would win the war which would be fought on their own soil. Therefore it would be in the best interest of the Osage Nation to continue their treaty commitments with President Madison, the white father in Washington.

Shelby hoped his speeches had made a favorable impression, but reading the impassive faces of Indians had never been a particular skill of his, in spite of spending several summers among the Lipan Apaches with Liza and Santiago. Often he wished that he possessed his brother-in-law's background so that he could deal more effectively with the Indians, but then he conceded ruefully, if he had been raised among them and lived as one with them, he would not be Jemmy Madison's emissary.

By the end of summer, the trail of the illusive English agent had taken him all the way across the Mississippi into Indiana Territory where he found the Sauk, Fox and Shawnee already firmly allied with the British. After a brief conference with William Henry Harrison, the territorial governor and military leader of the region, a harsh young martinet whom he instinctively disliked, Shelby realized that open and bloody warfare between American settlers and those tribes was already a foregone and unavoidable calamity, welcomed by both sides.

He had finally returned to Louisiana Territory the past month. If he could redeem nothing else, he must at least speak before the Osage grand tribal council. Someone there would be able to lead him to the Englishman. If he could keep the land west of the Mississippi at peace, he would have to trust that Governor Harrison could deal with Indiana Territory, although he entertained strong doubts about the latter. The arrogant Harrison had a well-organized militia prepared to fight, but they would pay a price. Samuel knew the cost of defeating the pro-British forces led by Tecumseh would be dear indeed.

"Santiago was right," he muttered to himself as he sat beside his morning campfire waiting for the coffee to boil.

"Our government has bungled the situation with the Shawnee Confederacy." American settlers had been allowed to usurp tribal land, then rely on the government to come in and enforce treaties, continually pushing the Red Man farther and farther to the west. "Now that we've taken claim to the whole upper Missouri all the way to the Pacific, what will be left for any of the Indians?" he wondered aloud, sipping the bitter rich coffee he had poured.

He swirled the black liquid around in the big tin cup and smiled, recalling the horrific muddy mess with which Olivia had almost choked him. Where was the little fire-haired hoyden by now? Certainly back in civilization. He wondered if there was any chance he might find her waiting for him in the house on Plum Street. Just thinking of her lying with all that flaming hair spread on the white sheets of his big bed made his pulse leap and his body grow hard.

If only he had been able to return within the few months he had projected for the mission. But circumstances had dictated otherwise and he had no way to find out if the beautiful mademoiselle was sleeping in his bed while he was out chasing about the wilderness. In all likelihood she had not spent any time in his house, he was forced to admit. She probably took the letter of credit and bought herself passage on the first steamer headed to New Orleans and that supposed uncle, who was more likely an old lover.

Somehow the thought of her exotic young beauty being enjoyed by a decadent older Creole gentleman made his guts clench. "Best I forget the damned vixen. I'll never see her again." He stook up and tossed the remaining coffee into the fire, knowing in his heart of hearts that he still hoped to find her waiting for him when he returned to St. Louis. *Fool.*

When the big piebald he had bought in Pawhuska's village whickered, Samuel looked around, his hand immediately going to the Martial Pistol in his sash. Although well out of hostile country, there were always small bands of renegade Osage not adverse to disobeying the elders' orders, eager to lift a white scalp. With a silent oath, he kicked out the remainder of the small campfire, the first such luxury he had allowed himself in several days. Someone was in the dense stand of hickory trees upwind from his horse. And, ominously, they were not showing themselves.

He picked up the rifle that had been leaning against the log on which he had been sitting, and cautiously walked toward the horse, which had its hackamore on. He could swing up on its back and ride hell-bent, if need dictated. Still no overt sign of movement. Suddenly a lone Osage warrior showed himself across the clearing, approaching unarmed. In spite of the Indian's friendly demeanor, a prickle of warning shivered up Shelby's spine. He recognized him as Man Whipper, a young troublemaker from the big Osage village. His worst fear was being captured by Osage renegades who would ignore Pawhuska's wishes. Slowly, Samuel shifted his grip on his rifle, holding it loosely in the crook of his arm, waiting to see what his visitor wanted.

Then without warning a blinding blaze of light seared his eyeballs as something struck the back of his head with sledgehammer impact. He stumbled to his knees and pitched forward. Everything faded to black.

Man Whipper grinned broadly as Bad Temper and a dozen of his followers filed into the clearing and peered down at the fallen Long Knife. A small pool of blood was forming at the crown of the soldier's head where the war club had found its mark. Hurled from a distance, it had not cleft his skull in two as it would have if wielded directly, but the blow was sufficient to render their foe unconscious.

They stood over him while Man Whipper used the toe of his moccasin to kick Shelby in the ribs, turning him onto his back. "This is the one Pardee told us of, the one who hunts him."

"Let us take the Long Knife's scalp to the Englishman. He will be pleased," one of the others said.

"No!" Bad Temper replied. "His hair is black, not bright. It will make only an ordinary trophy. Better that we have some sport before he dies. Wake him," he commanded.

When Man Whipper nodded, two of the braves hauled Shelby up by his arms and a third poured the remains of his waterskin over the unconscious man's head.

Samuel awakened with a severe headache pounding from the nape of his neck, wrapping all the way around to his eyeballs. The brackish taste of stale water combined with the subtly sweet substance of blood trickling into his mouth. He shook his head, then instantly regretted the rash act as a thousand war drums reverberated inside.

His arms felt as if they were being pulled from their sockets. He knew he was being restrained. Then gradually he recalled the scene with the lone Osage, and he knew it had been a trap. They had hit him from behind and disarmed him, then awakened him. But at least he was not dead yet.

Slowly he raised his head and shook free of the two men holding him up, then stood his ground and sized them up. If only his vision would clear so he could count straight. Even if he was not seeing double, there were still too damn many Indians!

"I am Shelby, emissary from the great white father in Washington," he began in Spanish, the commonest European language spoken among the Osage. "I travel under safe conduct from White Hair, peace chief of the Little Ones. I have seen you in the village of the great chief. You know I speak truly."

Bad Temper scoffed. "You are our prisoner. White Hair is not here."

"You are still honor bound to free me because of his word," Samuel replied, stalling for time, wondering what their game was.

"Our honor is our own," Man Whipper replied arrogantly. "Something white men do not share. Your fate lies in my hands, not that of any other man."

"I think it does lie with another man . . . another white man. The one known as the Englishman. He has sent you after me, hasn't he? Is he then too much a coward to fight his own battle with me, face-to-face? Then all might see who is strongest—his king or my president."

"We care for no king or president—for no white chief of any sort. We are Osage and this is our land," Bad Temper said belligerently.

"So, the Long Knife would fight," Man Whipper interjected, stepping between the soldier and the other warrior. Although Shelby was over six feet, Man Whipper had a good two inches on him and took full advantage of the fact, puffing up his chest and posturing as he continued, "We will give you a chance to save your life . . . if you are bold enough to take it."

"What chance?" Shelby asked with careless bravado, knowing that to show fear or reluctance would more quickly seal his fate.

"How fast can you run, Long Knife?" Bad Temper asked, smiling nastily.

Within minutes they had stripped him of his shirt and boots, leaving him barefoot and completely unarmed, clad only in his buckskin breeches. Two rows of Indians lined up five feet apart, each man brandishing a stick, spear or club with great relish. He would have to run the gauntlet between a dozen armed men. If he survived it, then what?

As if intuiting his question, Man Whipper said, "Pass through this ordeal and we will see how strong your medicine is. We will see how fleet your feet are. After the first trial you must outrun us . . . . if you have the heart to do either."

Shelby looked from his own bare feet to the Osage's thick moccasins with scathing contempt. "My heart is strong enough. It is you who lack, else you'd not have taken my boots." It was a gamble. The savage might simply shoot him out of hand. Or, perhaps not. Man Whipper was young and full of himself. Perhaps he might be bothered to hear the unfairness of the contest so boldly pointed out.

The inscrutable expression on his face revealed nothing for a moment. Then he nodded. "Pass through the rain of blows still standing and we will give you from here to the great oak." He gestured across the open meadow of thistles and snakeroot to the tree, a distance of roughly three hundred yards.

Not much of an advantage, especially if he received any more blows to his head but it was all the edge Samuel was going to get. He knew he had best try and make the most of it. He nodded to Man Whipper, then said, "You have that amulet for medicine," pointing to a small beaded pouch fastened around the Osage's neck. Spending the past months among their villages had been an education that might save his life.

Man Whipper touched his talisman. "Yes. White men do not believe in medicine," he replied scornfully.

"The Long Knives who fight for the great white father in Washington do. Our medicine is in our uniform." He pointed to his heavy dress tunic, lying on the ground where it had been pulled from his pack by several of the marauding Osages who had examined his shaving equipment and other personal belongings with great interest. Shelby's eyes dared Man Whipper insolently. "You wear your medicine. Are you afraid to let me wear mine?"

A nasty feral smile spread across the Osage's face. "Take it. We will see how powerful the medicine of the white father is," he said with contempt.

Samuel picked up the heavy jacket with its braided epaulets and medals. He had brought the damned gaudy thing only to wear on ceremonial occasions in front of chiefs and their councils. Perhaps at last he would find a practical use for it. He walked to the head of the dual line of waiting warriors and stood with his feet braced apart, then nodded to Man Whipper. If he survived the gauntlet, he knew this tallest and longest legged of the warriors would be the man to beat in a footrace. Shelby did not don the jacket, only held it loosely on one arm.

The tall Osage raised his hand above his head, then dropped his arm in a signal. Samuel took off down the line wrapping the jacket partially around his right arm to use as a shield. He zigzagged around the worst of the blows and slashes, many of which glanced off the stiff braid and double worsted wool. Several of the Indians aimed low trying to trip him or injure his knees or ankles. He used the loose arms of the tunic snapping them in front of him to absorb the blows and entangle the arms of the men who were bent over low, easily throwing them off balance.

He felt a dull ache from a club striking the back of his right shoulder, then a series of other splintering pains to his head and upper body as he weaved and dodged, flinging the loose coat sleeves before him. He set his mind to ignore everything else and concentrate only on freedom at the end of the line. When he had almost gotten through it, a white-hot sheering agony suddenly sucked the air from his lungs as a skinning knife slashed deeply across his left side. Samuel flung his tunic away, hitting the warrior on the opposite side full in the face. He clenched his jaw and sucked in a big breath of air, willing the red haze before his eyes to abate while he lunged past the last man.

So far he was still on his feet, but for how long? Not allowing himself time to consider his throbbing injuries, he walked across the clearing and up the hill into the field beyond. Spiky thistles bit into the soles of his feet and the sharp edges of dry prairie grass slashed his ankles and the tops of his feet with myriad tiny cuts.

Shelby willed himself to feel nothing. He knew the lean graceful Osage prided themselves on having swift runners. One as tall and powerful as Man Whipper would be fleet as a deer and enduring as a mustang. He must outdistance all the rest before he could turn and face that lone adversary.

Mercifully, the prairie meadow was broken by several stands of timber. If he could disappear from their view, they would have to split up their pursuit. Cunning, as well as endurance, would be needed here.

He concentrated on putting one foot in front of the other until he cleared the oak tree. Then without a backward glance he broke into a swift sprint. A series of loud whoops sounded behind him, signaling that his foes had taken up pursuit. The hunt was on and this time Samuel Shelby was the prey, not the predator.

The long stretch across the hard dry plain was thistle filled and pockmarked by prairie dog holes. He was forced to run flat out, risking not only the continued pain from the sharp thorns but also the chance of slipping into a warren and going down with a broken ankle. Yet he dared not look down. All he could do was expend every ounce of his will in that first great burst of speed.

With his long legs and powerful chest, Samuel had always been a swift runner but never before had he been forced to run for his life. By the time he neared the first wooded section of land, his sides began to stitch and he felt a slow burning sensation in the muscles of his legs. Soon his lungs felt as if they were afire. Every breath became an exercise in excruciating agony. But still he did not slow down. When he reached the trees he zigzagged through the heavy brush growing between them until he hoped that his pursuers could not be certain in which direction he had turned.

At last he slowed, blinking his blurred eyes in the damp gloom of the woods. Avoiding the dead trees and rotted stumps blocking his path, he cut sharply to the left, remembering that way lay a fork in the Niangua River he had been following before he camped last night. If he could reach it, he might be able to hide his trail and slake the burning thirst that seared his swollen tongue and throat.

Clearing the woods he again fell into a ground-devouring all-out run, hearing the yelling and the crashing in the brush behind him. His pursuers had drawn closer! The ground fell away now, a long gradual slope down to the marshy willow-shrouded reaches of the river. As his momentum caused him to pick up speed he thought his lungs would explode in his chest. Feeling a cool wetness on his burning chest he glanced down and saw that his nose was bleeding so profusely it had stained his whole upper body with sticky red blood. The evil slash inflicted on his side had already soaked his breeches. He felt light-headed, dizzy. Only the beckoning coolness of the river kept him pounding on until he broke into the timber. By now he had lost at least half his pursuers, judging by the noise of pounding feet behind him. He took no time to look back and count.

The sound of the river was sweet music. The cold current ran swift and, in spots, deep enough to conceal a man . . . if he were lucky to find such a spot. Samuel hit the water in a flat, shallow dive. The icy contact numbed the pain throbbing through every inch of his body but the shock of it nearly caused him to black out. He swallowed a few mouthfuls of water and looked around. Soon they would be on him. He could run no farther.

But he could float. A small pine tree had broken loose from the bank in one of the sudden rainstorms common to the plains. As it floated by, he seized hold of it and hung on, struggling to hide himself amidst its boughs so that he would not be visible from the riverbank. The dense spiky green branches served as cover. He submerged his body and held onto one small limb, coming up only to gulp quick painful breaths of air, then slip back beneath the surface.

The current was swift with several rocky rapids, twisting along the wooded valley floor. If only he could hang on until he was carried downstream far enough, past his pursuers, he might reach the fork where the Niangua ran into the Osage River. He heard Man Whipper yelling orders to several of his warriors, then nothing else.

Samuel was not certain how long he was under water or how he had kept his hold on the branch, but gradually the rushing current slowed and blended with another countercurrent. Had he reached the fork? With superhuman effort he raised his head through the pine boughs and looked around. It must be the Osage River. Untangling himself from the sanctuary of the tree was difficult but he worked his way free and began paddling to shore.

He stood in the shallows, bloody and bruised, his vision blurred and his head ringing, trying to focus on which direction he needed to take when a triumphant cry echoed from the bluff overhead. Man Whipper, panting with exhaustion but otherwise unscathed, stood with knife in hand, ready to lunge down the embankment at him.

Bracing himself, Shelby waited, sucking air into his tortured lungs. Every breath cost him dearly as the slashes and bruises covering his body throbbed and pulled each time his chest rose and fell. He stood alone on the bare muddy bank of the river, without a weapon, waiting.

∽ *Chapter 13* ∽

Man Whipper began sliding down the grassy slope of the bank, still winded but grinning. "You are clever . . . for a white man, but I have won this race. Now I will take your scalp to Pardee."

"I don't think so," Shelby said, scooping up a fistful of mud from the shallows and flinging it full into Man Whipper's face before he could duck aside in his headlong down-hill rush.

The Osage cursed and clawed at his eyes with his free hand, still holding the knife out in front of him, slashing in an arc to protect himself until he cleared his vision. Samuel stepped forward on the rocky bank and reached down, picking up two jagged fist-sized stones. Clutching one in each hand he stepped back from Man Whipper and let the first one fly. It caught the Osage in the center of his forehead, flinging him backward onto the bank. He rolled up, dazed, still clutching the knife. But before he could rise, Shelby hurled the second stone hard and fast. It struck square in the center of the big man's chest.

Man Whipper grunted, struggling to draw breath but before he could do so, Shelby was on him, his hand seizing his foe's wrist, smashing it back against a rock until the Osage dropped his knife. They rolled across the ground, both punching and gouging, each trying to come up on top of his foe long enough to finish him. Shelby's wounds were bleeding profusely again but the much smaller injury to Man Whipper's forehead poured blood freely into his eyes, blurring his vision. He lashed out at his foe while groping for the lost knife. Samuel saw it first, just out of reach. If he could only get free long enough to lunge to his right he'd have it, but the Indian's legs were entwined with his as they thrashed.

At last Shelby came up on the top near the knife but Man Whipper's palm skimming the ground to his left seized the weapon first and raised it with a loud cry. The sound died on his lips when Shelby's right hand came smashing down into his throat with a dagger of another sort. A sharp sliver of jagged shale pierced the warrior's windpipe, and Samuel twisted it until it broke apart in his hand. By then a fountain of blood gushed out of the wound, along with a long, slow sigh as Man Whipper's spirit departed his body.

Shelby climbed to his feet and looked down at the dead man who still clutched the knife in a clawlike hand, eyes staring sightlessly at the bright azure of the morning sky. The exhausted soldier bent double, his hands resting on his knees as he sucked in air.

"Yeah . . . you won the race . . . but I won the rock-throwing contest."

He pried the knife from the lifeless fingers and shoved it in his belt, then began stumbling up the embankment.

Dawn glowed on the horizon, pale golden with deep crimson streaks emblazoned into the inky vault of the heavens. Olivia licked her lips nervously and rechecked her gear again. She felt almost naked, stripped down to nothing but a sleeveless buckskin vest and knee-high britches, her concessions to modesty among the Osage hunters who wore only breech-clouts. Everyone had shed the excess weight of clothing as well as stripping their mounts of all saddle gear. The specially trained buffalo ponies carried only small blankets held on their backs by soft, wide rawhide strips. A hackamore was the only means by which they were guided during the mad melee of the hunt.

Soon. It would be no more than a few moments until they rode out. She checked her carbine for what seemed the hundredth time. After nearly six months of intense practice she could load, prime and fire the weapon from the back of a galloping horse as skillfully as most of the men she had observed. Micajah said she was a natural born shot, just as she had always been a natural born rider.

"Jest remember whut I tole yew 'n yew'll do right smart," he murmured to reassure her. "Stay off ta th' side near th' river. Gives yew room to move if'n one o' them bulls decides ta charge out."

"And always aim just behind the shoulder for the lights," she parroted, remembering all the lessons learned over the summer of hunting deer. But nothing compared to the thrill of joining their Osage friends from Pawhuska's village in the largest late hunt for the mighty buffalo. Midwinter was the season for taking large middle-aged bulls, summer the time for young bulls and heifers, but this was when the fat sleek cows provided the best meat. Yesterday they had scouted the large herd on this open stretch along the Missouri River. Everyone was primed for action.

Micajah watched his Lil' Sparky, hiding his misgivings beneath the surge of pride he felt in her. What an extraordinary young woman she had proven herself to be since he rescued her from that bear last spring. He had taught her to shoot and cook and survive in the wilderness, but there was nothing he could teach her about horses. She had the gift of communicating with critters of all sorts, from his antisocial hound, Dirt Devil, to the beautiful little ebony mare he had bought for her from a band of Sioux. Olivia had spent the summer working with the spirited horse until it obeyed her every command, whether by a touch on the hackamore or the slightest knee pressure.

The Sioux had already trained the mare to run buffalo and he had taught his Sparky everything he knew about surviving a hunt. Still, he was frightened for her. But she had her heart set on bringing down her own animal. And, perverse heathen that their Osage friends could be, several of them thought his white "boy-daughter's" participation would bring good medicine for the fall hunt. He vowed to stay close on his big buckskin gelding in case anything unforeseen should happen.

Then Traveling Rain, the hunt leader, gave the silent signal for the riders to split into two parties and head quietly toward the peacefully grazing herd. They were downwind and with luck would get within yards if everyone rode in a slow, even line making no sudden move. As they flanked the milling buffalo herd on two sides and closed in, each participant picked out his target. Olivia selected a small, plump young cow near one end of the herd and drew close, closer . . .

When the wind shifted, one of the bulls caught the scent of the hunters. Everything erupted in chaos as the herd metamorphosed from a peaceful browse to a pell-mell plunge across the flat open plain. The hunters kneed their steeds into a gallop and loud yips and cries of excitement sounded over the dull roaring thunder of stampeding hooves.

Olivia, mindful of Micajah's admonitions, kept away from the thick of the melee where dust rose in billowing clouds, and men wove their horses in wild patterns between the running buffalo. Leaning low on horseback, the hunters sighted in on the spot just behind the shoulder, using their heavy caliber rifles to puncture lungs or if very lucky to score a direct shot to the heart.

Few of the big beasts went down easily and many were blood mad, veering to attack their tormentors with demented fury and sharp, deadly horns. She waited for a clearing in the herd when the fat cow she had chosen came into her sights, then carefully aimed and squeezed the trigger. To her delight the cow simply collapsed, a clean kill.

She reloaded at once, a precaution Micajah had drilled into her. As soon as the task was complete, she scanned the billowing clouds of dust looking for Johnstone's huge figure. Stripped down to his breeches and moccasins, he looked almost as hairy as the bison themselves. Not only his chest and arms, but his shoulders and back as well were covered with a thick fuzzy pelt. She waved her rifle in a triumphant salute as soon as she spotted him.

Micajah had been watching her progress carefully as he rode down his own quarry and took it with a single shot. Damn if his Sparky didn't do it just as well! One half the experienced hunters in the party took two or more shots to accomplish the feat. Just as he returned her wave, Against the Wind, a youth of fifteen summers darted in front of him, intent on finishing off a large bull he had already shot twice. He fired again. The pain crazed animal lunged to gore the nearest thing to him—Johnstone and his horse. Against the Wind was swept along with the surrounding herd. The wounded buffalo grazed Micajah's gelding, then went down directly in the path of galloping horse and rider. Johnstone's mount stumbled.

Micajah vaulted from his horse as it went down, flinging himself onto the back of a big rangy old bull, digging his fists into the shaggy beast's grizzled fur and holding on for dear life. Too busy racing to escape the deafening crash of rifle shot and terrifying bloody carnage around him, the bull ignored his passenger as he broke from the thick of the herd. Micajah heard Sparky's scream and knew she was coming for him. Damn the fool girl!

Olivia kneed her mare forward, frantically working her way through the carnage toward her mentor, praying all the while that he would not be trampled before she could reach him.

Once she sighted him atop the big bison, she seized her

chance. Clearing the herd, she paced the bull, keeping just behind his neck. He neither saw nor smelled her as she drew abreast, waiting for Micajah to jump, her rifle ready to shoot should the bull turn and charge him once he was afoot.

Micajah watched as the herd broke up and thinned out, scattering to the four winds as the hunters culled their prey from all sides now. When enough of a clearing appeared, he began sliding backward down over the bull's great hump toward its small stringy hindquarters, holding hand over hand to patches of woolly fur until he could slide off the rump.

At once Olivia turned her horse and rode between him and several other stampeding animals headed in their direction. He sprang aboard the mare as she slid forward and kicked the black into a gallop. They rode several hundred feet until they reached a rise on the plain topped by several scrub pines.

"Whoowe, gal! Thet was th' beatin'est damn ride I *ever* took!" Micajah bellowed as he slid off the lathered little mare who had labored beneath his considerable weight.

"Ride? Ride! You crazy *bouffon,* you missed being prairie paste by a gnat's ass!" she shrieked, equal parts infuriated, amused and terrified as she threw herself into his arms and hugged him, still clutching the rifle. He held her up and swung her around as if she weighed no more than that proverbial gnat.

"Sorry I give yew sech a skeer, Sparky. Durn fool thang, I was watchin' ta see no harm come ta yew 'n purt' near got myself pounded inta pemmican. But I'm nigh onta as good a rider as yew." He put her down and fixed her with merry brown eyes. "Betcha yew never rode no buff'lo bull neither, did yew?"

"No, Micajah, and I never want to either."

"Good. I ain't 'zactly fixed on doin' it agin myself!"

They both burst into gales of relieved laughter. Then the dust cleared as the herd raced over the horizon, leaving a field of dead buffalo to be butchered and carried back to the village. Micajah's big gelding, none the worse for his spill and near goring, stood patiently beside the buffalo Against the Wind had shot. The mountain man whistled and the gelding trotted toward him.

After checking the shallow nick on the horse's flank, he

said, "C'mon. Let's see thet fat young cow yew brung down."

"Will they sing songs about Ember Woman's hunting skill around the campfire?" she asked teasingly.

"More like they'll sing songs 'bout her stupidity—ridin' inter a big stampede on a little bitty mare ta carry off an ole worthless grizzly th' size o' me," he said warmly. "Yew saved my life, Sparky."

"Perhaps, but that doesn't begin to even the score. You've saved mine every single day since you rescued a silly, useless girl from a bear last spring."

Together they walked toward the cow Olivia had shot, prepared to set to work.

Time had no meaning. Samuel crouched in the welcome warmth of the sun, feeling it penetrate his bruised and lacerated flesh. Although it felt good, he knew in a few short hours when dusk came, the air would turn bitterly cold for a man clad only in the ragged shreds of britches. He had been forced to cut off most of his pant legs and use them to make coverings for his feet which had been so festered and sore from thistles and stone cuts that he could not walk on them for nearly a week.

He had managed to catch a few fish with his bare hands the first few days by the river. These he ate raw. However, once he was forced to leave the stream because of the proximity of Indians—hostile or friendly, he could not tell which—he found nothing to eat except a few handfuls of wild berries and some tubers he dug up with his knife. That was about the time his head began to pound and his vision blur. The blow from that war club had done more damage than he had first thought. Only semiconscious and nauseously dizzy, he had spent countless days wandering in circles, reduced to crawling on his hands and knees at times when he was too weak and disoriented to walk. Several times he had slept through entire days. He was not certain how many.

Deep in the western woodlands that bordered the Great Plains, he had no idea how he could reach civilization before his badly drained reserves of strength utterly gave out. The slash on his side was steadily growing more painful and inflamed. Already he feared that the wound might prove fatal if not cleaned and treated. He had been avoiding Indian encampments, suspecting that they, like Man Whipper and his renegades, could be under the Englishman's influence. But now he had no choice.

"It's either possible torture and death or certain starvation and blood poisoning," he mumbled grimly.

His tongue felt fuzzy and his mouth was dry and sour. Chills alternated with fever, but at least the damnable hammering in the back of his skull had abated. He could walk upright—if he was strong enough to stand . . .

The fire burned brightly, a huge blaze leaping skyward as glowing orange coals popped and hissed where the fat from the roasting meat sizzled and dripped. Several huge slabs of buffalo meat were spitted over the fire while dozens of big stew kettles around them gave off rich aromas. Everyone in the camp would feast tonight.

Olivia and Micajah were enjoying their last evening of celebration before packing up their share of the buffalo and heading east toward their cabin on the Gasconade. Much had been made of Great Bear's "boy-daughter" whose medicine was spoken of with awe. None of the warriors, however, had offered Micajah a bride price for her since she brought down the cow and rescued the mountain man from the stampede. Micajah told her that they feared being shown up by a slender wisp of a female who was a better hunter than most warriors. Such a wife might prove difficult to control.

Olivia looked forward to returning to the peace and privacy of their cabin, away from the crowded socializing and rituals in the Osage great lodges. Compared to the war and peace chief's houses, which were twenty feet wide and over one hundred feet long, their simple log structure was small indeed, but then it slept only two, not dozens. Each night she shared one end of Chief Pawhuska's lodge with half a dozen of his daughters. They snored worse than Micajah. And when they weren't sleeping they were giggling.

The only subject young girls thought of, it seemed to Olivia, was men. Of course, she had never been so foolish. There had always been so many more interesting things to do as she was growing up than to moon over the gaggle of suitors who had pursued her, such as riding Wescott's fine thoroughbreds or going to the gaming hells with her parents. Life had been filled with such promise then, she thought wistfully. She had always believed that someday she would meet a man, doubtless of noble birth and fine breeding, who would sweep her off her feet the way *Père* had *Maman*.

Without warning the swarthy rugged features of Samuel Shelby flashed into her mind, his beautiful lips dazzling her with one of those blinding white smiles. She tamped down the image, forcing herself to look away from the leaping flames which seemed to conjure him. Still a warm liquid rush filled her belly and made her breasts ache when she remembered that dark velvety night in the small tent when he had almost—*Stop it!*

Restlessly, she stood up and made her way through the crowded center of the big village. Everyone congregated around the two chiefs' lodges, which were built side by side in front of the great campfire, a sort of town square where all feasting and ceremonial events took place. She walked past the smaller lodges where women were busy finishing up last minute chores, feeding infants, putting away the skinning and curing tools they used to work the buffalo hides, and setting their homes in order before joining the great feast.

Several women called out greetings and she returned them in the Osage tongue. Micajah and Iron Kite had taught her the rudiments of the Siouxian dialect. Having a natural affinity for languages, she had learned quickly. Now her Osage was nearly as fluent as the European languages she had learned as a child.

But Olivia St. Etienne was no longer a child. Feeling some strange compulsion drawing her, she walked toward the river. It would be peaceful down by the water. She needed to be alone, to think about the future, about what she wanted to do with her life. She stood by the bank and looked at her dim reflection in the twilight, running her hands over the butter soft buckskin dress Wind Singer, Iron Kite's sister, had made for her. Suddenly a loud crashing noise coming from the brush caused her to whirl around and reach for her knife. She had come out unarmed, all tricked out like some fool Osage princess! Peering into the thicket of elderberry and willow saplings, she began to backtrack slowly.

Samuel stared through the gathering gloom at the apparition in front of him. Not ten yards away the fantastical creature stood poised for flight. She was breathtaking, garbed in an elaborately fringed and beaded dress, like the wife or daughter of some very rich Osage chief. But she was no

Indian. Her long fire-red hair shown like a beacon in the twilight, bound in two fat braids which fell over her shoulders down to the tips of her pertly upthrust breasts. He blinked and squinted, certain the fever was causing him to hallucinate. It was Olivia St. Etienne's face with that stubborn chin stuck out defiantly and those slanted green eyes peering warily at his hiding place.

"Well, if I'm that far gone with fever, I might as well show myself and see if there's any help available," he muttered, taking several more steps, wincing with every one, for his makeshift moccasins had been lost two days ago fording a creek. He leaned heavily on the stout birch pole he had hacked off a dead tree a few days back. Without the crude walking stick he would never have made it this far. He stumbled out into the open and tried to speak to the apparition that looked like Olivia.

This must be my punishment for past sins.

All that emerged was a dry raspy croak. The earth rushed up to meet him as he slid down the pole and sprawled on his knees, weaving back and forth, struggling not to lose consciousness.

Olivia did not recognize him at first. In fact, she was not even certain he was a white man but thought he might have been a captive of the Sioux or the Kaws who escaped and wandered into Osage territory. His hair, uncut since the previous spring, hung below his shoulders in tangled burr infested clumps and his skin was so sun darkened and covered with abrasions that the discolorations made it impossible to tell his race. He was virtually naked except for the ragged buckskins hanging on his bony hips.

He made an incoherent croak, then slid down the walking stick he had been using to drag himself toward her, head pitched forward. Olivia knew he was too badly hurt to be any threat to her safety. She started to walk toward him as he fell to the ground. When he rolled over on his back and the dying rays of light fell on his face, she gave a gasp of recognition.

"Samuel!" Dear God he was half-dead, so emaciated and cut up it was a wonder he was still alive. What could have happened to him? She knelt beside him, cradling his head on her lap all the while screaming for help.

Micajah was the first one to reach her, his long brawny legs eating up the ground in devouring strides. "Sparky gal, yew all right?" He saw her crumpled on the ground, sobbing, and his heart stopped for an instant, until he realized she was tenderly stroking the man's face, holding him protectively.

She looked up at him with tear blurred eyes. "Oh, Micajah, it's Samuel. He's burning up with fever. He's been starved and beaten—"

"Hush, now. Hit's not thet bad. He's jest been out in th' woods afoot fer a spell," he said, kneeling beside her to examine the tall dark stranger while a crowd of Osage clustered around them, looking on curiously.

"He's been run pretty skinny. I seen more meat stuck on a cook stick then he's got left on his bones." Micajah picked up each of Shelby's feet and checked the raw festering soles. "If'n these here wuz moccasins, they'd have holes clean up ta his ankles." He ran his big hands up Samuel's legs and arms, then his torso, probing for broken bones and serious cuts and punctures. "Damn, child, this here's one hell of a uglified mess!"

"He's burning up with fever and that slash on his side is awful looking. Will . . . will he live?" she gulped out, holding her breath.

"I reckon I seen worse." *But not damn often,* he added to himself, noting that for all her words of scorn and betrayal, his Sparky still seemed awfully attached to this young Long Knife. "He needs some tendin'. I done taught yew 'bout herbs 'n sech. Reckon yew feel up ta helpin' me fix him up?"

"What do you want me to do?" she replied, her voice steady even though her heart still pounded fearfully.

"Thet's my gal." He looked up to where Iron Kite stood, scowling down at the white man Ember Woman held so lovingly. Speaking in Osage, Micajah made a series of requests.

Soon they had carried Samuel to the lodge of the Peace Chief, Pawhuska, whose head wife was steeping cherry bark, a fever reducing infusion. Several of the other Osage women gathered around, eager to help tend the hurts of Great Bear's friend. Olivia politely, but firmly shooed them away and took the woven basin filled with fresh water to bathe him herself.

Micajah assisted her, checking the countless angry red cuts and scratches marring his skin. "Them on his arms 'n chest ain't nothin' ta worry over," he said, beginning to tug down what was left of the tattered buckskin britches. He could sense Olivia's embarrassment but ignored it. "We got ta see if'n he's taken any pizen around his privates. Hit'll kill a feller quicker 'n anythin . . . or make him wish he wuz dead, anyways."

Olivia could not stop staring at Samuel's body. How pale his skin was below the waistband of his pants, almost as white as her own! Her eyes followed the slide of pants over the hard washboard of his belly, tracing that enticing narrow vee of body hair that seemed to travel like an arrow from the thick pelt on his chest downward to the black bush between his legs where his sex lay exposed as Micajah methodically examined him.

She remembered with scorching intensity how big and hard the now flaccid and innocent looking shaft had felt when he had loomed over her in the confines of the tent. She wet her dry lips and asked hoarsely, "Is he . . . hurt?"

"Onliest thang serious, sides bein' half-starved, is th' knife slice here in his side," the old man said, pressing along the red swollen edges of the slash, which oozed a vile looking pussy liquid. He rolled Samuel onto his right side and raised his left arm, stretching open the deep ugly wound. "Hit's in need 'o some cleanin', then sewin'. Yore right good with buff'lo skins. Reckon yew cud sew up a man?" He cocked one shaggy grizzled eyebrow and studied her pale face with shrewd brown eyes.

Olivia almost swallowed her tongue. "Sew him up?" she squeaked. "I—I suppose so." She looked at the angry slash and felt her gorge rise, an unusual occurrence since learning to live in the wilds with Micajah. But gutting and skinning bison and deer were quite different than working with a man's flesh and blood, especially when that man was Samuel Shelby.

"Wall, don't fret jest yet. First off we gotta poultice hit 'n git th' fever down." Then he swore to himself. "Damned if'n I didn't fergit my medicine bundle when I packed up my possibles."

"Don't the Osage have the same herbs and such?"

"Some, not all, but whutever they is, they'll have ta do till we kin git him back ta th' cabin."

Olivia continued to bathe his body, taking special care with the deeper cuts and the infected slash on his left side. When she got to his raw, lacerated feet, she nearly wept, realizing what he must have endured.

Micajah went in search of the tribal healer to secure what

herbs he could to stave off further infection and help Shelby fight the fever. After conferring with Sun Carrier, Micajah waited while the old man prepared his potions. Just as they were about to leave the medicine lodge, Pawhuska entered.

Dismissing Sun Carrier and several of the women, he turned to Micajah and said, "I would speak for your ears alone." The tall old man's hawkish countenance was grave. He was past sixty winters, a great age among the Plains Indians, yet his hair for which he was named, was thick and shiny as January snow. A great beak of a nose was balanced by a strong square jaw. His brow was high and straight and his eyes were fathomless ebony. He studied Johnstone intently as he took a seat on a big pile of buffalo robes before the smoldering fire in the center of the lodge. Then he gestured for Micajah to join him as he prepared a pipe for them to share.

"My brother White Hair does me honor," Micajah said in Osage as he hunkered down on the soft skins and took a puff from the proffered pipe.

"I would speak of the Long Knife Ember Woman discovered. The father in Washington will not be pleased to find one of his soldiers near death in our camp."

Micajah's shaggy eyebrows rose fractionally as he passed the pipe back to Pawhuska. "He wore no uniform. How do you know he is a soldier?"

"The one called Samuel Shelby visited our village many months ago, wearing the blue coat of a soldier. My daughter Meadow Dancer came to tell me she recognized him, although he is so badly hurt no one else has."

Micajah scratched a gnarled hand in his bushy beard. "What did he want of my Osage brothers when he was here last?" Sparky had speculated about Shelby's mysterious reasons for leaving Lisa's party to search for the Osage.

"He searches for the one he calls the Englishman, but that is not what he told us," Pawhuska replied with startling candor.

It had been Johnstone's experience of Indians—and he had much—that they seldom spoke directly to an issue but rather skirted around it obliquely, alluding to the point with metaphoric language, approaching it gradually. He nodded, waiting to see if the old chief would say more.

Pawhuska obliged him. "He made a fine speech for our elders, asking that we remember our treaty with the father in

Washington. He said that the Englishman would come among us spreading lies and making empty promises."

"And has he?"

Pawhuska nodded his head. "Yes, and he returns. There are young men among my people who have listened to the words of this Englishman . . . and drunk the firewater he brings," he added bitterly. "There will be a war between the Americans and the English, I think. And my people will be squeezed between the two."

Isolated as he was, Micajah had heard vague rumors of such from the occasional trader or trapper whom he encountered in the wilderness. He felt sorry for the Osage, for all the tribes. Whenever white governments went to war, it was always the Indians who lost the most. "Will you choose sides or not?" he asked.

"I have touched the feather. My pledge was made to the Americans. But"—Pawhuska leaned forward earnestly—"I am one old man. A chief, yes, but still there are many voices who will be heard at our council fires. The young warriors grow tired of seeing more and more white settlers cross the Father of Waters, pushing us farther and farther away from the great rivers, toward the setting sun. Some elders on our council listen to their complaints."

"Then you believe the Osage may choose to fight against the Americans," Johnstone said.

"I will do what I can to stop it." He smiled sadly. "Not because I believe the father in Washington is better than the father across the great ocean. But your great chief is closer and it is his children who will remain after the war is fought, not the English."

Micajah digested all that the wily old man had told him . . . and what he had not told him. Since Pawhuska had spoken plainly, he decided to follow suit. "Why do you tell me this, my friend? I am not a bluecoat. I have no part in the white men's wars."

"I wish you to take the Long Knife Shelby away from our village. He is sick and unable to speak for himself before the council. I fear for his safety when the Englishman comes and I would not see him harmed."

So that was the way the wind blew. Micajah knew the Osage put great store in spit and polish. Shelby had probably arrived last summer dressed in his best blues, but now he had reappeared in rags, feverish and wandering in the wilderness, perhaps chased by the very English agent who was coming to speak before the Osage council of elders. Johnstone cleared his throat. "I can see your point. He would make a poor showing against his foe right now and those hotheads who want to join the English might just carry the day, if they knew who he was." And they might well kill Shelby as well as him and Sparky, since they too were Americans. "We will take him to safety. Can you prevent your daughter from telling anyone else about Shelby's identity?"

The old man simply looked at him.

"Good."

The two men rose and bowed to each other gravely and Micajah took his leave. There was much to prepare and little time in which to do it.

By dawn the next day they were ready to set out. Micajah had rigged a travois to a stout packhorse which was a gift from Pawhuska. On it they carried Samuel while their own horses were laden with their booty from the buffalo hunt. No one but old White Hair and his daughter Meadow Dancer knew that their unconscious passenger was an emissary of the great father in Washington. With luck, it would stay that way.

∽ *Chapter 14* ∽

Samuel felt as if he were on fire, thrashing and rolling to escape the flames that seared his body. Someone must be prodding him with a burning firebrand. Osage torture? He struggled to open his eyes and focus on his tormentor, but emerging from the blackness was impossible. Then he felt a small cool hand touch him softly, pressing him back down, a low naggingly familiar voice speaking French endearments. A woman's voice. Not his mother, nor Liza. Certainly not Tish. Who? Then blessed oblivion claimed him again and he drifted.

Olivia felt tears sting her eyes as she held him in her arms lest his fevered thrashing tear open the healing stitches in his side. He was in such awful pain. She could still feel the pressure of the needle puncturing his skin, the pull of the thread as it drew the ragged sides of the wound back together. What it had cost her to stitch his living flesh was beyond imagining. Thank God, he had remained unconscious most of the time. When she was half-finished, he had awakened and Micajah had restrained him, holding his body still so she could complete the task. Blessedly, he had quickly fainted.

Micajah had assured her he was too feverish to really be awake and would remember nothing of the pain when he recovered, but she had been white and shaking after forcing herself to complete the task. She waited until he lay very still once more, then continued peeling away the poultice adhering to the wound. The redness and pussy swelling were gone.

"Micajah's strange ideas really do work," she murmured to herself as she cleaned the healing slash with compresses of warm water, then applied fresh herbs to the area.

She had been dubious when Johnstone had gone to the river and brought back a jar filled with an evil slimy gray substance, saying that it was a certain cure for infections. She had been horrified when he had explained that it was frog eggs.

"This won't cure him—it'll give him warts!" she had shrieked.

Micajah had laughed. "Nope. They's somethin' in 'em thet kills th' pizen. Don't rightly know whut, but my ma's folks brung hit along from the old country hunerts of years ago."

She had watched doubtfully as he packed the goo around the wound, but the next morning her fears turned to amazement when the fiery red swelling was nearly gone. Now the stitches were drawing tightly together, almost knit and ready to be removed. If only he would regain consciousness.

Squeezing her eyes closed, she shook her head, trying to dislodge the searing visions from his feverish ravings. He had called out for his sister and his father, but then came the awful revelations . . .

"*Maman . . . Maman.*" His voice had been so hoarse and soft she could barely make it out at first. As she had leaned closer attempting to soothe him with cool washcloths pressed to his feverish skin, he rambled on. "Why did you go away, *Maman?* You broke Papa's heart. How could you take Liza and leave me behind?"

Her heart wrenched at the little boy wistfulness in his voice as he talked about his first Christmas as a thirteen-year-old alone with a taciturn bereaved father in a big empty house. But if that betrayal cut to the quick, it paled by comparison to the next shocking revelation.

"I know you're disappointed in me, Tish, but I'm a soldier . . . not presidential material. Hell, I won't even make general. You married the wrong man . . . tried to make you understand. . . ."

The words about his mother had touched her deeply but this, this was his wife, far too personal and painful for her to hear. She arose to leave the cabin and call Micajah to take over but before she could reach the door, he thrashed restlessly, kicking off the covers and his voice rose. She rushed back to his side.

"You bitch! You bloody bitch. You killed my child! May Wretz is an abortionist . . . can't lie to me. I know you went to her while I was away. Did you kill the first child, too . . . that tragic *miscarriage* you suffered when we were first married . . . you swore you couldn't bear to carry another babe and lose it . . . kept your word, Tish . . . you kept . . . your . . . word . . ."

His voice had faded as he dropped off into deeper unconsciousness. Trembling, Olivia had finished sponging him, then carefully replaced the covers and kept her bedside vigil until Micajah returned.

Now she understood the reason Samuel Shelby was such an embittered misogynist. He had hated his dead wife bitterly, and he mistrusted all women except his sister.

He will never love you.

Olivia trembled when the thought suddenly flashed into her mind. *Fool,* she berated herself, then added, *as if I loved* him!

Looking down, she took a deep breath and finished packing the herbs against the healing sutures before picking up the clean strips of linen to rebandage the wound. She leaned across his chest and reached over to begin wrapping the bandage when suddenly she sensed his eyes on her. At very close range, Olivia looked into Samuel's harsh blue gaze.

He was speechless, as much from amazement as from the parched rawness of his throat. "I'll be damned," he finally rasped, "I wasn't hallucinating about the Osage princess."

His eyes swept over her as she sat bolt-upright on the edge of the big bed where he lay. She no longer wore the exotic beaded buckskin dress, but she scarcely looked like any conventional white female either. Her hair was bound in a single fat braid that lay across one shoulder, tied with a rawhide thong decorated with an eagle feather. She wore an age softened buckskin shirt, open at the throat, revealing an enticing patch of sun-gilded skin. Her nose was dusted with small gold freckles and that glorious red hair was streaked with bits of deep amber as if she had spent long hours in the hot sun.

Olivia watched him survey her, certain that he found her most unfeminine and repugnant in the comfortable and practical britches and shirt she had cut down from a set of Micajah's far larger garments. "I'm hardly a princess, but my father was a baron," she replied with all the self-possession she could muster. *I don't care a fig what he thinks of me.*

He felt a fiery stab of pain when he started to move, then reached over to clutch his left side, but she quickly grabbed his hand.

"Don't. You might tear open the wound. I was just changing the dressing." She lifted the bandage by way of explanation as he lay his right arm back on the mattress.

"Where am I?" he asked, looking around the interior of a small cabin, obviously not an Osage lodge.

The walls were made of whole logs, laid horizontally with tight mud and straw chinking between them, sealing out the weather. The floor was packed earth, hardened and polished to a dark maroon shine by "curing" it with buffalo blood, a trick he'd seen in numerous Indian villages along the Santa Fe trail. The only furniture consisted of a sturdy puncheon log table and four chairs, along with two plank shelves stretching across one wall, stocked with supplies and cooking implements. A big limestone fireplace filled one wall. A low bank of coals glowed in it and a heavy iron kettle hung over them, giving off a spicy fragrance that made his stomach growl. Several rifles and an old musket hung on the opposite wall, along with an Osage war lance, a tomahawk and several gleaming knives, all decorated with shells and feathers. Two rather large windows let in golden sunlight and amazingly he could see the bright blooms of fall flowers peeping over the window sill.

"You're in our cabin," she replied matter-of-factly, as she resumed bandaging his chest. *Let him ask.*

"*Our* cabin?" He felt poleaxed. What was this helpless European aristocrat doing garbed in buckskins, living in a settler's cabin in the wilderness . . . somewhere?

"Actually Micajah built it. Micajah Johnstone," she replied as if that explained everything.

"And who the hell is Micajah Johnstone?" he asked with rising irritation. *Your new lover?*

"Raise up carefully so I can slide the wrapping under you," she instructed, reaching across his broad chest, trying unsuccessfully to remain unaffected by his male scent and body heat. "Micajah is a mountain man or woodsman . . . sort of."

"Sort of?"

"What I mean is, Micajah has spent years here living at peace with the various Indian tribes and white trappers, but he doesn't trap for a living."

"Has he a rich family back east who sends him money?" Samuel asked cynically. Already he was beginning to dislike this Johnstone fellow.

"Don't be absurd. We grow our own corn and vegetables, hunt for meat and hides. We even have a bee tree," she added with pride. "Nature provides."

"We?"

"Is there an echo in here? Strange, I never noticed it before," she added serenely, proud of her steady hand on the wrapping. "I live here, too. He saved my life after you abandoned me on the Missouri."

"I did not abandon you. I left you in Manuel Lisa's care."

"Well, I didn't choose to remain 'in his care,' " she snapped back. "I left on my own."

"I can imagine you didn't get very far," he said dryly, grateful she had not been killed or taken captive by hostiles.

"Oh, I managed for three days," she exaggerated, "until I ran afoul of a she-bear with cubs." Olivia was rewarded when a look of horror flashed across his face. She was strangely pleased. "*That's* when Micajah saved my life. I've lived here ever since—except for when we're off on a hunt or trading in the Osage villages. It's lucky for you we were in Pawhuska's town when you straggled in. If Micajah and I hadn't brought you here, they'd probably have killed you," she said blithely, leaning back to inspect her bandaging.

"You live with this Johnstone. How cozy." He sounded like a churlish prude even to his own ears—or worse yet, he sounded just plain jealous.

Olivia stiffened. "Yes, it is—or it was until you horned it. We should've left you to the mercies of the English agent and his young Osage warriors."

His fever fogged brain suddenly became crystal clear. "What do you know about this Englishman?"

She shrugged. "Only what Micajah was told by old White Hair. He's been stirring up the young firebrands among the Osage who are tired of the Americans breaking their treaty promises."

"He was coming to Pawhuska's town?" he asked, trying to sit up.

"He's probably there now, but you're hardly in any shape to go chasing after him," she said, noting with satisfaction that he had the good sense to give in to the pain and lean back against the pillows. She felt a sudden need to place some distance between them. She stood up and walked over to the hearth where her stew pot bubbled, then ladled a small amount of broth into a bowl.

Samuel cursed silently at his failure to complete his mission. "If the Englishman wins over the Osage, the Missouri will run red with blood."

"And you could change all that?" She looked at him skeptically, holding the bowl in front of her.

"If I had caught up with the bastard, yes, I might have," replied stubbornly. "How long have I been here?"

"Several weeks, give or take a few days. We don't have much need to look at calendars around here," she said dryly, approaching the side of the bed with a bowl and spoon in hand. "Now, open wide. You need some nourishment."

"What I need is to get the hell up and back to Pawhuska's village."

"Try not to make yourself an even bigger ass than nature already has made you," she said sweetly. "You're starved, slashed and fevered. Not to mention that your feet look like cabbage slaw. You couldn't even stand on them, much less walk. Open wide." She held a spoonful of broth up to his mouth.

He considered protesting her high-handed assumption that he would be a docile patient but just then his stomach, so long without food, gave a low insistent rumble. He capitulated and opened his mouth. "That's delicious. Did you make it?" The question was meant to be sarcastic.

And so Olivia took it. "Remembering my coffee?" She tried to keep the tartness from her voice. "Micajah has taught me how to cook what I shoot, as well as how to dress the skins and preserve the meat."

"I can't help but wonder what else Micajah's taught you," he muttered beneath his breath.

Olivia heard him and angrily jerked the spoon away from his mouth, spilling the scalding broth across his chest. "I should've left you lying by the riverbank and let that Englishman carve you up!" She slammed the spoon down into the broth, splattering his bare chest with even more hot liquid. "Here, feed yourself." She shoved the bowl into his hand when he raised it to wipe off the burning broth.

"Ouch! Dammit, that hurts," he yelled, his voice cracking. When he tried to hold the bowl up, he found to his horror that his hands were so weak he almost dropped the whole scalding hot mess all over himself. Resting the bowl on his chest, he called out to her, "I'm sorry. Please, come take this before I add burns to all my other injuries."

At once Olivia felt contrite. He had nearly died of his wounds. The fever had broken only that morning and here she was expecting him to be able to sit up and eat by himself.

But he made her so infuriatingly angry that she could [
him every time they passed more than half an hour togeth[
"Here, I'll feed you," she said ungraciously, taking the bo[
from him and sitting down on the edge of the bed once mo[

God, how haggard and pale he looked. "What happen[
to you—how did you end up half-dead and naked, wande[
ing afoot through the woods?"

"I was careless," he said disgustedly. "Some of th[
damned Englishman's allies—those young Osage hothea[
you mentioned—captured me."

"And you escaped?" she prompted, continuing to spoo[
the broth down him.

"Sort of."

"Sort of?" she mimicked.

"They stripped my boots and shirt, then had me run[
gauntlet between a dozen armed warriors."

"A dozen! I can't believe you made it."

"Neither can I," he replied grimly. "That's how I got the[
slash in my side to add to the lovely little tap with a war clu[
that brought me down in the first place. But I did manage to[
get past them. They graciously gave me a couple of hundred[
yards lead before giving chase. I've never run so hard or so[
long in my life."

"That's how you got all those thistles in your feet." She
winced thinking of running across a field of the tough spiny
weeds barefooted.

"That was the least of my problems, believe me." Briefly
he outlined the rest of his escape, the fight with Man Whipper and his subsequent blackouts and wandering until he
found the Osage village.

When he had finished the tale and the broth, his small
reserve of strength was spent. Olivia could see his eyelids
growing heavy. Just as she started to rise from the bed, Micajah walked into the cabin. His big frame filled the doorway
as he peered at Shelby and his Sparky sitting so cozily by
his side.

"So, our soldier boy finally waked up." He noticed how
quickly she scooted off the bed, making a big production of
washing the bowl and spoon in the pan of water sitting on
the kitchen table.

"He won't be awake for long. He's still too weak to hold
his head up," she said matter-of-factly.

Samuel stared at the great grizzly of a man looming over

him. Good lord, he was old enough to be Olivia's father—
her grandfather! At once his snide words came back to haunt
him. Damn, why did he blurt out such tomfool stupid things
around that woman? "You must be Micajah Johnstone. I'm
greatly obliged for the hospitality. You've saved my life."

"Warn't me. Sparky here's th' one whut took keer o'
yew."

Sparky?

Micajah continued on, "She sat up ever' night sinc't we
come home from th' Osage town. Acted plumb skittish ever'
time thet litter we wuz carryin' yew on took a leetle bump.
She sewed up thet cut on yer side. Didn't want ta do hit
neither, till I held up one o' these." He gestured with his
huge meaty hand. "This here's more o' a bar paw than hit is
anythin' human. I 'spect if I wuz ta try stitchin' up yer side
yew'd o' felt like yew'd been mauled. Onc't she seen my
drift, Sparky here took thet needle 'n did a right proper job
of hit. Course, she wuz real worried 'bout—"

"Micajah, I think Colonel Shelby needs to rest," Olivia
interrupted, mortified to have him recount the way she had
fussed over that arrogant ingrate.

Samuel's curiosity was burning, but his mind began to
grow fuzzy with weariness as he looked from the loquacious
old man to the tense young woman. He moved his left shoulder experimentally and was rewarded with a tight stab of
pain from his side.

At his hiss of agony, she quickly rushed back to the bedside before even thinking about it. "Don't roll around so or
you'll break the dry stitches. They'll need to come out in a
few days, I think." She fought the urge to run her hands over
his body as she had done so often in the past days while
bathing him and treating his hurts. Now she knew every inch
of that splendidly male anatomy, knew it so well she had but
to close her eyes to see it, to conjure the touch, smell and
texture of him. Damn, what was wrong with her!

Micajah watched Olivia hovering over Shelby as the injured man's eyelids flickered closed. She looked pale and
had smudges of fatigue beneath her vivid green eyes from
staying awake nights, ready to jump up and tend him if he
made the slightest sound in his feverish sleep. Now his
Sparky was a sweet loving girl who felt anyone's pain—man
or critter—he knew that, but what she felt for the handsome

soldier went beyond the compassion of her woman's soft heart. He was as sure of that as he was of sunrise.

Was Shelby worthy of her love? Judiciously he decided to take the man's measure before passing judgment. After all, he had only heard her version of what passed between the two of them. She had a fierce temper and pride enough for an Osage war chief. And the soldier fellow had to be tough as a boiled owl to survive what he had. Micajah could imagine the two of them striking sparks off each other, he thought with an inner chuckle. Time would tell. He had the whole winter to study on the matter.

Samuel awakened to the aroma of freshly brewed coffee and baking corn bread. His stomach growled and he was salivating as he blinked a few times and gingerly raised his head to look around the cabin.

While she was unaware of his perusal, he observed Olivia. She was dressed in a pair of old britches, probably one of the ones she had brought with her from St. Louis, along with a soft plaid shirt he had never seen before. The sleeves were rolled up to her elbows, revealing her slim golden forearms.

The clothes, while old and much mended, appeared to fit her better than the ones she wore when she had been disguised as "Ollie." Odd, but there was something peculiarly tempting about the way a woman filled out a shirt and britches, especially a tall, slim, curvaceous female with yards of fire-colored hair and slanted emerald gypsy's eyes.

Damn, I sound moony as a lovesick schoolboy!

She had learned a thing or two from that old bear Johnstone. He watched the efficient way she checked the bubbling coffeepot, moving it away from the flames onto low coals. Then she shoved a big tined fork beneath the golden loaf of corn bread baking on a shallow cast iron pan to check the bottom side for doneness. Satisfied, she sat it on the side of the hearth and turned her attention to the smoked meat sizzling in the skillet. He watched her turn crispy strips of what he judged to be venison.

"Looks like Johnstone's created a culinary miracle."

Olivia turned around quickly, brandishing the big fork in one hand like a weapon. At once she felt a fool under his sardonically amused stare. "Micajah is different than you. I never wanted to poison him," she replied tartly, mocking his raised eyebrow by lifting her own disdainfully.

She returned his penetrating stare, studying the gauntness

of his face, what she could see of it beneath the thick stubble of black beard once more growing on the lower half. The night they returned to the cabin, she and Micajah had to ascertain the extent of his injuries, which meant they had to wash his hair and shave off his matted curly beard. Now it had all grown back. He was a heavily whiskered man. Remembering the feel of that beard stubble beneath her fingertips made her flush with a warmth that did not come from sitting so near the hearth. She looked away and returned to cooking breakfast.

"Poison or not, it smells more than good enough to eat."

"You could use some meat on your bones. Your ribs stick out." The minute she blurted out the retort, she could have bitten her tongue.

Samuel watched her blush to the roots of her hair. "So, what are you waiting for? Come over here and fatten me up," he said in a low, suggestive voice, taunting her.

"The only critters we fatten up around here are the ones we butcher for our winter larder. Not a bad idea in your case, except that you appear to be too tough to kill." As they exchanged double-edged banter, she dished up some venison, placed a thick slab of corn bread on the plate beside it and drizzled it with honey, then poured a mug of steamy black coffee.

"Dare I hope that's for me?"

"It's for Micajah. You get more broth and a bit of this cornpone soaked in milk."

He made a face.

Just then the giant came walking through the cabin door, carrying a rolled-up buffalo hide. "Where do yew want ta work on this? I thought hit'd be cooler beneath th' cottonwoods by th' creek, but if'n yew want hit closer ter th' cabin, I cud peg hit out front." He held the heavy soft skin on one arm as if it weighed no more than a patchwork quilt, although even dressed and tanned out a full-sized buffalo robe easily went one hundred-fifty pounds.

"Why don't we stretch it down by the creek. I could use some fresh air away from the cabin," she replied with a scathing glance toward Shelby.

"Mornin', son. Glad ta see yew waked up agin. Reckon yore stomach done thought some Injun'd slit yore throat. Sparky here's a real fine cook." He tossed the half-cured robe across one sturdy chair, then took the plate she handed him and walked over to Shelby with it.

"I don't think it's a good idea to give him solid food so soon," she countered.

"Wal, mebbee not th' meat, but pone's th' staff o' life," he averred. "So's coffee. We got fresh milk ta go with hit?"

"Yes. Sukey was balky again. I had to hobble her and she tried to horn me," Olivia replied.

"You have a cow?" Samuel asked, incredulous at the idea of Olivia as a milkmaid.

"Nope," Micajah answered. "A she-goat. Bought her off'n a Spaniard whut wandered through these parts a couply years ago. She gives good rich milk but she's a mite tetchy 'bout hit. All depends on how yew handle her," he added, looking Shelby directly in the eye.

"Aren't all females," Samuel muttered as he struggled to sit up.

"Here, better let me help yew," Micajah said affably. He walked over to Shelby and literally scooped him up with surprising ease and gentleness, sitting him against the back of the log bed frame. "Sparky, git some o' them extry pillers ta put behind his back."

Although sweat beaded his face from the searing pain in his side, Samuel gritted his teeth and said nothing.

Olivia hurried over and began to fluff several large corn husk filled pillows which she stuffed behind him. She could see the muscles and tendons standing out on his neck and along his jawline as he suppressed groans of pain. "Stitches burn?" she asked conversationally.

"Yes, a little," he replied through clenched teeth.

"Then you'd better eat to build up your strength. It's time for them to be pulled out today."

She was enjoying his misery, damn her. He could tell it by the smirk in her voice and the dancing light in those green eyes. "And you, I suppose will extract them?" His look was killing.

She smiled. "Who better? I sewed them in the first place."

"An' a right steady hand she's got, too. Yew never fear," Micajah interjected, grinning.

Olivia brought over a slab of corn bread torn into small pieces, soaked with a mixture of honey and milk. Taking a spoon, she sat down beside him and offered him a bite. "Go slowly. I don't want you throwing up all over the clean bedding."

In spite of the pain in his side, he felt amazingly rested and stronger than before. He almost offered to feed himself—until he noticed her nervousness as she gingerly positioned herself on the very edge of the bed, careful not to make bodily contact with him. Now it was his turn to grin . . . wolfishly. He cocked his head to one side and studied her. "I'm waiting. And I'm very hungry."

She forced her hand to remain steady and aimed for his mouth, watching as those elegantly sculpted lips closed over the spoon. Those lips had scorched her skin, brushing across her throat, temples, her cheeks, pressing against her mouth, demanding entrance so his tongue could plunder and taste of her. She watched him chew slowly, savoring the honey soaked bread, rolling it around on his tongue, then swallowing. Her eyes followed the sinewy bronzed column of his throat muscles as the food went down. How could the simple act of eating be so sexually charged?

She felt his eyes on her and broke the hypnotic trance that seemed to suspend time. "Here. You seem strong enough to feed yourself this morning," she said, jabbing the bowl at his bare hairy chest until he took it with one hand and secured the spoon with the other. As she stood up and quickly moved away from the bed she thought she heard him murmur very low, "Coward."

The sun was at its apex in the autumn sky as Olivia squatted over the heavy buffalo hide. It had been stretched tightly on a frame Micajah had made especially for the purpose of working a buffalo skin after it had been scraped clean. She smeared the greasy grayish mixture of brains and lye ash across the absorbent hide, then began to work it in to cold cure and soften. After it soaked long enough, she would scrape it completely clean again and let it dry out, then build a very low fire with green wood and let it burn down to smoldering coals. The hide would then be carefully suspended over the dense smoke. Ever after, it would remain soft even if soaked in the rain.

Micajah watched her labor, rubbing fiercely with both small fists, elbows stiff, throwing her whole back into the hard task. "Yew 'pear ta me ta have a wasp in yore britches, Sparky. Hit got anythin' ta do with thet pretty soldier boy?" There was a twinkle in his eyes as he looked down at her.

She straightened up and shoved a loose lock of red hair away from her forehead with the back of her arm. "Samuel Shelby is no boy."

Johnstone seemed to be considering this revelation thoughtfully. "Come ta think on hit, I reckon yore plum right 'bout thet. He's got his full growth." The big man clawed at his chin through the tangle of beard and then added softly, as if thinking aloud. "Shore 'nough, parts o' him got full growth."

The blood surged so quickly to Olivia's face that she thought her skin was being boiled from the inside. "Micajah Johnstone!" she almost shouted. "Colonel Shelby's 'parts' are no concern of mine—at least now that I've escaped his immoral snares." That declaration had not sounded exactly as she had intended, and the blood in her cheeks "boiled" even more fiercely.

Micajah ignored her discomfort and pressed on. "Hit don't look thet away from where I'm a squattin'. Th' two o' yew 'er circlin' each other like a couple o' bobcats fixin' ta den up in th' same cave."

"He's arrogant and insufferable and I may be stuck with him in our cabin all winter. He mistrusts all women because of his dead wife who was—so he says—quite blatantly wicked." Since she had gleaned that piece of information from his rather explicit feverish ravings, she did not truly doubt its veracity, but his low opinion of women in general and her in particular angered her with its unfairness. And it hurt her, too, but she would never consciously admit it.

Micajah scratched his head consideringly. "Then mebbe hit's up ta yew to change his mind."

"I don't give a fig what he thinks of any woman."

Micajah didn't reply but knelt down beside her and dipped his hand into the pot of brains and ash, withdrawing a big blob of goo. "Let me work on this fer a spell. You cud use a coolin' down in th' creek. This here warm sun ain't a gonna last much longer so late in th' year. Might's well enjoy hit whilst yew kin."

The idea of a bath did appeal. She could wash her hair with that small piece of scented soap she'd gotten from the last trader who happened by. Obviously she did not want to primp for Samuel Shelby. She only wanted to be clean. She desired a little luxury. Thus rationalizing, she smiled at Micajah and said, "A good wash sounds wonderful."

Olivia wiped off her hands and stood up but just as she started to walk toward the cabin in search of soap and towel and clean clothes, Micajah casually mentioned, "When yew take a mind, them stitches have got ta come outta Shelby's side," He watched her stiffen, then nod.

"If he's up to it, so am I."

As she stalked up the hill, Micajah grinned to himself and set to work, whistling.

When she reached the cabin, Samuel was asleep. Grateful that she did not have to face those mocking blue eyes, she slipped quietly inside and gathered her necessaries, then headed to the bliss of cool, clear water. As the sun dropped lower toward the beckoning trees, she climbed out, smugly recalling Samuel's mocking of the fact she had not learned to swim. Now she was as fast and graceful as an otter in the water, thanks to Micajah.

Olivia dried her hair by brushing it until it crackled and gleamed like polished copper. Then she slipped into her fresh clothes, the newest doeskin leggins and tunic she had sewn. The knee-length tunic tip was embroidered with beads and quills, a skill old White Hair's wife had taught her. Although she was a novice, she thought the simple pattern had turned out pretty well.

"I love to wear things that I've created for myself," she murmured, smoothing the butter soft skin over the curve of her hip. She certainly had not put it on for Samuel Shelby's gratification!

Now there was the matter of taking out those blasted stitches. With a grim smile she gathered up her things and headed back to the cabin.

When she walked through the door, the sun was at her back, gilding the masses of her hair until it glowed like molten red-gold flame, spilling across her shoulders. She looked flushed, pink from a bath and the soft pale cream-colored skins of her tunic clung lovingly to the sweet curves of her body. Samuel felt his throat close up and his heartbeat accelerate, not to mention a sudden throbbing in the lower regions of his anatomy, which leaped all too eagerly to attention. Thank heavens he was half covered by a heavy quilt!

"You look like that Osage princess from my fever dreams again," he said, trying for a light tone to cover up the effect she was having on him.

"This outfit isn't half so fancy. I can't sew like the women who made that dress," she said dismissively.

"Implying that you did sew this one?"

"Yes, as a matter of fact, I did. And it's damn comfortable, too."

"I'm impressed."

She opened the medicine possibles sack and pulled out a small, wickedly sharp penknife and ran her fingertip along the side of the blade, then said with a falsely sweet grin, "I couldn't care less. All I came in to do was cut out those stitches. Micajah said you were bellyaching about them hurting."

That quickly took the steel out of his erection! She advanced on him smiling cooly with the knife gleaming evilly in her small hand. "Why do I think you're going to enjoy this even more than you did sewing me up?"

"Because this time you'll be awake to feel it?" she answered his rhetorical question with her own.

He leaned back and crossed his arms on his chest. "After surviving a dozen bloodthirsty Osage bucks, don't think you can frighten me." He patted a spot close to him on the big bed. "Come on. I'm ready . . . if you are."

Dare her, would he? Clutching her little knife and a small tweezers, she walked over and sat down, although not as close as he indicated. "Pull down the blanket. You haven't got anything under it I haven't already seen," she said boldly, hoping to make him feel as flustered and embarrassed as he made her feel.

"Then you won't mind seeing it again." Calmly he flung the quilt away, baring his body to the top of his thighs.

"Not that far down!" she said much too quickly, her voice much too high as she angrily yanked the blanket back up to his waist, trying not to notice the washboard hard ridges of his chest and belly and the seductive patterns in that black body hair. "Roll on your good side," she commanded. "Before I decide to snip something more than stitches."

He did as ordered, facing away from her. She noted that he moved his body with considerable care. That healing slash was still quite tender.

"Hold still. This is going to hurt," she said with false relish. Samuel muttered something unintelligible, but did as he was told.

Willing her hands to remain steady, she began to work on

the first small stitch, biting her lip in concentration. As the flesh had knit together and healed over, the small strands of sinew she had used as thread had drawn tight and worked their way deep into his skin. Carefully she inserted the tip of the razor sharp knife beneath the tight sinew and twisted up and out.

Feeling a sharp pinch of pain as the thread snapped, he grunted.

"I said hold still," she repeated crossly, snipping the next stitch the same way. The thread would not come free as easily. No help for it, she had to touch him to steady herself. Although no longer hot with fever, his skin was still warm and smooth beneath the palm of her left hand. She could feel the hardness of muscle over rib bones as her fingers pressed down. Laying aside the knife, she used the tweezers to pull the sinew free.

Olivia could feel the rhythmic rise and fall of his chest as he breathed, feel the quivering tension in his body while she worked the stitch free, pulling on the pink tender flesh until she knew it must indeed hurt him far more than she had anticipated.

The pain was bearable. He had felt a lot worse on numerous occasions, but having her so close, hovering over him, touching him with her soft, cool hands, was sheer torture. He could smell the faint fragrance of wildflowers and feel the brushing of her hair as it fell against his back and shoulder, tickling his sensitized skin until he thought he would scream with frustration.

His erection was back, never mind her knife or the pain. Then he heard her voice, choked and low as she murmured, "I . . . I'm sorry. Really, I don't mean to hurt you."

Olivia worked as fast as she could, snipping and pulling until the last stitch, which would not budge. She chewed her lip in vexation. "I can't get it loose."

"Pull harder."

"I might make it bleed again."

No chance. All his blood had rushed somewhere else, but Samuel was not about to tell her that! "Just do it," he said, he hoped calmly.

Olivia took a steadying breath and leaned over his side, squinting in concentration, then placed two splayed fingers carefully on either side of the healing flesh where the stitch stuck out defiantly. Using her other hand she gripped the tweezers firmly and pulled harder.

As she worked, she was unaware of repositioning her body closer to his. Samuel felt her squirming behind him and all but forgot the burning in his side. One long fiery lock of hair fell onto his chest and he took it in his hand, wrapping it around his fist and raising it to stroke the silk against his lips.

The stitch gave way and pulled free. Olivia would have lost her balance and tumbled from her kneeling position on the edge of the bed if not for the anchor of her hair in Samuel's fist. She yelped when her scalp tingled in pain, and jumped forward in reflex at the same time he rolled onto his back, trying to let go of the tangled hair in his hand, but it was too late.

Suddenly she was above him, staring into his eyes, their gazes locked, inches apart, their mouths also inches apart. For a heartbeat neither moved. Then instead of releasing her hair he pulled gently on it, drawing her down until her upper body was sprawled across his, her breasts pressing against the black pelt of his chest hair. Time was suspended. They had no idea for how long as they continued to stare into each other's eyes until at last the warmth of their breaths met and intermingled. What happened next was inevitable.

✑ *Chapter 15* ✑

Micajah hallooed into the cabin. "We got us a real treat fer supper. Lookee whut my trot line done give us." He held up a stringer of dark greenish catfish. When he stepped inside, he could see Olivia leaping from the bedside as if snakebit, her hair tangled and her face flushed. She had bathed and selected one of her best outfits, and she was breathless, unable to meet his eyes, as if guilty of some heinous crime. Shelby didn't look too comfortable either, sitting huddled in the center of the bed, scowling fierce as a treed cougar. Micajah smiled to himself.

"I was just removing those stitches as you asked me to do," she said, replacing the medical implements in their sack and unrolling a length of clean bandages. "I'll get to work on frying those fish as soon as you gut them and give Devil his treat."

"No need ta rush. Thet hound·kin wait. Jest take care o' yore patient first," Micajah replied genially, tossing the wriggling catfish onto the table while the dog sat watching him from the doorway, ears at attention and head cocked expectantly. Micajah looked at Shelby and said, "Sparky fries th' best catfish I ever et. Jest wait till yew sink a tooth inta one."

"Right now I'm so starved I'd eat one raw—skin, guts and all," Samuel replied.

"I don't think your stomach is up to anything as greasy as fried fish yet," Olivia said neutrally as she held out the bandage for his side.

Micajah whistled jovially, seeming to ignore them as he poured himself a cup of coffee from the pot ever steaming at the edge of the hearth. "I'll let yew two settle up betwixt yoreselves," he said with deliberate vagueness, then slung the fish across his shoulder and headed out the door with Dirt Devil at his heels.

Samuel raised his arm and looked down at the healing wound in his side, then flexed the muscles across his shoulder and back. "I'm feeling a lot stronger." He waited for her to sit down beside him again and apply the wrapping, then added suggestively, "So's my appetite."

Olivia could see the challenge in his eyes. Taunt her, would he? She would show him she was no fainting miss. If only her heart would cease its triphammer beat and her skin lose the heated flush that tingled everywhere from her face to her most intimate parts. She could still feel the warmth of his breath mingling with hers, the pressure and command of his mouth in that interrupted kiss . . . a kiss she had ached for. It was madness to desire him. He would only hurt her again.

Forcing herself to remember the cold betrayal of his ugly bargain with Emory Wescott, she sat on the edge of the bed and reached out to wrap the bandage around his waist. There was no way to do it without coming far too close to the muscled hardness of his black furred chest. She unconsciously chewed her lip as she held one end of the cloth strip pressed against the wound and began to reach around him with the bandage.

Samuel could feel his heartbeat accelerate, keeping a pulsing rhythm with the lower part of his mutinous anatomy. He shifted uncomfortably beneath the covers, cursing himself for seven kinds of a fool for taunting her, then drew in his breath sharply when her hair softly brushed his chest as she leaned forward.

"Hold still so I can fasten this" she commanded crossly, struggling to keep her hands steady as she tied the bandages, then scooted quickly off the bed.

He could sense the unease beneath her cool veneer but was uncertain of exactly what motivated her to be warm and pliant in his arms one moment, then skittish as a schoolgirl the next. Probably having Johnstone around made her feel guilty, rather like being chaperoned by her father, but then when he imagined the sort of father she had described to him, a profligate French aristocrat who lived from hand to mouth, he could not help but feel the irony in it. Micajah was no doubt a far better protector of her dubious virtue than St. Etienne had ever been.

That thought gave him pause. As long as he was under the old woodsman's sights, he had better tread very lightly around "his Sparky." No more sexual teasing. In fact, the sooner he was strong enough to leave them both behind, the better. After all, he still had an assignment to complete.

Channeling his thoughts along that line he said, "Tell me about the camp gossip regarding the Englishman. I know the Osage women must have discussed him."

She shrugged. "I didn't spend much time with the women. All I know is what Micajah told me and I've already told you that." She scrutinized him from the corner of her eye as she prepared to fry the fish Micajah would shortly bring in. "Is that the only reason you came with Lisa? To search for this English agent?" *Not to search for me.*

"He needs to be stopped," he replied evenly, as his thoughts returned again to Emory Wescott. Could she possibly be in league with a whole damn cadre of English spies? He settled back in the bed and feigned sleep. Yes, the sooner he escaped from here the better it would be for more reasons than one.

Against Olivia's better judgment, Samuel ate solid food that evening as he and Micajah discussed unrest among the Osage. The old man knew more about the English traders who were wooing the malcontent young bucks away from more peaceful tribal leadership, but he volunteered little to Shelby, not wishing to violate Pawhuska's trust and endanger the Osage. He explained that Pawhuska was concerned that the Americans not blame the whole tribe for the hostility of a few renegades in the matter of Shelby's attack. Like Santiago Quinn, Micajah Johnstone was more sympathetic to the Indians than to the United States.

Over the following days Samuel's strength began to build with increasing rapidity. So did his reaction to Olivia. Living in such close proximity was even more hellish now than it had been back with the rivermen. Then he had seen her as merely a spoiled useless belle, bedraggled and ill-tempered. Now she had become a woman like no other he had ever known, competent and comfortable under the most primitive wilderness conditions, a beguiling temptress in beaded doeskins who warily kept her distance from him. Perversely, the more she did so, the more he desired her.

Although Olivia kept herself busy as possible trying not to think of Samuel or acknowledge his presence, living in close quarters with him was increasingly difficult for her, too. She watched his recovery with mixed emotions, telling herself she would be overjoyed to have him leave her in peace; yet she knew that when he departed her heart would be hollow.

One morning after breakfast Samuel stood up and stretched, flexing his left arm. The wound had not required bandaging for several days, much to his relief, and seemingly, Olivia's. "God, but I itch like a hibernating bear in the spring."

She could not resist saying, "You smell like one, too."

Micajah, sitting across the table from them, slapped his thigh and laughed. "If'n yew wuz still under th' weather, all feverish like, Sparky here'd still be givin yew baths from head ta—"

"I think the colonel can manage his own bathing from now on," she interrupted hastily, sliding back her chair and walking over to one of the parfleches hanging on the wall. Extracting a bar of homemade lye soap she tossed it to him. "Here, go wash in the creek. The day's warm enough and Micajah can help you walk that far."

Samuel caught the soap with his left hand easily, then grinned. "I can make it to the creek by myself." He turned to Micajah and asked, "Could I trouble you for that razor? I'd love to hack these boar bristles off my face while I'm at it. They've grown back pretty fast."

"Durn fool nuisance, shavin'. 'Course, if'n my mug wuz as purty 'neath these whiskers as yores, mebbe I'd take th' time." He fetched the razor and gave it to Shelby.

Stubborn man, Olivia thought. Samuel had refused Micajah's offer of help and sent the older man on his way to check his rabbit snares. He had slipped on a pair of moccasins that Johnstone had obtained at the Osage village and strolled casually out the door. She stood staring after him as he walked slowly across the meadow toward the small, swift-running tributary that fed into the larger Gasconade River. "It'd serve him right if he fell in and drowned," she muttered to herself, holding at bay images of his body, naked in the water, gleaming with every fluid movement.

She had seen him naked, of course, but that was when he was ill and unconscious. Then she had been so terrified that he was going to die of his feverish wounds that she had little time to consider the prurient pleasures of simply looking at his magnificent male body. Now she remembered, wickedly. As his recovery became more complete, she distanced herself from him more and more, spending time away from the cabin, helping Micajah with simple chores, unwilling to watch him regain his strength so he could leave.

"I have to get away and do something or I'll go crazy," she muttered to herself, picking up a woven reed basket. There were still a few apples left on the trees. A fresh apple pie would taste good with supper. She headed toward the woods along the banks of the Gasconade, downstream from the creek where Samuel would be bathing. Soon she had enough to fill her container. Just as she was about to turn back toward the cabin she heard the sound of splashing water and a male voice humming.

Samuel's voice. What was he doing down here on the big river? Setting down the fruit basket, she made her way quietly through the undergrowth to the clearing. There was a broad sandbar at the river's edge where Micajah beached his canoe. Samuel was standing waist-deep in the swift-running current, singing lustily now as he sudsed his body from his scalp down. She swallowed convulsively as her eyes riveted on the soap bubbles gliding across that muscular chest with its fascinating pelt of black hair. Then he ducked beneath the water.

For an insane instant she thought he was drowning and almost raced out to dive in after him, but he quickly resurfaced, shaking droplets of water from his head and shoulders like a great wet shaggy dog as he waded toward the shore. Olivia stood riveted behind the trunk of a cottonwood, peeking out at his emerging body. He had been so thin only a few weeks ago. How had he regained all that muscle so swiftly?

Samuel looked sleek and splendid in spite of his newly healing scars. Her eyes traveled from his chest, sweeping over his long powerful thighs and legs, then returned to that vital male center of him, always mysterious and magnetic, as if all the patterns of his body hair led to that same inevitable destination. Heat infused her body and it had nothing to do with the warm sunlight filtering through the trees. She stood frozen to the ground as he walked casually up to the overturned canoe, upon which he had laid a towel, a change of clothing and shaving gear. Briskly he rubbed himself down, then slipped on a pair of Micajah's buckskins. Like all the clothes he had borrowed from his host, they were too large but he solved the problem by rolling up the pant legs and cinching a belt at his narrow waist.

Samuel picked up the razor and soap and strolled casually over to the nearest tree. He had positioned a small polished steel mirror in a convenient fork. Working up a lather with his hands, he covered the prickly beard with thick suds, then picked up the razor and set to work, wondering idly if it had been Micajah or Olivia who had shaved him when he had been unconscious. *She'd probably have used the razor to slit my throat.* He smiled grimly and continued tugging the blade over his dense beard, glancing into the depth of the mirror as he worked.

Olivia's mouth had gone dry, the moisture fled to a lower part of her anatomy as she watched him. The low rasping scrape of cool steel against warm skin was incredibly erotic, quite different from the last time when he had lain so pale and still while Micajah shaved him. She could feel every pull of the blade right down to her toes, which curled unconsciously inside her soft moccasins.

I have to get out of here, leave . . . But she did not move, could not move. Then his voice, low and amused, cut through the chaotic jumble of her thoughts.

"Do you approve of what you've seen, Livy?" he asked conversationally as he wiped the last of the suds from his face with the towel, then slung it casually across one shoulder. He leaned against the tree trunk with his arms crossed negligently over his chest, staring directly into the thicket where she hid—or thought she hid.

"How did you know I was here?" The question asked itself before she could stop the flow of words.

Samuel grinned and looked back at the mirror. "Even with the poor reflection, that fiery color stood out. You'll never make a real woodsman as long as you go with that hair unbound. It showed through the dry brush like a flaming torch."

Olivia felt like a coward hiding behind the tree trunk but was loathe to face the cheeky devil who stood so arrogantly across the clearing. *Brazen it out, don't let him gloat.* She stepped into the open and walked closer . . . but not too close. "As to your first question. Yes, I do approve of what I've seen. You're recovering thanks to my medical skill. When we brought you home you were nothing but a rack of bones covered with a pretty beat up hide."

"So, you enjoyed what you saw," he said smugly.

She shrugged as negligently as she could, willing herself not to let her fair skin betray her with any more schoolgirl blushes. "I don't have much to compare you against. I never saw a naked man before." The cynical glint in his blue eyes at once gave away his disbelief. Her anger flared white-hot without warning. "You don't believe me, do you?" she added contemptuously, knowing full well the answer to her question. "What a fool you are to swallow Emory Wescott's lies."

As Olivia spun around to leave, his words echoed mockingly across the space between them. "Why did you follow me to the river if you're such an innocent?"

"I didn't. I was picking apples from my own trees when I heard your splashing. You weren't supposed to be anywhere near here. You were supposed to be in the creek. When you went underwater, I thought you were about to drown," she said, never breaking stride as she retraced her path through the trees and scooped up her basket of apples. Holding them on one hip she glared at him with narrowed eyes, hard as bottle glass. "Now I wish you *had* drowned."

Samuel almost ran after her, then thought better of it. The chit was nothing but trouble. Every time he was near her he lost control and did something completely, irrationally stupid. But she had saved his life, according to Micajah, who recounted the hours of ministrations she had performed while he lay in feverish helplessness. His behavior had been inexcusable. He vowed to apologize after she had cooled down.

The day passed before Olivia returned to the cabin. She was not avoiding Samuel, she was acting in Christian charity. If he spoke another word to her, she knew she'd take that English screw barrel pistol Micajah had given her and kill him. There was always plenty of work to do around the place. She walked to the bee tree down by the creek and garnered a small pot of honey, then checked the snares and found two fat rabbits which she killed and dressed for dinner. Finally when she knew she could procrastinate no longer, Olivia headed home laden down with the bounty of nature.

The ring of an ax echoed from behind the cabin. Micajah must be chopping more firewood. She went indoors and deposited the honey and meat on the table, then stepped over to the window to call out a greeting to her friend. But it was not Micajah who wielded the ax. Samuel raised the heavy handle and swung it in a downward arc with rhythmic ease, setting up and splitting the pile of logs at his feet one by one. He wore no shirt and his back gleamed with sweat as his muscles bunched and flexed with every blow. In the late afternoon sunlight his skin looked as dark as an Osage's and his long shaggy hair gleamed like a raven's wing.

Lest he again catch her spying and accuse her of lascivious thoughts, she quickly withdrew from the window and set to work fixing supper. Where in tarnation was Micajah anyway? It seemed that he was spending an inordinate amount of time away from the cabin the past few days, almost as if he wanted her to be left alone with Samuel. But that was absurd. Whatever for? She had already made it quite clear that Shelby would never marry her—not that she wanted him either, the arrogant misogynist.

Just then her ruminations were cut short when the cause of her frustration walked into the cabin, his arms laden with wood. He had donned his shirt which clung damply to his body and hung open, revealing more chest hair than was at all proper. Far be it from her to comment and receive another of those smirking looks from him again!

Samuel watched her paring potatoes with small, incredibly soft hands. He had learned from Micajah that she treated them with mink oil each night to keep the heavy chores from reddening her sensitive skin. He cleared his throat after depositing the wood on the hearth. "There is something between us, Olivia, that seems to bring out the worst in me. I apologize for my behavior this morning."

She plopped the last potato in the cookpot and started to lift it toward the fire. He gently took it from her and slid it in place on the iron rod, then turned back to her.

"Why do you always assume the worst about me?"

He shrugged uncomfortably. "You aren't exactly a conventional female, Olivia. By your own admission you spent your childhood in Europe's capitals, either living the high life or fleeing your father's gambling debts in the dead of night. As an adult you've dressed in boy's clothes to race horses at rough frontier tracks and flirted with bevies of drooling men in elegant ballrooms. Forgive me for sounding arrogant, but you did seem to pursue me that night at Chouteau's. Was I to fall in line with all the other men panting after you? Was that Wescott's plan?"

"When will you get it through your thick head that Emory Wescott never informed me of his plans," she replied coldly. "I overheard them for myself—and your reply to them. My uncle knew you were married. I did not, more the fool I."

"Yes, I was married," he echoed bitterly.

"And you never intend to be again. You made that perfectly clear."

"Tish was the perfect southern belle, when surrounded by suitors. She was meek and charming, everything I thought a wife should be."

She could see the incredible bleakness darkening his eyes. "But you were wrong and she hurt you. When you were feverish, you talked about her," she said softly. "But is it fair to blame all women because of Tish's betrayal?"

"It wasn't only my wife," he replied tightly, not wanting to discuss this, uncomfortable with the empathy in her eyes, the softness in her smile.

"It seems you've spent your life dallying with the wrong sort of women. Perhaps because of the places a man like you frequents?" She could sense his withdrawal and wanted to share his pain. "What other women betrayed you?" she prodded gently.

"My mother," he said flatly. "She was a self-centered, calculating French aristocrat. As wily as her sometime lover Prince Tallyrand. To date, she's survived the rise and fall of three governments. When I was thirteen, she took my sister and sailed away from Virginia back to the gaiety of Paris, leaving me and my father behind. He died of a broken heart. Mine mended. Or maybe it just shriveled up until I quit missing it . . . and her." He grinned but the smile was without warmth. "By that time I'd discovered a whole new use for women. I didn't need a mother anymore."

"Or a heart? I'm not so sure that little boy isn't still locked inside you . . . still searching for love." So much about him made sense now, the glib charm, the evasive answers, the hard-edged antagonism. At his cynical look she amended, "Well, perhaps not motherly love . . ."

"I'm not looking for any kind of love, Olivia. I took the plunge once, married a proper girl from a good family and settled down to have children—or so I thought. I was a fool."

"You've been hurt and disillusioned, but that doesn't make you a fool, Samuel," she argued, drawing nearer, longing to hold him in her arms and comfort him. She could see by the rigid way he stood with his fists clenched at his sides that he was struggling to hold onto the black anger, the bitter pain from his past. "It doesn't mean you can't trust another woman."

He looked down at the earnest expression on her face, aching to drown himself in her sweet allure, to accept the marvelous oblivion of her silken flesh. But she was Emory Wescott's ward, perhaps his victim, perhaps his accomplice. He smiled but not with his eyes. "I'm afraid I'm a rotten judge of women. I've always been attracted to the sort who draw blood."

The implication was as unmistakable as the rejection. The pain slammed into her heart with a sudden rush. Instinctively she raised her hand and slapped him hard, then spun around and ran from the cabin. Her parting words, "Yes, you are a rotten judge of women," seemed to hang suspended on a choked sob in the empty room.

Samuel debated going after her but knew it was no use. He had spent the entire time he'd known the infuriating woman alternately insulting her and then apologizing to her. They were just no good for each other—even if she was what she claimed to be. And his years as a spy made him highly suspicious of that.

Skimming along the periphery of his consciousness was a nagging accusation—as long as he held firmly to the belief that she was in league with her guardian, he had a secure wall erected to protect himself from the maddening attraction to her which had plagued him since the first time he laid eyes on her.

Shaking his head, he looked about for something to occupy his mind until Micajah returned. Then he spied the woodsman's rifle standing in the corner. Perhaps it could use a good cleaning.

Outside Olivia ran, heedless of where she was headed. Tears blurred her vision and she swiped at them with the back of her hands as she stumbled through the woods near the cabin. When she heard the low burbling sound of the creek, she sank down onto the ground and crumpled over. The tears fell silently, bitterly. She wrapped her arms around herself and rocked back and forth, unable to bear the desolate realization.

I'm still in love with him. I always will be.

Finally, her tears subsided enough for her to blink them back and compose herself. Micajah would be home expecting supper and here she was sitting out in the sand, blubbering like a fool schoolgirl. Just as she started to rise a low feral growl emanated from down by the side of the creek.

Olivia looked into the glazed eyes of a coyote standing with its legs rigidly braced, its fangs bared in a snarl. Normally coyotes were timid animals who hunted by night and avoided any contact with humans. But this one was out in broad daylight, openly challenging her. Something was definitely wrong. Then she saw the saliva dripping in long strings from its open mouth, foaming down over its chest. Micajah had described what a rabid animal looked and acted like. Frantically she glanced around her for a weapon but nothing larger than a twig was in sight.

Samuel had just finished reloading and priming the rifle when he heard Olivia's scream. Reacting to the sheer terror in her cry, he seized the weapon and raced toward the creek. He saw her first, crouched on an open sandy stretch of the bank, staring with fixed intensity into the shadows a dozen feet away. The coyote growled again, more like a gurgling moan, as it stepped forward, stiff legged. Samuel's blood froze.

"Don't move a muscle," he commanded. His voice was breathless and ragged as he slowly raised the rifle and aimed, praying. Only one chance. If he missed . . . it did not bear thinking on.

Samuel squeezed the trigger gently and a loud report echoed across the clearing. Smoke stung his eyes. He charged through the cloud as he quickly reversed his hold on the rifle, preparing to use the stock as a cudgel to bludgeon the dangerous beast if his shot had missed its mark. It had not. The coyote had been flung backward against a hollow log where it lay stone still as blood gushed from its chest.

Carefully he walked over to it, the rifle stock still raised. Then he lowered it and used it to prod the carcass, making certain it was dead. Once assured, he dropped the gun and rushed to where Olivia still knelt. Without a word he enfolded her in his arms and held onto her for dear life.

Olivia felt the solid, life-affirming warmth of his big hard body when he pulled her to him. Of their own volition her arms came up, wrapping around his neck as she pulled him closer, wanting nothing more than to melt into the cocooning safety of his embrace.

He repeated her name over and over, murmuring soft love words mixed with curses, almost indistinguishable as he buried his face in her long glorious hair. His hands traced the soft curve of her spine, then cupped her buttocks, lifting her tighter against him. *If you had been killed . . . If I had lost you . . .* He did not know if he spoke the words aloud or not, for he was drugged by the euphoria of her warmth, her life, the way she clung to him.

She could not make out the words, but her body understood the urgency of his as they caressed each other. When his hands left her hair and glided down to pull her against him, she tipped her head up and looked into his eyes. They were dark, stormy blue, burning with an intensity that lit an answering spark in her. She felt it leap between them as she raised her mouth and he lowered his. What happened next was inevitable.

His lips claimed hers with a slowly building desperation, tentative and gentle at first brush, as if waiting to sense her answering hunger. The instant her lips parted and he felt the soft heat of her mouth, the sweet tingle of her tongue tasting hesitantly of him, he was lost. He savaged her with his kiss, plunging his own tongue inside her mouth with a low possessive growl.

She was afire, enveloped in living flame, so near death, now never more alive. And life was Samuel. Her nails dug into the muscle of his shoulders, then her hands swept up to his shaggy mane of hair and her fingers tangled in it, pulling him nearer as the kiss grew in white-hot intensity.

They sank from their knees to the soft sandy earth, lost to everything around them, both murmuring indistinctly, speaking in the age-old language of lovers everywhere. She felt his hands on her breasts, cupping them from the sides, then gliding inside the soft tunic to touch the aching tips, hard and burning with need. Cool evening air brushed her upper body as he tugged the lacings of the tunic free but then his warmth replaced it as he lowered himself on top of her, pressing her to the ground.

Olivia longed to feel the abrasion of his crisply furred chest against her bare breasts. Her hands clawed at his partially buttoned shirt, easily stripping it away from his shoulders as he raised his head to look down at her beautiful lithe body, spread open before him, inviting him, waiting for him to take her. Her nails raked through the hair of his chest, then her hands slid around to his back, pulling him down to her once more.

Samuel kissed her throat, feeling the pulse beat wildly, then lowered his head to taste the sweet fruits of her delicate pink nipples. When she moaned and arched up with the sudden new surge of pleasure, he could wait no longer. One hand swept down the subtle curve of her hip and over her thigh to push up the barrier of the fringed skirt.

Before he could complete his task the sharp click of a rifle hammer being pulled back intruded, followed by Micajah Johnstone's voice, low and almost congenial, saying, "I reckon yew kin save thet part till after th' weddin', Shelby. Now, jist git up real slow and straighten yer britches as best as possible."

Olivia felt the icy cold dash of humiliation, exacerbated by the sudden removal of Samuel's body heat as he rolled off her. Cool air touched her breasts—thighs. At once shamed and mortified she struggled to pull down her tunic and close the gaping front of the garment so her breasts were covered. Clutching the tunic front closed, she struggled to her knees before Micajah's words finally registered. *Wedding!*

Samuel shrugged his shirt back on his shoulders but there was little he could do about the obvious bulge in his tight buckskins until nature took its course, which it did with sudden impact when Johnstone's pronouncement struck him. *Wedding!*

Both young people mouthed the word in horrified unison, then glanced from Micajah back to each other, staring at the incriminating flushed dishabille of their situation. Samuel was the first to gather his thoughts enough to speak coherently, looking quickly away from Olivia back at Micajah.

"Look, Johnstone. Nothing happened. We were just overcome by the danger of the moment. She could've died horribly," he said, gesturing to where the dead coyote lay. "But luckily for us, you came along to return us to our senses before things got out of hand. There's no need for me to make an honest woman of her. Her virtue didn't suffer at my hands."

Olivia sat huddled in misery, unable to meet Micajah's eyes, fumbling to relace her tunic so that she was decently covered while Samuel spoke. *Her virtue didn't suffer at my hands.* But he believed it had suffered somewhere else before, no doubt about that! How could she have been so blindly stupid as to fall into his arms yet again? He would never love her, didn't think she was good enough to be his wife. He desired her—and hated himself for the weakness.

But he could never feel half so disgraced or foolish as she did for sharing that weakness. Her excuse might be better, for she did love him, but that changed nothing.

"There won't be any need for you to dishonor the vaunted Shelby name by bestowing it on me," she said scathingly. Forcing her eyes to meet his, she held her chin high and stood up on rubbery legs. Olivia St. Etienne knelt before no man. "The blood of the French nobility flows in my veins and although you've made it abundantly clear how much you despise it, I take pride in my heritage. I would not wed with you if my life depended on it."

"Hit 'pears ta me thet neither one o' yew younguns is payin' much mind ta th' plain facts," Micajah said patiently, still holding his rifle leveled at Shelby's chest. "Now *yore* life might not depend on marryin' him, Sparky, but I kin promise thet his does depend on his marryin' yew. I seen whut I seen and hit ain't comin' 'round no other way."

There was sufficient steel in his tone of voice to make both of them realize the gravity of the situation. Micajah Johnstone was formidable and he was pig stubborn and he was holding the only loaded rifle.

Samuel looked at him in blatant amazement. "Is this some sort of trap you've cooked up between you? Because if it is—"

"Why, certainly," Olivia cut in sharply, "we planned and rehearsed the whole thing with that charming coyote. I even infected him with the rabies!"

Samuel made a sardonic sweep of her with eyebrows raised. "Now *that* I *would* believe."

"I despise you. Whatever makes you think I'd plot to lure you into marriage? No, don't answer, I already know. Your overweening male arrogance!"

She started to flounce away but Micajah's voice stopped her. "I ain't funnin' with this, Sparky. Yew warn't 'xactly fightin' Shelby here off. Yew both know what would've happened if'n I hadn't come along."

Her cheeks blazed crimson. She held Micajah Johnstone's good opinion in higher esteem than anyone else's on earth, and she had shamed him, the man who had taken her in, treated her like his own daughter, taught her everything she knew to restore her sense of self-worth. In return she had betrayed his trust in her.

Micajah could see his stern voice was having the desired

effect on Sparky. As for the mule-headed soldier boy, well the rifle would work well enough for now. "Sparky, fetch me a rope from the smoke shed."

"You're not going to tie him up?" she choked, horrified at the picture of Colonel Samuel Shelby delivered before a priest bound hand and foot.

Johnstone shrugged his massive shoulders like the great bear for which the Osage had named him. "Don't make me no never mind. I kin always cudgel him a good smack ta thet hard head o' his'n. Either way, we's all headin' ta an old French mission a couply days north. They got them a priest there. Ole Father Louie'll marry yew onc't I tell him th' way thangs are."

Early the following morning they set out for the small mission outpost on the Missouri. Olivia St. Etienne sat in the prow of the canoe, back ramrod stiff, eyes staring straight ahead like a French aristocrat on her way to the guillotine. The colonel lay in the bottom of the craft trussed hand and foot, body rigid, a silently furious "cargo."

Johnstone chuckled to himself. He had accomplished what he set out to do without having to fire a shot or wait half as long as a patient man such as he had been prepared to do. When Samuel had rushed out to rescue Olivia from the coyote, Micajah had already seen the menace since he had been going out into the woods to observe the two of them, hoping to catch them in precisely the compromising position he had. His rifle had been sighted on the rabid animal ready to fire if Shelby's shot had missed its mark.

No, sir, he hadn't had to fire a shot. He was pleased as a possum inside a pig carcass.

Chapter 16

Emory Wescott sat in his dining room, a Spode demitasse cup paused at his mouth, inhaling the delicate fragrance of the specially blended French coffee he had brought upriver from New Orleans—among other items. It was those other items, fifty barrels of rotgut whiskey and twenty cases of old Brown Bess muskets, that had caused him some loss of sleep the past nights. That accursed shipment was delayed. Again. It seemed every enterprise he undertook in recent months had turned sour.

Wescott had made a tidy profit as a smuggler during Jefferson's embargo the past decade, and in so doing had cemented excellent contacts in the highest circles of British industry. But during Madison's administration the international economy had gone into a slump. To further add to his woes, he had made a series of bad investments and only this dangerous dealing with Stuart Pardee on the frontier stood between him and the wolf that was beginning to sniff at his door. At least such was true until war broke out, which was bound to occur within the next six months if not sooner.

The way Wescott saw it, allying himself with the British in the conflict was his hedge against the future. Whether the English army could invade New Orleans and march all the way up the Mississippi Valley to unite with British forces in Canada was problematic. If such could be accomplished, excellent, but even if the British failed to take the big river, they would certainly defeat the puny American forces on the Gulf and hold the key port city of New Orleans, thus placing a stranglehold on America's western commerce. Then men of vision like him would become the arbiters of trade and he would grow rich as Croesus.

But that eventuality might take several years. In the meanwhile, he was alarmingly short of cash and in need of proving his good faith to his British allies, namely Stuart Pardee, the distasteful lummox. Where were those damned guns and whiskey for Pardee's savages?

As he sat drumming his fingers impatiently on the polished mahogany surface of the table, the butler entered with a missive. Bowing perfunctorily, the dignified black man handed it to his master, then stood quietly as it was read, waiting to see if a reply would need to be delivered.

A slow smile splayed across Wescott's jowly countenance. He had sent word to his agents in New Orleans, hoping to locate his runaway ward through the uncle who had disowned her scapegrace family. This was interesting news from that quarter, indeed.

The troublesome chit had vanished without a trace, leaving him with the unpleasant prospect of facing Samuel Shelby upon his return to St. Louis, but Shelby had not to date come back. Perhaps he had perished in the wilderness at the hands of savages—or Pardee. But no, Pardee had agreed it would be better to keep Shelby alive and use Olivia as a conduit for information about American plans on the frontier. He had, in fact, sent word to the Englishman regarding his ward's most untimely disappearance and offered a handsome reward for her return. Once war broke out, Olivia would be especially valuable to both of them.

Now it appeared she was even more valuable than Wescott had ever imagined. He skimmed the message again, then dismissed the butler and sat back to consider his next move. Charles Durand, the not so dearly beloved uncle in New Orleans, was dead without any direct heirs. His only existing blood kin was his sister's child, Olivia Patrice St. Etienne.

Charles Durand had been a fantastically wealthy man. He had, it seemed, somehow managed to abscond from France with a sizable portion of the Bourbon family's personal wealth and set himself up in exile, living the high life in the Creole backwater of New Orleans, awaiting the overthrow of that upstart Napoleon and the restoration of the rightful Bourbon monarchy. In the meanwhile, he had invested the wealth and multiplied it several times over.

"A pity he didn't live to see his dreams come true," Wescott said mockingly to himself.

Now the fortune was Olivia's. And he, as her legal guardian, meant to have it. The first matter at hand was to locate the girl, no mean feat since she had obviously not gone to her uncle. If she had not headed south on the river, she must for some reason have headed in the opposite direction. In anticipation of that, he had dispatched agents to check the few settlements on the Missouri and upper Mississippi for a boy matching Ollie's description, as well as notifying Pardee. Sooner or later someone would run her to ground. Stuart Pardee would not act so high and mighty around Emory Wescott once he had the Durand fortune within his grasp.

He stood up and headed to his library. It was time to send another inquiry upriver regarding Olivia's whereabouts. Since he had a vested interest in her return, perhaps Pardee had already located the chit. No need to tell the Englishman their plan had now been altered.

Stuart Pardee sat outside the Ste. Francoise trading post surveying the sunset. Small and rude as the little mission stockade was, it afforded some few amenities of civilization. Founded by French Jesuits in the last century, the post was austere and small, but at least he had slept for a few nights on a bed with a roof over his head, albeit the bed was a narrow corn husk mattress and the roof a crude log shelter.

He was heartily sick of smoky Indian lodges, greasy stews made of wild game and pot puppies and the everlasting quest to keep his majesty's childlike, undisciplined allies loyal, such loyalty being purchased with old muskets and new whiskey. Since Ste. Francoise was on the river, mail boats arrived at odd intervals, keeping him in touch with Wescott in St. Louis. He detested having to report his failure to locate that fire-haired ward of Wescott's, but he was beginning to doubt that she had ever come upriver unless she was with one of the trading parties enroute to the headwaters of the Missouri, a most unlikely event which would place her well outside his reach, anyway.

What he really needed now was not that damned woman, but the latest shipment of guns and whiskey from Wescott. As usual the bastard was behind schedule. He leaned back against the rough log wall and peered out the open gate of the post to the river flowing by several hundred yards away. A canoe banked and three figures emerged. He looked away. Just more voyageurs coming from upriver, probably carrying a load of pelts to sell in St. Louis. Perhaps they had seen or heard something about a red-haired woman on the upper Missouri.

Pardee decided to question them, but just as he stood up he noticed that one of the three was walking ahead of the other two and his wrists were bound behind him. Something was nigglingly familiar about the tall black-haired man who walked with such arrogant confidence in spite of being a prisoner.

Shelby!

His eyes narrowed as he studied the colonel's companions, a great grizzled mountain of a man who looked as if he had not seen civilization since the colonial revolt and a slight figure partially obscured by the two tall men. Then he caught a flash of flaming red hair glinting in the setting sunlight. A slow smile spread across his wide mouth. Two problems solved at once. He slipped into the shadows between the trading post and the small log cabin which served as a crude rectory for Father Louie.

"Ain't no use yer tryin' ta talk me outta this," Micajah said doggedly as they walked through the gate of the post.

"I'm only telling you the priest won't marry two people at gunpoint. It wouldn't be considered a valid marriage even if he did," Samuel said with equal tenacity.

"It would be no true sacrament, Micajah," Olivia added in a subdued tone of voice.

"Where I come from, once't a preacher says th' words over yew, yore hitched. Don't make me no never mind 'bout sac'rements er sech." He stopped as they neared the little church and fixed Shelby with shrewd brown eyes. "Yew really want ta walk in there all trussed up like a Christmas goose—er will yew give me yore word ta act like a man?"

The barb struck home. Shelby felt the sting of heat on his face. He had been badgering Johnstone continuously for the past two days, rather like a schoolboy caught in an infraction, trying to wriggle out of it. According to the old mountain man's simple code of morality, he was guilty of a grievous sin and Micajah meant to see justice done. Sighing, Shelby replied, "I'll tell the truth to the priest. You don't have to drag me before him."

"Good 'nough." Micajah nodded and slipped the long hunting knife from his belt to cut Samuel's bonds.

Olivia stood silently through their exchange. Still chastened and humiliated by her foolish passion which had precipitated this whole debacle, she had said little during the journey to Ste. Francoise. She could not bear the idea of marrying Samuel when he believed her to be nothing more than a scheming harlot, but neither could she bear to see Micajah's pain and disillusionment if she flatly refused to do what his honor demanded.

Samuel rubbed his chaffed wrists and looked from Johnstone to the quiet woman. Olivia stood staring at the bright molten ball of orange dipping below the uneven spikes of the post's fence. The sun's dying rays turned her hair to living flame and limned her proud patrician profile in gold. She was so beautiful she fair robbed him of breath. And possibly she was just as treacherous.

"Let's talk to your priest, Johnstone," he said grimly.

Father Louie was a slight dark-haired man with a hooked nose and shrewd black eyes. His face was swarthy, burned by the sun and seamed by wind. Deep grooves around his mouth gave the appearance of harshness until he smiled.

"*Bon soir,* Monsieur Johnstone. To what do I owe the pleasure of this visit? Perhaps you are interested in taking instruction and being baptized at last, *mon ami*?" The merry glint in his eyes belied that he seriously believed such to be the case.

"You preachers jist never give up," Micajah said with a grin as he reached out to envelope the diminutive man's hand in his huge one. "Nope, I come on serious bidness though. Hit's about these two tomfool young'uns." He motioned to Samuel and Olivia. "They need ta git hitched."

Father Louie looked at the handsome couple standing well apart from each other. They scarcely looked like lovebirds. In fact they seemed to be rather antagonistic at the moment, casting each other furtive, angry glances.

"This here's Sparky, er, Mam'sel Olivia St. Et-tane," he said, stumbling over her full French name as he shoved her forward to meet the priest. "She's my 'dopted daughter. 'N this big buck is Samuel Shelby, an American soldier boy. A colonel he is, tho'sorty out o' uniform fer the time bein'."

"Charmed, Mademoiselle St. Etienne," the priest said graciously. "I did not know this old rogue had such a lovely daughter in his charge." He turned to Samuel. "Colonel Shelby. We do not get many Americans here save for an occasional trapper, but then if you wish a marriage performed, I shall be most happy to oblige."

"Our wishes on the matter need to be discussed," Samuel said in a measured voice.

"How so?" Father Louie inquired as Micajah growled a low warning.

"The lady and I don't want to get married. We aren't at all suited to each other."

"Cudda fooled me when I seen yew rasslin' 'round on th' ground like a pair o' bobcats in heat. Yew fit together right well then," Micajah interjected sourly.

Father Louie's expression became grave as he turned back to Samuel. "Is what he says true, my son?"

"No—well, yes," he admitted grudgingly. "But we didn't intend to let it get out of hand," he amended lamely. "Anyway, he interrupted us before the act was consummated." Samuel felt his face breaking out in a cold sweat.

"What he says is true. Micajah saved me from committing a terrible folly," Olivia added, staring at the priest, giving no more than a scathing glance to Samuel.

Father Louie stroked his chin consideringly, looking from the murderously intent expression on Micajah's face to the nervously squirming young people. "And if Micajah had not so fortunately come along to insist on the proprieties, would you then have stopped before the act was consummated?" His shrewd black eyes moved between Olivia and Samuel. She blushed and looked away, shaking her head.

Shelby muttered an oath beneath his breath and returned the priest's stare. After a moment he sighed dejectedly and admitted, "No, I wouldn't have."

"I see," Father Louie replied consideringly. "You do know that God considers intent in sin almost as serious as the act itself?"

Was there the slightest bit of irony in those last three words?

"The point is that in fact I did not compromise Mademoiselle St. Etienne," Samuel said tenaciously, refusing to be drawn into a theological debate.

"The point is I wouldn't marry you even if you had!" Olivia replied furiously.

"How long have you known Colonel Shelby, child?" Father Louie asked gently. A woman of her obvious education and breeding scarcely seemed the sort to succumb to a handsome stranger's casual blandishments.

There was something about the priest that made it impossible for her to withhold the truth from him. "We met in Washington last winter. Then again when he came to St. Louis in the spring."

"So, you have been, er, acquainted for nearly a year and"—he turned suddenly to Samuel—"you followed the lady from the East Coast all the way across the Mississippi?"

What could he say without revealing his mission in the region? Damn and damn again! "Not precisely. I was posted to the Cantonment at Fort Bellefontaine outside St. Louis, but I did expect to meet her again while I was in the city." He, too, found it impossible to lie with those fathomless dark eyes on him.

"Th' two damnfool young'uns 's too stubborn ta admit they got feelin's fer each other—but when th' chance comes, they ain't too stubborn ta act on 'em," Micajah averred triumphantly.

"I cannot perform a marriage if you refuse, of course, but it would seem there are a great many reasons for you to agree. To what do you object?" he asked Olivia.

"To him!" she said, glaring at Samuel. "He thinks I'm—" She broke off, unable to repeat the hateful innuendoes.

"And you, my son?" the priest asked when Olivia was unable to go on. "A man who does what you have done has the moral obligation to put it right, especially considering the duration of the relationship." He waited, patiently studying the unhappy young soldier while at the same time catching Micajah's nod of approval from the corner of his eye.

Father Louie had been friends with the frontiersman for nearly twenty years, and he knew Micajah to be nobody's fool. If Johnstone believed these young people to be in love and suited for each other, that was good enough for him.

Samuel struggled with his conscience. The very last thing on earth he wanted was another wife, especially one who might be involved in British espionage. But Micajah and Olivia had saved his life—she had in fact saved it twice. He owed them both a debt of honor on that count and he had behaved badly toward the woman, regardless of her provocation. Protecting her reputation would make Johnstone happy and he could offer Olivia a comfortable settlement to live on once he became established in the Santa Fe trade with Santiago. She would have her freedom from Wescott—if she truly wanted it—and he would not need to be encumbered with a second wife . . . or so he told himself.

"I have no further objections. I'll marry her," he replied stoically.

Olivia's head jerked up and she stared at him in stunned amazement. "Well, I won't marry you."

"You're behaving childishly, Olivia. Consider the alternatives," he said, looking from the grave priest to the scowling Johnstone.

Of all the ways she had imagined her wedding day, this was certainly not one! This was a nightmare. But one from which she would not simply awaken. *He plans to annul the marriage,* she realized at once. Well, why not? She could certainly prove her virginity if it came to an examination! He would never learn the truth about her until it was too late . . . or so she told herself.

Without warning the pain clawed at her heart and a giant lump formed in her throat, making it difficult for her to say, "Very well. I will marry you, Colonel."

They recited their vows in the small rude chapel made of mud-chinked logs. Neither of them could have said what went on during the ceremony as they walked through the motions, but soon Micajah was slapping Samuel on the back and hugging Olivia joyously.

"Father Louie here says they's an empty cabin jest across th' post, where th' manager o' th' mercantile 'n his wife lived till he up 'n quit last month. Traders in St. Louis ain't sent anyone to replace 'em yet, so yew kin use hit fer to-night."

"Where will you sleep, Micajah?" Olivia asked, refusing to consider how she and her new husband would make their sleeping arrangements in a small trader's cabin.

"Shucks, I kin bunk with th' good father here. I ain't fixin' ta waste any more time watchin' out fer th' two of yew. Don't need ta no more." He winked at Samuel and then patted Olivia's hand gently. "Tamorah we'll say our good-byes 'n plan fer our next rendezvous. I 'spect ta be bouncin' a grandbaby on my knee afore th' snow flies next year."

She nodded and forced a smile to her lips. How could she bear to hurt him with the truth? When he and the priest bade them good night in front of the small cabin, she turned to Samuel, not knowing what to say.

Samuel. Her husband.

In name only, she reminded herself. There would be no grandbabies for Micajah, no love for her. She would not humiliate herself further by crying. Her "husband" was not worth her tears. "Well, do you have a coin to flip? Heads I get the bed, tails you do."

He looked down at her with an unreadable expression on his face. "You do understand we can reach an agreement.

When I'm able to return to St. Louis I'll make arrangements for your support. Although I'm not a wealthy man, I'll have a comfortable living from my investment in my brother-in-law's trading company."

She was taken aback by his words which seemed to imply that he did not intend to end the sham marriage. "I don't want your money, Samuel, living as your wife *or* your mistress." She turned and walked through the open door into the cabin.

Father Louie had asked one of the clerks from the mercantile to prepare the place. A lone candle burned on the table in the center of the room and a cheerful fire crackled its welcome from the hearth. In the far corner, a modest-sized double bed had been made up with a patchwork quilt and the covers turned back. Suddenly the room seemed suffocatingly intimate. Her breath caught and she turned to face him, unable to stop herself from saying in a breathless rush, "Just have the marriage annulled and leave me in peace."

Her angry denunciation startled him. "Why? I have no plans to ever marry again. We can live separately without any problems. My military career and my future business will keep me away from St. Louis most of the year. I'll secure you a house of your own."

How cold-blooded he sounded, patiently explaining a soulless, loveless arrangement to her while her heart shattered in a million shards. "I want the marriage annulled," she gritted out.

He had been trying to be patient under such difficult circumstances, but her anger fanned the spark of his temper. "Might that not prove a bit awkward? To get an annulment you would have to prove the marriage had never been consummated."

"Well, it sure as hell won't be consummated!" she snapped before the implication of his remark sunk in. When it did, her hands curved into claws as she took a step toward him, itching to slap the insulting look of cynical disgust from his face.

"I wouldn't try it," he purred softly.

Suddenly an overwhelming rush of tears threatened to engulf her. Olivia turned away quickly lest he see the incriminating evidence of her stupidity. How could she have fallen in love with such a black-hearted, mule-headed, cold-blooded . . . "Leave me alone," she said hoarsely, praying her composure did not crack.

As soon as he had made the cruel insinuation, Samuel had regretted it. Their situation was unpleasant enough without making a mortal enemy of her. They would have to learn to deal civilly together, at least until they got back to St. Louis. Making her killingly angry and ready to fly at him was stupid for a man who had always prided himself on his coolness in adverse situations. Why was it that he had lost his temper more times in the scant year he'd know Olivia St. Etienne than he had in all the rest of his life?

"Look, we've been through a lot the past few days," he said placatingly. "Get yourself ready for sleep—you take the bed. I'll take the settee. While you're doing that I'll go over to Father Louie's kitchen and bring back that wedding supper his cook has supposedly prepared for us."

"Fine," she replied, looking dubiously at the rickety little settee by the front window, which surely could not accommodate a man of Samuel's size. When she heard the door close, she turned around, almost as if she were hungry to capture his lingering scent on the chill evening air. "I really *am* a fool."

She walked over to where her possibles sack lay on the table and opened the heavy leather pouch, rummaging until she found the simple cotton nightrail she had sewn from a bolt of cloth Micajah had taken in trade. The fabric was yellowed with age but soft and comfortable. She held up the long-sleeved, high-necked sleepwear and wrinkled her nose. Hardly the sort of gown she had imagined wearing on her wedding night, but then this was hardly the sort of wedding night any woman envisioned.

Going through with the ceremony had been a mistake. She could see that now. She should have refused flatly, would have if she had ever imagined the way Samuel would react once they were alone. "It's all over and done with now," she murmured, slipping off her buckskin tunic and moccasins, then reaching for the gown. She had just slipped it over her head when a light rapping sounded on the door. Surely not Samuel back so soon.

Olivia opened the heavy door, only to be knocked backward into the room and seized by a tall rawboned man in greasy buckskins. He kicked the door closed with his foot while holding onto her with both hands.

"Make one little peep, my dear, and it will be your last," he said as his eyes quickly scanned the room. "I can snap that pretty neck before you get out a scream."

"Stuart Pardee! What on earth do you think you're doing?" she gasped, but she knew he had ogled her from a distance on numerous occasions and she suspected that he was involved in some mysterious business dealings with Emory Wescott. Every instinct told her that her guardian had sent him to recapture her!

"Looks like you're getting ready for your wedding night with Shelby," he said, ignoring her question. "Too bad I have to interrupt the festivities." His eyes swept over her body, swathed in the voluminous white cotton. One big bony hand held her slender throat lightly but menacingly while the other glided across the curve of her hip and over her belly, then moved upward to fondle a breast.

Olivia bit her lip, trying not to flinch. If she could only stall him for a few minutes, Samuel might return. "There won't be a wedding night, Pardee," she said quietly.

His free hand stopped. "That so."

She could smell the feral lust oozing from him. He reeked of whiskey and old greasy buckskins that he must have slept in for weeks. "Samuel and I had a fight. I was just . . . retiring for the night," she added suggestively, glimpsing the long shiny knife on his belt. If he released her neck for a fraction of a second, she could slide it free and slash him. Micajah had taught her the rudiments of self-defense.

"Well now . . ." he said in a low growl, "most peculiar that you never would look at me before when I saw you with Wescott." His free hand reached up and pulled the tie at her neck open, then slid the gown down, baring one creamy shoulder.

Olivia leaned into him, letting her breasts bunch against his chest. She could feel his body go rigid and his breathing quicken. *Now!*

Just as she slipped her hand upward toward the knife, the door opened. Samuel stood frozen in the sash, incredulously taking in his half-naked wife in an embrace with the ruffian from the racetrack. "First you try to break her neck, now you're sampling her feminine charms. We seem to have something in common, my friend," he said with false geniality as he stepped inside the door, still holding their covered tray of food.

"Samuel, this is Stuart Pardee. He works for Emory Wescott."

"Pardee," Shelby purred, at once remembering the name Man Whipper had used. A slow, chilling smile moved across his face. "So at last I'm privileged to meet the Englishman, although I'd expected it to be under slightly different circumstances. Get your hands off my wife."

"And if I do not?" Pardee said with a taunt in his voice, still holding Olivia's neck in his big hand.

"I'll beat you to death with my bare hands for touching her," he replied in a conversational tone belied by the icy look in his eyes.

"You're amazingly difficult to kill. Man Whipper was one of my most trusted allies among the Osage. A pity about him," Pardee said with negligent regret. "Bad Temper reported that you survived the gauntlet and then killed his companion and eluded the war party. Quite a resourceful feat. I expect you would prove a worthy adversary." His grip on Olivia's neck tightened fractionally. "I am inclined to linger and test your mettle, but I really must be on my way. So sorry to disrupt your wedding night but . . ." He slid the pistol from his belt and raised it intending to fire point-blank at Samuel. Olivia used that instant of inattention to break free of his choke hold and smash her fist into his gun arm, deflecting the shot, which discharged into the roof.

As soon as she moved, so did Samuel. He flung the tray he was holding into Pardee's face, then lunged for him as Olivia jumped out of the way. The gun was knocked to the floor, spent.

The two men went down on the floor rolling and punching. "Samuel, he has a knife!" she shrieked as Pardee slid it from its sheath and scrambled to his feet, grinning evilly. Shelby rose too, keeping just out of reach of the blade as he circled Pardee. Olivia frantically looked around the room, searching for another weapon. Inside her possibles sack she had a primed pistol, but that was in the opposite corner. Plastering herself to the wall she started edging slowly around.

Before she got more than a few feet, Pardee lunged, slicing Samuel's forearm lightly as Shelby deflected the blade. Seizing Pardee's knife arm with both hands, Shelby twisted it upward while at the same time he used his right leg to sweep behind the Englishman's left knee. Again they went down onto the floor but this time Samuel came up on top.

Pardee had lost his blade when he had been slammed to the ground. The knife slid across the floor, stopping near Olivia's feet. She reached out and scooped it up but saw no way to use it without risking Samuel. The two men were on their feet again, circling each other in fast arching movements, punching and retreating, knocking aside the chairs, overturning the table. They moved with blurring erratic speed, each searching for an advantage.

"You are good, Colonel, but a bloody damned inconvenience. And I am a man who dislikes being inconvenienced," Pardee said as one long arm snaked out, punching with lightning rapidity.

Olivia winced at the sickening sound of bone smashing into bone. Samuel staggered back but stayed on his feet, lunging in low and landing several hard body punches that drove the air from his foe's lungs in loud wheezing grunts. It was apparent that this was a no-holds-barred contest. Both men were utterly ruthless, using every advantage they could find. If only someone heard that shot and came to investigate! She held the knife ready, waiting for a clean chance to use it on Pardee.

They went down onto the floor again, rolling around in the muck created by the spilled coffee from the tray Samuel had thrown. Pardee seized hold of a piece of shattered crockery and tried to use the jagged edge like a knife, drawing a bloody furrow across Shelby's chest, missing his throat by scant inches when Samuel jerked away, but by this time the American was on top. He slammed his knee into the Englishman's groin, then smashed his fist into his foe's face over and over until the jagged piece of crockery fell limply from Pardee's hand.

Stuart Pardee was unconscious but Samuel continued battering him. "I told you I'd beat you to death with my bare hands," he grated out between blows.

"Samuel, stop—you're killing him," Olivia screamed, attempting to pull him off Pardee's inert body.

"You must admit . . . the idea . . . has merit," Samuel panted out, but he stopped, slumping over the unconscious Englishman, laboring for breath.

Just then the sound of footfalls echoed outside and one of the voyageurs came through the door. "I think I hear a shot, but maybe not. Then I hear a white woman scream and know something is wrong."

As he climbed off Pardee, Samuel looked up at the wiry trapper. "Does this post have someplace that can serve as a jail?"

The man shrugged. "*Oui*. Father Louie has no need of such, but now and then the voyageurs, they get drunk and fight. Monsieur Califon's agents, they put such bad ones in the smokehouse. Come, I will show you."

By this time several more white men had arrived, along with a smattering of local Indians who traded at the post. The sound of Micajah's voice drew nearer as the big man thrust everyone else aside to enter the room. "Sparky, yew all right, gal?" His eyes fastened on her pale face and the bruise forming on her throat, then he enveloped her in a hug. "Me 'n th' padre went outside th' post fer a walk by th' river. Thought we heerd a shot but figgered it wuz some drunk trapper—till yew screamed."

"I'm not hurt," she said, then quickly explained what had occurred with Pardee.

"Good thang yore husband got him 'stead o' me. I'd o' scalped th' bastard with a flint hide scraper fer whut he done ta yew," he said grimly, turning to Samuel. "Whut yew figger on doin' with his lordship, here?"

"Lock him up in the smokehouse until morning. Then take him downriver to St. Louis. The army will have some very pointed questions to ask him about his dealings with the Indians in this area."

"Reckon I kin take keer o' thet. Yew look like yew cud use some tendin'," Micajah said, observing Samuel's bloody and battered condition. With that he knelt down and hauled up Pardee's long-limbed body as if it weighed no more than a feather comforter. Slinging the Englishman across his shoulder, he strode from the room after giving Olivia a reassuring wink. "See yew both in the mornin'!"

As Johnstone ushered the rest of the gawkers from the wrecked cabin and closed the door, his voice carried on the night air. "Leave them young'uns be. They's jist been hitched."

Father Louie's voice added, "*Oui*, this is their wedding night."

One of the voyageurs said as their voices faded, "Then it is good that the bed was not broken!"

Samuel and Olivia stood in the center of the room, facing each other. Their features were cast in shadows, since the only light remaining was that of the flickering fire, which had burned low. Neither could read the other's thoughts and both spoke at once.

"I'll get some water to wash those cuts—"

"Let me stoke up the fire before it dies—"

Nodding, Olivia walked over to the dry sink in the far corner of the room where a basin and pitcher of water stood. She poured the fresh water into the basin while he added logs to the fire until it crackled brightly again. Then he sat down on the hearth and leaned back against the stone wall surrounding the fireplace, sighing wearily. She searched for linen with which to cleanse his injuries, finding a small stash of folded towels beneath the dry sink.

This is their wedding night.

Such a wedding night, Olivia thought dejectedly. She looked at Samuel sitting on the hearth. His profile was outlined by the firelight, boldly handsome, yet angry, forbidding. He was a stranger to her and always would be even though they were legally bound together. She could never again return to the simple life at Micajah's cabin. Once again Samuel Shelby had robbed her of her place, disrupted her life. She should hate him . . . but she could not.

Nervously she approached, setting the basin and linens on the hearth. "Let me wash those cuts," she said softly, reaching out with a wet cloth in her hand.

"Cover yourself," he snapped as his eyes caught sight of the creamy swell of her breast when her nightrail gaped open.

She gasped and clutched the torn drawstring, dropping the cloth back into the bowl and fumbling to cover herself. "Pardee ripped it when he . . ." She shuddered in revulsion.

"You didn't seem to be repelled by his touch when I interrupted you," he said, his eyes studying her intently.

"I wanted his knife and there was only one way to get close enough to grab it. *Merde,* you cannot think I have a tendresse for that loathsome man who nearly caused Gypsy Lady to break a leg! I saved your wretched life when I hit his gun hand. He would've killed you. I should've let him," she added, willing her anger to burn away the pain.

"I have reason to suspect you if Pardee works for Wescott."

"I told you he did and I have sufficient reason to hate Emory Wescott for what he tried to do to me." She finished tying the gown the best she could and picked up the wash-cloth again. As she reached out and took his hand, pulling the cut arm closer so she could wash it, she glanced up and his dark blue gaze held hers. Trying to ignore the warm tension that sprung between them whenever they touched, she asked, "Do you ever trust anyone, Samuel?"

He sighed, staring at her small pale face, shadowed by the firelight, then said softly, "Very seldom. I've found it safest in my line of work."

"You're not just a soldier, are you?"

Damn, he hated her astuteness! "Samuel Sheridan Shelby, Colonel, Army of the United States, nothing more," he replied with a lazy mocking drawl. "If anyone is not what she appears to be, it's you, a French aristocrat playing at being a frontier woman," he said, knowing that would goad her to anger and shift the conversation away from his work.

"Playing! Do you think the life I've carved out with Micajah was just some sort of game to me? I've learned to cook and cure hides. I'm a darned good shot and I can track a deer through the woods for hours, if need be, until I bring it down," she said with pride.

"For the warm months, it was a good diversion, but I suspect you might begin to miss civilization during the long cold winter in that cabin."

"How shallow you must think me," she murmured more to herself than to him as she concentrated on her task. Finishing with the arm that had been cut, she took his right hand in hers and examined the bruised, swollen knuckles.

He winced slightly when she pressed a fresh cold cloth onto them.

She continued the pressure, saying, "You nearly carried out your threat to beat him to death bare-handed. Was it because of me?" What had made her ask *that!?* She held her breath, drawn against her will to look up and meet his eyes.

❧ *Chapter 17* ❧

Time hung suspended as they sat in the firelight amid the wreckage of the cabin. She held his larger hand in both of hers, the washcloth now forgotten.

"What is it about you?" he murmured low, more to himself than to her, almost unaware he had spoken the words aloud. He looked into her fathomless green eyes, reliving the shock and horror of seeing her in Pardee's arms, her body half-naked, leaning into the renegade as if ready to surrender herself to him. Did he believe her story about reaching for the Englishman's knife? Hell, he did not know. And right now he did not care.

Olivia watched him, trying to gauge his mood. Was he still angry with her, still jealous, mistrustful? She was uncertain of how to react to his apparent confusion. She said the first thing that came into her mind. "Our supper is all over the floor. Are you still hungry? I'm sure the cook—"

"No, I want no food. My hunger is of another sort." His eyes continued to study her face while he felt the pulse in her wrists accelerate at his remark.

Was this his answer to her earlier foolish question? Best that he did not answer it at all; yet some perverse, self-punishing instinct drove her to press. "We have very little to base a relationship on . . ." she said, faltering over the words.

"We have this," he replied raggedly, taking her chin in one hand, tilting it up as his lips descended, slowly, inexorably.

His mouth brushed hers with surprising gentleness, almost as if he waited for her to protest, withdraw. She did neither. Instead her body leaned forward, returning the soft kiss as her fingers tightened their grip on his hand, the soft pads massaging his bruised knuckles and scraped skin. He had been frighteningly angry when he found her in Pardee's arms, but he had also been possessive.

Get your hands off my wife.

She was his wife in name. It would take so little right now to make her his wife in fact. He would learn the truth. All his ugly suspicions about her virtue would have to end. Once she had vowed never to let him know that truth, but that was not when he was so near, drowning her with his male vitality, drinking her in as if she were the last drop of water and he a man lost in the desert. *I am the one who's lost.*

Samuel felt her melting into his arms. He was all too willing to draw her against his body and hold her next to his heart as it slammed in his chest. He was trembling with need for her in a way he had not ever needed a woman before, not even when he had been a green and randy schoolboy. "Oh, hell, it isn't as if we'll ever get an annulment anyway," he muttered against her lips as he kissed her again, this time with greater intensity, letting himself submerge in the hypnotic allure of her lithe, lovely young body.

His words did not quite register with Olivia because as he spoke, he drew her closer, tangling his fingers in the long flaming skein of her hair, pulling on it until her head tipped back, exposing the vulnerable column of her neck. His mouth moved along her jaw, trailing soft wet kisses downward along her throat, pausing at the frantic pulse beating at its base. His lips were scorching hot, his breath meltingly delicious on her skin as he caressed her collarbone, pulling open the drawstring that she had refastened and shoving the sheer cotton nightrail away to reach for her breast.

When his hand cupped her breast, lifting it with soft pressure, she arched against his palm. Then his fingers grazed over the hard distended peak of her nipple, returning to circle and tweak it, until she gasped with the sharp jolts of a pleasure so keen it took her breath away. He shoved the gown down to her waist and his hand moved on to the other breast while his mouth claimed the first one. She was liquid, soft as water running over smooth stones in a swiftly flowing stream. The pressure of his mouth suckling on her breast sent small achingly sweet frissons of raw pleasure radiating through her body, but centering low in her belly. A deep hungry clenching began to grow there as she dug her fingers into the thick shaggy black hair of his head, pulling him closer to her, closer yet.

Samuel felt her eager assent as her arms wrapped around his shoulders. He reached down and scooped her up, then stood and strode from the glow of the firelight to the bed where he knelt, pressing one knee into the soft mattress. He placed her in the center, then bent over her, studying her in the dim light as he pulled the nightrail the rest of the way down her body, past her slender waist to the soft hollows at the sides of her flat belly, over the flair of her hips, revealing the downy thatch of fiery red curls at the juncture of her thighs. When the gown was free, he tossed it away, feasting his eyes on her long slender legs with the delicate ankle-bones and sweetly curved calves. Her thighs were slim yet strong, able to clutch a man tightly between them while he plunged into the welcoming wetness of her woman's core.

"You are perfection," he murmured as one hand glided up her leg. He watched her eyes close for a moment, replete with the pleasure of his caressing, like a well-petted cat.

Olivia could feel his hungry eyes on her all the while he stripped down the nightrail, devouring her nakedness. He loomed over her like some large pagan god, all strength and darkness. His back was to the fire, his expression obscured to her vision yet those dark blue eyes glowed as he examined every inch of her flesh.

She felt suddenly vulnerable. No man had ever before seen her naked. Would he find her too thin? Too tall and gawky? Many men liked pillowy softness and plump curves. When he finally touched her again, running his hand up her leg, the warmth of the contact reassured her for a moment. She closed her eyes, trying to calm the frantic beating of her heart.

Then his hand moved upward to her mound and caressed the curls at the seat of her womanhood, where all the restless unfamiliar sensations were gathering. Her eyes flew open and met his. He was fully clothed, she completely naked. He was calm; she was disoriented. Olivia tried to cover herself with her hands and arms. "I've never had anyone look at me this way," she admitted in a low, husky voice.

Samuel chuckled with amusement. "Turnabout's fair play. You watched me stripped buck naked walking out of the river that day—and you enjoyed looking, don't deny it."

"I . . . I won't," she whispered as he pulled her arms away from her breasts and then eased his hand between her clenched thighs, once again caressing the curls there.

"Now I'm enjoying this . . . a very great deal," he murmured raggedly, lowering his mouth to her navel and flicking the tip of his tongue inside until she shivered and moaned. His hands held hers pinned at her sides as he raised up once more claiming her breasts, suckling them until she whimpered and arched against him.

With a muttered oath he sat up and began tearing off the tattered remains of his shirt, then pulling off his boots and hose.

Feeling the loss of his body heat so abruptly, Olivia's eyes opened again as he rose from the bed and began to strip off his tight buckskin trousers. When he turned back to her, her eyes widened in amazement at the transformation from the last time she had seen his male member lying flaccidly in the black hair of his groin. Now it jutted out, big and dark red, almost menacing . . . yet not quite.

"Touch me," he commanded softly, seeming to understand the fascination which drew her. When she hesitated, he reached out and took her hand, pulling it to the scalding heat of his thigh as he placed one knee on the edge of the bed and sank down on it. Then he moved her hand upward, toward his aching shaft and wrapped her small soft fingers around the pulsing engorgement.

Olivia felt the sleek muscles of his thigh, but nothing prepared her for the shock of touching his sex. Like steel in velvet, silky smooth and hot, so vibrantly alive with power. She watched his jaw clench and then he threw back his head, shuddering. "Did I hurt you?" she whispered, trying to withdraw her hand.

But he would not release it. "God, no!" he ground out, showing her how to slide her hand up and down the length of him rhythmically. When she caught the motion, he released his hand from hers and clenched his fists at his sides, breathing rapidly, reveling in the pleasure of her touch until he knew he could stand it no longer without losing complete control. He reached down and caught her wrist, pulling her hand away and pinioning it and her other one above her head as he covered her, sinking onto her on the soft mattress.

She felt a small frisson of fear as his big body pressed against hers but it passed quickly as his mouth once more found hers. This time there was no gentleness in the kiss. It was as hot and hungry as those they had shared all the times past. And yet it was different, too, as they lay together naked, poised on the brink of yet another discovery. She felt protected by the hardness of him, hair roughened and muscled, the opposite of her silky smooth and softly rounded body. She gave herself over to the kiss.

He could sense the tension in her body when he first moved over her, but when his mouth claimed hers, she opened to the insinuating caress of his tongue, allowing it access to the sweetness inside, to plunge and plunder above as he soon would below. He slanted his mouth across hers, deepening the kiss. When he released his hold on her wrists to bury his hands in her hair, he felt her arms encircle his waist and her palms glide up his back until her fingernails dug into his shoulders. She was ready . . . and he was more than ready.

When Samuel's knee separated her thighs, opening her for his touch, she was beyond coherent thought, lost in a maelstrom of passionate new sensations, oblivious to the eminent sundering of her maidenhead. His hand glided down her body, pausing at the curve of her breast to flick the pebble hard nipple and let his fingertips glide around the aching mound. She whimpered as jagged bolts of pleasure mixed with an inexplicable need centered low where she could feel the heaviness of his phallus pressing against her core.

Then his hand swept down, brushing the curls as his fingers quested deeper, separating her labia with a soft gliding touch made smooth and wet by the creamy moisture her body gave off. He was pleased that she was so responsive and forced himself not to consider how many other men might have trespassed where irrationally he felt only he had ever possessed the right to be. He guided the tip of his aching staff against her sweet welcome, teasing her with the gliding friction until she spread her legs wider and arched up involuntarily, crying out his name.

Her last movements drove him past all control. He had to have her that very instant. Without further delay he positioned himself and plunged deep inside her. When he began the slick glorious penetration she was incredibly tight, almost as if there were a barrier, but that could not be.

Olivia tossed her head back and forth against the pillows, her whole body like a bowstring drawn taut, ready to be released in some unknown soaring flight. She writhed in ecstasy against his hand and then against his scalding hot maleness as waves of unbelievable pleasure swamped her. But when he poised the tip of his staff at her center and drove deeply into her, the intensity of feeling moved abruptly from joy to sharp unexpected pain, almost as if she were being torn in two.

She looked up into his face and saw in his eyes the sudden comprehension she had known would vindicate her, but the pain was a cost far dearer than she had thought to pay.

He felt her whole body stiffen as he tore into her tender flesh and knew at once the enormity of what he had done. She did not cry out but bit her lip, then turned her head away, no longer able to meet the shocked surprise and guilt on his face. At once he lay still within her, not moving his lower body as he struggled to regain control. His breaths came in great shuddering pants as the heat and softness of her body enveloped him. Every nerve cried out for him to move, to plunge up and down for the surcease he had craved all these many months.

But he could not do it. He gazed down at her lovely profile. Her face was pressed against the pillow and her eyes, those magical green eyes, remained squeezed tightly closed. He could see the faint glistening of tears gathered beneath her thick dark red lashes. She made not a sound. He reached down with one hand and stroked her cheek gently, then bent and kissed her lashes, releasing a single diamond bright teardrop, which he lapped up with the tip of his tongue.

"Salty and sweet, just like you," he murmured softly.

Olivia could withstand anything but his tenderness. He did not love her, nor did he trust her. She could not bear that he should pity her, feel sorry for her pain or guilty because he had inflicted it. Yet when his lips continued their soft seductive caressing, moving across her cheek, temple, nose, to press once again at the edge of her mouth, she felt that old familiar warmth eddying inside of her.

The pain began to recede slowly but the feeling of being stretched almost beyond endurance remained. She moved ever so slightly, restive beneath the weight of him, the fullness of his body invading hers. At once she heard his ragged intake of breath.

"Don't move, please, not yet," he commanded raggedly. "I . . . I can't control myself if you do. Give me time and I will make it good for you, Livy, I promise."

His voice was low and husky, the words swiftly spoken, the shortening of her name almost an unconscious endearment. She turned her face to meet his kiss head-on, and opened her mouth when his tongue glided along the seam of her lips. Now when he plundered inside, she understood what the action mimicked. How could the one be so pleasurable when the other hurt? Yet a stealing warmth had begun to invade her senses once more, making her body liquid and heavy. She felt the tightening in her belly begin to ease, but the ache of wanting did not. It grew and grew with every fierce kiss and caress he bestowed on her, until she was returning them with abandon.

Samuel could feel her respond and that refueled his ardor until it burned out of control once more. He moved slowly at first, waiting for a sign from her that it was good. When her hands stole up around his neck once more and her thighs tightened around his hips, he knew he need hesitate no longer. His tempo picked up slowly, building gradually, waiting for her responses.

Olivia felt the hot coiling tension in her lower body blaze into open flames, the inferno stoked by Samuel's movements. His body was perspiring in the cool room as he, too, seemed ready to blaze with the same scorching need. He savaged her mouth with fierce kisses, then moved to her neck. She loved the feel of his rapacious mouth on the sensitive skin of her throat and wanted to taste of him the same way.

Her lips brushed against the bristling whiskers on his cheek and jaw, then moved to the corded column of his neck. She touched the tip of her tongue to his hot skin and it tasted salty with perspiration, male and vital. This was Samuel, her love, her husband. She bit down on the thick bunched muscles where his neck and shoulder joined as the blinding surges of ecstasy spiraled out of control from deep within the center of her body. He continued to stroke with ever faster rhythm until she thought she might faint or die from the pleasure he brought her.

But she did neither, only waited for some mysterious culmination that her body intuited, even though her mind had never known of its existence . . . until that moment. She bit down, her teeth drawing blood as they dug into his skin, tasting even more of him as the dizzying contractions seemed to shatter her into a million diamond bright shards.

Samuel felt her sheath's rhythmic pulsing begin deep inside of her, squeezing his staff so exquisitely he could not endure the pleasure without spilling himself. When she made an incoherent cry and bit into his shoulder, her whole body rigid with climax, he gave in to the glory of joining her, shuddering and pulsing his seed into her until he was more utterly drained than he could ever remember being in his life.

Olivia felt his body stiffen and his staff swell even more as it pulsed its life deep inside her womb. As he collapsed onto her body, cradling her beneath him, she held him locked tightly in her arms and legs. *I could be carrying your child now.* The thought stole over her unaware. Although it took her by surprise, the idea was not unwelcome. A small black-haired replica of her love would be a part of him she could keep, even if he chose to leave her.

Seeming to echo her last melancholy thought, he pulled out of her and rolled over onto his back, flinging one arm across his eyes. She felt the sudden chill of night air on her perspiration slicked flesh, once more vulnerable. Her first impulse was to slip from the bed and clean herself up, then don the ripped nightrail to cover her nakedness. But just as she started to move, his words froze her.

"I wouldn't have hurt you if I'd known. I'm sorry, Livy."

The words stung her with his guilt and she retorted in kind, quickly, without thinking, "Sorry you hurt me or sorry you've inadvertantly let slip your chance for an annulment?"

He sat up in the bed, resting his arm loosely across his bent knee but the casual pose belied the tension simmering inside him. "If you had explained to me that you were a virgin instead of coming at me with claws bared—"

"Explained? As if you would have believed anything I said! I told you I wanted an annulment and you laughed that cynical, patronizing laugh of yours. Nothing I could have said would have made any difference to you. Nothing any woman says ever will. You are nothing but an emotional cripple, Samuel Shelby, a man who hates all women because of your mother and your wife."

"You're my wife now—and I'd hardly call what just passed between us hate," he said softly, watching the heat creep up into her cheeks as she realized that she was kneeling on the edge of the bed facing him stark naked.

"You believe in no one, nothing. I pity your lonely life," she said, slipping from the bed to scoop up her gown and hold it in front of her like a shield.

He, too, removed himself from the bed and grabbed his discarded clothes, cursing himself for the fit of lust which had made him fling them with such hasty abandon all about the floor. "I do have scruples, whether or not you believe it, else I'd never have married you," he said angrily, as he slipped on his breeches and reached for his shirt.

"So, duty before dishonor . . ." she said brittlely, willing the pain of his callous words not to bite so deeply. "Are you a spy, Samuel? Is that why you are so suspicious?" She was grasping at straws and she knew it.

He grew very still, his shirt hanging open and unlaced as he stared at her with slate blue eyes that cut through the dim light of the dying fire. Damn, he had been right not to trust her! "Don't confuse my dismay over our circumstances with some deep, sinister motives on my part," he said with biting sarcasm. "Stuart Pardee is allied with your guardian, who offered your luscious little body to me after losing a bet which he himself had insisted on. I've since learned that Pardee is distributing guns and whiskey among the Osage in direct violation of the law. I'd be an unbelievable fool to trust a word you say."

He had learned over the years that the best way to deflect an unwanted line of inquiry was to attack the inquirer. It worked all too well this time. Olivia grew silent and the glitter in her eyes brightened with tears which she held at bay by sheer force of will. She stood clutching the pitiful remnants of her nightrail—the nightrail he had ripped off her body—just staring at him in hurt amazement. He wished she would scream, throw things, curse him or come at him with her nails, anything but the stony silence she chose instead.

"Repair yourself, then get some rest. I'll be back in the morning," he said gruffly as he pulled on his boots and headed to the door.

"Where are you going?" she could not help but ask.

He turned to her with one eyebrow raised sardonically. "Why, to get drunk, my dear wife. Damn good and drunk."

With that he was gone.

She was left alone with the dying embers in the fireplace casting their pale gray light on the wreckage of the room . . . and the shambles of her dreams.

Olivia lay alone in the bed, which seemed so much larger without Samuel's big body in it. After bathing herself and straightening up the room as best she could, she had climbed back into the bed, so emotionally and physically exhausted that sleep should have claimed her instantly. But it did not. Instead, she had lain awake for hours, reliving every encounter she had ever had with Samuel Sheridan Shelby, from their first electric meeting in that crowded Washington ballroom to the shocking betrayal when her guardian had tried to sell her to Samuel. Was her husband partially right—had Wescott wanted to use her to gain entree to the colonel's secrets?

Samuel had far more freedom to pursue a broader scope of assignments than any regular army officer she had ever encountered. Whom did he work for? The secretary of war? Perhaps even President Madison himself? She imagined such a life might harden a man predisposed to mistrust those close to him from the onset.

But I would die before I betrayed you, my love.

As tears slowly seeped from her eyes she finally fell into a restless slumber. Hours passed. Or was it only moments before she was suddenly awakened with something cold touching her throat and a horribly familiar voice whispering in her ear?

"My knife is quite sharp and I'd hate to mar that lovely little neck, so do be quiet while my friend here ties you up."

Stuart Pardee's mocking British accent and repellently acrid smell raised her to full consciousness, but before she could move, another pair of hands was groping beneath the covers, throwing them off and tying her feet with buckskin thongs. As Pardee pressed the keen edge of his blade to her throat, his "friend" rolled her on her side, pulled her arms behind her, and bound her wrists with another abrasive thong. Only when his accomplice had stuffed her mouth with a large wad of cloth and had bound that tightly in place with a strip of buckskin did Pardee relax his vigilance and remove his knife from Olivia's throat. There had been no chance to fight, no chance even to scream.

"A good thing Bad Temper here traveled with me to the post. I might never have gotten out of that makeshift prison without his help, but I never intend to answer any of your colonel's questions, so I left nothing to chance. Now, it is time for us to be on our way."

She wanted to ask where he was taking her—but did she really want to know? Surely it was back to Emory Wescott. But why would her guardian want her abducted now that she was Samuel's wife? Perhaps the renegade Pardee had some even more terrible fate in store for her among the hostile Indians who were his allies.

As he slung her across his shoulder and slipped silently from the cabin, she fought down her fear. Her captors would not always be so vigilant as they had been during the abduction. She would keep her head. Her chance would come. Until then, she would survive one day at a time, just as Micajah had taught her.

Samuel awoke in the backroom of the mercantile, lying on a pile of partially cured beaver plews. Their smell added nothing to his already pounding headache and roiling stomach. As he climbed unsteadily to his feet, he looked around the warehouse, wondering how the hell he had ended up here. His mouth tasted brackish as a sink pond in midsummer's heat.

Around him, littering the dirt floor were several whiskey bottles. Gradually the whole ugly scene with Olivia came back to him, along with his foolish storming out in search of the oblivion to be found in a bottle. As usual it solved nothing. In fact, it only made things distinctly worse. He would have to face her. The sooner it was done, the better.

Then he could make arrangements to transport Pardee downriver to St. Louis. Forcing himself to concentrate on how he might wring an admission of Wescott's complicity out of the Englishman, he walked out of the warehouse into the glare of the sunrise, only to hear loud shouts and Micajah's voice bellowing across the compound from the cabin.

Damn, had Olivia gone sobbing to her protector about how he had abused her? Somehow Samuel doubted she would do it. His wife had too much stubborn pride for that. A premonition of disaster raised the hackles on his neck as he began to run across the compound to where a group of trappers and merchants clustered about the manager's cabin. He shoved his way past them and entered to find Micajah standing in the center of the deserted room with murder in his eyes.

"Where in tarnation have yew been?"

"Where's Olivia?" Samuel replied with dread.

"Gone. 'N so's thet Englishman o' yourn. Some o' his Injun pals cut the guard's throat 'n let him outta th' jail. First thang I thought o' when I found out wuz Sparky. He tried to kidnap her last night 'n now she's gone, too. Yew left her alone agin, didn't yew?" Johnstone accused.

"Yes, I left her," he admitted, combing his fingers through

his hair distractedly. *But was she abducted or did she go with Pardee willingly?* Samuel was too judicious to voice that question aloud to the giant in front of him. "They have several hours start on us. We'd best start looking for a trail at once," he said instead, walking across the room to look for his rifle and other gear, which he had placed in the corner.

"Yew start off from here 'n see if yew kin pick up any sign. I'm headin' upriver fast as I kin fer Dirt Devil. If anyone kin find Sparky, thet dawg's hit. He'll foller her trail till hell frosts."

Grimly the men parted, both dreading in their hearts what they might find when they caught up with the infamous Englishman.

∾ *Chapter 18* ∾

Olivia lost track of time. Her captors had carried her through the dense overgrowth of woodlands for what seemed forever. Her thin nightrail had been torn to shreds and her tender skin scratched and abraded as they trotted past hawthorn trees and blackberry bushes. She was cold, and the gag made it difficult for her to breathe. To compound her misery, her bound hands and feet had gone completely numb. Finally, by dusk that following evening, they reached a river. Judging by its size and muddy color it was the Missouri. A well-provisioned canoe awaited them along with several more young Osages.

To her horror, they did not race downriver toward St. Louis. Instead they began to paddle against the powerful current, headed northwest, farther into Indian country. Her heart had frozen with terror. What did Pardee plan to do with her? As if intuiting her thoughts, he had run a filthy gnarled hand over her breasts, leering nastily as he explained that he had a rendezvous with his supplier of whiskey and guns to the north, where he would deliver the contraband to a group of Osage renegades. After his essential business was concluded, he promised her, there would be time for the two of them to become better acquainted.

She had felt bile rise up in her throat, choking her behind the gag. He would rape her, use her and then kill her in retaliation for the way she had scorned him back in St. Louis. She would be so broken and soiled by his touch that death would be welcome. Samuel would never want her after Pardee finished with her.

Samuel never wanted you anyway.

But she was his wife. Would he come for her? If not him, then Micajah? Her beloved old friend would never rest until he found her. She vowed again to survive no matter what. After spending most of the night paddling by moonlight, along the twisty, tortuous course of the river, the party finally pulled ashore.

There Pardee had surprisingly produced a pair of baggy old buckskin breeches and a filthy cotton shirt, saying, "You're used to dressing up like a male. Cover yourself before I'm forced to fight off half the Osage nation to keep that fire-haired scalp off some buck's lodgepole."

He had untied her bonds, removed the gag and thrown the clothes at her, even allowed her privacy away from the Indians' hard obsidian eyes, to change into the outfit. Turning her back on the Englishman, she had tugged the britches on beneath the tattered filthy nightrail, then slipped it off and quickly donned the heavy shirt, thankful for its protection against the chill. A small piece of hemp served as a belt to hold the baggy clothes on her slender frame.

Her feet remained bare, however, as he said, "Easier to keep you from running off this way. Anyway, I always was partial to barefooted women . . . not to mention bare assed ones," he'd added with a nasty chuckle.

When they returned to the camp, Bad Temper looked at her with renewed interest, never before having seen a female in men's clothing. Unaware she understood his language, the Osage began urging Pardee to share the captive with his red brothers. Her heart froze with terror at the prospect of having not only Pardee but the three Osage all take their turns at her. They would tear her apart! But Pardee said that no one was to touch her.

He finally prevailed, threatening the renegades with the loss of their destructive contraband if they despoiled the property of the man who sent them firewater and rifles. They, in turn, out of disgruntled spite, secured his pledge not to touch her either. Olivia uttered a silent prayer of thanks and wondered if the supplier could be Wescott.

The small party slept for a few hours, rising at dawn to resume their upriver journey. All the while she plotted escape, formulating and rejecting plans, knowing there would be no second chance if she failed the first time. When they camped the following night to eat and take a brief rest, she was prepared.

She ate a few mouthfuls of the rancid greasy pemmican offered her, then pretending to be exhausted, she curled up a distance from the fire, her hands and feet securely tied. But this time, her wrists were bound in front of her. After all, even if she were free, she would not get far barefooted. One Osage guard was posted but he took his station away from the small fire, looking out toward the river, from where they most reasonably expected pursuit to come. Once she was certain the others, especially Pardee, were asleep, she took a small sharp piece of shale from her pocket. She had managed to secret it away that morning when she had deliberately fallen on the riverbank while they were boarding the canoes.

Gritting her teeth, Olivia began the long, laborious task of sawing through her bonds, those on her feet first, although if she was unable to free her hands, she knew running away bound would surely end in failure. It took several hours, but when the final hide binding on her wrists gave way, she sat quietly rubbing her hands and feet to restore circulation while her eyes scanned the camp for any possible weapons to take with her. There was no hope of killing four armed men single-handedly, or she would gladly have rid the world of the deadly renegades. Several muskets were stacked against the trunk of a sycamore by Pardee.

If she dared move closer to the fire where Bad Temper slept, a knife gleamed at his side. It had fallen from a loose sheath at his waist as he rolled over. Dare she risk it? Survival in the woods was going to be difficult enough even with a rifle. A knife to gut and clean her kills would be a tremendous asset. She began to crawl slowly toward the fire, scarcely daring to breathe as she inched her hand forward to slide the knife away from the sleeping Indian. Placing it in her belt, she retreated into the shadows and circled around for Pardee's rifle, a sturdy .69 caliber flintlock, far better than the crude old Brown Bess muskets the Osage carried.

For one horrifying instant she thought the Englishman had awakened, but he merely snorted and tossed abruptly on his other side, then resumed his loud even snoring. Trembling, she took the rifle with its shot pouch and the powder horn hanging alongside it and vanished silently into the darkness.

Three days had passed since Olivia had disappeared. Samuel did not know whether to hope she had gone willingly with Pardee and was safe or that his wife had actually been abducted by the renegade, even though that meant her life was at grave risk.

His wife. She was in fact his wife now, and he was not nearly as certain that he regretted the fact as he had been after they had consummated their vows. He had been angry at Micajah's coercion, mistrustful of her motives and then after he took her innocence, shocked and guilty at what his own lust had wrought.

But had it been only simple lust? The question kept nagging him as he tracked her and Pardee through the wilderness. Hell, nothing about Olivia had ever been simple from the first moment he'd laid eyes on her. She was the most complex and fascinating woman he had ever met, and he was determined that he would get her back, no matter if it took him a year in the wilderness.

Where the hell was the accursed Englishman going with her? Not downriver back to Wescott, that much had been obvious after a few hours of tracking them in a northwardly direction. But what if the shady merchant had come upriver? Or, dispatched Pardee to deliver even more of his illicit cargoes among the Osage encampments stretching all along the banks of the Missouri and its tributaries to the northwest? His heart had sunk when he had reached the bank of the Missouri that second morning and seen the unmistakable signs of a heavily laden Osage canoe shoved off into the water. Their trail ended.

He cursed bitterly, realizing how difficult it was going to be to find her. No matter about Wescott or Pardee or the guns or the war. His first priority was Olivia, his wife. She had turned his life upside down since he'd been brought more dead than alive to Micajah Johnstone's cabin. Perhaps with Dirt Devil tracking her Micajah might have had better luck than he. Maybe she was already safely back at the cabin waiting for him.

As he rode his borrowed horse upriver through the woodlands, he prayed for a miracle. By tonight he could reach a smaller Osage town that he had visited last spring. If Chief Rich Man was still in charge, he might be able to secure some help in his search. Rich Man was an old friend of Santiago Quinn's. Right now, Shelby was banking rather heavily on that friendship. Olivia's life might well hang in the balance.

He tried not to think of what some tribes did to captive females, or even worse, of what a man like Pardee was capable. In that lay madness. No, he must remain calm and use his head, not race off in a blind panic. When he closed his eyes he could still see the expression on her face when he had breached her maidenhead, the look of surprise, the shocked bewilderment and pain she had tried so valiantly to hide—his brave, beautiful wife.

Samuel was exhausted, his strength still not fully recovered from his earlier ordeal with Man Whipper and his companions. He had been virtually without sleep for three days now, only allowing himself to rest an hour or two when the moon set and he could not see to travel. Once he realized he must have help and a canoe to journey upriver, he had set his horse toward Rich Man's village and dozed fitfully in the saddle, something he was inured to doing.

When he heard the sound of some creature crashing through the brush, it jarred him to instant wakefulness. He reined in his horse and listened, then saw a blur through a thicket of chokecherry, a slim figure in ragged britches—with long red hair blazing like a banner behind her as she leaped agilely through the rocks, clutching a rifle in one hand as she ran.

His own rifle was primed and ready to fire at her pursuer as he kneed his mount to intersect her at a stand of scrub oak for which she was headed. Just then an Indian broke through the brush behind her. He raised his weapon to fire but before he could sight it in, she had rolled down behind a rock, taken aim and fired at a range of fifty feet, hitting her target in the chest. Without waiting a beat she was up on her feet, reloading, and then spinning around to continue her flight.

Samuel urged his horse forward, then saw a second pursuer raising a rifle and sighting in on Olivia's back. Shelby fired, knocking the Osage against a tree trunk. Olivia turned toward the sound of the shot, incredulous joy infusing her face when she saw her husband riding toward her, smoking rifle still in his hand. He bent down to scoop her up in front of him as she ran toward him.

"There are a dozen more! Pardee must've run into the renegades he was delivering his guns and whiskey to," she said breathlessly as they took off at a gallop toward the trees.

Another shot rang out, then another. The big gelding screamed in pain and stumbled as blood gushed from its neck. Samuel kicked free of the stirrups and jumped, carrying Olivia with him as the animal went down. They scrambled to their feet and started running toward a stand of scrub oak as the dirt around them was peppered by several more shots.

When they reached the cover of the trees, she turned and

took aim at their pursuers. While he reloaded, she fired. They took turns until the woods grew quiet. Three dead Osage lay sprawled in the meadows behind them.

"If they wait us out, we'll eventually run out of ammunition," he said bleakly, his mind racing. Taking her hand he gritted out, "I outran the sons of bitches once. Damn if the two of us won't do it now."

Trying to ignore the screaming pain in her cut and bleeding feet, Olivia said, "My legs are too short to outrun them, but maybe we can outsmart them."

"What do you mean?"

"Micajah told me a story once . . . about a friend named John Colter."

"I've met the man," Samuel replied as they began to trot deeper into the woods. "What about him?"

"He hid from his pursuers in a river up north. If we can make it back near where Pardee and his friends came ashore—"

"They left a canoe!" Samuel exclaimed eagerly.

"No," she replied calmly, "that's the first place they'll search. They've probably spread out and one group is half-way there by now."

"Then what?" he asked impatiently, slapping a low branch out of his way.

"There's a beaver dam in an embarras on one of the tributaries, just below where we landed. I saw it as we were coming upriver."

Shelby looked at her oddly but said nothing, then scanned the woods for more hostiles. "So, if we find this embarras, you figure we can hide in it until they give up looking for us? Pretty dangerous with savages popping up all around the damn thing. I think we'd be safer to keep running. We may lose them in these woods."

"I did manage to lose them for nearly a day but they still caught up to me." She flinched as a jagged piece of rock bit into her instep, but kept on jogging beside him.

For the first time he looked down at her feet and cursed. "Why didn't you say you were barefooted?"

"It didn't exactly come up in the conversation," she replied acerbically. "If you recall, Pardee kidnapped me from bed. I was wearing only a nightrail."

Our marriage bed, he thought guiltily. And he had left her there for Pardee. "How did you acquire these clothes then?" he asked at once.

Her eyes met his as the implications of the question struck her like a lightning bolt. "Damn you? You think I went willingly with him?"

"No, not now," he said sighing wearily. "I'll confess it did occur to me at first. There were no signs of a struggle."

"He slipped in with an Osage warrior while I was asleep. They both had me before I could make a sound or even move," she said bitterly. "Pardee gave me some of his old clothes. He left me barefooted thinking I couldn't run that way. I took a page from your book and fooled them." She had a look of grim pride on her face.

"You sure as hell did, Livy," he replied softly.

"About that embarras," she said, returning to the subject doggedly, unwilling to let him know how much his continuing suspicions could still hurt her, or how much his implied praise pleased her. "If we can make it to the river, we can hide in the beaver lodges—some of them looked pretty big from what I could see."

"Well, hell, I guess it's a better chance than thrashing around in this brush. How far downriver?"

"Half a day . . . I think . . . on foot."

He stopped and she followed suit. They listened for any sounds to indicate the presence of men in the surrounding woods. They had zigzagged and changed course since killing the last of the Osage whom they had seen. Nothing disturbed the low hum of nature.

"Time to take a breather—and see to your feet," he said, pulling her down beneath the cover of elderberry bushes beside a small trickling creek. They both quenched their thirst before he raised one of her small feet by a delicate anklebone and inspected it with a grimace.

"Not half as bad as yours were," she said as he checked the other foot. "No thistles sticking out thick as porcupine quills."

"But you are cut and bruised. Damn, if only we hadn't lost the horse. My saddlebags had medicines."

"If I just bathe them in the cool water, it'll help. Some yarrow would be good to stop the cuts from bleeding." She glanced around the creek bank.

Samuel saw the tall gold-crowned weeds the same time she did and walked down a few dozen yards to cut some.

"Becoming a regular woodlore expert, aren't you?" he asked as he began pounding the flower tops into a powder on a smooth rock.

"I have already survived a revolution, a cholera epidemic, several attempts to kill me, even one to sell me," she could not resist adding. "I'll survive this, too."

He quirked one eyebrow. "If you had been sensible enough to come to me with the truth when Wescott tried to *sell* you, you could've saved us both a lot of trouble."

"So very simple," she scoffed. "The only way you accept the truth is when it stares you straight in the face—with incontrovertible bloody evidence."

He thought of her ripped maidenhead and the blood smeared on the sheets afterward and his face darkened with a guilty flush as he shrugged off his shirt and began ripping it to make bandages for her feet. "I'd give you my boots, but they're so much too big you'd break your neck trying to walk in them," he said gruffly. Taking one slender foot which she had been dangling in the creek, he dried it off, and applied the yarrow paste. Then he began swaddling it with long strips of the heavy cotton cloth.

All the while he worked, she watched the play of bronzed muscles rippling across his chest. Olivia remembered how the crisp black hair there had felt when she pressed her face against that warm solid wall, listening to his heart slam furiously when he had made love to her.

They spoke no more as they resumed walking, following the small creek which would eventually empty into the river. When they reached a rocky area where they had to ford the creek, he gave her his rifle, scooped her up in his arms and carried her.

Olivia let out a squeak of surprise as his arms lifted her against his chest. "Put me down! I can walk. You're not fully recovered from your injuries. You need to save your strength."

"I'm fine. I don't need you to lay open one of your feet and undo all my careful bandaging. After all, I don't happen to have a spare shirt on me," he added dryly.

Olivia was all too aware of that as she held onto the smooth muscles of his shoulders. He was as powerful as a great black panther. She was acutely conscious of the heat of his skin, the male smell of his bare upper body pressed so closely to hers. Her stiff resistance quickly gave way to acquiescence as his long easy strides ate up the ground.

She always felt protected and safe when he held her. *Fool. He's a greater danger to you than the hostile Osage and Pardee combined!*

He stayed in the creek bed shallows for a mile or so saying, "This should keep them from tracking us quickly even if they happen to see signs farther back. How far do you estimate to the smaller river with the embarras?"

"If we cut overland to the south, maybe another mile, but you can't—"

"Yes, I can," he replied, holding her fast as he jumped from the creek across several flat rocks, careful to leave no sign of where he left the water. "Of course, this will make it damned hard for Dirt Devil to pick up our trail if Micajah is following."

"If he is, that dog will find us," she said with assurance, praying that they would all be reunited safely.

Within an hour they had reached the confluence of the small river and the larger Missouri. As Olivia had observed, a large thicket of driftwood and other debris floated at the mouth of the lesser body of water. Near one end a sawyer bobbed precariously, beating time on the rippling current. At the opposite end a huge complex of beaver lodges stuck up, giving the impression of a small city. Several of the lodges were a goodly size.

Samuel set Olivia on her feet, on a long flat stretch of rock, and relieved her of both the rifles she had been carrying. "I vote for that big one in the center," she said, pointing to one huge brown dome that rose above all the other surrounding lodges. "The trick will be finding a way in," she continued, starting to roll up her pant legs.

He cocked an eyebrow at her. "If I recall correctly, you can't swim."

"I can now," she replied calmly. "Like a fish."

"More like a beaver, I hope." Then he hesitated again, weighing the options.

"If we do this, we lose the use of our rifles," he reminded her, but already he had concluded that they were both too exhausted to go any farther.

Olivia shrugged. "We're almost out of powder anyway. There wasn't much in Pardee's powder horn to begin with. He's a careless woodsman."

He tied their shot pouches and powder horns to the weapons, then carefully submerged them in murky water beneath the brush snarled undergrowth of the embarras. Hopefully they could retrieve them when they left. Then they waded out into the river, diving into the cold green current. Samuel kept an eye on Olivia, moving close to her. She swam with graceful ease, slithering past slow-moving mudcats who drifted along the silty brown bottom. Underwater weeds undulated around them, twisting like silken gauze in a summer breeze. When they moved beneath the shadow of the embarras, all light vanished and the only source of reckoning was pure instinct, as they aimed for the center of the largest beaver lodge. Both prayed they could feel its underwater entrance.

Groping along the tightly meshed network of twigs, wood and hard-packed mud, Samuel found an opening big enough to stick his head into. Fitting his shoulders would be a tight squeeze. His lungs were beginning to scream for air. He turned, reached out for Olivia, not sensing her nearby at first. Then suddenly the current surged and he felt something brush his arm.

Confused by the inky blackness, Olivia grasped for something to orient herself. Although she had become a strong swimmer over the summer months, she had never spent this long underwater, beneath light breaking cover such as this. All sense of up and down had vanished and she fought panic. Perhaps using the beaver lodge had not been such a great idea after all. Then she felt Samuel's hand grasping her arm and shoving her into an opening. She was half-pushed while she half-propelled herself upward until she suddenly broke through the water. Blessed warm air rushed into her strained, burning lungs.

Quickly shimmying up into the dim cavern, she felt Samuel right behind her. He struggled to work his way through the funnellike opening. Frantically, she reached down into the water and tugged at his shoulder, pulling with all her strength beneath his armpit until he, too, surfaced, filling his lungs with huge gulps of air.

"Damn, I thought I'd never work my way through that pinhole opening," he gasped, coughing up water as he blinked to acclimatize his eyes to the faint light filtering into the lodge from a narrow air hole in the center of the dome-like roof. He could make out Olivia's shadowy outline as she huddled across from him.

"For a while there I was reconsidering the wisdom of trying to find this place," she said.

"Hell, I don't know. If they trail us this far, they'll have no way of being sure that we entered the river on this embarras. I expect it'll take them a day or two to split up and look for a sign before they get close. Meanwhile we can rest." He could see that she was shivering in spite of the stuffy brackish air inside the lodge. "Best we get out of these wet clothes," he said, beginning to pull off the sodden britches and boots he'd hurriedly secured from the Ste. Francoise mercantile.

Olivia sat very still, suddenly aware of how intimate their circumstances were in spite of the size of the lodge. She looked nervously around, gauging the ceiling to be ten feet at its apex. The round room was perhaps as large as forty feet across at the base. The floor of the lodge was sturdily built of painstakingly layered roots, twigs, wood shavings and moss, so tightly packed as to be rock solid, but wet from seepage from the river bottom. "Will the beavers come back at dark, do you think?" she asked nervously.

"I doubt they'll want houseguests. They'll avoid this lodge and use the others until we're long gone." He, too, studied their quarters, noting the sleeping loft the beavers had built a foot or so above the wet floor. Walking over to the surface which ringed the perimeter of the circular room, he tested its sturdiness. "Alder bark. Soft and dry. Should easily hold our weight, too. Good carpenters, these beavers. At least we can sleep in comfort."

He looked at her again, noting that she had made no move to get out of her wet clothes. Suddenly their proximity struck him, too. Clearing his throat nervously, he said, "I'm going to search for dinner. You'd better shuck those clothes or you'll catch your death."

"Dinner?"

"Yes, if I remember correctly what Santiago and his trapper friends have told me, the tunnel opening over there should lead to a food cache."

"Oh." She could think of nothing else to say. Her throat was suddenly dry. With trembling fingers she began to unfasten the buttons on the filthy shirt. Relieved when he turned his back to go into the adjoining lodge, she pulled it over her head, then lay back and skinned off the sopping britches. At least the light was faint. He would not be able to see much of her naked body . . . she hoped.

In a few moments Samuel returned with the bounty from the beaver's cache—berries, iris bulbs, sedges, watercress and mushrooms. "Not exactly a banquet but it'll fill us up," he said, setting down the vegetarian delight.

Her stomach gave a sudden growl and she reached out for a handful of the berries, stuffing them greedily in her mouth. "I haven't eaten since I grabbed some wild persimmons yesterday."

"Try the mushrooms. They're almost like meat—at least the chewiness makes it seem that way," he said between mouthfuls.

They shared the repast, making casual conversation about the bitterness of iris bulb or the sweetness of the dried choke-cherries, gradually becoming more aware of each other's nakedness and their proximity, sitting in the middle of the cavernous room. Outside, a leopard frog snorted and rattled while a chorus of wood frogs kept up a steady chickenlike clucking in the background. The gentle hum of the river's current was broken by the erratic slapping of sawyers on the embarras, pounding the water as they rose and fell with the tug of the current.

Another current, hot and electric as a summer storm was pulsing inside the lodge. Suddenly as they each reached onto the pile of food their fingers touched. Both pulled away as if burned, speaking at once.

"I didn't—"

"You must—"

They stared at each other, their eyes glowing, meeting across the gloom, dark stormy blue and glittering deep emerald.

"What are we going to do, Livy?" he asked at length, breaking the spell of silence.

"I . . . I don't know," she whispered, fighting the urge to cover herself in spite of the cloaking gloom.

"I want you," he admitted, unwilling to formulate his thoughts any further than the obvious.

"You say that as if you begrudge your own desire." Her voice was at once hurt and scornful. "You don't trust me, Samuel. You don't *want* to want me." *You don't love me.*

"I admire you—your courage, your resourcefulness. As to

trust . . ." he hesitated, then admitted, "I have reason to suspect your guardian of treason. Considering the circumstance that first brought us together, can you blame me for being suspicious?"

"I suppose not . . . but I have just as much reason to detest Emory Wescott as you and things have changed over the past months . . ." *I have fallen in love with you.*

"They sure have changed over the past days. We *are* married, Livy," he reminded her.

"Don't call me that." The pet endearment hurt. "My father used to call me Livy." *And* he *loved me.* Not wanting to dwell on that she quickly added, "Neither of us wanted this marriage. We were foolish to consummate it."

He smiled in the darkness. "Then you admit I wasn't the only one who participated that night?"

"You're the most insufferably arrogant man I've ever known."

"I'm the *only* man you've ever known . . . at least in the biblical sense." The idea pleased him suddenly. He reached out and slipped his hand around her slender wrist, pulling her toward him as he stood up.

Olivia did not resist. His heat drew her, cool and shivering, up against his body. His scent, his hard male vitality seemed to surround her as he enfolded her in his arms and slanted his mouth over hers, tangling his fingers in her long wet hair. When he rimmed her lips with the tip of his tongue, then pressed the seam, prying them apart with gentle insistence, she opened to him.

Samuel tightened his arms around her as he claimed her mouth, and felt her small cool palms press against the muscles of his back as her silky body molded itself against his. He could feel the tilt of her pelvis as he cupped her buttocks, lifting her to press against the aching insistence of his erection, groaning low in his throat as her hips unconsciously undulated against him.

When he swept her up into his arms and walked over to the narrow loft edging the room, she clung to him, returning his kisses with wicked abandon. He had to crouch low as the domed ceiling curved downward. Then he knelt and lay her onto the soft, dry bed of fine bark shavings. She closed her eyes as he loomed above her, his hands moving with deft sure strokes across her belly and up to her breasts, circling them, cupping and molding them until his mouth, hot and seeking, fastened on one nipple, drawing a sharp exclamation of bliss from her.

He felt her fingers dig into his scalp, pulling his head closer as he moved between her breasts, feasting on one, then the other, back and forth as she arched up and thrashed with the pleasure he was giving her. His hand slid lower, caressing the concave hollow of her belly, letting his lips trail soft, wet kisses down to her navel. When he circled it with his tongue she quivered.

His fingers found her wet, warm center, parting and delving inside in slick, delicate rhythm. She undulated against the erotic pressure, expecting him to cover her and fill her again. But he did not. Instead his mouth nuzzled the curls shielding her treasure, before delving lower. His head dipped between her thighs as his hands pressed them apart. Olivia was too shocked to resist when the heat of his mouth found the velvety folds of her sex, suckling and drawing on it, his tongue working maddeningly around the small nub where ecstasy centered.

When she moaned, he felt a surge of pleasure that he could give her this, some small atonement for the pain he had inflicted on their wedding night. He worked patiently, slowly, subtly, all the while gauging her reactions. Gradually her legs opened wider and wider and her hands clutched frantically at his shoulders. He could feel her whole body stretched taut as a bowstring. Using the flat of his tongue, he massaged the swelling little bud with long, soft, slow strokes, until it began to spasm.

Olivia came up from the mat, a keening sound torn from her throat as the most intense pleasure rode in sharp little waves, jolting through her whole body, right down to her toes. Just when she thought she could stand no more, or go mad with it, he pulled away.

She lay open to him, throbbing in her release as he mounted her, guiding his rigid phallus into the pulsing heat of her body. He could still feel the fading aftershocks of her climax as he began to move slowly, deeply, willing himself to be patient, to make it last as long as he humanly could.

Nothing could surpass what she had just experienced. Or so she thought until his hard length pressed into her, this time sliding effortlessly deep. There was no barrier, no pain, only the enrapturing pleasure of his body joined to hers. Soon the lethargy of repletion began to fade, once more sharpening into renewed need. Olivia looked up at his shadowed face, able to make out only the glow of his eyes as he moved over her. Her arms raised, encircling his neck, pulling him down. Their lips met in a slow, tentative kiss that grew along with the building ecstasy they shared in the coupling.

Samuel felt her thighs tighten on his hips and his thrusting grew harder, faster. He reached up with both hands and placed his palms against her bent knees, pressing them backward so her hips raised higher, her body opened further, allowing him deeper access, increasing the maddeningly pleasurable friction, tightening the velvety sheath that surrounded his staff, drawing him ever deeper into her beckoning softness until he knew that he was lost.

This time she knew what the spiraling tightness, the thrumming ache meant, where it would lead her, where she would most willingly follow. She rocked her hips against him with each thrust, greedy for it, impatient, mindless with the sweet pain of need and fulfillment blended all together at once, until it burst upon her again. The splendor of climax was heightened even more with his answering response.

Samuel threw back his head and felt himself swell in that last glorious stroke which brought him finally home, spilling his seed in the highest seat of her womb, pulsing life into her in long powerful throbs, until he was utterly spent, panting and breathless as she.

When her smooth legs slid down the hair roughened sides of his and she felt his chest press against her breasts, she clutched his head against her neck, running her fingers through his thick night dark hair. She felt the warm flutter of his breath as he murmured against her throat indistinctly.

"Livy . . ."

Or had she imagined it? Somehow the endearment no longer seemed inappropriate as she drifted off to sleep, cocooned by his warmth.

Chapter 19

"**D**amned if we ain't a gittin' close, Dirt Devil." Micajah squatted, examining the body of a slain Osage warrior while the hound paced excitedly, eager to continue. "Now jest stick ta Sparky's trail. She fer certain got shut o' them varmints," he instructed as they resumed their search.

Micajah had to find her before Pardee and those renegades recaptured her. He had read the signs of her escape and encounter with Shelby, a matter of some good luck. Having his horse shot out from under them certainly was not lucky, but at least with two weapons they stood a better chance. As the dog sniffed and dashed, Micajah trotted behind him in ground-devouring strides.

Suddenly the hound stopped, growling low in his throat, his fur bristling up along the ridge of his spine. At once Johnstone crouched behind the scant cover of a clump of buttonbush as a shot whistled by his shoulder. He held his rifle steady, gauging from where the attack had come, not wasting his own fire. The dog took off circling around, swift and silent. *Flush 'em out, Dev.*

After several minutes he heard the sound of a feral growl followed by a human scream. He took off in the direction of the snarling sounds of battle, but just as he crested the rise he hard a loud yelp, then ominous silence. Dirt Devil lay sprawled on the grass with blood pooling at the side of his head. A badly chewed up Osage with a tomahawk in his fist was climbing to his feet.

Micajah quickly took aim and started to squeeze the trigger but before he could get off the shot, another rang out from his left side. The impact of the ball slammed the big man against the trunk of a sycamore. He slid down the rough bark as blackness hazed his eyes. The last thing he saw was that Osage who had clubbed Devil coming at him with his scalping knife in his hand.

The Indian who had shot the fallen man in the back reached the victim before his hound-chewed companion. He toed the big man's body, and when there was no response, he set aside his rifle and started to draw his own scalping knife. He sensed rather than heard the danger behind him and whirled about, too late. His terrified scream was cut short. The other Osage turned and ran as fast as his fleet feet could carry him, all thoughts of a fine trophy scalp forgotten.

Micajah Johnstone lay still as death at the base of the tree, while blood oozed from the hole in his back in a life-ebbing trickle. The hound, covered with its own caked on gore, crawled across the clearing to his master and began licking the bearded face and whimpering low, piteous cries.

Micajah did not respond.

Samuel awakened to the sounds of the river at dawn, the splashing of sawyers, the low hum of the current and the counterpoint of cooing mourning doves in the tall cottonwoods that overhung the bank. He started to move, then felt the softness of Olivia's body burrowed against his side. The long tangled skein of her hair lay across his chest. A new shaft of sunlight trickling in from the air hole above burnished it like living flame.

His legs lay possessively across her slim thighs and her head was pillowed on his arm, which was numb when he flexed his fingers and tried gingerly to withdraw it. She awakened slowly, blinking her eyes in the dim light as he rolled up and reached for his pants. As he tugged them on she raised her upper body on her elbows and watched, uncertain of what to say after what had passed between them last night.

Finally, he broke the silence after shoving on his miserably wet, stiff boots. "I'll bring us some more of the beaver's hoard for breakfast while you get dressed."

"Then what?" The question seemed to ask itself, pregnant with many meanings.

He grinned at her. "Then we eat."

She struggled to slide into the still damp britches and shirt and refasten the makeshift clothes with the rope belt, then examined her feet. The yarrow had done its work. Already they looked less red and raw but she still had no shoes and they faced a long trek. As she considered the dilemma, he returned and they both found themselves famished, quickly devouring a pile of berries, mushrooms and other roots and tubers the beavers had gathered.

When they had finished, he looked at her and said, "When

I was tracking you and Pardee, I prayed he hadn't hurt you—that I found you before—"

"He never touched me," she quickly interrupted, then shuddered in revulsion. "Not that he didn't intend to. I overheard when he talked with the Osage. They didn't know I could understand their language. He told them I was not to be touched, but I think it was only because he wanted to keep them from fighting over me."

"And maybe he'd promised to deliver you safe and sound back to Wescott," he suggested.

"I wondered about that, but he never said what he was going to do with me after the rendezvous with the rest of the Osage renegades. He never mentioned Wescott's name. I only know that he intimated to me that he would use me when we were alone together."

Samuel could sense the loathing in her voice. "But he didn't and he never will. I'll kill him before he touches you again."

She looked at him sharply, seeing the tightly leashed fury in his burning eyes and clenched jaw. His whole body was taut with it. "You don't have to defend my honor," she said softly.

He looked at her with an unreadable expression on his face, all the previous open anger submerged. "Why? Because I despoiled you myself?"

"You were forced into the marriage but you *are* my husband. Whatever you do now, you can't despoil me, Samuel."

"Why did you run from me back in St. Louis?"

"Why did you lie to me about being married?" she countered. That betrayal still stung.

He sighed, realizing they were falling into the same old accusatory circular arguments as they had before. "I should have told you . . . but I was in the process of petitioning for a divorce from Tish."

She had learned from his feverish ravings how his first wife had hurt him, the pain and shame Tish had inflicted on a proud and very private man, but she knew she could not speak of that. "I was listening outside the door when my guardian offered me to you as a mistress. That he would do such a thing was a terrible betrayal . . ."

"And that I would accept an even more terrible one," he supplied for her and saw the confirmation in her haunted eyes. "If you had come to me that night, I wouldn't have fallen on you like a lust crazed animal, Olivia. I already had doubts about Wescott's reliability. I intended to ask you if you wanted to stay with me, not force you."

She stiffened. "How noble of you, considering that you already believed me to be less than virtuous and possibly in league with Wescott. He is the one the men in Washington sent you after isn't he?"

He shrugged in defeat, admiring her quick mind as much as her prickly pride. "Yes, I was sent to stop British agents from convincing the Osage Nation to join the crown against us in the coming war." Then he smiled and stared into her eyes, saying gravely, "But I'm learning to trust you, Olivia. I don't believe you're a British agent or that you took part in Wescott's schemes."

"You told him that you would never marry again. All you ever intended to offer me was my keep as a mistress. But now I'm your wife. Where do we go from here, Samuel?" She could not believe she had possessed the boldness to ask such a direct question, no matter how desperately she wanted the answer.

Before Samuel could reply, loud yipping erupted from the riverbank and the smell of smoke began to filter inside the lodge.

"It looks as if Pardee's friends have found us, although I don't think they know we're inside. It's just a precaution in case we might happen to be."

"And a way to drive us out," she replied grimly.

Samuel grabbed her hand and ran to the entrance of the lodge. "Wait until I have a hold on you once we're underwater," he commanded, then began to shimmy down the narrow passage.

She quickly followed as smoke began billowing in the chamber above. The Englishman's Osage were firing the whole top of the embarras! She felt Samuel's hand clamp on her ankle, pulling her quickly into his arms, then propelling her next to him as they moved through the cold, murky water, which glowed an eerie dull orange, reflecting the flames which leaped above them.

They swam underwater as far as their lungs would allow, until they were well clear of the fiery inferno of the beaver lodges and the embarras. Their lungs burned as intently as the licking flames behind them when they finally broke water, far downstream. Not a hundred yards away lay the

Missouri's wide muddy channel, but the river was too cold and wide, the currents too treacherous for them to hope to swim across.

Treading water, Samuel looked back to where the renegades were chopping their way into the tops of the lodges, then putting each one to the torch as they found it empty. All along the dense brushy embarras the flames licked skyward in the clear early morning light, darkening the blue with thick sooty smoke. Indians whooped and yipped, leaping from log to log across the floating debris until one man made the mistake of stepping on a sawyer, which submerged, then quickly sprung back up, catapulting him into the air. When he fell back, his leg was crushed beneath the weight of a massive dead cottonwood limb. Several of his fellows tried to reach him.

Using the diversion, the fugitives swam furiously for the opposite shore. Dense scrub pines and cattails covered the water's edge as they scrambled, breathless and dripping, into the shallows. Olivia slipped as her foot struck a moss covered rock and Samuel reached out, catching her in his arms.

"How touchingly solicitous. The perfect officer and gentleman. My, my, Colonel, you are a difficult man to kill," Stuart Pardee said conversationally. "But I do plan to kill you . . . very, very slowly." The venom in his eyes was magnified by the swelling surrounding them and the yellow and purple bruises covering his face, souvenirs of his last, less successful, encounter with Shelby. He signaled half a dozen Osage, who emerged from the dense rushes all with muskets aimed at the couple. "I rather imagined our little bonfire would bring you across the creek if you happened to be hiding inside."

Samuel tried to shield Olivia when two of the Indians reached for her, but as his knife slashed at them, a third came up behind him, clubbing him on the head as the first two seized the kicking, punching woman and dragged her to shore.

"Tie him securely. I have a bit of unfinished business with him before I amuse myself killing him. There are one or two questions Mr. Madison's special agent needs must answer."

Olivia's blood ran cold as she listened to Pardee's hate. Her hunch had been right. Samuel was a spy—and soon he would be a dead one if she did not do something. But what?

They were bound hand and foot in front of a campfire that

night before Samuel came around. For a while Olivia had feared that the second blow to his head had caused some permanent damage and he might never awaken at all . . . not that their future looked that much less bleak when he did regain consciousness.

She had been studying him worriedly when she first noted that his back tensed and his eyes opened, but he only raised his head an imperceptible bit, then murmured to her, "Where have they taken us?"

"We're only a mile or two upstream from where they captured us, on the banks of the Missouri."

"Then Pardee is still late for his rendezvous with that shipment of contraband."

"I rather doubt we can prevent him from reaching it," she replied dryly, refusing to give in to her fear. "How does your head feel?"

"Like a herd of buffalo stampeded over it but at least I'm not seeing double like I did the last time." He slowly scooted around so his hands were in the shadows away from the fire, then began to work his wrists methodically back and forth, testing the buckskin bonds.

"I've already tried that," she said.

"Yes, but I've had more practice."

Their sotto voce discussion was interrupted by the arrival of a large delegation of Osage, several dozen men who had not been with Pardee during his pursuit of the fugitives.

"Looks like the rendezvous has come to the Englishman," Samuel said, cursing beneath his breath. All the while he covertly studied the activity across the fire, he continued to work at his bonds.

"Do you recognize any of them?" she asked, noticing the way he studied one shorter, stocky man, obviously a chief.

"The fellow with the disfigured ears I met with my brother-in-law a few years back. I doubt Chief No Ears will remember me, but who knows?"

"Would he free us?"

"I'm sure he hasn't the power even if he were so inclined. No, he's come here to see what Pardee has to offer just like the rest."

The new delegation took seats and an animated exchange ensued, although the prisoners were too far away to understand much of it. "What are they saying?" Samuel asked

Olivia as she strained to make sense of the occasional phrase carried on the breeze.

"A few are from Pawhuska's village—not yet committed to joining the English and breaking with the old chiefs and the Council of Elders. Your friend No Ears is open to offers, too. They've all come to see what Pardee's message is from the English king," she murmured. "Beyond that, I'm not certain what he is answering—his back is to me and I can't make out his words."

Samuel concentrated on releasing the last of the bindings on his wrists, trying to formulate a way to use the information she had just given him when she suddenly gasped. "What is it?"

"One of the men asked what was to be done with the fire-haired warrior woman who is Great Bear's daughter."

"And?" he prodded, dreading the reply.

"They're arguing on it . . . I can't make out—"

"No one will have her for she is my adopted daughter," a familiar voice boomed in the stillness of the night speaking in Osage. Micajah Johnstone walked boldly into the midst of the assembly, along with another group of Osage. Samuel and Olivia recognized two of them as members of the Council of Elders from Pawhuska's town.

"The white woman and the American Long Knife are my prisoners. You no longer have a claim on her," Pardee said in English, then quickly repeated himself in the Osage tongue. He stood up to face the behemoth in front of him, realizing that the situation had suddenly taken a turn which might not be in his favor.

"When I came after my daughter, one of your men thought to kill me by stealth, shooting me in the back like the cowards you are. My totem, the great bear, took his life with one swipe of her mighty paw—just as I will do to you . . . I wish to win my daughter's freedom by right of combat. Or is the servant of the English father king afraid to fight the Great Bear of the Osage?" Micajah gestured broadly, casting his eyes around the circle of impassive faces as he spoke in their language. As he had hoped, a murmuring rose as the warriors from both factions looked at the Englishman to see how he would respond to the challenge.

Knowing he could not back down, Pardee studied Johnstone whose ruddy seamed countenance looked gray and pale beneath the sun and wind blasted skin. His bloody clothes had been changed for fresh buckskins but the Englishman knew Micajah had to be weakened by the bullet he had taken only two days earlier. "I accept your challenge. Prepare to die and remember that I shall possess your fire-haired daughter while scavengers pick your great carcass clean."

"I claim the right to make the challenge," Samuel interrupted in Spanish, a language all the Osage understood. Striding forward, he shoved aside two of Pardee's Indians who moved to seize him again.

Everyone was amazed that the Long Knife walked free, none more so than the silently enraged British agent. "I have already said I would fight the Great Bear for his daughter. You are still my prisoner."

Shelby smiled nastily, raising his thong burned wrists dramatically in front of the Indians ringing the campfire, striding arrogantly forward when Pardee's warriors hesitated to stop him. "Do I look a prisoner?" he scoffed.

"Who are you to make the challenge in her father's place?" one of the elders asked in broken but serviceable Spanish.

"I am her husband—and my body is whole, not injured as is the Great Bear's. Would the coyote be brave enough to bare his fangs at the bear if he did not see the bear was wounded?" With that he strolled over to spit at Pardee's feet.

Now the murmuring grew louder as Shelby took his place beside Micajah. "While I keep Pardee busy, you see that Olivia is cut free. Get her out of here, Johnstone."

Micajah was still dizzy from blood loss and exhausted by the swift journey in pursuit of the captives. "I'll see ta Sparky," he said quietly. "Yew jest tend ta killin' thet rattler Pardee."

The Englishman knew his credibility with these savages depended on swift retribution against the American who dared call him coward. "I accept your challenge for the woman," he replied in English. His gestures made clear that he was going to fight his challenger. "When I kill you she will belong to me all the more—and so will her father," he added with a sneer. "Then his life will be forfeit, too."

"First you have to kill me. As you already said, not an easy thing to do," Shelby purred.

"But could your other opponents fight like an Osage? This will not be a barroom brawl like that night in the cabin. Let us try knives." Pardee signaled to Bad Temper, who pulled a long, wicked looking blade from his belt and tossed it to his friend, who caught it easily by the handle. He pulled out his own weapon as he offered the other to Shelby.

Samuel took the knife, testing its weight and feel in his hand as he eyed the big rawboned man who moved with such surprising grace. As they began to circle each other cautiously, the ring of spectators spread out, away from what everyone knew would be a no quarter contest between two deadly men.

A number of the Osage placed bets among themselves. Micajah quickly slipped over to where Olivia sat watching in spellbound horror. He cut her free and assisted her to her feet.

"You have to help him, Micajah. Pardee's vicious," she whispered.

"Sam'l beat him once't. I reckon he kin do hit agin. I'll jest make sure th' odds don't change," he said as his eyes narrowed on Bad Temper, who watched the contest with avid interest. Another knife had now magically appeared at his waist in lieu of the one he had tossed to Pardee.

Pardee made the first move, testing Samuel's reflexes and his own reach, which was several inches greater as his arms were abnormally long in proportion to his body. Shelby parried the thrust but not before Pardee opened a superficial cut across his collarbone. The Englishman waited, grinning, for his foe to make the next move. "I'm going to skin you, Colonel, flay you alive . . . inch by bloody inch," he taunted, still waiting.

"The only way you'll kill me, Limey, is to talk me to death." Samuel knew he had to compensate for the disparity in reach but Pardee was lightning quick as well as longer armed. He would just have to be trickier. Everything depended on it. Olivia. Micajah. His mission. Peace along the Missouri. He feinted high, then came in low, and drew Pardee's blood from a long, shallow furrow down his left arm. The Englishman had only one weakness. The swelling around his right eye impaired his vision slightly, a reminder of the beating the American had given him. Now, could Samuel use it to his advantage?

The two men circled, feinting, thrusting, parrying as the firelight reflected the sheen of their sweat soaked bodies, casting the rippling play of muscle, bone and sinew in shadow and light. Olivia stood at the sidelines, afraid to breathe as she watched the deadly ballet being played out before her horrified eyes. Although both combatants were white, they seemed far more savage in expression than the Osage who surrounded them. When Pardee again nicked Samuel, she bit down on her lip to silence her cry.

Both men were well bloodied now, hungry for the kill. Suddenly Pardee lunged, his blade arced high, coming in for a throat slashing kill as his body weight slammed into Shelby. The American seized his foe's wrist, halting the descent of the blade as they went down, rolling on the ground. Each had a death grip on the other's knife hand as they rolled across the dusty earth near the fire. When they were close enough to feel its heat, Pardee used the impetus of the last roll to smash Shelby's knife arm against one of the rocks ringing the fire pit.

Samuel felt his hand go numb, almost losing purchase on his blade. Gritting his teeth, he held on, using his left shoulder to roll them over again. This time he came up on top. His blade drew nearer and nearer Pardee's throat. In a contest of sheer brute strength they were well matched.

From the sidelines Micajah watched Bad Temper move stealthily nearer as it appeared Shelby might break Pardee's grip and plunge his blade into the Englishman's throat. Moving with amazing speed, Johnstone seized the dagger poised in the Osage's hand. Bad Temper jerked away, caught by surprise as several onlookers saw his dishonorable act and murmured in disgust.

"Jest yew let 'em fight man ta man," Johnstone said, shoving him into the waiting hands of several of his angry tribesmen who held him fast.

Although sweat broke out anew across the Englishman's brow, he held Shelby's deadly blade at bay. Suddenly he arched up, rolling them both on their sides, jamming his knee between his foe's legs. Samuel caught the blow to his groin partially on his thigh but the pain was still blinding. He dove away from Pardee and rolled onto all fours struggling to regain the breath that had been sucked from him.

Quick as a snake, the Englishman was up, coming at him again. Shelby barely had time to rise to his feet and parry the deadly slash that could have gutted him. Again they circled, panting, their wet bodies now covered with a thin veneer of mud as the dust from the earth clung to them.

So, you want to use your knees, eh, Pardee? Samuel drew near, daring the deadly arc of his foe's blade. If only that right eye really was impaired enough. Maybe he could help it along. He took another slash of Pardee's blade across his chest to achieve his end as his left fist connected with the injured eye, rocking the Englishman backward with a snarled oath of pain.

When Pardee's eye began to seep water, running in a muddy rivulet down his cheek, Shelby smiled. They closed again, each holding the other's blade at bay but this time as they maneuvered, Samuel butted his opponent in the damaged eye and his left foot swept out, catching the back of Pardee's knee and hooking it forward.

With a grunt of surprise, the Englishman's leg buckled and he lost his balance, stumbling backward. With his balance broken, Pardee's strength slackened and Shelby twisted his knife hand free of his opponent's grasp with surprising ease. He drove his blade into the Englishman's belly, ripping upward to the breastbone.

Pardee teetered on his knees, eyes wide, glazed with disbelief as Shelby stepped back and said, "No, Englishman. I fight like the Osage. You fight like a white man."

Stuart Pardee toppled lifelessly onto the dusty ground.

Samuel stood over him, his cold blue eyes moving from man to man around the campfire. In spite of his blood smeared body—or perhaps because of it—he held their attention riveted when he began to speak, once more in Spanish.

"This man deals in death and now death has claimed him as one of its own. He brought whiskey and weapons to you, promising that with help from his king you could drive out the Americans. I tell you this was a lie. The guns of the English king will never drive out my countrymen who are as numerous as blades of grass or grains of sand along the bank of the Father of Waters. The English king's whiskey will destroy you for it robs great warriors of their reason and sickens the strongest among you. The Osage and the white father in Washington have touched the feather, pledging friendship and peace. I ask you to honor the word given by your elders. What say you to this?" Samuel asked, turning to Chief No Ears and the two elders from Pawhuska's village.

"I have seen you defeat the father king's man in an honorable fight although one of our own sought to bring dishonor on it," one tall old man said, casting a look of pure loathing on Bad Temper, who stood stoically under restraint, his mouth pressed closed in silence.

Then one of the elders from Pawhuska's village stepped forward. "We hear much about this war that is to come between the Long Knives of the seventeen fires of the Americans and the Long Knives of the father king across the great waters. I say it is no fight of ours. My Chief White Hair has already pledged peace with the American Long Knives. I say we should honor it. If children of the two Long Knife leaders wish to kill each other, that is their concern. All is finished here." He gestured to Pardee's body.

Another and then another of the Osage leaders stepped forward to speak. They were in favor of holding to peace with the Americans. Several of the young warriors were displeased, but none dared speak out with their English comrade lying dead at the hands of this American.

Finally, Chief No Ears stood up. The squat little man had a powerfully broad and muscled chest and an air of imposing command about him in spite of the disfigurement of his marred ears, cut off while he was a prisoner of the Kiowas in his youth. "It is true we cannot rely on the English. The Long Knife is right. They live far across the great waters and the Americans are here. But the Americans take our land and give us promises. Then they break them. We cannot rely on them either. What are we to do then? Be swept aside like the dust that settles after a herd of buffalo has raced across the open prairie? Be no more a nation?" His keen black eyes pierced into Samuel's soul.

"I do not know an answer to give you. What you say is true. My government has not been able to prevent settlers from overrunning Osage hunting grounds. But the father in Washington—Madison—wishes peace and prosperity for the Osage. I can only tell you what I do know. And I do know that allying with the English against us will cause more destruction for your people than holding the peace. In time we may learn to live side by side and respect each other's rights. All I can ask now is that you give us all that time."

Samuel waited, holding his breath. Hell, he was a soldier and a spy, not a damned diplomat! Quinn should be here. The White Apache knew how to communicate with these people far better—had lived among them all his life.

Just then Micajah stepped forward for the first time.

Everyone turned expectantly to him. He had the advantage of being able to speak their own language, as he said, "You all know me. You know my heart." He pounded his chest with one massive fist. "It is not in the cities of the white men which I left long ago. It is here in the woodlands, on the prairies, in the land of the Osage where I have lived in peace as a brother. Like you, I do not want the white men to come among us. But the Long Knife speaks true. They will come. You can stop them for a little while, but for every one you kill, they will send many, many more from the seventeen fires across the Father of Waters. In the end it will be the Osage who are destroyed. Peace with the Americans is the only chance for your children and your children's children. It is a wise thing to give the Long Knife the time he has asked."

As Micajah finished speaking, several of the men nodded, including No Ears. Finally, after conferring among themselves, the Osage leaders faced Shelby once again and No Ears spoke. "We will carry your words back to our winter camps where our warriors hone their weapons—not for war—but to hunt the buffalo. We will tell our young men that the Englishman is dead and there will be no more whiskey from him. We ask that your government send one to hold talks with us—one we know and can trust—the one we call the White Apache, a Spaniard you call Santiago Quinn."

Samuel smiled. "The White Apache is my brother, the husband of my sister. He will come. I promise it."

All the while the men spoke Olivia stood in the shadows, absorbing what went on, much relieved at the resolution. Two young warriors took the gory body of Stuart Pardee off to dispose of it and a pipe was lit as the leaders assembled at the fire. Samuel's mission had been accomplished, she thought wistfully. If only there were some resolution to their personal problems. A lump tightened in her throat. Samuel was engrossed in talking with the Osage, setting up a place for his brother-in-law to meet with their leaders. It was Micajah who came to see that she was all right and to bring her some food from the cook pot on the campfire.

"You should let me check that wound. You look awfully pale, Micajah," she said, noticing he winced as he sat down.

"Th' Osage medicine man fixed hit up right 'nough. Bullet passed clean through. Chipped my shoulder blade. Thet's th' part whut hurts somethin' fierce, but I done had worse.

Luckily I got Horse Whisperer and Water Bird ta back me when I come bustin' in here."

"Samuel said you'd gone to get Dirt Devil. Is he—"

"Thet ole rascal's livin' high as a Georgia pine 'bout now back in th' Injun camp. After I got ambushed, my friends lugged us both back there. He took a pretty considerable o' a hit on his skull, but hit's thick."

"Did a bear really save your life like you said?"

"Yep. Took out after them renegades jest afore they wuz fixin' ta' lift my scalp. Hit wuz a she-bar, too."

"Do you think it was the same one you rescued me from?"

He scratched his head consideringly. "Thangs got a way o' commin' 'round. I 'spect it wuz. Wouldn't hit be justice?"

"Yes, Micajah, it would," she said bemused, then dug into the stew. "I'm so grateful you saved us, and grateful she saved you."

He watched her eyes stray again and again back to Shelby as he sat at the fire with the Osage leaders.

"What will happen to Bad Temper?" she asked him, not having worked up her courage to discuss the issue really preying on her mind—her relationship with Samuel.

"Prob'ly nothin'. He's been shamed in front o' his own. Ain't nobody goin' ta listen if he starts talkin' war now. Hit'll be a ways afore he kin make up fer whut he done." He studied her with shrewd eyes, then said softly, "Yew ain't in'erested in thet Injun. Whut's got th' burr up yore rear is smokin' a pipe over yonder."

"He's accomplished his mission. Now he can go back to Washington for his next assignment from President Madison."

Johnstone harrumphed in disgust. " 'N leave his wife behind? I purely doubt hit."

She lifted her chin stubbornly. "It's me who'll be doing the leaving. He doesn't want a wife and I won't stay where I'm not wanted. Besides, I love my life at the cabin. I want to go back with you."

He sighed. *Durn fool young'uns.* "Whut yew love is a tall, purty-faced soldier boy—'n he's got feelin's fer yew, too—jest too pig stubborn ta admit hit ta hisself. But he will 'n then he'll tell yew. Meanwhile, yore married afore man 'n God. I ain't comin' betwixt yew."

Now it was Micajah's turn to look stubborn. Olivia sighed,

knowing argument was as useless as it had been that day at the cabin when he found them together. He had some fool romantic notion that she and Samuel were destined to love one another.

If only it were true.

Samuel finished talking with the Osage, then stood up, moving his aching shoulders gingerly. Not an inch of his body was unbruised, most of it cut or at least sticky with blood, both Pardee's and his own. His eyes swept the camp searching for Olivia.

His wife. The words did not sound so alien now. Grinning, he decided perhaps he was getting used to the idea. She and Micajah were seated in the shadows, talking intently. When he drew near they stopped. Olivia rose and walked up to him as the old man studied him with those unnerving dark eyes of his, saying nothing.

"You're hurt. I'll need to clean off that dried blood before I can see how badly," she said, touching the crusty dark smears on his arm.

He smiled at her. "I appreciate the wifely concern."

Her cheeks felt warm under his scrutiny. "Come with me to the stream so I can wash you. Micajah, we'll need something for bandages and some herbs to—"

"I got everthin' yew need in my possibles sack," he said. Picking up the buckskin pouch tossed on a nearby rock, he began to root through it, then handed her a jar of salve and a roll of clean white cloth. "Jest go git cleaned up. Moon's full 'nough ta see down by th' river. After all thet's happened, I 'spect yew two cud use a minit or two alone ta talk."

"Yes, I expect we could," Samuel echoed, taking Olivia's hand in his, pulling her into the trees, headed toward the soft hum of the rushing water.

∽ *Chapter 20* ∽

When they reached the river's edge, Samuel finally broke the silence. "Back there in the beaver lodge, before Pardee and his renegades found us . . . you asked me a question. I never had the opportunity to answer it."

Olivia wished desperately that she could see his face more clearly, not shadowed and dappled by moonlight as it was. "And now . . . ? What will we do about this marriage? You were forced—"

"We both were forced," he interrupted softly, "but that doesn't mean that things haven't changed since our wedding night."

"You acted as if you blamed me because I was what I had always been—as if you wanted me to be no better than you expected." The pain of his angry guilt still stung bitterly. "Then you left me alone."

"So Pardee could abduct you when it was my place to be there, to protect you." The guilt over that bit deeper than the guilt he felt for misjudging her innocence. "I was out getting drunk to drown my own filthy conscience."

The words seemed dragged from him, as if he were revealing a piece of his innermost soul to her and it was incredibly painful. She leaned toward him and her palms pressed against his chest, feeling the harsh slamming of his heartbeat. He was tensed like a mountain lion in a cage—a cage she and Micajah had unwittingly wrought. "I don't want your guilt or your sense of duty as an officer and a gentleman, Samuel. You know who I am now. If that's not enough, then no vows spoken before a priest will ever make it good enough for me to stay with you."

"And what would make it good enough, Livy?" he asked, reaching up to caress her cheek and cup her stubborn jaw, tilting her chin up so he could look into the dark fathomless depths of her eyes.

She did not answer in words but her lips parted slightly and her hand seemed to move of its own volition, small and pale over his larger, dark one, covering it, pressing it more firmly against her face, drawing nearer to him, begging to be kissed as he ached to kiss her.

Samuel, too, answered without words as his mouth brushed hers, softly rimming the sweet bow of her upper lip with the tip of his tongue, tracing the plush full outline of the lower, then gliding along the moistened seam between them to skim over her teeth, before he deepened the kiss. Slowly, savoringly, he plunged inside to ravish her with languid sweeps, drawing her total response as she opened to him, her own tongue twining with his, tasting of him and hungering for more, so very much more.

They held each other that way, their hands cradling each other's faces, kissing slowly, deeply, communicating in the poignant caress what neither had been able to say aloud. Then, gradually he ended the kisses, pulling his mouth from hers like a man denying himself the gates of paradise.

Murmuring against her mouth, he said, "Oh, Livy, Livy, stay with me, be my wife. I need you—I love you." He shook his head ruefully, then met her eyes. "I swore an oath I would never say that to another woman as long as I lived."

"I love you, Samuel. I think I always knew from the first moment I saw you across that ballroom floor in Washington."

He grinned down at her, unable to keep his hands from caressing her throat, brushing her tangled hair away from her face. "I guess that's why we've always been so explosive together. I've never been able to control myself around you the way I could with other women."

"And you hate not being in control." She knew him so well, this mysterious stranger, this soldier-spy who owned her heart.

"Ever since I met you my world's been turned upside down. When I found you with Lisa's men I couldn't believe it. God, I hated myself for wanting you so badly then," he confessed raggedly.

"Was that why you were such a beast to me?" she asked sweetly.

"That and the fact you nearly poisoned me, drowned me, and got my brains beaten in by a dozen trappers," he replied with a lopsided smile.

When he raised his arms and drew her against him, the slash along his collarbone twinged and he winced at the unexpected pain. "I'd better see to your wounds before Micajah sends half the Osage Little Old Men out searching for us." She knelt down at the water's edge and began to soak a clean piece of cloth, then instructed him to kneel so she could cleanse away the dried blood.

"It might be better if I just stripped and swam into the deep. I'm pretty gory from head to foot."

Olivia shuddered, remembering how terrifying the grisly fight with Pardee had been. "You could've been the one dead, not him." Suddenly she needed the assurance of his warm male vitality, the solid protective wall of his flesh pressed to her own. "Hold me, Samuel," she whispered, wrapping her arms around his back and lying her head against his chest, heedless of the caked and seeping blood on it.

He obliged, enveloping her in his embrace, squeezing his eyes closed, feeling a sense of peace steal over him that he had never before in his life felt.

Livy was his wife, for always.

After a few moments she stepped back. "You need to get cleaned up so I can tend your wounds." She watched him as he slipped off his pants and waded into the current, swimming out far enough to let the cool rushing water cleanse away the blood. Olivia knelt on the shore with Micajah's salves.

"Why not join me?" he invited.

"Samuel, it's getting late in the season for a moonlight swim. I can see your goose bumps even in this light."

Samuel laughed. "The water's only cold until you get in deep. Come in and join me and I'll let you feel my bump!"

She longed to bathe away the contamination of Pardee's touch even if the only clothes she had with her belonged to the dead man. Quickly she unfastened the rope at her slim waist and tugged off the baggy britches and shirt. Her feet were still bare but healing nicely since Samuel had tended them. She let out a squeak of shock at the chill when she stepped into the current, then quickly submerged herself and swam out to meet him where he lounged against a dead log wedged into a mud bank jutting ten feet or so out in the river.

He opened his arms and she glided up against him, at once feeling the hardness of his phallus pressing against her belly, scorching hot even in the chilly water. She undulated against him and he took her arms, lifting her against him. "Come on to me, Livy," he whispered hoarsely. She obeyed, wrapping her legs around him as he impaled her smoothly in one long swift thrust.

She threw back her head, arching into the sweet heat, clutching his shoulders, digging in with her nails as she tightened her thighs at his waist, falling in sync with the rocking tempo of his thrusting hips. Her breasts bobbed at the surface of the water, the nipples puckered into tight aching nubs. The warmth of his mouth covering one, then the other, released a swift shock of pleasure that radiated through her body, intensifying the incredible pressure building deep inside her belly until it burst upon her in long lovely waves that seemed to build with the steady lapping of the current eddying around them.

Olivia waited in that little death, soaring yet experienced enough by now to know that he would join her. Then she felt it, the tumescent swelling and pulsing of his staff deep inside her, his body convulsively stiffening as he gasped out her name and spilled his seed into her womb. She threw her head across his shoulder and clung to him in joy. And the river gave its benediction as its life-giving water flowed serenely around them.

Micajah was ready to travel at dawn the next day. Most of the Osage had already vanished into the gray morning fog, leaving him and the two men who would escort him back to their village to collect Dirt Devil. He watched in satisfaction as Samuel slept with Olivia cocooned protectively in the curve of his body. They had returned from the river last night touching and smiling in subtle ways that spoke clearly to the shrewd old man. Still, he felt constrained to speak his piece to Shelby before he entrusted his beloved Sparky to the colonel's care.

He sat hunkered beside the fire with a tin mug almost concealed by his big hands, drinking the steaming inky brew black and bitter, wishing for a bit of his honey to sweeten it, while he let the young lovers sleep. Neither had gotten much rest in past days. Of course, some of that was their own doing, he thought with a smile, remembering how it was to be young and in love.

Shelby stirred, gently disentangled himself from Olivia, then climbed from beneath the blanket Chief No Ears had given them. He shivered in the foggy stillness. The winter that had been so long in coming would soon be upon them.

Micajah threw him a buckskin shirt which was a bit tight across his broad chest but provided welcome warmth none-theless. He accepted a cup of coffee from the old man and sat down across from him expectantly. "You have something to say, Johnstone, spit it out."

Micajah chuckled quietly. "Fer a feller without th' sense ta see truth when hit slapped him upside th' haid, yew kin be plenty sharp from time ta time."

"I was wrong about Olivia. I misjudged her . . . in many ways, underestimated her."

" 'N now yew know who she really is?"

Samuel smiled. "She's my wife. All right, Johnstone, you were right to drag us to that priest. I admit it."

"Jest so's yew treat her like she deserves else yew'd have me ta answer ta—'n yew would purely never want thet. I cud think o' thangs even th' Osage 'n the Sioux never imagined . . . if yew take my meanin'." He smiled benevolently with his eyes twinkling.

Shelby returned the grin. "Yes, Micajah, I take your mean-ing. We have to go downriver to St. Louis as fast as we can get there. I have to report Pardee's death and arrange for my brother-in-law to bring a representative from the War Department to talk with the Osage."

"While they wuz fixin' me up, them Injuns whut found me offered me one o' their secret caches below them bluffs up yonder. Got a canoe, food, even a few furs to keep a body warm . . . not thet I do believe yew two'll need 'em."

"With a canoe we could make good time, be back in St. Louis in a few days," Shelby replied, excited at the prospect. "Livy wouldn't have to walk on her injured feet either."

Micajah nodded his head. "Hit's settled then. Yew 'n' me go dig up th' cache whilst Sparky fixes breakfast." He turned to grin at her as she climbed sleepily from beneath the covers.

God above, St. Louis was a squalid and barbaric outpost clinging to the banks of a wild, treacherous river. Richard Bullock despised it, just as he despised the jowly pompous merchant perched on the chair across from him like a giant green toad. But Emory Wescott did have his uses. At present, he was Bullock's only link to Colonel Samuel Shelby.

"And you say this ward of yours has married Colonel

Shelby," he repeated, sipping fragrant tea from a delicate china cup as he stared across the rim at Wescott.

Emory set his cup down with a slight clatter, angry beyond words at the latest piece of news he had just received from upriver, another complication he did not need. Pardee had failed. Perhaps Bullock would be the man to rid him of the impediment of Olivia's husband.

"Yes, Olivia was always a headstrong girl, reckless and spoiled just like her mother. She ran off on a lark. I was able to send word to one of my acquaintances who located her in a godforsaken outpost on the Missouri. She and the colonel had just been wed by a Catholic priest in Ste. Francoise."

With Pardee now dead and their last shipment of contraband lost, Wescott's interest in the British war effort had taken a decidedly cool turn. If only he could get his hands on Olivia, free and clear of Shelby's meddling, he would hurry her down to New Orleans where the fabulous wealth of the Durand estate would be his.

"Then you expect the honeymooners to return here soon?" Richard asked neutrally.

"I would imagine Olivia and her soldier will arrive shortly. As you can well imagine, her marriage will create all sorts of embarrassing complications—complications I wish to avoid. After all, I am still her guardian and I do have her best interests at heart."

Bullock smiled, a chilly curling of his thin, beautifully sculpted lips, but it was a smile that never touched the pale ice in his eyes. He could well imagine how sincerely solicitous the cagey old bastard was toward the chit. "I'm certain you do, Mr. Wescott. And I have an equally strong interest in the colonel . . . for entirely different reasons. Perhaps we can reach some accord regarding a resolution of this situation," he purred, setting down his cup as he rose to take his leave. "I shall attend to Colonel Shelby in due course, never fear."

After the icy Virginian had departed, Wescott stared moodily into the tea leaves at the bottom of his cup, then rang for a brandy, although it was barely past the noon hour. Bullock was a cipher. Wescott understood his professed reasons for wanting Shelby dead, but he had never been one to trust any man's superficial motives. They had met at a social function at the home of the acting governor, Frederick Bates, honoring territorial militia general William Clark. Wescott rubbed his forehead, not even wanting to contemplate his fate if General Clark learned about his involvement in gun running among the Osage. If only he knew how much Pardee had revealed before he was killed.

One thing was clear—Emory Wescott had no time to wait for Richard Bullock's *due course*.

In spite of the long overdue turn in the weather, Samuel and Olivia's journey downriver was an idyll of smooth currents and crisp but sunny days. They paddled on the open river, only once having to portage past a dangerous embarras. On the first day out, they ate from the dried fruits and meat from the Osage cache, but the second morning, Samuel shot a pair of rabbits before they set out. Olivia efficiently cleaned and cooked them over the campfire, throwing a fistful of wild sage onto the coals to add a wonderfully pungent flavor to the meat.

At night they pulled the canoe up on the bank, and slept out beneath the starry canopy of the sky. To waken every morning in each other's arms was a new experience for both of them. Samuel had never slept with Tish even in the early days of their marriage since she had always insisted that a lady deserved the privacy of her own bedroom. From Olivia's childhood in lavish European accommodations to her months in Micajah's cheery cabin, she had always spent her nights alone. Never had she dreamed how wonderful this could be, how warm and reassuring the feel of her husband's heart beating in rhythm with her own.

She wished they could drift forever on the river, living off the bounty of nature, picking wild gooseberries and currants, shooting fat rabbits and watching the brown and gold grandeur of the woodlands around them. Otters and muskrats played in the current, diving and chasing one another, putting on a show for their human audience. From the shore a black bear peered at them from behind the carcass of a deer, his mouth smeared with blood. Olivia had watched, fascinated by the stark contrasts of nature, beautiful and brutal in alternate turns.

"I'll miss Micajah," she said pensively on the third afternoon as they moved swiftly in the main channel. Samuel paddled skillfully while she lay in the bottom of the canoe, basking comfortably in the midday sun. "Saying good-bye was harder than anything like it before. I was ten when we left the Count of San Giorno's estate in Tuscany. He was the one who taught me to ride. I called him Uncle Angelo." She smiled in fond remembrance. "I cried inconsolably for days."

"Why did you have to leave?" Samuel had a pretty good idea but he wanted to learn more about her family.

"My *père* was bored living so far out in the country. He longed for witty conversation and ladies decked in jewels, for the city life; in truth he longed for the gaming tables in Rome. And so we made our way across Europe. It seemed the longer we traveled, the more rootless we became, the less time we spent in any single place."

He could understand now why Micajah's simple cabin had meant so much to her and felt guilty for his accusations about getting bored with the adventure and longing to return to her easy life in St. Louis. "Micajah was a better father to you than Julien St. Etienne," he said.

"Yes, that's true, although I would never have believed it possible before. I adored *Père* . . . but I never knew who I was until I met Micajah Johnstone."

"We'll see him in the spring, Livy. He promised to come to St. Louis for a visit. I'm sorry we had no time to return to the cabin with him, but I have to send a report to my superiors and arrange for the Osage to meet with my brother-in-law."

"I said I would miss him, not that I would be lonely, Samuel." She reached up to take his hand, distracting him from paddling. "Let the canoe drift with the current. It's moving fast enough," she said with a lazy chuckle.

Shelby scanned the river ahead. As far as he could see, it flowed free. He set the paddle down and then slid from his seat to settle in the bottom of the small skin-covered craft, drawing her into his arms. Together they watched as meadows of prickly pear and tall stands of cottonwoods on the shore passed by, content just to hold each other in the dying light of the late afternoon sun.

They reached St. Louis at dusk the following day. The waterfront was crowded with moored keelboats and flatboats. Samuel eased their canoe in between two of the heavy flatboats and as soon as they had jumped ashore, he pulled the light craft up onto the bank lest it be damaged. The riverfront was deserted but up on the hill the noise of drunken revelry from Main Street could be heard echoing across the black stillness of the Mississippi.

"We'll go to my house first. I need a clean uniform before I can report to Bates and Clark." He grinned at her, the dim light showing the white slash of his teeth as he said, "Maybe I'll even carry my new bride over the threshold."

"Maybe I'll hold you to that—and a bath. I am not only filthy; I'm freezing. Lord above, how I long for a hot, lazy soak with real soap."

They made their way up the steep hill, avoiding the rowdy district where the rivermen caroused, heading south toward his rented house on Plum Street. "While you're luxuriating in my tub I have quite a bit of business to attend. I don't think we should let your so-called guardian know about our marriage until I've made my report to the acting governor and General Clark. If he sent Pardee after you, I want to find out why."

"You're afraid he might hurt me, aren't you?"

She was far too perceptive. "It's possible. Just stay inside the house until I return. It may be late. I'll also have to explain to Santiago about the parlay he'll lead."

"Will he be willing to do it? I thought you said he distrusted the American government."

Samuel grinned. "Liza will see to it that he does. Hardbitten Spanish outcast that he is, Quinn will do anything for his wife."

"I'm anxious to get to know my new sister-in-law," she said primly.

"Just don't go letting her fill your head with crazy ideas. I'm not as indulgent as Santiago."

She smiled secretively but made no rejoinder as they trudged down Second to Plum. When they arrived, he did carry her across the threshold amid laughter and tenderness.

Samuel quickly cleaned up and shaved, then donned a fresh uniform while the elderly man he had employed to watch over the house drew a hot bath for Olivia. Samuel left her soaking blissfully and headed straight to the Quinns'. Liza and her canny Spaniard knew more about what went on in the city than anyone.

Won't she be amazed that I married again. But then he reconsidered. Perhaps she would not be. His sister had been the first to notice the attraction between him and Olivia. He climbed the well-worn stone steps to their front porch and knocked eagerly.

When Orlena Quinn opened the door for her uncle, a broad smile of joy wreathed her cherubic face. "Unca Samuel!" the five-year-old squealed in delight as he picked her up and swung her around in the air.

Elise stood in the doorway down the hall watching fondly as her eldest child bombarded her brother with questions. She bit her lip worriedly. *How shall I break the news to him?*

Samuel looked up and caught sight of her the same time that little Orlena did. "Mamma, Mamma, Unca Samuel's back all the way from visiting the Osage Indians."

At once he sensed something was amiss. "Is Santiago all right—the boys?"

She nodded. "Yes, of course, they're all fine. And so it seems, are you. Oh, Samuel, I was so worried. You've been gone for months with only that one sparse note."

"I didn't know if it got through or not. I had to entrust it to a French-Canadian trader I met headed down the Missouri last summer. He was the only white man I encountered until the Englishman."

She paled. "You found him then."

"He's dead," he said flatly. "So are his schemes to take the Osage into a British alliance."

Knowing they had serious business to discuss, Elise picked up Orlena and rang for the nanny to get her ready for bed, promising to come in later to hear the child's prayers and tuck her in. Samuel waited for his sister in the library, wishing Santiago had not chosen tonight of all nights to work late at the warehouse. Then again, perhaps it was better to enlist Liza to his cause before the Spaniard returned home.

Hearing her at the door, he turned, glass in hand and asked, "Does Orlena forgive me for precipitating her early bedtime?"

"She knows well enough she can only remain up half an hour past her little brothers," Elise said smiling. "She was greatly mollified by that pretty quilled Osage necklace you brought her. You do spoil her outrageously."

"Maybe it's practice for having children of my own," he said lightly, watching with relish the poleaxed expression on her face. "While I was upriver I got married again, Liza. Olivia St. Etienne is now Mrs. Samuel Shelby."

She paled. "Oh, Samuel, no."

Seeing her dismay, he set down his brandy glass and walked over to her in consternation. "I thought you favored the match, Liza."

"Oh, I do, very much I do, but . . ."

"But what?"

Her shoulders slumped as she took his hands in hers. "Tish is alive, Samuel. She's here in St. Louis with her stepbrother. They arrived several months ago. I had no way to send you word. I'm afraid the colonel's lady has become quite the toast of local society in your absence," she added bitterly.

Now he was the one poleaxed. "But the letter last spring said she had . . . Then that means—"

"Yes, your marriage to Olivia is invalid. Her guardian has been quite mum about her sudden departure last spring. Said she'd gone to visit relatives in New Orleans, but somehow I never believed him. Where is she now, Samuel?"

"At my house on Plum." He cursed and pounded Santiago's heavy oak desk. "If people ever find out we've been bigamously married, her reputation will be in shreds. Bad enough she has a panderer for a guardian."

"What do you mean? Why did she vanish last spring?" Elise's clear violet eyes studied her brother, who looked distinctly uncomfortable, much as he had when they were children and their father called him on the carpet for some infraction.

Quickly, not sparing his own culpability, Samuel outlined Wescott's proposition to him, his acceptance and the dangerous aftermath. "So, after Micajah was able to rescue us from Pardee's Osage friends, we headed back to St. Louis."

Elise took it all in, not accusing or condemning. She knew her brother to be an honorable man who would not have taken advantage of an innocent girl under any circumstances, least of all one for whom he already had feelings whether or not he acknowledged them at the time. When he finished, she had decided upon a course of action. "I must bring Olivia here at once. She can stay as our guest until we sort out this tangle. That will spare her reputation and protect her from any claim of her guardian. You'll have to deal with Tish."

He sighed and finished off the brandy. "The divorce will take months."

"I'm certain Olivia will wait, Samuel," Elise consoled.

"But do I have the right to ask that? You know the stigma attached to a divorced man. As you said, the first Mrs. Shelby has made quite a splash among the city's elite. They won't forgive this easily—if at all."

"I know Olivia will not care and anyone else who would hold you to Letitia Soames is not worth bothering about," she replied crossly. "Now you go report to General Clark and Secretary Bates while I fetch Olivia here. We'll concoct some story to give out regarding her absence while we wait for you and Santiago to return."

"I must be the one to tell her about Tish, Liza. I owe her that."

"I understand. I'll bring her here and say only that you have something of moment to discuss with her. I'll do my best to reassure her, Samuel."

"What would I do without such a marvelous sister?" he said, kissing her forehead and hugging her.

She patted his cheek, noting the haunted look darkening his eyes. "We'll work this out, Samuel," she assured him. *The good Lord knows you deserve a chance at the happiness our papa never had.*

It was well past midnight by the time Samuel finished discussing the Indian situation on the Missouri with his superiors. Santiago, summoned by his wife, had arrived at Secretary Bates's residence shortly after Shelby and remained there planning the expedition upriver. Now Samuel had to face Olivia. What would her reaction be? How could he ask her to endure the ugliness of a divorce as it dragged through the distant Virginia legislature?

When he arrived at the Quinn residence one lone light burned softly from the library window. He knew Olivia was waiting for him. Inside the house was deathly quiet, Elise, her children and the servants all asleep. He walked down the darkened hallway and opened the library door.

Olivia heard his footfalls at the front door and moistened her lips nervously. She knew it must at last be Samuel. There was something about the way he moved that she would always recognize, even in the dark. She had spent the past hours in desperate fear that he had changed his mind about their marriage, that he was going to make some provision and leave her, but then why bring her to his sister's home?

Elise had gone to great lengths to reassure her of how much Samuel loved her. She pressed her fingertips to her aching temples, then smoothed the simple yellow muslin gown that her sister-in-law had given her. It fit quite well since they were both tall and slender. She had bathed and washed her hair, eagerly anticipating Samuel's lovemaking in their own bed when he returned. Now she sat in a strange house, dressed formally for a confrontation with him . . . and she had no idea of how to react, what to do.

Oh, my love, what has happened?

When he stepped inside the room, she could tell at once that something was terribly wrong. Her heart seemed to stop beating as she stood up and took a step toward him, then stopped in midstride, afraid to fly into his arms. He stood ramrod straight, looking so splendidly handsome in his blue uniform, just as he had that first night when she had seen him across a crowded ballroom floor. And fallen in love at first glimpse.

He ached to take her in his arms, but he had no right. With his fists balled impotently at his sides, he struggled to regain control. "Livy . . . Olivia, I'm sorry Liza had to bring you here in the middle of the night this way."

"What has happened, Samuel?" He stood across the room from her. But she knew they were separated by more than a few yards.

He nervously combed his fingers through his long shaggy black hair, pacing back and forth across the thick Navajo rug on the polished floor, trying to frame the words. There simply was no way to soften the blow. He forced himself to meet those fathomless green eyes and said, "Tish is alive, Olivia. She's been here in St. Louis for months. Everyone knows she's my wife. That's why Liza had to get you out of my house before anyone saw you."

When he spoke, the words at first refused to register, so great was the shock, but then they did, especially the last ones . . . *before anyone saw you.* "You're returning to her, then," she said flatly, numb with shock.

He blinked incredulously. "Going back to her? God, no! I despise her as much as she does me." He walked over to her and took her in his arms, pulling her against his heart and holding tight. "You smell like jasmine," he murmured against her fiery hair, kissing the tumbled curls and pressing them against his face.

"Then why did you have me—"

"Little fool," he said fondly, relieved at her simple misunderstanding. "Livy, your reputation would be destroyed if word of a bigamous marriage got out, even an unintentional bigamous marriage. No one in St. Louis would ever receive you again."

"Since I've already scandalized proper society at the racetrack, they probably won't receive me anyway. I don't care." She looked up into his eyes, her own blazing with defiance.

"Well, I do care. Think, Livy. I wouldn't be able to secure a divorce if you were implicated. The whole thing could become very ugly. Regardless, it will take months, probably a year. Her father is a very powerful man in Virginia and he'll fight us every step of the way."

Suddenly Olivia could feel his trembling. He was afraid for her. She reached up and stroked his cheek. "I don't care how rumors fly or how long it takes—whatever it takes, I will wait for you, Samuel."

He felt her arms tighten around his neck as she pulled his head down to her and kissed him with a soft desperation that quickly turned to white-hot ardor. As always they were explosive together, melding to each other, bodies entwined as the kiss deepened and they felt themselves spiraling out of control.

His mind hammered a desperate message to his body. *Stop before it's too late.* He pulled away from her in a sudden rush, holding her trembling lithe young body at arm's length. Her lips were swollen with his kisses and her eyes dark, fathomless with passion and love. Nothing had ever been harder in his life. He struggled for breath, air searing his lungs in great gulps as if he'd just run the Osage gauntlet once more.

"I can't—I have to go, Livy. If I stay . . . I have no right to lie with you . . . it's not the way I want it to be between us. I want you for my wife, not my mistress."

Her heart shattered with the bittersweet pain of his declaration. Once she had run from him because he wanted what she was now all too willing to give. But everything had changed. "You have all the right on earth . . . but I will wait, if that's the way it must be."

He smiled a wistful, lopsided smile that made her heart turn over and said, "I love you, Livy . . . and that's the way it must be."

Outside in the darkness a figure crouched behind the bare

brushy branches of a lilac bush, watching the scene being played out in the Quinns' library. He scowled in satisfaction when the lovers embraced passionately. So this was the woman Shelby had married, thinking his first wife was dead. It was obvious he would never go back to Tish. "In any case the colonel must die," he murmured to himself as he watched the touching leave-taking going on inside.

Then he waited.

Samuel swung up on his horse and rode slowly down the street, lost in thought. He was bone weary. Nothing would have been more wonderful, more natural than to sleep with Livy's soft warmth nestled against his body, but that was not to be. A deep, slowly simmering rage rose inside him, thinking of Tish's scheming lies. He knew it had been her doing, this "mistake" about her death.

"God rot me, I still wish she *were* dead," he muttered to the horse disconsolately as the big stallion's hoofbeats plodded down the dusty street. When he turned the corner onto Plum he ducked his head to avoid a dead grapevine swinging from the locust tree overhead. At that same instant the crack of a shot erupted and the vine snapped in two, splinters flying from the force of impact.

Samuel wheeled his horse around and kicked him into a gallop, lying low against his neck as he rode directly toward the wooded lot from which the shot had come. The undergrowth was thick, choked with dry blackberry brambles and tall goldenrod now autumn brown. By the time he had reached the wooded lot, he could already hear a horse racing down the next street, headed toward the waterfront. To the north First Street was crowded with buildings, tall warehouses and smaller offices and tanneries. Whoever it was would be long gone by the time he reached the road.

He was getting damned tired of being used for target practice, especially since all that had saved his life the past several times was blind chance. His assassin was uncommonly unlucky, but an accursedly good shot, whoever the hell he was.

Turning back his horse, Samuel girded himself to face Tish in the morning.

∽ *Chapter 21* ∽

Samuel rode up to the front yard of the Parker mansion and dismounted. Tish waited for him inside. He could no longer think of her as his wife—not since marrying Olivia. It was a very fortunate thing Tish had considered his humble lodgings unworthy of being graced by her presence, else she would have found out about Olivia. The huge two-story stone monolith standing before him, built by a prosperous "Boston" for his socially ambitious wife, was grand enough to suit a Soames. The Parkers had welcomed Colonel Shelby's lady into their home and introduced her to St. Louis society.

Scowling, he knocked on the door, knowing Tish would still be abed since it was scarcely eight A.M., an utterly uncivilized hour by her reckoning. A punctilious butler admitted him, then ushered him into the front parlor to cool his heels while Mrs. Shelby was informed of her long-absent husband's return. He paced restlessly while he waited, anxious to have the nasty confrontation over.

Surprisingly, Tish came downstairs within a quarter hour, her hair in an artless dishabille of silvery curls, spilling over her shoulders. She wore only a lavender brocade dressing gown and soft carpet slippers. "Darling, I've been absolutely desperate to see you! It's been nearly four months since we arrived and no word from you. I was terrified you'd been killed!" She flew across the bric-a-brac filled parlor with arms outstretched. When he made no attempt to return the embrace but stepped stiffly back, she retreated a step with a wounded look on her face. "After I've risked life and limb traveling thousands of miles through the wilderness to reach you, this is the welcome I receive?"

"For a dead woman, you appear amazingly hale and hearty, Tish. How did you manage the resurrection?" he asked sardonically.

"You're angry with me," she said with a small moue, stepping closer again, letting her dressing gown gap open the tiniest bit as she shrugged one elegant shoulder. "The whole thing was a terrible misunderstanding. I wasn't on the boat that went down, but I had planned to be. Daddy was beside himself when he received the news. By the time everyone realized that I hadn't drowned with the others, the letter to you had already been posted. That's when I decided to come to St. Louis in person."

She had excellent timing, Samuel would give her that. All the theatrical gestures, the cajoling and tears—she could hold a stage with the best of them. Old Senator Soames always fell for it. So did Richard. So had he, at first. Shelby watched as she wrung her hands and moistened her lips with a pleading look in her eyes.

"We've both had time apart to reconsider our lives. I . . . I wanted to prove to you that I could change, could learn to make a home here in the West. You believed you had lost me forever and I've feared so much that you might have been killed . . . I must say your sister and that foreigner she's married to weren't at all forthcoming about where you'd gone or when you might return. They wouldn't tell me anything."

He arched one eyebrow cynically, standing with his arms crossed and feet braced apart. "You scarcely seemed to be pining away in my absence. Liza tells me you've become the belle of the Mississippi. Every prominent family in the city has feted you while I was upriver."

"Well, I did have to meet your friends and business associates. If we're to build a new life here—"

"We are not building anything, Tish. I told you back in Washington, our marriage has for all practical purposes been over for three years."

"You can't do this to me!" She almost stamped her foot, but restrained herself and forced the tears to well up instead. "I've done exactly as you wished. I've come to you in St. Louis. I risked my life traveling up that hellish, savage-infested river. I've given up Washington, broken poor Daddy's heart leaving him the way I did—just for you, Samuel. All for you."

"All too late, Tish. You know it, too. Is that why you concocted the lie about drowning? To buy yourself time so you could get here and insinuate yourself back into my life before the divorce bill was brought to the Virginia legislature?"

Tish paled, balling her hands into tight fists to keep from

clawing at him. How had he guessed? When had she become so transparent to him? So careless of him as to let matters get this disastrously out of hand? She swallowed the bile rising in her throat and cried prettily. "How can you be so cruel? I have nowhere to go. Daddy will be ruined by the scandal of a divorce. He'll disown me."

"Your father would never disown his precious Tishabelle, not even if you sprouted a tail and horns and walked down Pennsylvania Avenue stark naked." Samuel watched her growing frustration as all her well-rehearsed, teary scenarios failed, one by one. "Anyway, you'll always have Richard to console you. He is here with you, isn't he?"

"You've always hated my brother," she accused.

He shrugged. "Bullock may always do what you want, Tish, but I will not. Best you have him take you home to Daddy. I'm going through with the divorce."

The words were delivered with flat finality. She stared at him with pale calculating eyes narrowed. "It's her, isn't it? That little French slut you took upriver with you—the one you *thought* you'd married." Tish smiled in satisfaction at his lack of reaction. She had long ago learned that he never revealed his most deep-seated emotions. Richard had been right, damn it all. Her husband was well and truly lost to her.

"What do you think you know, Tish?" he asked carefully.

"I know everything. One of the prominent men I've become acquainted with happens to be the little fool's guardian. Mr. Wescott has been most concerned about his ward's absence. Imagine his horror to learn that she had contracted a bigamous marriage with *my* husband," she finished in catty triumph.

Samuel's guts clenched, but he fought to remain calm, although it had never been more difficult in his life. "You don't intend to rusticate here in St. Louis, Tish," he began, carefully neutral. He had to buy time for Olivia, to get Tish back to Washington, away from St. Louis where she could ruin his innocent love. "I'm frankly amazed you lasted for these few months."

"Now that I've been reunited with my husband and his mission here is completed, I had hopes *we* might return to civilization." She stressed the *we* maliciously.

"And if I don't dance attendance on you?" His voice was low, deadly.

"Why, Samuel darling, it's quite simple. I shall take

shameless advantage of what the distraught Mr. Wescott told me and announce to the world that Olivia St. Etienne married you and lived as your wife thinking all the while that I was dead . . . which I most obviously am not."

"A situation I itch to remedy, my dear," he replied bitterly.

"Ah, but you won't, Samuel dearest. I know that you're too honorable to stoop to murder."

A sudden flash of intuition caused him to ask, "But you aren't, are you, Tish? Neither is your lapdog, Bullock."

She feigned confusion. "I'm quite certain I don't know what you're talking about. All I want is my husband returned safely to me. And now I have him, don't I, Samuel?"

"What you have, Tish, is a stalemate. I won't petition for divorce and you won't besmirch Olivia's reputation. When do you wish to return to Washington?" he asked with bitter resignation.

"I think by the first of the week. I shall have to have time to pack. And we must attend the gala the Parkers are giving tomorrow night. You will escort me, of course." She looked up at him coyly. "I suppose I should move into that quaint little cottage of yours now that you've returned."

"Don't put yourself out, Tish. You could never survive without a retinue of servants and I've no room for them—not to mention no place for your beloved brother either."

"Very well. But don't think to publicly humiliate me by sleeping with your French whore. You'd not like my retaliation, I vow."

Samuel stepped closer to her and seized a fistful of silver gilt hair, twisting it around his fist. He pulled her head back, forcing her to look him full in the face. "Don't ever threaten me or Olivia again, Tish. We have an agreement. I'll not tarnish her reputation. You had better not either."

With that, he released her and stalked out, leaving her to rub her aching scalp while she seethed.

"I already told you I don't care a fig for my reputation. Don't let her do this to us, Samuel," Olivia pleaded.

Shelby stopped pacing across the Quinns' library and sat down on the small settee beside her. "I have no choice, Livy. Neither do you. If I don't return with her to Washington, I'll just be giving her father more ammunition to use against us. God, a court might consider my failure to escort her as desertion. If I'm ever to get free of her, I have to fight Senator Soames on his home ground, away from any possible scandal here."

"You promised me you would never return to her and now she's blackmailing you into it." Olivia knew she sounded stubborn, petulant even, but she could not seem to help it.

"I'm doing only what I must. You know I would never touch her," he said patiently.

"Nor me either until this whole ugly mess is over," she replied disconsolately.

"It could take a year, Livy." There was anxiety in his voice, his manner, as he watched her. "I have no right . . ."

Her heart turned over and she seized his hands, raising them, kissing the callused palms one at a time. "Samuel, sometimes you have no more sense than a chicken. You have every right. And I *will* wait no matter how long it takes."

After Samuel had departed, Elise found Olivia staring out the window, lost in thought. "You're sad," she said sympathetically. "Do you want to talk?"

Olivia turned to Samuel's sister as the tears she had held at bay so long battled for release. "I love him so much and I may lose him. If only he weren't so pigheadedly honorable, she couldn't do this to us."

"Being pigheadedly honorable is one of my brother's failings, but neither of us would love him half so much if he were any different," Elise replied, remembering an earlier time. "Once he risked his life to save my reputation. He'll do no less for you, Olivia. It will all work out in the end," she added, praying that it was true.

"In the meanwhile he and Tish will masquerade as husband and wife. What can she hope to gain by it?"

Elise shook her head. "I never understood Letitia Soames. There's something about her . . . something dark and sick beneath all that gilded beauty." For some reason Richard Bullock's handsome face flashed through her mind and she shivered, then forced the thought aside, wanting to reassure Olivia. "Samuel knows her for what she is now. He'll deal with her. In the meanwhile, we can't have you pining away like some recluse. I recommend a shopping trip. It's marvelous therapy."

Their conversation was interrupted by a servant rapping

lightly on Olivia's bedroom door, asking to talk with Madame Quinn.

"There's a gentleman asking to see Mademoiselle St. Etienne, Madame. Monsieur Wescott, her guardian."

Elise turned to Olivia. "You don't have to see him if you don't want to."

"No. I'm not afraid to face him," Olivia replied. "In fact, I'd rather enjoy it."

Downstairs Emory Wescott stood in the Quinns' parlor, mentally rehearsing his speech for Olivia, half expecting that she would refuse to see him. At least he had to try it the easy way. Perhaps he could bring her around with the lure of the New Orleans trip now that Shelby's first wife had so conveniently broken up their little romance.

"Good afternoon, Mr. Wescott." The coolness of her voice brought him swiveling around to face her.

"Mr. Wescott, Olivia? Come, come now. What happened to Uncle Emory?" he cajoled, walking closer to give her a fatherly embrace.

Olivia neatly sidestepped him without backing away. "He's dead. An uncle would never try to sell his niece as if she were a common harlot. I must say I admire your gall coming here as if you hadn't tried to pander me to Samuel."

His face turned the color of aged bricks. "See here, Olivia, I'll not accept that kind of talk from Julian St. Etienne's daughter, whom I took in when her father died in penury. You owe me a debt of gratitude, gel."

"I may owe you money for my upkeep, perhaps, but gratitude? I think not after you attempted to collect the debt the way you did."

"You went to Shelby willingly enough after all was said and done," he snapped testily. "I saw you and Shelby pawing at each other on several occasions."

The thought of this twisted, greedy man spying on them made Olivia feel violated. She blanched as Wescott smirked triumphantly and continued.

"He even married you in some backwoods ceremony, didn't he? A pity it was bigamous. If anyone in the city learned about your scandalous liaison with Shelby, you'd be quite ruined. That's why I came to take you back under my protection."

"I don't need your protection."

"I beg to differ. You're a hot-blooded little chit who needs guidance. You should be thank—"

"This interview is at an end," she said coldly. "Get out. Right now."

"You ungrateful little—"

"You will leave this instant or I'll show you a few of the tricks I learned from Micajah Johnstone. You won't like them." Olivia extracted a small, slender dagger from her sleeve. "Micajah's first lesson was to always be armed. Shall I show you the second?"

Emory Wescott jumped away, backing toward the door, red-faced and furious. His eyes darkened to dull pewter, narrowing on her as he turned in the hallway. "You willful, foolish little bitch, you'll pay for this."

When he was gone, Olivia replaced the knife in her sleeve, then sat down on a chair, trembling from head to foot.

"Don't weaken now. That was quite an excellent showing," Elise said from the doorway. "I couldn't have done better myself and I was accounted pretty good with a knife by some people who should know." A small smile of remembrance tinged her lips as she pulled up another chair beside her friend. "I didn't mean to spy on you, but I was concerned. Wescott isn't to be trusted. I've always had a feeling about him."

"Samuel thinks he's the one who was supplying Stuart Pardee."

Elise digested the fact that her secretive brother had shared his suspicions with Olivia. "How much do you know about what Samuel does for the army?" she asked point-blank.

"You mean that he spies for President Madison?" Olivia replied artlessly.

"My, he has confided a great deal," Elise murmured dryly.

Olivia smiled wistfully. "He didn't exactly confide so much as I intuited and pieced and extracted."

"That's always been the better way of making sense of a man," Elise replied with a chuckle.

The two women chatted and exchanged confidences about Samuel and husbands in general. Elise shared childhood memories of growing up with a troublesome younger brother, and before they realized it, the day was half-spent, past time for the shopping spree Elise had promised Olivia.

* * *

Across town an exchange of confidences of quite another sort took place. At the Parker estate Tish stood in the sitting room of her suite, impatiently tapping her slipper as her stepbrother carefully removed his gloves and tossed them inside the beaver hat he had set on the table after slipping up the back stairs into her quarters undetected.

"Where have you been? I waited for you last night . . . all night alone in that big lonely bed," she said, her voice softening from petulance to purring, as she gestured at the bedroom door across the small sitting room.

"I do have a life of my own to attend, pet," Richard replied lightly, evading her question as he reached out and ran his pale slender fingers across the swell of her breasts, which were bulging from the top of her low-cut bodice. Only the sheerest wisp of cream lace covered the pinkness of her nipples. He reached inside and tweaked one, then the other, watching her eyes close for an instant, involuntarily.

Tish forced her body to obey her mind, stepping quickly away from the hypnotic spell of his touch. "Later, there will be time for that later," she said breathlessly, still feeling the throb of hunger deep within her as her nipples stung from the rough handling.

"How did your interview with Shelby go?" he asked as he poured himself a glass of the expensive sherry Mr. Parker kept on a Lannuier pier table between the windows.

"As well as could be expected, I suppose," she replied guardedly.

Bullock studied her, his glittering eyes hooded beneath heavy lids. "He threw your touching offer of a reconciliation back in your face, didn't he? I told you the whole bloody ruse of faking your death and returning would only enrage him. You should have let me kill him, rather than debase yourself in front of him."

"You tried twice and failed," she reminded him coldly.

Thinking of his unsuccessful attempt the preceding night, Bullock knew he would never admit his third failed attempt to Tish, even if she had agreed to let him kill Shelby. "I will succeed the next time," he said arrogantly.

"You will do nothing. He's agreed to continue our marriage and to return to Washington with me . . . but there is one obstacle."

He studied her as she paced. "You mean the St. Etienne

girl? She's quite a beauty. You were scarcely cold in your supposed grave before your beloved husband married her," he could not resist jibing.

Tish turned on him with a furious oath. "She is a nobody, nothing!" she hissed furiously, then calmed, smoothing her hands over the gauzy clinging fabric of her rose pink gown. "I've already made plans with Emory Wescott to dispose of her. Once she's out of the way, Samuel will come to heel quickly enough."

"I beg to differ, my pet. If I know you . . . and I do, quite well . . . you've blackmailed your noble husband with the chit. If you kill her, you'll lose whatever tenuous hold you have on him."

This time she came at him with nails bared, but he was ready for her. Seizing her wrists, he twisted her hands behind her back, bending her backward across his arm while his mouth ravaged her exposed breasts, nuzzling them free of their scant confinement, then biting the nipples until she whimpered in a frenzy of pain and excitement.

"Ah, Letitia, my beloved, I burn for you. I will eventually burn in all eternity for you, no doubt . . . but I will have you now," he rasped as they sank together onto the carpet, their hands greedily tearing at each other's clothes.

Not a bad forgery, all in all, Emory Wescott considered, examining the poignantly worded letter to Samuel Shelby for the dozenth time. As Olivia St. Etienne's guardian, he had ample samples of her handwriting to copy from in concocting the missive. Over the years in trading ventures, Wescott had become adept at forging various bills of lading and payment receipts.

"One might even say I have a talent for forgery," he said chuckling to himself.

Now to the matter at hand—the way to lure Olivia out from under the watchdog eyes of Madame Quinn. It was a good thing her husband, that deadly Spanish renegade, had left to parlay with the Osage. Smiling to himself, he thought about the irony. A failure in one area led to success in another. The British failure to incite the Osage against the United States meant nothing to him. When Olivia brought him the Durand fortune, he could say to hell with the whiskey trade forever. Let the English and the Americans all kill one another and the miserable savages in the process! He would live like a king in Queen New Orleans.

He folded up the letter and placed it in the envelope he had painstakingly addressed to Shelby in Olivia's hand. So much for deflecting the troublesome American from following the chit once he had abducted her. Now he had to lure her into his trap. The colonel would be at the Parkers' gala tonight, an unwilling escort for his wife. Olivia was no doubt repining over that fact. But what if Shelby sent her a note, requesting a tryst after the party? Surely she would slip out of the Quinn house and meet her lover.

"I think the racetrack up on the bluffs would call forth some fond memories, Olivia," he murmured. Certainly the dark, deserted area would be perfect for his plans. He would have her on that keelboat headed to New Orleans within twenty-four hours while Shelby was mourning the loss of his fickle lover. Smiling, he took another piece of paper and began to compose a second forgery.

Samuel sat in the parlor of his house on Plum Street. A pouch of dispatches from Fort Bellefontaine had been delivered in his absence and sat on the desk in front of him. Looking around the simple room he remembered Olivia's delighted reaction to it when he had carried her across the threshold the other night. She had been thrilled with everything. Hell, she had been happy in a one-room cabin with Micajah Johnstone. He massaged his temples and crossed his eyes, willing away the bittersweet memories of their brief time together. How could their lives have changed so radically in such a few days? Tish alive. Livy not legally his wife.

Livy. No matter what society or the courts might say, she would always be the wife of his heart. At least for the present he could content himself that she was safe with his sister and that Tish had indeed preferred the Parkers' accommodations to his humble abode. The thought of traveling all the way back to Washington in such close proximity to that woman was enough to send him to the liquor cabinet to refill his snifter with brandy.

"Why not? It's half-past three in the morning," he muttered disconsolately. He had spent the past evening in full dress uniform as befitted the husband of Letitia Soames Shelby. Just spending a few hours in her company made him realize how impossible her demands on him were. She wanted him to be a man who never existed, a figment of her imagination, someone who could magically carry her all the way to the White House.

Sipping the pungent brandy, he returned to the desk where his reports on Stuart Pardee and his further suspicions regarding Emory Wescott lay, half-written. The verbal accounts he had given in such detail the night of his arrival had to be followed up with a mound of written reports. He had put the chore off for too long.

What a glamorous life, he thought with a grimace, a spy who was more apt to expire from choking on paperwork than die of a gunshot. He opened the dispatch from Washington first, giving it a quick perusal before completing his own task.

The news was not heartening. President Madison had convened Congress early to prepare for war. He scanned the report, glad that he could at least send back a small piece of good news regarding the Osage alliance, especially considering the information in the second dispatch. It had come from Indiana Territory where the young hotheaded governor and militia leader William Henry Harrison had incited the Shawnee to join the British by burning their village at Prophetstown. His forces experienced heavy casualties at a battle on Tippecanoe Creek, resulting in a stalemate which would soon erupt into a full-scale Shawnee uprising once the absent Tecumseh returned to regroup the embittered and undefeated Shawnee and their allies.

"The damn fool," Shelby muttered in disgust, throwing down the papers and running his fingers through his hair. War would soon be here and Tish would be lobbying for him to take a military command on the front lines. "If not for Livy, I might just do it to escape."

He polished off the brandy, then resumed writing his report for Jemmy Madison. He would probably be able to deliver it in person rather than rely on a courier, he thought glumly. His troubled ruminations were interrupted by a soft insistent rapping on the front door. It was scarcely the hour for social calls. "Who is it?" he asked, reaching for the pistol lying beside him on the desk.

At once he recognized his sister's voice and rushed to throw open the door. Elise slipped inside, shivering from the cold damp mist that had enveloped the city, bringing a taste of winter. "What's happened?" he asked, knowing it must bode ill indeed for her to be out at this hour.

"Olivia's gone," she said urgently as her eyes swept around the parlor and then returned to meet his. "I had hoped she'd come to you but I see she hasn't."

"What do you mean, *gone*? Has she been kidnapped from your house?"

"No. She rode away alone. I saw her slip out from the stable behind the house."

"But where would she go in the middle of the night?"

Elise betrayed some agitation now. "I don't know. It was quite accidental that I saw her leave. Otherwise I wouldn't have known she was gone until morning. Orlena's kitten wandered away from her room and she awakened me crying for it. I searched the house and just happened to be passing the kitchen window when I saw someone open the stable door. By the time I got to the backyard it was too late to stop her. I don't think she even heard me call her name."

Samuel's expression hardened. "This smells like some sort of trap."

"That's what I fear, too. It has to be Wescott, but how did he get her to come to him?" she asked, as much of herself as of him.

"I don't know but I'm sure as hell going to find out," he said, strapping on his sidearm and then reaching for the Bartlett rifle hanging on the wall above his desk. He turned at the door and added, "Stay here, Liza—just in case she turns up. I'll be back as soon as I learn anything."

She nodded. "I'll send Justus back to tell the children's nurse where I am."

Dawn came quickly, gray and sullen, as if forecasting bad news. Elise had a pot of coffee bubbling on the hearth when the sound of hoofbeats broke the early morning stillness. Rushing to the front door, she was disappointed to find that it was not Samuel or Olivia but rather a young boy, fourteen or fifteen, thin with stringy tan hair and freckles. He carried a sealed envelope.

"I'm looking for a Colonel Shelby," he said in a soft drawl.

"I am his sister, Madame Elise Quinn. You may leave it with me," she said, turning to open her reticule and pull out a piece of silver. The youth looked dubious, but when she handed him the silver coin, he smiled. "Who gave you this letter to deliver?" She held another coin in her open palm.

"A lady like yoreself, m'am. Real pretty she was."

"What did she look like?"

"Like I said, pretty, finely dressed. Oh, she had red hair. Real red hair."

"Where did she find you?"

"At the Owl and Bear late last night. She said I was to get it to the colonel this morning."

"Was anyone with her?"

He nodded. "There was a fellow—an older gent with her. But it was the lady what give me my orders."

"This older gentleman, describe him."

By this time the boy was growing restive under her terse inquisition. He eyed the coin with longing but started to back off the porch, as if afraid he had blundered into something in which he did not want to be involved. "He . . . he was kinda big, stocky with thick gray hair. Dressed real good just like the lady. I thought he was her father."

Elise nodded and tossed him the coin. He caught it deftly and leaped from the porch and onto his horse's back, kicking the spavined old beast into a brisk getaway.

Elise stood studying the letter as dread squeezed her heart. It had been Olivia and Wescott, no doubt of it. But why? She itched to break the seal. What if there was some news that should be acted upon at once? Perhaps they could prevent Olivia from being forced to go with Wescott, for she was certain that Olivia would never willingly have accompanied him.

She was just about to tear into it when Samuel rode up, exhausted, with dark circles beneath his eyes and a day's growth of black whiskers making his face look both piratical and haggard. "This just came from Olivia. I questioned the messenger—she was with Wescott. He's forcing her to do something terrible, Samuel, I know it!"

She thrust the letter at him and he took it woodenly, making no attempt to open it. "She embarked with him . . . on a keelboat. They left when the moon was full up," he said in a hollow voice. "I talked to the man who made the arrangements yesterday for Wescott. He assured me the lady went of her own free will," he added bitterly.

Elise looked at him with a mixture of pain and impatience on her face. He had so few reasons to trust, so many not to that it broke her heart. She knew how much he loved Olivia St. Etienne. That hurt worst of all as she watched the last tenuous threads of open emotion being severed. Samuel retreated behind the hardened shell he had donned over the years. She was all too familiar with that skill for she, too, had worn it once and cut herself off from all tender feelings.

Placing her hand on his arm, she squeezed it. "This isn't as it seems, Samuel. I know Olivia loves you and would not do this willingly. Let us read what she wrote—or was forced to write, then decide what to do."

As he tore open the wax seal, she ushered him inside. "I've coffee on. Come, you look as if you could use some."

He sat down wearily at the table and read the letter, then tossed it aside and cradled his head in his hands.

Elise picked it up and read:

My Dearest Samuel,

When you read this, I will be on my way to New Orleans. My uncle Charles has asked me to come live with him. Under the present circumstances, I think this is the best solution to our untenable situation. Uncle Emory has been so kind as to make arrangements to escort me there. If you can end your marriage to Tish, I shall hope to see you one day.

Until then, lovingly,
Olivia

"He made several mistakes," she said.

Samuel looked up, distractedly. "It's Livy's handwriting, Liza."

"Perhaps, but she calls him Uncle Emory. I overheard her parting argument with him, Samuel. She despises him and specifically told him she would never again consider him her 'uncle.' Also she signed it Olivia, not Livy. Would I sign a letter to you 'Elise'?" By this time she had his attention.

"No, Liza, you wouldn't. What else?" he asked, tensing up, ready to spring into action.

"Charles Durand, this uncle . . . if she is his only heir and he is older or in poor health . . ."

"Wescott could eliminate him and even Livy once he was certain the estate would come into his hands."

"Yes, I suspect so," she said worriedly.

"See that these reports get to the president, Liza. You know as much about the situation as I do. You can complete them. I have a boat being outfitted right now. It should be ready to shove off within the hour," he said, standing up, then heading toward his bedroom to pack a few things for the long trip.

She smiled at him as the tightness around her heart eased a bit. "So, you were going after her anyway."

His expression was haunted with fear and uncertainty, but also with love. "How could I not? I do love her, Liza."

Chapter 22

As Elise departed to see to her children, Samuel threw a few changes of clothing into a pack, then gathered his weapons, two .65 caliber Martial Pistols and the Bartlett flintlock. After checking to be certain they were loaded and ready to fire, he collected sufficient powder and shot for what might turn into a serious fight. Just as he was preparing to leave, footsteps sounded on the front porch. By this time the street was busy with early morning traffic so he had not noticed the carriage pulling up in front of the house.

The brougham was a gaudy expensive model, befitting a senator's daughter. As a servant opened the door for her, Tish swept in as if she owned the place. Two burly black men were busy unloading trunks and boxes from inside the large conveyance.

Thrusting the pistols into his sash, he put the rifle down on the table and stared impatiently at her. "What the hell do you think you're doing here, Tish?"

She stiffened at the insulting tone of voice. "Please, Samuel, must you swear in front of a lady."

"When I see one, I'll amend my manners," he replied curtly, once more gathering up his gear.

"I've come to live in your house until we can arrange suitable passage home to Washington." She glanced for the first time at the pack slung across his shoulder and the arsenal of weapons. "Where are you going?" she asked tightly, already guessing the answer.

"After Olivia. Wescott has her . . . but then I expect you already knew that." His eyes were ice-cold, impaling her like daggers.

She took a small step back, placing one pale white hand at her throat protectively. There was no use trying to feign innocence regarding the damned little bitch. "Yes, I knew she agreed to accompany her guardian to New Orleans. According to Mr. Wescott, she'll be heir to millions." She knew how much he resented the Soames wealth. *Let this work.* "She'll be beyond your reach. Give her up, Samuel."

He paused. "If she left of her own choice, I'll let her go, but not until I hear it from her."

"This is insane! You can't go traipsing off after her like some lovesick schoolboy. You'll look the fool."

"And so will you—more to the point, isn't it, Tish?"

"I warn you, Samuel—"

"And I warn *you*, Tish." He moved suddenly across the space separating them, grasping her shoulders in his hands, squeezing the soft pale flesh cruelly. "If you so much as breathe a word about Olivia while I'm gone, I will snap that white . . . slender . . . swanlike neck of yours with my bare hands." One large dark hand glided up from her shoulder to her throat, stroking it almost delicately, yet the menace behind the caress was palpable. He could feel her shudder and swallow convulsively before she spoke.

"You can't threaten me, Samuel. I am your wife. We made a bargain."

"So we did. And if Olivia is unharmed, I'll return to it. But, Tish . . . if she's been harmed, you and Emory Wescott will both wish you'd never been born." With that he shoved her away and seized his rifle, then left the house without a backward glance at the pale trembling woman.

Tears of sheer rage gathered in Tish's pale eyes. As they overflowed she blinked them away furiously, noticing for the first time the slaves standing awkwardly in the corner of the room, beside her trunks. "What are you staring at, imbeciles?" she shrieked, grabbing a candlestick from the table and hurling it in their direction.

They scattered, dashing out the door to huddle by the carriage as she fell into a full-blown temper tantrum, hurling every loose object around her at the walls until she finally collapsed, red-faced, spent and sobbing on a chair. That was how Richard Bullock found her half an hour later.

After dismissing the servants he knelt beside her and took her in his arms. "I told you it was a mistake coming here. You should've stayed with me at the Parkers' residence. This place is little better than a woodsman's cabin."

"He's gone after her, Richard," she said in an eerily calm voice. Her face was red and puffy from crying but her eyes were ice-cold now, calculating.

"The St. Etienne girl? I was afraid Wescott's forged letter wouldn't deter him. He'll never give her up, Tish. You know that now, don't you?" he crooned, stroking her cheek tenderly.

She nodded slowly, then broke free of his embrace and stood up. "I shall need you to kill him after all, Richard." She sighed in regret, rather the way she often did when a favorite knickknack was broken or a lavish gown ripped or stained. "A pity. He had the best potential of any of them."

Richard Bullock watched her stop in front of a window, her pale hair gilded in the morning sun which was beginning to break through the fog in strong golden shafts. She stood in profile, so patrician and perfect, so cold and controlled. His heartbeat began to accelerate furiously and his mouth suddenly went dry.

Now is the time to tell her, an inner voice screamed at him. Dare he do it? There would never be a better opportunity.

"Tisha," he said softly, coming up behind her to enfold her in his arms, letting his mouth tease the sensitive skin of her nape as his hands kneaded her breasts.

"Don't, Richard. Someone might see you," she said, breaking free from him and stepping away from the window.

"Damn if anyone does. Who cares what the rustics here think? I'll kill Shelby for you, my pet. I want you free of him. It was a mistake to marry him in the first place."

"I know that now," she said, sighing. "I have always depended on you so, my darling. What would I do without you?" She glanced at the front door. He had closed it and slid the bolt when he entered. With a slow smile of invitation she began unfastening the buttons at the front of her bodice, letting the lush white bounty of her heavy breasts spill free.

He stalked over to her with glazed eyes, taking a large breast in each hand, hefting them and squeezing painfully with his slender strong fingers until she whimpered just the way he knew she would. *Say it, now!*

"Tisha, after I kill him . . . I want you."

"You have always had me, my darling Richard, always," she rasped, thrusting her hips against him as she writhed beneath the sharp, delicious pain he inflicted on her sensitive breasts, twisting them, then pinching the large distended nipples between his fingertips.

"But I don't want it to be like this—a few moments snatched in secret, all the rest of the time pretending to be your beloved brother, so damn punctilious, so bloody proper. I want you for me . . . only for me . . . all for me . . . we can go away together, Tisha. I have money enough from my father's estate. It doesn't matter if the senator disowns you. We can go to London, Paris, Rome—wherever you want. No one will know us. We can be together, pet, just the two of us."

All the while he talked, he continued the painful kneading of her breasts just the way he knew she liked it, but he could sense her gradual stiffening. The ecstasy-filled writhing stopped and her hands began to push at his shoulders as an expression of incredulity filled her face.

"You can't be serious." She felt his grip loosen and backed away from him, her breasts swaying obscenely, her nakedness forgotten.

"I love you, Tisha. I always have. I'll do anything for you—even kill. God how I've ached to kill Shelby ever since your wedding night. The thought of that bastard touching you sickened me. I was glad when he quit your bed. You belong to me, Tisha. Me!"

"You're mad," she said flatly. "Do you think I could marry my stepbrother?" There was contempt in her voice.

"No one would know if we went abroad." He hated the pleading in his voice.

"I don't want to live abroad. I want to live in Washington, to take the position I've been groomed for all of my life, where Daddy expects me to be—at the side of a president!"

"You've failed with Shelby, need I remind you?" he said nastily as a sick rage began to boil his blood.

"But I won't fail with Senator Phillips. His period of mourning for his dead wife is almost over. I'll be done mourning for Samuel just in time for a New Year's wedding in 1813. That should give us plenty of time to handle matters here," she said briskly, dismissing her stepbrother's impossibly ridiculous suit out of hand.

"Phillips is an old man! Why he's practically doddering," Richard replied, aghast. This was the first she had ever mentioned the old senator to him.

Tish smiled slumberously at him. "All the better for us, my darling. He is a genuine war hero, even if it was the War for Independence. I shall manage him quite well and with Daddy's backing, well, he'll win the nomination and the election quite handily."

"No. I won't stand for it—that old goat pawing you. No more husbands, Tish. You're mine," he snarled, furious that she and Worthington Soames had cooked up this scheme behind his back. He grabbed her arm and yanked her against him roughly, pressing her lower body to his with one arm while his other hand seized a breast and squeezed it. He lowered his head and bit her neck, growing rougher as she struggled, cursing at him, kicking and trying to break free.

"You *are* mad," she screamed, clawing at his face, raking a bloody furrow across his cheek.

But he seemed impervious to the injury as he continued savaging her breasts and throat, drawing blood as his teeth fastened on a nipple and clamped.

Tish pushed and kicked, all the while groping for the small English pistol he always carried in his satin waistcoat. Her hands finally found it and fastened around it with clawlike desperation. He was making low ferocious noises now, deep in his throat, snarling like a lion staking his claim on a downed piece of game.

"You belong to me—do you hear? Me!" he growled, looking up into her wild eyes, his own glittering with a bizarre mixture of crazed lust and utter despair.

"No, Richard. I belong to no man," she said, pulling the gun free and shoving it against his chest. "Let me go."

One hand still pressed her against his body as the other slid free of her hair where he had entangled it. He slipped it down toward the gun and tried to pry it from her white frantic fingers. "Let go, my pet, before you do something we'll both regret," he said, a bit of the old smooth swagger back in his voice.

"Let *me* go, Richard," she replied frantically, still trying to twist away from him as he maintained his grip on the gun she clutched.

"No Tisha, my love—"

Suddenly the loud report of a shot echoed in the small room and a look of surprise widened her pale gold eyes. Then the thick silvery lashes fluttered and she sagged against him . . . dead weight.

Richard looked down with horror at the small crimson hole in her breast, directly in front of her heart. How milky pale the skin looked around the angry red wound. "No, Tisha, no . . . no . . . no." He crooned to her softly as they both sank to the floor.

His hold on her never slackened as he lowered her onto his lap. Then he took the gun, which had become twisted and turned inadvertently on her, and he pried it free of her lifeless fingers. Tossing it away, he began stroking her naked breasts which were now liberally smeared with blood.

"So beautiful, my beloved. Even in death, you are so utterly perfect." He bent down and kissed her lips, then the tips of those magnificent breasts. They were beginning to show the marks of his hands with purplish bruises. Tenderly he caressed them, then pulled her bodice closed and fastened it once more.

For a moment he held her and stared across the room at the gun. Slowly he shifted Tish's body from his lap and stretched her out carefully on the floor. He got to his feet and retrieved the small pistol. He righted an overturned chair and then sat, a smile spreading slowly across his handsome face.

"Yes, my pet, it is true. Blood calls out for blood."

With a calmness borne of utter madness and despair, Richard Bullock carefully reloaded and primed his pistol . . .

Olivia looked up at the darkening sky and shivered. There were no clouds per se; the sun simply vanished behind a lowering slate gray veil. Not a breath of wind stirred but a strange hint of sulfur hung ominously in the cold, damp river air.

"Chilly, my dear? You'd best go back inside else you'll take a lung fever," Wescott said solicitously, walking up behind her as she stood in the door of the keelboat cabin, looking at the dark churning waters of the mighty river that bore them relentlessly downstream, farther and farther away from Samuel.

"And we couldn't have me take ill and die before claiming my inheritance, could we?" she replied acerbically, pulling her woolen shawl more tightly around her shoulders. Before he arranged her abduction, Wescott had seen to it that the best of the wardrobe she had left behind at his house was carefully packed for the trip.

"What's this talk of dying?" he scoffed jovially. The last thing he wanted was for the troublesome chit to get the idea that he planned to kill her once the Durand wealth was securely in his hands.

She raised one eyebrow disdainfully and fixed him with a cold green glare. "You're the one who talks of dying. You threatened to have Samuel murdered if I didn't cooperate—

you even leveled your own pistol on that poor messenger boy at the tavern. You'd have shot him in a trice if I hadn't given him that note for Samuel, pretending it was from me."

Samuel. Would he come after her? Or did he believe Wescott's awful letter? She had been foolish enough to fall for his skillful forgery and place herself in his hands. For the hundredth time since he had seized her at the deserted racetrack, she cursed her folly. *You wanted the note to be true so badly that you abandoned all common sense.*

"That ugliness is past and behind us now, gel. Once you see the bright lights and elegant refinements of the Queen City, you'll soon forget about your colonel. You'll be rich beyond your wildest dreams, Olivia."

"No, *you'll* be rich, *Uncle* Emory," she said, emphasizing the formerly affectionate title with utter contempt. She had to stop him before they reached New Orleans—even sooner if Samuel was following her. If Wescott got Shelby in his sights, she knew he would kill her love.

He muttered to himself and walked off to the front of the boat where several of the men were sharing a bottle, leaving her alone with her thoughts. Tonight when they moored up for the night she would escape. She had eluded Pardee and his Osage. Surely she could outsmart the likes of Emory Wescott and the pack of half-drunken river rats he had hired. Olivia stared at the river that carried her south, looking to the northern horizon. Would he come?

Darkness fell, sullen and cold. Not a star shone in the night sky. They were nearing the Chickasaw Bluffs, a particularly rough stretch of river called the Devil's Race. No one, not even the most experienced rivermen dared to attempt it at night. They moored up beneath a steep bluff and began preparing an evening meal. One of the men, a lecherous looking little weasel with dirty yellow hair and a pockmarked face, was assigned to watch her. His name was Gruener.

Olivia sat in the bow of the boat on a small barrel, clutching a tin pan filled with burned beans and a greasy unappetizing hunk of pork. She pushed the noisome mess about with her fork after taking a few mouthfuls of the less charred beans for sustenance.

"You are not hungry tonight, *leibchen?*" Gruener said in a thick Westphalian accent.

She shoved the plate at the ugly riverman. "Here, you eat

it. I'm going to get some sleep." She walked calmly to the cabin box and slipped inside the darkness, knowing he would not dare to follow, but would position himself outside the door. Emory and the boat's captain would sleep at the opposite end, effectively sealing off that exit to her. The best she could do was prepare herself for when everyone slept except for the sentry on land and Gruener.

Olivia felt around in the dark for the flint, then used it to light a tallow candle. Setting it down beside her trunk, she opened the lid after making certain no one else was inside the crowded room. There beneath a froth of lace gowns and undergarments lay her secret weapon—a high-heeled boot made with a decorative nickel plating on the bottom edge of the heel. Hefting it against her palm, she felt the cool weight and smiled grimly. If wielded properly it should put Herr Gruener to sleep for quite a while, perhaps forever, and at this point, she cared not which.

Dousing the candle, she crawled beneath the covers, preparing for a long night's wait. Gradually the men retired one by one, falling into drunken slumber. Wescott and the captain were among the last to go to bed. Unfortunately, she could tell from beneath veiled lashes that although the captain was in his cups, Emory remained sober. She would just have to be very quiet when she disposed of Gruener.

On the shore, Samuel climbed through a thick stand of cattails and reeds, then peered at the keelboat Wescott's men had secured for the night. Shelby waited patiently, watching them retire for the evening. A sentry was posted ashore and a squat little man sat watch in front of the cabin box where Olivia must be held.

Several times during the course of the afternoon he had caught sight of Wescott's boat from his own. Using the spyglass he had brought along, he saw her on deck, seemingly unharmed. He had not dared to approach closer in the smaller, swifter craft for fear of what Wescott might do to her. Instead he had bided his time, waiting until they moored up for the night.

As he crouched in the wet cold, Samuel felt an eerie premonition of doom. The sky had been dark all day and the air peculiarly becalmed with a nasty acrid aroma permeating it. All the wildlife was restless, too, as if sensing that something unnatural was about to occur. In the faint reflection from the water, he watched a rabbit bound out in the darkness, dashing erratically across an open stretch of shoreline grass, heedless of danger. Frogs croaked loudly, though they should be in hibernation by now, and swarm after swarm of wild birds and geese moved across the sky, screeching deafeningly as they flew blindly in the darkness.

Nervously he rubbed the back of his neck, then turned his attention back to the boat. One dim lantern flickered on the prow of Wescott's keelboat. He began moving through the brackish water toward the sentry, coming upon him from behind. Since there were seven men aboard with Wescott, Samuel knew he must move swiftly and silently to get Olivia free without alerting anyone.

Just as he reached the tree stumps where the guard sat dozing lightly, leaning on his musket, Samuel saw Olivia appear in the cabin doorway. She raised some sort of a cudgel and smashed it against the squat bloke's head. Taking his cue from her, Shelby raised the butt of his pistol to crack the sentry, but in that very instant a noise like the scraping of a boat running aground filled the night air, a rasping, irritating sound, followed by a dull roar. The earth began to vibrate, at first only a low tremor, but quickly accelerated in intensity.

The sentry jumped up, snorting with surprise as the earth beneath his feet moved. Shelby whacked him hard on the back of the head and he crumpled silently. Samuel almost followed him down, so great were the tremors growing. He struggled to stand, then took off running toward the dim gleam of the lantern on the boat where Olivia was attempting to regain her balance on the shifting deck.

Suddenly all the forces of hell broke loose. The ground began to buck up and down like a crazed horse. The earth rumbled, hissed and cracked open with a sound like hollow deafening thunder. Now the sulfurous smell became overpowering as a miasmic vapor filled the air, issuing from the crevices. Whole circular sections of ground around Samuel simply disappeared as if being sucked into the bowels of the earth which belched forth mud, water, sand and a hard black substance that looked like coal.

One such giant sink dropped right beside him. He scrambled away from the vile debris being hurled skyward thirty yards into the air. Nearby a giant cottonwood split at its roots as the earth opened beneath it, splintering the tree upward until it was rent in two like a ninety-foot matchstick.

Looking with horror at the scene unfolding on the river, Samuel struggled to reach the riverbank where the keelboat was moored. He could not see Olivia, but he could hear the cries of Wescott's men when several were thrown overboard. The roar of angry water grew louder. Across the wide expanse of the river an entire bluff collapsed, a massive avalanche of trees and earth sliding into the foamy, boiling waters with a deafening noise, creating a tidal wave. In the middle of the channel the waters rose up, a solid wall rolling toward the boat. Where was Olivia?

Screaming for her, he jumped and dodged, struggling to keep his footing as he drew nearer. The heavy keelboat was picked up on the crest of the water with a sickening crack. He clawed at the bow, feeling it lift, knowing if he did not hold fast, he would be swept away downriver to certain death.

Suddenly Olivia was there, her hands frantically seizing hold of him, hauling him aboard as the boat pitched wildly, flying toward the bluff in front of them. He took her in his arms, throwing them both onto the deck and covered her with his body. In an instant the craft landed, crashing loudly into the soft wet earth on top of the bluff.

Olivia felt the force of impact knock the breath from her body, then heard the sharp splintering as the cabin box broke free of the deck. The sides of the craft split like kindling wood, sending debris flying through the air. When the boat finally settled on the continuously vibrating ground, Samuel raised up and looked down at her. With the lantern extinguished, all was in blackness.

He could hear a few faint groans from the men around them but none seemed nearby or inclined to menace them. "Are you hurt?"

"I don't think so—no," she replied, sitting up next to him, feeling numb from shock. "This is like the end of the world," she rasped hoarsely.

He could barely hear her over the low insistent rumbles echoing up and down the churning river below them. The acrid stench of sulfur was chokingly strong now, borne aloft on the wind, which had picked up just as the cataclysm began. "It's what the mountain men in the far west call a shake, the biggest one I've ever heard of," he replied as he struggled unsteadily to his feet and pulled her with him.

"I can't see anything," she said, coughing and blinking her eyes in the dark.

"Neither can I but I know we need to get off this bluff. It could be pulled down into the river like the one on the other side."

They groped through the jagged wreckage of the boat, climbing free of it, then stumbled across the uneven heaving, bucking earth, away from the roar of the river. After struggling for several hundred feet, they collapsed in the darkness, amid the screams of wildlife, the cracking of timber and the ever present rumble from the belly of the earth. High-pitched whistling noises heralded further eruptions from the sinkholes still opening up and down the river valley.

"We're away from any tall stands of trees but the ground could sink or crack open anyplace. All we can do is wait it out and pray we can stay one jump ahead of the shake until daylight," he said.

"That's at least two or three hours," she replied. "Do you think any of the others escaped alive?"

"No way to tell until morning," he said fatalistically, wondering about the grizzled old boatman he had hired to bring him downriver after her.

"Hold me, Samuel."

He did, enfolding her in his arms. "I love you, Livy," he whispered.

She dug her nails into his shoulders, molding herself against the reassuring beat of his heart. "I love you, Samuel."

Over the next few hours the ground quieted for brief intervals, then resumed its self-destructive fury, splitting and erupting all around them. Twice a sinkhole opened up near enough to spray them with water and sand, but the earth they rested upon remained intact. In the distance the river roared and hissed unceasingly like a wild beast in a frenzy of torment.

They waited it out, holding onto each other, shivering in the damp December air, murmuring indistinct love words and reassurances barely audible over the chaos of nature. Then the first low gray threads of light filtered across the eastern horizon and they could see the cataclysm they had thus far lived through.

The landscape looked as if a berserk giant had trod across

it, uprooting whole stands of timber and kicking them into the river, leaving his giant footprints thirty feet deep where the earth had dropped into the sinkholes which had spewed up sand, coal and mud, then filled with water. In other places, low swampy swales had ballooned up, raising the overgrown vegetation into haphazardly formed hillocks. But the change on the river was the most dramatic of all.

"My God in heaven," Olivia breathed. "Look at those islands. They weren't there when we moored up last night. That stretch was open water."

"The whole course of the river's been altered," Samuel said, squinting to see in the dim sulfurous light. "The main channel never used to curve to the east like that. Look at the chasm where it left its original path."

As they stood overwhelmed by the destruction of nature's fury, the rumbling resumed, more fiercely than ever. Suddenly a fissure several yards wide began to zigzag its way toward them. Seizing Olivia's hand, Samuel began to run at a right angle away from it, praying it would not shift its general direction which now headed toward the river.

They outran it, then stopped, panting with exhaustion, able to see what they had only heard and felt before. The earth buckled up, sunk in and cracked open, releasing more noxious fumes. The river, too, erupted. Whirlpools formed when the bottom of the channel dropped into sinkholes with a loud sucking noise. Islands vanished and others were formed in moments as if the hand of an erratic god stretched itself upon the face of the churning deep, creating and then destroying at whim.

Then as another great cracking shudder threw them to the ground, the noise of the current stilled for an instant. When Samuel and Olivia were able to stand, they stared in stunned amazement at the Father of Waters.

"It's flowing upstream!" Olivia said in awe.

"This is one for the history books. The whole Mississippi has reversed its course from south to north!"

"Can it stay this way?"

"I doubt it—the force of gravity eventually has to make it flow downstream again, but who knows what upheavals farther downriver caused this—or how long it'll last?"

Olivia bit her lip. "I wonder how long *we'll* last."

"The sky's getting lighter and the shake seems to be subsiding. We'll need supplies to build some shelter and to eat.

I'm certain we won't be able to travel on the river safely for a while—at least not until it reverses its course downstream."

"Look, Samuel," she said, pointing to the southern horizon where a black cloud began to fill the sky, accompanied by shrill cries. "Geese, thousands and thousands of them."

"All the wildlife's panicked. Even before the shake I noticed how jumpy and erratic the rabbits, deer—even frogs—were, as if they knew it was coming."

"I wonder if Micajah's all right," Olivia said worriedly.

"Surely, he's too far away to be harmed. I suspect we were almost at the center of the damn thing, but I bet they felt the vibrations pretty far away."

Samuel looked across the jagged landscape toward where the wreckage of the keelboat lay like a smashed toy. "If there's anything left of their food and weapons, not to mention blankets, we need to find the stuff."

"Be careful, Samuel. If any of Wescott's men are alive they'd just as soon shoot as not. He told them to be on the lookout for you."

He turned back to her with a smile. "Did you believe I'd come for you?"

"You mean after that letter? I didn't write it, Samuel. Emory forged it—a skill he acquired as a smuggler. He bragged to me about it." Quickly she outlined to him how she had been duped and taken prisoner so that Wescott could use her to gain control of the Durand fortune.

As she explained, he realized Liza had been right. He had failed to trust Livy as he should have. *Once a spy, always a cynic* he thought sadly, vowing to change his suspicious nature.

As they approached the boat he could see several of Wescott's men lying on the ground. All of them appeared to be dead, their bodies thrown clear of the wreckage like rag dolls tossed away, heads and arms jutting at grotesque, twisted angles. He did not see Wescott.

"Stay here while I look inside the cabin box. It seems to have survived relatively intact," he instructed. The small wooden rectangle lay on its side a dozen or so yards away from the shattered prow of the boat.

"I can't believe we survived that landing with nothing more than a few bruises," she said, climbing over the splintering debris.

"You both have the devil's own luck, as do I, my dear,"

Emory Wescott said in a businesslike manner as he stepped out from behind a clump of coyote willow where he had lain in wait for them. He held an expensive over-and-under barreled pistol in his hand aimed directly at Samüel's heart.

"I need my impetuous young charge to accompany me to New Orleans, but as for you, Colonel, well, you've been a thorn in my side for far too long as it is."

Wescott raised the pistol and took aim.

≈ *Chapter 23* ≈

Just as Wescott pulled back the hammer, Olivia slipped the knife she'd taken from Gruener out of her boot and threw it quickly, aiming for Wescott's chest. Seeing the blurry motion from the corner of his eye, Wescott jumped aside, firing wildly. That was all the opening Samuel needed as he dove toward his foe, intent on beating the vicious schemer insensate before he could discharge the second barrel of his weapon. The two men went down, kicking and punching, just as another tremor began to rock the already riven earth.

So intent were they on each other, Shelby and Wescott felt the shaking earth only as an extension of their own fury. They rolled forward and back, locked in an embrace of hate. Shelby had the advantage of height but Wescott was barrel-chested and exceedingly powerful, fighting with the desperation of a cornered animal. Olivia quickly retrieved the knife which had missed its mark, the only weapon she had managed to keep during the night's upheaval. Samuel had his own blade strapped to his hip, but as yet he could not draw it. He was too caught up in staving off Wescott's attempts to cock the pistol he still clutched.

Frantically she waited for an opening, some secure way to plunge the dagger into Wescott without risking injury to Samuel. She was down on her hands and knees now, unable to stand as the quake intensified. The river was a loud hissing inferno in the distance. The sharp reports of more trees snapping filled the sulfurous air.

Severed at the base by the force of the vibrations, one big oak less than fifty feet away fell with a deafening crash toward Olivia and the men. With a scream she jumped out of the way, terrified that Samuel had been injured. She climbed over the broken limbs with her heart pounding. The heavy trunk had narrowly missed the combatants.

The sudden explosion of flying twigs, bark and dry winter leaves momentarily blinded Samuel. He blinked furiously trying to clear his tearing eyes as Wescott slipped out of his reach. Then he heard Olivia's scream.

"Samuel, he's going to shoot!" She had no clear way to throw her knife in the tangle of tree limbs she was scrambling through. The scene was horrifying, almost frozen in time—Samuel shaking his head and squeezing his eyes as the tears gushed, Wescott malevolently grinning as he stood on the undulating earth, trying to steady himself for a shot.

Olivia fought her way through the last imprisoning branches, knife raised ready to throw. Then the ground opened up like a gaping maw directly in front of Wescott, separating him from Shelby, whose vision was finally restored. Samuel jumped back as the crevice widened, yelling for Olivia. She clawed her way free of the tree as he seized her wrist, pulling her with him. They began to run around the fallen tree, trying to escape the ever widening fissure which was belching noisome vapors in thick gray clouds.

Wescott bellowed his rage as they escaped to the other side of the tree. His pistol was ineffectual as he fought to stand upright on the careening earth. In spite of it, he raised the cocked weapon again and took aim at Shelby's broad back but the bucking ground suddenly dislodged the tree which began rolling toward the fissure.

Samuel saw the tree start to move at the same time he lost his footing on the wildly shaking ground. Just as he and Olivia went down they heard the report of Wescott's pistol. The shot flew harmlessly over their heads, a puny sound indeed amid the roaring of unleashed natural fury. Wescott stood at the edge of the abyss now, oblivious of his precarious position as he raved at his nemesis and his prize. Without Olivia, he was destitute, bankrupt. Everything he had worked and schemed for all these years would come to an ignominious end in a jail cell if he could not kill Shelby and reclaim the girl.

Samuel and Olivia watched in amazed horror when the mighty oak tumbled into the giant rent in the earth. One of its long outstretched limbs plucked Emory Wescott from his position on the opposite edge, dragging him into the steamy bowels of hell. His screams wailed thinly over the tumult all around them.

Struggling to his feet, Samuel approached the edge with Olivia trailing him closely. Wescott clung to one sturdy branch like a demented leech, shrieking curses through the sulfurous clouds, clawing his way upward on the limb. It was too thin at its outer extremity to bear his considerable weight and began to give way just as the earth inexorably closed, crushing the giant oak branches as if they were mere twigs. Before Olivia and Samuel's eyes, the crevice fused shut, burying Emory Wescott for all eternity.

The stink of sulfur assailed their nostrils as they watched the door to hell close. "I expect he's arrived now where he was always destined to be," she said with a shiver.

"Just in case that fault reopens, let's get the hell away from here," Samuel said to her.

"By all means! I wouldn't want to join him," she replied, still shuddering as they struggled to walk on the careening earth.

By that afternoon the quakes had subsided and the river reversed its course to flow once more naturally toward the Gulf to the south. Everywhere around them signs of nature's rampage had left their mark, but nowhere more visibly than on the great river itself. Not only was the channel radically altered, but whole series of large islands had been utterly destroyed, including several pirate's nests inhabited by cutthroats who would nevermore terrorize hapless travelers. In place of the vanished islands, new ones had been thrust up, muddy and gray with the sediment of eons once more exposed to daylight. The river flowed turbulently, the channel clogged with dense debris—whole forests of uprooted trees and bushes, the remnants of smashed keelboats and flatboats, even parts of settlers' cabins, which had been swept from the shore or sunken down when vast tracts of land were sucked below water level.

The sky remained darkly overcast and a chill wind gave some relief from the poisonous fumes from beneath the earth. Olivia foraged through the damaged supplies in the cabin box while Samuel went in search of Billy Weeks, the riverman he had hired to pursue Wescott's boat. By the time he returned to report that Weeks, too, was dead, she had a small campfire burning and was stirring a skillet of beans as coffee simmered fragrantly in the coals.

"It isn't much, but at least we won't starve. I found a few dry blankets, too. We're miles from the nearest settlement. What do you think we should do?" she asked, handing him a steaming plate of beans.

"New Madrid would be a day's journey north by boat, but judging from the wreckage we've seen floating downriver, I fear there'll be no help there—if anyone is even left alive," he added grimly.

"I don't want to chance it, Samuel. We might find less damage downriver—if it's safe to travel on the river again. What do you think?"

"We can stay here until we're sure the shakes are passed. The cabin box is intact enough to provide us shelter and we have Wescott's supplies. Meanwhile I can start gathering lumber to lash together a small raft. If the river calms, we can try it. Otherwise, we'll have to walk all the way down to Natchez—not exactly a prospect to relish."

"Aren't there any small settlements downriver?" she asked, searching her memory from the infrequent trips she had made as a pampered passenger who paid scant attention to the wilderness being traversed. Mostly she remembered it as flat monotonous swamps and woodland with little signs of human habitation.

Samuel shook his head. "As nearly as I can recall, the closest one is almost seventy-five miles south and it's on the eastern shore."

"We'll have to get back on the river then." Her tone of voice indicated how much the idea appealed. They ate in silence for several moments, both deep in thought. Finally she worked up her courage to ask, "What will happen when we reach New Orleans . . . assuming we *can* reach there alive?"

He set his plate aside, all appetite fled as he recalled the last vitriolic scene with Tish. "This rich uncle of yours, Wescott seemed certain he would take you in. It might be better than returning to St. Louis. When I came after you, Tish wasn't exactly pleased. I'm afraid of what she might do if I take you back there, especially now that Wescott's dead."

"Then you think I should live with Uncle Charles?" she asked, trying to hide her disappointment.

He studied her as she fidgeted with a half-empty mug of coffee. "You'll be a wealthy heiress."

"I don't care about the money. I don't even care about Uncle Charles. He turned away his own sister with her husband and child. Now I'm to be his heir by default because his own sons died in a yellow fever epidemic and he has no one else. I don't think I should like him much."

"He might not be alive. Yesterday, when I was following your keelboat, the thought occurred to me that there is every possibility he named you his heir and is already dead. That would better explain Wescott's attempts to drag you to New Orleans. I don't think he would have taken the risk of kidnapping you unless your inheritance was already a sure thing."

"I don't want his money." *I want only you, Samuel.* She waited, struggling for the patience Micajah had taught her. Somehow it had been easier when Samuel Shelby was not around.

He looked at her stubborn chin and felt his heart break. "But you need protection, Livy, a place to stay while I take Tish back to Washington and begin the divorce proceedings again."

"I could go back to Micajah. To hell with the gossiping old biddies in St. Louis."

He smiled sadly. "We couldn't live isolated in the wilderness for the rest of our lives, Livy. I'm still in the army, at least until the war is over. Then my interests in Santiago's business would dictate that we live in St. Louis. We could move to Spanish territory, settle in Santa Fe as my sister has done, but that still wouldn't rid me of Tish. We can't marry until I secure the divorce."

"I'd rather have you than a wedding ring." Tears choked her voice as she realized his duty and his sense of honor would both conspire to keep them apart for a long, long while.

He reached over and caressed her cheek softly. "I don't want you to live that way. You deserve better."

"At least we have this time before the war takes you away from me. Let's use every precious minute of it, Samuel," she whispered, pressing his palm against her lips.

"Come here," he commanded, pulling her into his embrace. Kneeling beside the crackling campfire, he framed her face with his hands and lowered his mouth to hers slowly, reverently.

She tilted her head back, opening her lips, tasting him as his tongue teased hers. In spite of the chill evening air she was on fire. His body seemed to give off heat as volcanic as that which had burst from the earth. She pressed her breasts to his chest, feeling the steady, accelerating thrum of his heartbeat. "I've made us a bed inside the cabin box. I even salvaged a lantern," she said shyly, eager to see the sleek symmetry of his harsh masculine beauty, to touch his hard muscles without the encumbrance of clothing between them.

Samuel stood and swept her into his arms as if she weighed no more than thistledown. He carried her to the cabin box, stooping to enter the narrow little door. Inside the broken log frame, she had cleared the smashed and damaged cargo and supplies, leaving room for a wide soft pallet in the middle of the space. The flickering light from the lantern cast a soft glow over the makeshift bed.

"You were busy while I was gone," he murmured, placing her on the pallet.

"See what an excellent little housewife I'll make for you." She pulled him down beside her and began to unfasten the buckskin lacings on the front of his shirt, revealing the crisp black pelt beneath. Running her fingers through it, she pressed kisses near his heart and nuzzled him, breathing in the scent which belonged to Samuel alone.

He yanked the shirt up and over his head, tossing it away without a thought, murmuring her name with a groan as his hands glided over her curves, reaching inside her jacket to tease the sharp points of her nipples with his thumbs. Then he pulled open the blouse and delved inside, loving her sharp intake of breath as he found her aching for his caress.

Slowly in the flickering light they undressed each other, taking deliberate time, kissing and exploring, affirming love and life in the wake of so much destruction and death.

Her hand feathered down from the waistband of his tight buckskins, which she had just unbuttoned. Reaching inside, she cupped him with eager inquisitive little fingers, taking delight in his acute gasp of pleasure—or was it pleasure? She was still quite new at this and her own boldness shocked her. Her hand stilled and she raised her head to look at his face, which was contorted in the shadows.

"Did—did I hurt you?"

He reached down, pressing her hand back where it had been, urging her on. "No! God, no!"

His hoarse breathless voice further emboldened her. She began to pull his trousers down over his narrow hips and long legs. He stopped her midway, saying, "The boots first, Livy," and sat up, quickly dispensing with his footgear and kicking away the tangled leather britches.

When he stretched out again, he lay before her completely naked, studying her with hooded eyes, waiting to see what

she would do. She blushed beneath that heated gaze but
could not keep her eyes from devouring his magnificent
body, so long and lean and powerful. Her fingertips traced
the subtle patterns in black body hair, the silky softness on
his forearms, the more abrasive growth on his legs, then
moved up to the heavy mat on his chest which narrowed to
a slender vee, pointing like an arrow to his groin. Standing
proudly in the thick black bush, his erection enticed her,
twitching and straining, beckoning her to touch it.

Samuel watched her nervously rim her lips with the tip of
her tongue as she stared down at him in a passion glazed
trance. He willed himself to remain immobile, waiting to see
what she would do, his beautiful Livy with her fiery hair
trailing across her bare breasts in long soft tendrils, her green
eyes glowing. When she hesitated for a moment, he said,
"Take off the rest of your clothes for me. I want to see all of
you—it's only fair."

She obeyed, peeling off the open blouse, then standing up
to free her heavy skirt and undergarments. He reclined on
his elbows, watching the revelation of sweet soft curves, so
smooth and feminine, yet at the same time so strong and
resilient. When she started to bend over to remove her shoes,
he said, "Allow me," reaching out to take one firm calf and
tiny ankle in his hands, lifting it so he could work the buttons
of her shoe free. He braced it against the flat washboard of
his belly, then set to work, all the while looking up at her
standing above in glorious nudity.

"The sun has turned your skin to gold," he said, as his
eyes traveled across her arms and over her collarbone where
the tan lines from her summer outdoors left a sudden demar-
cation between delicate warm tan and light creamy ivory.
The pale skin of her breasts and belly betrayed the rosy heat
of her blush as he removed the second shoe.

Olivia could feel the heat as she knelt in front of him, but
she kept to her resolve, pressing her palms against his chest
until he lay back down. When he reached up to splay his
hand against her hipbone and glide around the curve of her
buttock, she bit her lip, then whispered, "Lie back, my love,
I want to do something . . ."

He obliged. Once again she resumed her exploration of
his body, this time using her mouth the way she had her
hands, nuzzling and kissing, following the patterns of his
body hair until she reached the inevitable apex at the center

of his body. He could feel her hands grasp him and then her hair brushed between his legs as she knelt over him. He nearly exploded at that instant.

Olivia watched as sweat beaded his brow and his jaw clenched, making the tendons in his neck stand out. Beneath her hand his staff, already hard and distended, grew even larger, throbbing and straining for more of her touch. Deep within the core of her, an answering ache built up deliciously, but she ignored it, turning her attention to the dark ruby tip of his sex where one small pearlescent drop of semen glistened. Her tongue snaked out and swiped at it, tasting of him as he had of her that night in the beaver lodge.

One tiny flick and he was nearly undone! His body arched up off the blankets as he gasped at the raw ecstasy of the sensation. Control. He must exert control or else he would spill himself like a green boy. But never before with any woman had this felt so wonderful. Never before had it been done by a woman he loved, an innocent whose very hesitance and uncertainty made it all the sweeter. He reined in his rampant desire and concentrated on breathing deeply, letting her do as she would with his all too willing flesh.

Easier said than done! The breathtaking heat of her lips scorched him, then her mouth slowly enveloped him. He moaned her name softly, balling his hands into fists to resist tangling them in her hair. Instead he let her proceed at her own delicate and agonizingly slow pace, learning the taste and texture of him as he had of her, instructing her when she hesitated or retreated, urging her on with love words and helpless curses that were also endearments.

Olivia knew it must be good for him as she felt him bow up tautly, offering himself to her like some splendid pagan god. With growing confidence she increased the pressure of her lips, moving along the hard velvety length of his phallus, following his lead as he pleaded for her to do as she was doing. This was a remarkable new way to make love, one that put him utterly in her power. Her lean, muscular lover, always so in command, was now completely at her mercy.

As she marveled at the heady control she was exerting, he was losing his, step by glorious step. Her maddening lovemaking continued until he could hold off no longer. "Livy . . . I'm going to . . . if you don't want . . ."

She knew what he was trying to tell her, but she did not want to stop, not until it was complete, and then she felt it, that final intense pulsing swell that signaled his release. His ragged cry of ecstasy filled her with joy as she drank him down. When she raised her head to look at him, he was panting and felt as if he had run a long hard race.

"You look as if you've just outrun those Osage renegades again," she whispered impishly.

"This . . . I can assure you . . ." he gasped out, "was infinitely more strenuous . . . and obviously more pleasurable."

"Then you didn't mind my . . . inexperience." It was not quite a question, but she could not help wanting his further assurance, even his praise.

He reached up and twined a long lock of her hair about his wrist and pulled her down into his arms. "The greatest pleasure of all was that you gifted me with that inexperience, Livy," he replied simply, stroking her back as he rained soft, tender kisses across her face.

Shyly she burrowed her head against his chest and murmured, "I wanted to taste of you as you had of me."

He smiled wickedly. "So, you enjoyed my lovemaking in the lodge." It was not quite a question either, but he loved her *humm* of assent. Brushing the tips of her breasts with his hands, he sat up beside her, letting his mouth trail hot wet licks and bites down to her aching sensitive nipples, suckling them tenderly until she arched up, her fingers kneading his shoulders frantically as her whole body writhed with wanting.

Olivia was on fire, liquid fire and his hands and mouth were stoking the inferno until she feared she would incinerate. "Oh, Samuel, please, my love, please . . ." She did not know if she was pleading for him to continue the maddeningly slow seduction or to stop before she died—or to do what he did then, moving his mouth lower, skimming across her navel with a quick flick of his tongue until he reached that melting, throbbing center that wept for his touch.

As he made love to her, she buried her fingers in his hair, pulling him closer, urging him to continue the sweet spiraling madness that was lifting her higher and higher until at last she reached a shattering climax, crying out his name as the earth seemed to move beneath her.

As her body slowly subsided, she felt the ground with one hand. "I wanted to see if it was shaking again or if it was only me," she confessed sheepishly as he chuckled, moving up to embrace her.

"No more bad shakes, only good ones," he said, kissing her lips softly.

"You taste strange," she said dreamily against his mouth as he continued to kiss her.

"No. I taste of you," he replied, covering her body with his own, deepening the kiss.

She could feel the renewed hardness of his erection pressing into her belly and wriggled against it until he growled low in his throat when she grasped it, guiding it to her.

He paused before plunging in to murmur, "Are you ready to start the quaking all over again?"

"Yes, Samuel, please make the earth shake again," she said breathlessly, already wrapping her legs around his hips, urging him deeper.

The next morning brought pale winter sunlight to the devastation along the river. Samuel made a reconnaissance while Olivia efficiently saw to their camp. After a few hours he returned, shaking his head.

"It's as if the Mississippi is alive and has gone berserk. There are huge whirlpools dragging whole trees down into them and falls, my God, some as much as ten to twenty feet high all the way across the river!"

"But that's impossible. Micajah said the only falls on the whole river are way north near its headwaters."

Samuel shrugged. "The shakes must've reconfigured the land so completely it created new ones."

"Then it's impassable?"

"As it is now, we'd be taking a terrible chance. I felt a few more low rumbles while I was gone."

"So did I," she said worriedly.

"If we have some more shifting underground, the water may run more normally. Problem is, how long will it take?"

"We have enough beans and cornmeal to last us for a month or more—lots of shot and powder for your rifle and the one I found in the cabin box. We can hunt for meat. I vote we wait and see what the river does."

"Walking hundreds of miles through Indian country has definitely lost its appeal for me, too," he replied dryly, then grinned at her. "You wouldn't exactly have any ulterior motives for wanting to camp here, would you?"

His voice was a sexy purr and she responded by gliding into his arms. "I can think of lots of ways to pass the time of day while we watch the river . . ."

For nearly a week they camped beside the cabin box while Samuel used the tools and lumber from the wreckage of the keelboat's outer hull to fashion a small maneuverable raft. Olivia helped him lash it securely together. Unspoken between them lay the dread of once more getting back on the tortuous, debris-filled Mississippi, but in one of his longer scouting trips, Samuel had discovered that the falls seemed to stop about five miles downstream.

The giant sucks that had made the already turbulent waters into impassable whirlpools had all disappeared, but shrubs and trees as well as flotsam and jetsam from washed away settlements upriver still remained deadly impediments. It was nearly three hundred miles back to St. Louis and even farther down to New Orleans, both overland routes filled with hostile Indians and murderous outlaws. The river was their only choice.

Finally on a morning that dawned bright and clear with a slight wind blowing from the southwest, they set out on the raft with their supplies and weapons in oilskin wrappings. Portaging over the area around the falls was laborious but Olivia worked alongside Samuel, uncomplaining and amazingly resilient.

As he watched her pulling on the ropes, he knew her hands were blistered inside her gloves the same as his and marveled anew at her grit. The elegant belle surrounded by swains in that Washington ballroom should never have become this adaptable. There were depths to Olivia St. Etienne that he had yet to fathom. She was as complex, as deep as the river. If only they had a lifetime in which he could discover those depths.

But would they have that chance? The unresolved issue of Tish hovered over them. Neither spoke of her since their last stalemated exchange about the divorce. He worried about what sort of vicious havoc Tish might be stirring up in St. Louis in his absence. But perhaps she had already grown bored enough to pack up and have Richard take her home. What if they were caught someplace on the river when the previous week's chaos erupted? He smiled grimly at the thought, dismissing her actual drowning as too great a piece of luck.

Another matter niggled at the back of his conscience—the issue of Olivia's inheritance. What if Durand really was as rich as Wescott hoped and that fortune was waiting for her? Samuel had already wed one woman who tried to buy him with her wealth. Olivia was not that sort of woman, but still, she might be an heiress, a member of New Orleans Creole elite and he was still a simple soldier. Even with a lucrative share of his brother-in-law's business, his pay could not provide her the luxuries of that life.

What would happen when they reached New Orleans? Olivia would disavow the Durand estate for him in a heartbeat, he knew. But he also knew he could not allow her to do it. What if—his heart squeezed with dread as the sudden thought surfaced.

Olivia looked up at Samuel as they tied the raft to its moorings for the night. His expression was grim, his eyes slate colored and haunted. Instinctively she knew he was thinking of their future.

"What is it, Samuel? You look as if God just told you the quake was coming back." When he did not reply but continued securing the raft, she waited him out patiently. *Micajah would be proud of the way I've learned to control my temper,* she thought wryly. Well, around Samuel, perhaps not always.

She stepped away from the raft and knelt with her flint, gathering up bits of dried leaves and other materials for punk to start a campfire. While they worked together over simple camp chores, she noted his agitation. Something was bothering him. But he would have to spit it out in his own good time. After they ate supper, she laid out their blankets and prepared for bed by taking a quick wash beside a small cold stream flowing into the big river. When she climbed beneath the blankets, he remained seated at the fire, clutching a coffee cup in his hands.

"Come to bed, Samuel," she said huskily. No matter what else was wrong between them, they would always have this. And this was beautiful.

He tossed the silty grounds away and stood up, then walked reluctantly over to her and reached for one of the blankets. "Maybe it's better if we sleep apart from here on until we reach New Orleans . . . that is . . . oh hell, Livy," he cursed some more at the stricken look on her face. "It sure isn't because I don't want you . . ."

"Then what is it?" Her voice sounded brittle.

He sighed, then asked, "When was the last time you had your courses?" He knew it had not been since he rescued her from Wescott.

She looked baffled for a moment. "About two weeks ago. Why ever . . ."

"You could be carrying my child, Livy," he said gently.

"And you don't want that?"

"Not until I can give you my name. I can't marry you for another year, maybe longer."

He sounded defensive, her proud, lonely soldier, yet he looked so vulnerable that it hurt her heart. How much she loved him! "And you believe we can sleep apart from now until we reach New Orleans?"

He grinned wryly. "Difficult but not impossible."

"For you, maybe," she said, moving out from beneath her blanket and taking hold of the one he held, tugging it toward her. "I suddenly find I'm cold. Too cold for just one blanket. I need them both."

"Livy." His voice grew low and dangerous.

"What if I'm already pregnant? If you were going to cook up some crack brained idea like this, you should've thought of it two weeks ago. I vote we take our chances until you have to leave me—if you still want to leave me," she added roguishly. She stripped off his large shirt, which she was using as a nightrail, revealing the pale perfection of her body. When she drew his hands over her breasts and pressed them against the hardened nipples, he cursed and tried to pull away, but she threw her arms around his neck. "Hit's too late ta change horses in th' middle o' a buff'lo stampede," she said in a broad Carolina twang.

"Another of Micajah's bits of wisdom?" he asked, not really caring about the answer as her hands began unfastening his britches with great dexterity.

Hell, a saint couldn't last for three weeks out in the wilderness alone with Olivia St. Etienne. And he was sure as hell no saint, he mused, giving in, kissing her voraciously.

You want this to bind her to you, a nagging voice in the back of his mind scolded. Samuel did not listen.

❦ *Chapter 24* ❦

New Orleans at the opening of 1812 had a population of around twenty thousand people of highly diverse backgrounds. It was a city more cosmopolitan than any other in the fledging republic, a good part of its European flair derived from the fact that it had been part of the United States for only nine years. Essentially, it was French, but forty years of Spanish governance had left an indelible mark with the blending of French and Spanish cultures into the unique amalgam of Creole.

Yet in recent decades, as the restless Americans crossed the Appalachians and settled the Mississippi wilderness, they, too, had gravitated to the only seaport from which to sell their crops and purchase the necessities and luxuries of life. Rough Kaintucks in greasy buckskins rubbed elbows with narrow-eyed Bostons who spoke in flat Yankee accents and drove hard bargains with the tempestuous Creole businessmen.

The bustling port city drew merchants and seamen, drifters and opportunists from around the globe. In the sprawling public market on the massive embankment of the delta levee, French and Spanish blended with the various accents of English as well as with German, Italian, Greek and Creek Indian dialects. Everywhere the lilting patois of African free people of color sounded as they called out their wares while the more silent black slaves went about the drudgery of their appointed chores.

Samuel had often visited the city and had lived there briefly with his sister prior to her marriage. He took the sights, sounds and smells of "Queen" New Orleans in stride. Olivia's memories of the city were different. This was where her uncle had cruelly snubbed his only sister, leaving her family in desperate straits. Julian St. Etienne had won at the gambling tables for a few months, but it had done little to soften the blow of her brother's heartlessness for Solange.

As Samuel and Olivia moored their small raft, Olivia's mind was filled with bittersweet reminiscences. She watched an oysterman farther up the banks cracking open his wares and selling them to elegantly dressed Creole gentlemen and their families, who devoured the raw delicacies with epicurean relish. The pungent tang of fresh oranges and lemons blended with the oily richness of bananas.

Vendors clogged the levee as they made their way up the narrow streets of the city. Greeks hawked hot meat pastries and slave girls described the delights of their freshly baked ginger cakes. A bronzed Indian with the shaven head and roached topknot of a Muskogee moved silently through the motley throng as if born to it, passing two beautiful octoroon girls out strolling under the watchful eye of their *maman*. A gaggle of nuns hurried by, dressed in black robes and veils, impervious to the carnival atmosphere surrounding them.

"It's just as I remembered, only perhaps a bit more frenetic," she said as they cleared the market at last.

Samuel looked down at her. "The first thing we have to do is get you cleaned up and respectably chaperoned before we look up this uncle of yours."

His voice was detached and neutral. *Already he is distancing himself from me,* she thought with a pang. He would see that she was safe and provided for, but then he would leave her. What if his fears about Senator Soames proved valid and he could not secure the divorce? Stiff necked and honorable man that he was, Samuel Sheridan Shelby would nobly insist she find someone who could offer her what he could not . . . unless she were carrying his child. Olivia knew no force on earth could prevent him from claiming her then. She held fast to that fragile hope as they wended their way down a narrow street and entered a small shop.

While she stood shadowed in the musty interior, Samuel carried on a swift conversation in flawless French with the small wizened proprietor. His facility with language was as great as her own, and she had spent a lifetime traveling across the capitals of Europe to acquire hers. A useful tool for a man in Samuel's profession, she was certain.

Soon all was arranged and within the hour Olivia was settled in a small inn at the edge of the city, soaking off weeks of Mississippi River mud in a tub while her new maid laid out the clothing Samuel had purchased for her. She would hardly greet Uncle Charles in high style, but at least some semblance of respectability would accompany her. Perhaps it would have been best if she had refused to allow the charade and stalked up to the Durand mansion bedraggled from her ordeal on the river and confessed to the arrogant old Creole that she had traveled down the Mississippi as the colonel's paramour.

Uncle Charles would have disowned her on the spot, certain that the taint of Julian St. Etienne's blood had ruined her beyond redemption. How desperate the old man must be to seek her out after all these years. She supposed she should feel sorry for him, but she could not. Emory Wescott had explained that the entire Durand family had been wiped out in a yellow fever epidemic, leaving her uncle with only his estranged sister's child as the last heir to his fortune.

Olivia guessed that fortune was considerable and knew that it would prove an additional impediment to her relationship with Samuel. Tish, too, had been an heiress. She knew how much his wife's wealth had galled the proud man who insisted on providing for his wife without any outside help. The extravagant gifts from Senator Soames to Tish had been an affront. Silently she closed her eyes and sank back into the hot water, cursing Emory Wescott for the thousandth time for abducting her and bringing them to this wretched impasse in their lives.

When she heard Samuel's voice in the outer room, she rang for Tonette and dressed quickly, eager to hear his news. The moment she walked through the door, she knew it was not good.

"Your uncle has been dead for months," he said without preamble, knowing she would little mourn the loss of the snobbish old aristocrat.

"Then we were right about Wescott's motives," she said, chilled to realize how easy it would have been to arrange her death once Durand's fortune had been securely placed in the hands of her legal guardian.

"I've met with Durand's attorney, a Monsieur Jean-Claude Brionde, who explained to me about his client's demise. He's most eager to meet Charles Durand's long-lost niece."

"Long lost. Long discarded would be more accurate," she scoffed bitterly, then walked over and put her arms around his neck, ignoring the prim little maid, who hovered silently in the doorway. "Oh, Samuel, let's just leave, forget about my uncle's inheritance. Let's return to St. Louis. The river traffic is—"

"No, Livy," he said softly, removing her arms and setting her gently aside. "That's no good and you know it as well as I do. If I'm ever to secure a divorce, I have to go to Washington—and we have to stay apart until it's accomplished."

There was something guarded in his expression as she looked into those dark blue eyes. "There's more, isn't there?"

He smiled sadly. "You're getting as good at reading me as Liza." Then all trace of the smile vanished as he turned away from her. God, how could he tell her when he stood so close, breathing in the scent of her perfume? All he wanted to do was bury his hands in that fiery hair and pull her into his arms, never letting her go again!

"After I saw the Durand attorney, I reported to Governor Claiborne's office. It's a clearing house for any special messages that would be sent upriver to me." He glanced at Tonette, then said, "We need to discuss some sensitive matters."

Olivia's heart was pounding with dread as she politely dismissed the maid and closed the door, allowing them privacy in the small parlor. "A message from President Madison?" she asked.

He nodded, forcing himself not to be affected by her stiff demeanor. "I've been summoned back to Washington, Livy. It would seem Secretary Monroe needs an experienced go-between to make some rather ticklish arrangements with a French émigré who purports to have some incriminating documents."

"Incriminating. How?" Her voice sounded hollow. All she could think about was that he was leaving.

"This mysterious Frenchman supposedly acquired reports from an Anglo-Irishman who spied for the governor general of Canada. He spent the past couple of years in New England."

"Where the Federalists are keenly pro British," Olivia ventured, biting her lip. She could see where this was leading. New England shipping merchants were so incensed over the Republican administration's trade embargo that there had been murmuring about secession from the union.

Samuel could see that she understood the gravity of the situation. "Yes. If these papers contain any scraps of hard evidence at all, they must not fall into the wrong hands.

Madison can use them to expose British perfidy and at the same time throw his Federalist enemies into disgrace."

"And who but Colonel Shelby could handle such a delicate matter?" she said tremulously. "How soon do you have to leave?"

"There's a ship sailing on the morning tide, Livy. I must be on it."

Black spots floated before her eyes but she blinked them away and smiled. "Well then, that doesn't leave us very much time, does it?"

"No. Before we attend to the matter of your inheritance with Monsieur Brionde, I'm taking you to meet William Claiborne."

"The governor?"

"He's an old acquaintance who was so kind as to offer his protection to my sister some years ago. He can be trusted. Also, he's the only means through which you can get messages to me and I to you. I fear over the next several months I'll be moving around a great deal."

Olivia digested that, knowing it might be a very long time until she saw her love again. Swallowing for courage, she looked into his eyes but made no attempt to touch him. "Will you have time to attend to the divorce petition?"

This time he could not help himself. He had to hold her. She looked so alone and vulnerable, standing proudly with her slender back so straight, her chin upthrust. He embraced her and at once felt her arms slip around his waist. "Good God, of course! I'll see that the petition is drafted. Tom Jefferson will shepherd it through the legislature for me." He stroked her bright hair with one hand while his other arm pressed her tightly against him. She nestled her head on his shoulder as he said, "You feel as if you'd been made to fit here." Damn, she had been! She was going to be his wife.

"I was," she said, echoing his thoughts.

"Livy . . . there's one thing you must promise me . . ." He continued caressing her long soft curls.

"Anything," she murmured, lulled by the warmth and security of his embrace, the steady protective rhythm of his heartbeat.

"I must know if you're carrying my child . . ." He hesitated, feeling miserably inadequate, unable to protect her reputation.

Olivia was over a week late for her courses and he knew

it. She had hastened to assure him when he had casually questioned her regarding it that her cycle had always been irregular. He had not mentioned it since . . . until now . . . when he was leaving her. "It must gall you to besmirch your honor, being forced to sail away without knowing."

She felt him stiffen in her arms and knew blurting out that snide accusation had been cruel. "I'm sorry," she said, her voice husky with emotion. "I only said that because I'm afraid of losing you."

When she looked up into his face, her eyes were jewel bright with tears. He traced the exotic upward tilt of her high cheekbones with his fingertips, catching a crystalline tear-drop on his thumb. "Oh, Livy, there's nothing on earth I want more than to give you my name, to hold our child in my arms, to spend my life with you. Promise me you'll write as soon as you know." He hung his head in misery. "Even though I can't marry you now, I will do what I can to protect your reputation. I have family in Kentucky—in fact, my cousin Nestor Shelby is Governor Isaac Shelby's brother. Nestor owns a large plantation outside Lexington. He and his wife, Alva, would be more than happy to offer you hospitality."

"I don't care about my reputation, Samuel. I only care about your returning to me. Just keep safe and I will write you as soon as I know."

He smiled crookedly. "Even though I know it would be wrong for you to suffer, a part of me wants it to happen, you know? Our baby would be a means of binding you to me."

"Nothing, not even a child, could bind me to you more strongly than my love already does," she replied simply. Yet in her heart Olivia prayed that his seed had indeed taken root in her womb.

The visit to Governor Claiborne was brief but reassuring. The harried man was struggling through long-standing polit-ical antipathy with the Creole politicians who still mistrusted the "Boston" sent to rule over them. Yet in spite of being hampered by the recent loss of his trusted personal secretary, the pale and punctilious Claiborne was genuinely kind, wel-coming Olivia to New Orleans and assuring her and Samuel that he would do everything in his power to expedite com-munications between the two of them.

After they shared a late luncheon with Claiborne, they left

his sprawling office in the old Spanish governor's building on the main square and headed down Royale Street to the elegant law office of Charles Durand's attorney, Jean-Claude Brionde.

The little Creole was squat and corpulent, yet for all that, he possessed the innate grace and charm of a New Orleans native son. Once he examined the documentation proving that Olivia was indeed Solange Durand St. Etienne's daughter, he was effusively delighted.

"It is so wonderful that an honorable old family name such as Durand should not end with the death of your esteemed uncle, mademoiselle," he said in melodically accented English, believing that the American officer escorting Olivia was not fluent in French. Shelby did not disabuse him of the notion.

Olivia had noticed that Samuel often let others make erroneous assumptions, underestimating him, a useful method of operation for a man in his line of work. He would be in constant danger now with war looming so close on the horizon, perhaps even more peril than the soldiers who would face British guns on land and sea. When would he return safely to her? *Would* he return at all?

So absorbed was she in her fretful ruminations, Olivia did not really attend Attorney Brionde's words as the buoyant little Frenchman grew round-eyed and serious while he explained the extent of Charles Durand's holdings. But when she looked over at Samuel's tight expression, the rigid set of his body indicated that something was amiss. Then Brionde's words began to sink in.

"The local sugar plantations amount to ten thousand, five hundred sixty acres in all, but the refineries process far more cane than that brought downriver from the Durand holdings above. The shipping line runs a dozen packets in the coastal trade, as well as six schooners and two new steamboats. The speculation profits from land investments are outlined in some detail as are the banking ventures, but I expect mademoiselle will wish to have a man of business to attend such wearying financial matters for her.

"A *jeune fille* such as you must dance and laugh, attend the theater, enjoy all the pleasures of our beautiful city while you look for a suitable husband," the attorney said with an indulgent twinkle in his dark eyes. "Ah, mademoiselle, if I were only twenty years younger, I would court you myself—if my family were as distinguished as the house of Durand. *Alors,* it is not."

He shrugged with Gallic insouciance, but then his expression turned serious. "There is the matter of a guardian. You've explained about Monsieur Wescott's unfortunate demise just before your arrival. Is there no one else, no male family member who could see to your affairs and provide guidance?" His eyes strayed to the tall American colonel as he spoke. It was apparent that the young officer did not fit the job description.

Olivia was all too aware of Samuel's reaction, the stiff posture and cool neutral voice, the expressionless mask that had slipped over his face. He thought he was "unworthy" of her now that she was an heiress! Damn male pride and stupidity!

Samuel addressed Brionde, saying, "Mademoiselle St. Etienne is quite alone in the world now that her uncle has died. I was fortunate enough to be able to escort her and her maid to the city, but now—"

"You two need not speak of me as if I were an imbecile or a child," Olivia interjected. Her growing anger began to tamp down her despair over Samuel's eminent departure.

Although Samuel had coached her not to reveal any personal attachment to him beyond gratitude for acting as her escort downriver, Olivia cared far less about what the little attorney might think of her than she did about Samuel's withdrawal from her. *Damn Uncle Charles for being so bloody rich!*

"I spent the past years on the frontier, Monsieur Brionde, in St. Louis and then upriver on the Missouri living among the Indians. I care little for dancing and theater and I am not in the market for a husband. I—"

"I believe Mademoiselle St. Etienne is overwrought from her long journey and the blow of learning that her uncle has died," Samuel interjected smoothly, willing her to subside.

She met his level blue gaze defiantly, then realized how impossible the situation was. Suddenly she was truly weary, bone weary and disheartened.

Samuel felt acute relief. She would not ruin her chance for a life here in New Orleans. He quickly began to question the Creole regarding the legal transfer of Charles Durand's vast wealth to Olivia St. Etienne.

The son of a bitch did abscond with the whole damn Bour-

bon treasury! he thought bitterly. Olivia was one of the richest women in the United States, no doubt the richest in this vast new territory. The attorney's words about a "suitable husband" from a "distinguished family" had hit him with the impact of a cannonball. She was utterly out of his reach now, as much as if she were still a titled noblewoman residing at the court of the French emperor.

Once the attorney had answered all the questions about legal technicalities, Samuel said, "Mademoiselle St. Etienne requires rest. If you would be so kind as to direct us to the Durand city house?"

Within a quarter hour Samuel, Olivia and her maid, Tonette, rode in the elegant Durand landau Monsieur Brionde had summoned to take them to the city house. The trip was made in virtual silence as both Samuel and Olivia considered the impact of her inheritance on their future together. Olivia stared unseeing at the quaint charm of Creole New Orleans, its narrow winding streets filled with a motley press of people. The architecture of lacy wrought iron grillwork and triple-tiered galleries held no enchantment, nor did the burbling fountains and winter greenery in the half-hidden courtyards visible through narrow gangways between the buildings. She wondered with dread what sort of ostentatious palace Charles Durand had built here in the city. The chatty lawyer had already described the fabulous luxury of the plantation estate on Bayou Bienvenue.

When the driver pulled into the *porte cochère* of a beautiful three-story pastel brick house with wide galleries surrounding it on three sides, Samuel swung down lithely from the seat and assisted Olivia and her maid to descend. Tonette stared in awe at the life-sized bronze nude dispensing water through an urn in the courtyard pool, then looked up to the gallery where a bevy of black faces beamed down on them, murmuring softly in French. The Durand servants were eager to welcome the new mistress.

"It is rather daunting," Olivia said uncertainly, pressing her fingers on Samuel's arm, hoping for some reassurance from him.

He remained grimly silent as his eyes swept across the whitewashed wrought iron gallery railing into the wide standing doors beyond where opulent crystal chandeliers gleamed against the dusk of twilight. "It's quite magnificent," he replied at length. Even more imposing than that

monolithic pile of rocks Worthington Soames had built in
Washington.

"Samuel," she said urgently, leaning toward him, "get
those thoughts out of your mind. Don't . . ."

"The servants are watching, Livy," he reminded her
gently, taking her hand and placing it atop his arm to escort
her inside.

Tonette snapped out of her awestruck muteness long
enough to instruct a footman to carry the lady's trunk upstairs to her quarters, then silently trailed after Samuel and
Olivia across the wide gallery. Pots of aromatic rosemary
were positioned at the sides of the wide glass doors fronting
each spacious room on the courtyard. The plants grew lushly
in spite of the coolness of winter. A smiling ebony-faced
woman of Amazonian proportions welcomed them, intro-
ducing herself as Ceale, the head housekeeper for Monsieur
Durand's city place. She ushered them into an elegant drawing room and bid them take seats while another servant girl
was dispatched to bring refreshments. She personally
showed Tonette to the mistress's sleeping quarters to super-
vise the unpacking of mademoiselle's things.

Left alone, Samuel stood up and began to pace across the
polished floor of intricate oak marquetry. A marble fireplace
dominated the inside wall. A small blaze crackled invitingly,
casting a pale orange glow around the room. The light was
magnified by the magnificent crystal chandelier hanging
overhead. Fine mahogany furniture graced the room while
around them the portraits of dead Durands stared mutely at
them. To Shelby they seemed to be looking down their aristocratic French noses at the American interloper. He eyed
one tall silver-haired man with the delicately chiseled somewhat effete features he always associated with the French
nobility.

"Is that Uncle Charles?"

Olivia studied the cold patrician features. "Yes, although
I never met him. He looks a bit like *Maman,* but . . . aloof."
She felt so utterly alone, bereft. "Don't leave me here, Samuel," she pleaded, then waited for him to speak, knowing he
was marshaling his courage to say good-bye.

"I have to go, Livy. You know that. It isn't as if you won't
be comfortable," he added, gesturing around the beautiful
room.

"I was *comfortable* in Micajah's cabin. This . . . this

frightens me, Samuel." She hugged herself unconsciously, wrapping her arms around her waist in spite of the warmth in the room.

He knelt in front of her and took her hands. They were ice-cold as he lifted them to place a chaste kiss on top of each. "You must remain here, Livy. I can't take you back to Micajah and it's not safe for you to travel alone."

"You mean I should stay here because I'm rich, that I'll be able to live the life of a pampered aristocrat that I was born to?" Her voice was brittle.

"The money won't go away, Livy," he said darkly.

"I don't want it."

"That isn't for you to decide now. I can't give you my name or my protection. Wealth can be a shield and for now you need that shield."

She swallowed painfully. "The money will always be between us, won't it? It hurts your pride that I'm rich."

"I won't deny it. No man who is a man wants his woman to support him. He should do the providing."

"You think I'd lord it over you like Tish?" she asked, stung when he voiced his feelings aloud even though she already knew them.

"No, you're nothing like Tish! God, Livy, I *know* that, but there is no time to resolve this issue now," he said in frustration.

"Oh, Samuel, what are we going to do?" She stroked his face with her fingertips.

He smiled crookedly, that old dazzling grin that had always made her heart turn over. "You will become the belle of New Orleans. And I will go to Boston for Secretary Monroe. When I'm free to return for you, I will." He sobered then, and his eyes revealed the bleakness as he added, "But I cannot promise how long it may take. The divorce alone will go slowly. And there is a small matter of war . . ."

"I shall wait, no matter how long it takes."

He studied her face as if memorizing every nuance, each delicate aquiline feature, so strong and lovely. "I believe you, Livy. I'll write to you as often as I can, although I don't know how informative my letters will be given the nature of my work."

"Only keep safe. I shall write to you of how I long for Micajah's cabin and how bored I am with New Orleans social life," she said with forced levity.

"You must let me know at once if you are with child. If so, I'll send my cousin Nestor and his wife to bring you to their plantation."

"Don't look so worried. I've already told you how much I want your baby, Samuel."

He shook his head stubbornly. "Not this way. I was a selfish bastard for putting you at risk like this. Now that you have everything here you should never be forced to leave it and hide in the backwaters of Kentucky."

She smiled sadly. "You cannot doubt that I would choose you over the Durand millions—with or without a baby."

"You say that now and you mean it, but I don't want necessity to decide for you, Livy. I want it to be your choice."

"I made that choice long ago, Samuel . . . right in the middle . . . of a crowded . . . Washington . . . ballroom . . ." She punctuated the words with soft brushing kisses, cupping his face between her hands.

Samuel knew he must leave before he did something utterly reckless that would ruin her reputation even if she was not already carrying his child. He stood up and held her at arm's length. "I will carry the image of you with me wherever I go."

"And I, yours," she whispered, holding back the tears as he walked through the gallery door and disappeared into the chill New Orleans night.

Olivia slept poorly that night on a high tester bed in the elegant suite that had been Madam Durand's. Since she had preceded her husband in death by over a decade, the rooms had been cleaned meticulously by the servants, but Charles had kept Marie Latise Durand's quarters undisturbed as a shrine.

Upon arising the next day, Olivia inspected the beautiful Louis XIV furniture and Aubusson carpets. All the furnishings had been imported from France at no little expense, as if the Durand family held on to the fiction of life in the old country in this warmer Gulf coast climate.

"My first orders will be for all Aunt Marie's personal effects to be packed up and stored away," she murmured to herself, gazing down at a collection of miniatures, portraits of haughty Durand faces, exquisitely painted on ivory with gilt frames. She saw little family resemblance to her mother.

For several days Olivia kept busy learning the household

routine and the names and jobs of the servants as well as entertaining the endless stream of visitors from the city's social elite. Everyone who was anyone of consequence in New Orleans felt it obligatory to call on the new heiress, especially the matrons with eligible sons and the older widowers in the market for a wealthy young wife.

Olivia felt like a piece of veal hung up for display in the plaza market. She ached with loneliness and thought of nothing but Samuel. In her spare moments, especially when sleep eluded her late at night, she began a letter to him, really more of a series of entries rather like a diary. As soon as she had resolved the issue of pregnancy, she would include the news and post it to him.

She did compose a somewhat shorter letter to Micajah, explaining what had transpired on the Mississippi and in New Orleans. Governor Claiborne was to be the conduit for her mail to Samuel, but she felt reasonably secure in sending the letter upriver by regular post. However, just before mailing it, she decided on impulse to visit the governor's office. There was no sense in taking chances. In the best of times the postal service was uncertain and with the war fever sweeping across the West, things were becoming exceedingly unsettled.

When her driver pulled onto the Place d' Armes, the scene was one of bustling chaos, what she had come to associate with the lively international port city. If Samuel were here to share it with her, she would have enjoyed New Orleans. Several bold rather unsavory looking types wearing high boots, gold earrings and thin shirts bloused open in the warm morning sunshine, lounged against the pillars of the Pontalba, watching her with hooded eyes. Baratarians. Probably men in the employ of the mysterious Laffite brothers.

As Olivia stepped down from the carriage beneath their scrutiny, she marveled at the bizarre contradictions of this city. Its Creole leaders were so civilized and precise in their social conventions, yet willing to tolerate pirates and smugglers boldly walking the streets of this town in open defiance of American authority.

The young soldier standing outside the governor's palace bowed courteously and held the door open for her and Tonette. Olivia made her way to the governor's outer office with the little maid following behind her. It appeared that the position of secretary to Claiborne had been filled. A slender young man sat writing busily away in a ledger. When he heard her enter, he looked up distractedly, then smiled, revealing straight white teeth. A heavy shock of silver gilt hair fell artlessly across his forehead as he stood up to greet her.

Olivia was struck by the perfection of his features. He was as handsome as a stage performer, yet there was something unsettling about his good looks.

"Good morning, mademoiselle. I am Governor Claiborne's secretary, Edmond Darcy."

Olivia returned his warm smile, feeling more at ease as she introduced herself.

"Ah, yes, the Durand heiress. Every cafe has been buzzing with the tale of your harrowing journey downriver. How may I be of assistance to you?"

"I don't know if the governor has spoken to you regarding handling my mail?"

"As a matter of fact, he has, Mademoiselle St. Etienne," he replied, smiling, one slender pale hand extended to take the missive from her.

Olivia gave it to him. "I'm ever so grateful, Mr. Darcy."

"Would you care to see the governor? I believe he is between appointments with legislators about now."

"No, that's all right. I know he's a busy man. Please give him my best wishes and tell him I am going to open the plantation house on Bayou Bienvenue next week. If all is as efficiently handled there as at my uncle's city house, I shall be entertaining within the month."

"I am certain the governor will eagerly await your invitation," he said politely.

They bid each other good day and Olivia departed with her maid. Claiborne's secretary stood watching the flame-haired woman as she walked through the door and vanished down the long hallway. Then he looked down at the thick letter addressed to Micajah Johnstone in care of Father Louie at Fort St. Francoise, Upper Louisiana Territory.

Smiling grimly, he slid the letter inside his jacket pocket. There would be time later on to read it at his leisure, then decide whether or not to post it upriver. However, all of Mademoiselle St. Etienne's correspondence to Colonel Shelby was to be destroyed.

* * *

Washington had changed in the year he was absent. Not the physical appearance, which still remained the raw unfinished dream of architect Pierre-Charles L'Enfant. The buildings were a peculiar accretion of splendid stone and higgledy-piggledy frame threatened by the unrelenting encroachments of the Virginia tidewater swamp. Rather, the difference in the city was a tension in the air that crackled across the seats of power, a restless malaise, fearful yet conversely eager. Washington wanted a war.

Secretary of State James Monroe did not. However, the situation between the Madison administration and the British government had deteriorated rapidly over the past months, and the flames of war had been fanned by the Western expansionists who saw opportunities to seize British lands in Canada as well as Spain's colonies in Florida.

"If only Henry Clay and the rest of those posturing fools would stop prating about American honor," Monroe said, looking down at the documents which Colonel Shelby had brought back from his mission in Boston.

"The Western congressmen are screaming about British confiscation of American ships, ignoring the fact that Napoleon has taken nearly as many," Samuel replied with disgust, waiting for the methodical man's assessment of the Henry papers.

James Monroe was superficially the opposite of his president in every way. A careful but plodding thinker who possessed none of the brilliant scholarly insights of Jemmy Madison, Monroe was physically tall and rawboned, a robust man of action beside the small older Madison whose frail health had been steadily worsening as the strain of the presidency took its toll. Yet appearances—like intellectual estimations—could deceive. Lifelong friends, the two men worked in complete accord, complimenting each other's strengths and weaknesses. Monroe was nobody's fool.

"As a spy, our Anglo-Irishman has much to learn," the secretary of state said dryly.

"He's an amateur, no doubt of it, but I don't think his intermediary the count is."

Monroe's shrewd brown eyes fixed Shelby with keen interest. "What do you think—is he a French agent?"

"I made some discreet inquiries through old friends at the French embassy. They've never heard of a Count de Crillon, either before or after the revolution."

"Napoleon's secret police, then," Monroe replied, nodding. "Yes, it would make sense. Things aren't exactly going swimmingly for the little emperor these days—he needs a two-front war foisted on the British."

"And we're making it damnably convenient for him," Shelby said sourly, knowing his father-in-law was one of the most vociferous advocates of war in the Senate.

"I'm afraid it's too late to shift course now. The War Hawks in Congress have whipped the whole countryside into a frenzy. The only bastion of peace is in New England . . . and we see here how reliable they are."

"We've known since Jefferson's embargo how New England shipping interests felt about their commercial ties to England. No surprise in that, but the signed letters of instruction from the Canadian governor-general to Henry are a new element in the equation," Shelby said thoughtfully.

"The Henry papers will not only add fuel to the fires of the War Hawks, they can also strengthen the administrator's position," Monroe replied, always carefully balancing both sides of an issue as was his wont.

"You mean because the New England British sympathizers mentioned in Henry's reports are all members of the Federalist party?"

Monroe smiled grimly, his eyes taking on a hard glint as he replied, "Precisely so, Colonel. They've even been making noises about possible secession if war comes. Our administration may not be able to prevent the war, but we can damn well prevent the dismemberment of the federal union. You have once again done your country an inestimable service."

"How soon until the president asks for a formal declaration of war?"

"Difficult to say. The president still hopes Prime Minister Perceval will agree to rescind the Orders in Council and end the Royal Navy's attacks on American ships, but it's rumored that Foreign Secretary Wellesberg will resign, and he is the strongest advocate of negotiating with us. If he does resign"—Monroe shrugged—"I expect we'll have our hand forced by spring . . ."

Samuel waited, knowing Monroe would give him his next assignment in due course. For the present, he was simply instructed to remain available in the capital in case of any emergencies. Given the precarious tenor of the times, Shelby knew there would be a surfeit of emergencies.

After the secretary had left the small hotel where the colonel had taken rooms, Samuel sat back and poured himself a brandy. It was approaching midnight. He had ridden hard from Boston, taking the slower overland route, fearing to take ship with such valuable papers when British men-of-war occasionally managed to stop American ships within sight of the United States coastline.

Exhausted and disheartened by the senseless wrangling of politicians and their governments, he polished off the brandy, relishing the warm soothing burn of it deep in his belly. He longed with all his being to return to Olivia in New Orleans but knew that could not be. They had already been separated for two months. Upon reaching the capital yesterday he had eagerly inquired about a letter from her but was disappointed.

Surely she must know by now whether or not she carried his child. Why had she not written? Of course, the letter could have been lost in transit, but dispatches from Governor Claiborne's office had arrived on schedule. Nothing from Olivia had been included.

Rubbing his eyes, he picked up a pen and began to compose another letter to her, his third since leaving New Orleans. *Why the hell don't you respond, Livy?* A deep-seated dread tightened his chest as the pen scratched along the page.

⊷ *Chapter 25* ⊷

"**Y**ou *are* certain?" Olivia sat in Dr. Albert Freul's office, her face ashen as she received the news which only two months earlier she would have greeted with unconditional rejoicing. "I mean, I haven't felt sick in the mornings or had any symptoms . . ."

The kindly old Alsatian Frenchman smiled gently. "Not every woman has the morning sickness, my dear. You are a very strong and healthy young woman. You should experience no difficulties carrying the child."

"Except for the lack of a husband," Olivia said baldly, too bereft by Samuel's apparent desertion to care about propriety.

The big round-faced man's normally florid complexion darkened a bit as he patted her hand sympathetically. Mademoiselle St. Etienne had been a generous patron of his hospital for the indigent, and volunteered long hours caring for sick orphans the nuns brought to him for help. The doctor admired her spirit and her kindness. If only there was some way to help. "The child's father—he is not in New Orleans?" he asked gently.

"No. And even if he were, he could not marry me." She raised her eyes to meet his. Finding no condemnation, only sympathy, she added, "He already has a wife."

The elderly physician scratched the thick gray whiskers on his chin. "Ah, I see. And you have no family to turn to, my dear?"

"My parents preceded Uncle Charles in death. All our other relatives perished during the Terror back in France when I was a child. My only living family is an old woodsman up in the Missouri River country. I know he'd welcome me and I would love to go to him, but with the reports of new earthquakes, the river has been very dangerous. I couldn't find anyone to take me, no matter how much money I offered them."

She looked haunted and vulnerable. He knew what people would say when word got out that she was unwed and pregnant. Even the vaunted Durand wealth would not save her from being totally ostracized. "Perhaps . . ." he began slowly, "I could help . . . that is, if you do not wish to have the child . . ."

When his words registered, Olivia felt her hands go protectively to her belly. "No! That is—I do appreciate your concern but . . ."

The doctor smiled, relieved. "Then you want this man's baby?"

Dr. Freul's kindness was suddenly too much. All her defenses of pride and stoicism crumbled and Olivia suddenly found herself sobbing. "Yes, yes, I want the baby very much. It's all I have left of him." She scrubbed at her eyes with a lace handkerchief. "I don't know what's wrong with me. I never cry."

The hint of a smile touched his eyes as he said, "Heightened emotion is a symptom of pregnancy. Perhaps you are not as asymptomatic as we first believed. Now"—he rose, gently touching her shoulder in a fatherly fashion—"I am going to have Louise brew us some fine fresh coffee and then we will decide what is to be done for you and this little one."

A short while later Olivia found herself seated in the Freuls' cozy parlor sipping the fragrant French coffee everyone in New Orleans loved so well. The doctor and his spinster sister, Louise, were genuinely solicitous as they made her feel at home in the cheery little apartment above his business office.

"Now, you must tell me about this young man you've fallen in love with," Louise said after insisting Olivia eat a thick wedge of rich golden pound cake generously slathered with butter. Mademoiselle Freul was a formidable lady, tall and buxom with heavy iron gray hair fastened securely in a no-nonsense chignon at the crown of her head, but her dark eyes were merry and kind and she laughed frequently. Olivia had worked with her over the past two months at the foundlings hospital and had often thought Louise should have married and had a dozen children of her own to love.

With such sympathetic listeners, Olivia found she was eager to unburden herself. She had endured a long and lonely silence, surrounded by strangers who only cared for her because she was the Durand heiress, or shy servants who spoke in monosyllables. Her meeting with Colonel Samuel

Shelby and the events of the past year came rushing quickly to her lips. She told them everything.

When she described Samuel's departure, her voice broke. "I . . . I fear something may have happened to him. His work is dangerous. He may have been killed."

"We can't be certain of that—after all, it's only been two months and the mails are so uncertain. You yourself said he travels around a good deal. His letters to you and yours to him may be lost."

Olivia shook her head. "Surely not all of them. I've written him so many times, and we agreed to post them through Governor Claiborne's office. If he were alive, he would have written me. I've even tried to contact his sister in St. Louis, but she hasn't answered. The governor assures me his dispatches arrive from Washington regularly, but the pouches contain nothing from Samuel."

Dr. Freul paced, stroking his short curly beard as he cogitated. "We will not give him up yet. Maybe the president sent him abroad?"

Willing to grasp at any straw, Olivia nodded. "It is possible."

"Well, that will still not solve our immediate problem," Louise interjected practically. "The colonel has to secure a divorce. Even if he were here, he could not marry you."

The doctor looked at his sister and said, "There are many fine young men in the city from good families. Perhaps—"

"No! That is, even if a man would be willing to accept me and my child, I could never wed anyone but Samuel. Not if there is the least chance he's still alive . . ." She shook her head in despair. "Not even if I knew he was dead."

"Then we shall just have to invent you a husband," Louise said cheerfully.

Both Olivia and Dr. Freul looked at her, stunned.

"What devious scheme are you cooking up now, Lou-Lou?"

Louise raised her heavy dark eyebrows and regarded her brother fondly. He had not called her Lou-Lou since they were children. "I think the solution to our problem is straightforward enough. Olivia needs a temporary husband—one who will not burden her with marital duties, but who will offer the protection of his name for the coming child. If her colonel is alive and secures his divorce, she will be suitably widowed and can wed him.

"Yes, the very thing!" she continued, delighted with her own ingenuity. "A husband with the decency to die young! I think a Spanish officer would suit nicely. Hmm, yes, a don from a fine rich old family, stationed in Spanish Florida. We shall visit Pensacola. I have not seen Señora Valdez in several years, and I believe I shall require the companionship of an adventuresome young lady on the trip. Tell me, Olivia, are you up to a brief sojourn in Florida?"

Catching the drift of what Louise Freul was up to, Olivia's spirits suddenly felt lighter. She smiled at the merry twinkle in the older woman's eyes and replied, "I've already traveled all the way down the Mississippi during an earthquake. I don't believe the short sea voyage to Florida will be difficult."

"Don Rafael Obregón!" Louise crowed triumphantly. "Yes, I like the name. What do you think, my dear?"

"I shall wed this mysterious Don Rafael in Pensacola, then be tragically widowed and withdraw to my estate at Bayou Bienvenue to mourn."

As the two women plotted, Dr. Freul shook his head in perplexed admiration. The male, in his estimation, never possessed the tenacious survival instincts and toughness of the female of the species.

Governor William Claiborne had just spent one hellacious morning placating a roomful of Creole planters who were frantic about the impending war with the British. Where was the American army to protect them against this ancient enemy whose ships sailed unchallenged along the Gulf as if they owned it? After reassuring them that all was secure, a fact he very much doubted, the governor finally succeeded in assuaging their vapors and sent them on their way.

With the bill for statehood before the Congress, it would not be long until those very same volatile Creoles would sit in a Louisiana legislature, plaguing his life even more. He rubbed his head wearily as his secretary knocked discreetly, then entered.

"What is it now, Darcy? More of those infernal Frenchmen—or another Spanish ship's captain complaining about the Baratarian freebooters robbing them blind?"

The secretary smiled, producing a thick sheaf of papers. "Nothing quite so taxing, your excellency. Just a few official papers requiring your signature—the public notices you requested regarding that pirate, Jean Laffite, the commutation of sentence for Enrique Salazar, a summons for Paul Schmitt and a series of requisitions for supplies and payments to the quartermaster."

Claiborne scanned the notices. All goods purchased from Laffite's illegal smuggling operation would be subject to immediate seizure by the United States government. He signed it with a flourish. "The arrogant scoundrel wants a lesson in manners," he gritted out, then skimmed a few lines from the next long document, copied out painstakingly in Darcy's cribbed handwriting. The governor was rapidly developing a blinding headache.

If only his beloved Creole wife were still alive, but she had perished of a fever and he was widowed and alone for the second time in his life. Forcing aside personal considerations, he applied himself to signing the mountainous pile of papers where Darcy indicated. He had come to depend on his able and efficient new secretary over the past months since Edmond Darcy had begun working for him.

Explaining partially what each document entailed, the secretary opened it to the back page and held it for Claiborne's signature until the entire stack was complete. "That should do it for today, your excellency. Why don't you go home for the evening? It's getting late and I can finish up here."

"Thank you, Darcy. I believe a glass of Madeira and early to bed would not be at all amiss," the weary governor said, rising and heading for the door while his secretary meticulously straightened his desk.

After Claiborne was gone, Darcy slid one piece of paper carefully from the stack and smiled chillingly. The salutation was addressed to Colonel Samuel Shelby. "This was even easier than I'd thought," he murmured in satisfaction as he sat down at the big walnut desk and folded the letter, then slipped it into an envelope. "I do hope you don't take the news of your little French tart's marriage too hard, Colonel. Of course, the governor could have mentioned that she's already widowed and in seclusion at her country estate . . . or, he could have told you the truth—just as your beloved herself has. Poor thing, pouring out her heart to you in all those letters, pleading for you to come claim her and your bastard!"

His gold eyes glowed malevolently in the candlelight as

the pale, perfect features of his aquiline face were cast in shadows. He looked for all the world like a fallen angel. Satan's right hand.

Colonel Samuel Shelby walked out of Jemmy Madison's office by a side door, used only when the president did not wish a special visitor to be seen. Many men from imperial ambassadors to political enemies had slipped through the discreet rear entry since the White House was first occupied by Thomas Jefferson, but Samuel's mind was far from the military matters at hand as he walked, grim faced, down the long, twisting corridor.

Dolley Madison stood poised in the doorway of her salon, silently watching him approach. It was obvious that Samuel did not see her. The look in his eyes was a thousand miles away—in New Orleans if she did not miss her guess.

"I know the situation on the Canadian border is grave, but somehow I intuit that your thoughts veer in a southerly direction." Mrs. Madison stepped into the hallway and gave Samuel a motherly kiss on his cheek, then drew him into the salon and closed the door.

When he first returned to Washington, Samuel had confided in her that he was pressing for the divorce from Tish because he had met a woman he wished to marry, a woman who waited for him in New Orleans. The young colonel had always kept his own council and never more so than in matters of the heart. Dolley had deduced that Olivia St. Etienne must be an extraordinary female indeed. But now the new spark seemed to have died in his eyes and his mask of cynicism was once again in place. Beneath it lay a world of pain, of that she was certain, and she wanted to know the particulars so that she might help or at the least offer consolation.

"Tell me what has you looking so preoccupied," she commanded when they were seated on the cabriole sofa in the parlor, well out of earshot of servants once she dismissed her maid. "And don't you dare give me another summary about the debacle when General Hull surrendered Fort Detroit to the British. Jemmy has already spoken more than enough about that!"

He smiled at her. "I could never fool you, could I?" he said fondly, his smile fading as a bittersweet look haunted his eyes before he shuttered them once more. "I no longer need pursue the divorce. Tish really is dead this time."

Dolley gasped softly. "What happened?"

"I'm not certain really. I only learned of it yesterday when I was accosted by Worthington Soames. The senator was livid about my filing the petition with the legislature, screaming at me about defaming his beloved paragon of a daughter even in death."

"But you've already told me how they faked her death once before," she said uncertainly.

He shook his head. "There's no fakery this time. He was like a wild man, red eyed and unshaven, crazed with grief. Tish is dead, all right. She was shot in St. Louis after I went downriver. He was too upset to give me any coherent details, but it appears to have been a robbery. Her body's being sent back to Virginia for burial in the family mausoleum."

"I know this sounds callous, Samuel, but now that she is truly gone, you could send for Olivia . . ." The bleak look in his eyes when he raised them to meet hers robbed her of breath. Surely it was not grief for Letitia Soames.

Echoing her thoughts he said, "I won't be a hypocrite and say I'm sorry Tish's gone but . . . I can't very well send for a married woman. Ironic, isn't it? First I was the one not free, now it's her."

"But how? Are you certain? Did she write this to you?" Her heart was breaking as she saw the anguish of his soul laid bare when the mask slipped for a moment.

"I haven't received a word from Olivia since I left, even though I've sent a dozen letters. Governor Claiborne kindly and rather regretfully informed me of the particulars at the lady's request. I suppose she found it awkward . . ." He stood up, unable to sit still any longer, and began to pace, needing to talk even though it was impossibly difficult to frame his thoughts.

Dolley was a patient listener who had spent years drawing out the shy and very private James Madison. As Samuel gathered his composure, she poured them each a glass of sherry from a decanter on the pier table against the wall. Silently she handed him one.

He took it absently. "He's a Spanish nobleman, Don Rafael Obregón. I always thought she'd look to her own kind. After all, her parents were of the Ancient Régime, a baron and baroness, while I'm just the son of a land poor Virginia planter. When she was impoverished with little hope of reentry into the humble ranks of St. Louis society, I suppose she changed—or we both wanted to believe she did.

"But once I learned about her uncle's money on the journey downriver, I had this . . ." his voice faded for a moment as he groped for the right words, "this apprehension, a feeling deep in my guts that she just wasn't meant to be mine. Then when I realized the extent of the Durand fortune and saw the way the Creole elite kowtowed to her, I wasn't sure I could live in the shadow of her money, or that I had the right to ask her to give it up."

"But she offered to, didn't she?" Somehow Dolley knew it was true.

He laughed a hollow, bitter rasp, then finished off the sherry and set the glass down on a dainty table. "Yes, she did, but that was when . . . oh hell, forgive my lack of delicacy, Dolley, that was when we both thought she could be carrying my child. I suppose until she knew that wasn't true, she was ready to walk away from all the wealth and position she'd been born to. But remember, I was gone with only the promise to secure a divorce. It might have taken a year or longer before I could marry her, if I wasn't killed first." He shook his head, the pain and bewilderment of the betrayal still numbing.

"And being in New Orleans, rich, young and beautiful, surrounded by swains, she succumbed without even the courtesy of sending you one word by her own hand." Righteous motherly anger warred with a niggling thread of hope that there was still some chance this was all a horrible misunderstanding.

"If it had been the ordinary post, I'd have assumed all our correspondence had been lost, but I've seen Claiborne's courier pouches arrive, filled with official documents and personal mail—but no word from Olivia . . . until she asked the governor to inform me of her marriage."

Dolley walked to his side and squeezed his arm. "Samuel, I am so very sorry. You deserve so much better from life." Almost afraid to ask, she nevertheless did. "What are you going to do now?" There was a coiled urgency in him, tensile and ready to explode. So palpable was his despair, she could feel it.

He smiled with his lips but his eyes were bleak as a storm swept sky. "I'm going to serve with Harrison in Indiana Territory. It seems after my success on the Missouri with the

Osage, I'm perceived by the war department as the perfect man to learn the battle strategy of Tecumseh and the Shawnee Confederacy. I'm going over the British lines into Canada."

Dolley blanched. "Samuel, that is virtual suicide. You cannot!"

"I am . . . and I must, Dolley. We've already suffered incalculable setbacks on the high seas. Our navy is outmanned and outgunned by more than twenty-to-one. We can't dare lose our strategic positions on land or the British will cut a corridor all the way from Upper Canada down the Mississippi to the Gulf. I have to go."

"Be safe, Samuel. Don't take any foolish chances, no matter how disillusioned you feel right now, promise me. I shan't let you go lest you give me your word," she commanded sternly.

Samuel smiled with a small bit of his old charm. "Ah, Dolley, if only I could have met you before Jemmy did . . ." He raised her hands to his lips and kissed the backs of them.

"Such flattery for an old married lady, Samuel, but you can't deter me. Have I your pledge—no rash heroics to endanger yourself?"

Bowing to her he nodded. "No more than I've ever endangered myself."

As he departed, the president's lady stared after him, bemused, her mind turning over various reasons why Olivia St. Etienne would have betrayed him. "A rich suitor from an aristocratic background similar to her own? A secure life free of the worries Samuel's work would bring to a marriage? No, none of it made sense if the girl were anything like the way he had previously described her.

Then another thought struck her. *She could be carrying Samuel's child.* What if the girl found herself pregnant and alone in a strange city with no friends or family to turn to and the child's father was a thousand miles away—not to mention already married and unable to offer her and her baby the protection of his name? Would she wed the first man who offered her such protection? Dolley simply did not know enough about Olivia to make the judgment. Yet there seemed no other answer.

During the next three years the war became a long and bloody stalemate, not the quick, easy march to Quebec that the War Hawks in Congress had envisioned. Canadians, much to the chagrin of the American Army and population, fought determinedly beside the British to repel Yankee invaders. Although American privateers inflicted substantial losses on British shipping, the Royal Navy effectively blockaded the whole Atlantic seaboard. A peace negotiation dragged on its desultory course in the Low Countries while both Britain and the United States strove for more clear-cut victories to strengthen their positions at the bargaining table.

Samuel spent over a year on the Canadian border, slipping information quietly back through the American lines, intelligence which eventually resulted in several British defeats. By October of 1813 at the Battle of the Thames, the Indian Confederacy of Tecumseh was broken and the great Shawnee war chief himself perished valiantly in the fighting. After the threat of an Anglo-Indian alliance in the north was over, he was sent south where the Red Sticks of the Creek Confederacy, allied with Britain and Spain, had left the Florida-Mississippi border running red with blood. His fluency in Spanish enabled him to pass himself off as an imperial officer from Madrid. By the fall of 1814, Shelby had gathered some priceless information and headed posthaste back into American territory, desperate to reach Madison and Monroe. . . .

Samuel reined in his lathered horse and listened for sounds of pursuit. After his escape from the Pensacola jail, he had headed for Mississippi Territory where he knew American forces were gathering to finish off the last of the Red Sticks. The swampy country along the Gulf Coast was nearly impassable and he had not slept in at least three days. Leading his stolen mount, he had hacked his way through junglelike undergrowth rife with poisonous snakes and dangerous bears and cougars. Altogether not the route home he would have chosen, Shelby thought wryly as he crested a slight ridge and looked down on yet another twisting river.

He used a glass to check the area spread below him, then consulted his map. "This must be the Tallapoosa River," he murmured, knowing it was the site of a series of Creek villages friendly to the Red Sticks. Avoiding them and locating the Americans proved easier than he might have anticipated when he heard the belching of cannon fire. Several small artillery pieces were pounding a long breastwork, seemingly to little avail. Musket fire and the loud keening cries of Indians filled the air between the booming reports.

Carefully, Shelby made his way down the hill toward the American forces. He grabbed hold of the first soldier he found, a militiaman. "Who's in command here?"

"Genr'l Andy Jackson, Ole Hickory hisself," the man said, spitting a wad of brown tobacco juice near Shelby's feet and looking at him with suspicious eyes, even though both men wore the same sort of travel stained, age softened buckskins. "Who th' hell air ye?"

Samuel had grown used to the insolent, undisciplined manners of the militia or "dirty shirts" as the British disdainfully called them. Although difficult to control and keep under enlistment, there were no more deadly guerilla fighters anywhere on earth . . . when they decided to join the war. "I am Colonel Shelby, regular army, and I have vital dispatches for General Jackson. Where is he?"

Something in the big dark-haired man's voice bestirred the militiaman to decide it might be wisest to answer the officer. "Over there. Th' skinny feller," he said, pointing to where an officer was barking furious orders to his men.

Samuel made his way toward Jackson, past the milling troops to where the general's small tent had been haphazardly erected. A rickety campaign table stood in front of it with several maps and other papers lying on it. Andrew Jackson was tall and thin to the point of emaciation, with craggy angular features and a ramrod straight posture so severe even the thick mane of iron gray hair on his head stood starkly upright as if at full military attention. He riveted Shelby with a pair of intense blue eyes that fairly shot sparks like a lightning storm. "And who the hell air ye?" he asked in a nasal Tennessee hill country twang. His eyes raked Shelby's mudstained buckskins and unshaven face disdainfully, although after weeks of marching and camping on muddy riverbanks his own grooming was little better.

Shelby saluted. "Colonel Samuel Shelby, regular army, General Jackson."

"Ye're a touch out of uniform, Colonel."

"I was sent from the war department on a special mission, General."

"Then ye're also damned far from yer headquarters," Jackson snapped, completely unimpressed by any connection to the military bigwigs in the capital.

"I've just come from Spanish Florida and I have urgent information that must reach Washington. If you could spare me a fresh mount and some ammunition, I'd be most grateful."

One shaggy gray eyebrow lifted and those incredibly fierce eyes blazed hot enough to scorch steel. "I've nothing to spare, Colonel."

Samuel struggled to contain his impatience, knowing how he must appear to Jackson. "With all due respect, sir, what I've learned about British plans could change the course of the war before year's end. Napoleon's been defeated decisively. Britain and her allies are overrunning France itself."

"By the Eternal, I don't care if the damned Europeans cut one another's throats down to the last man jack of 'em! To use a phrase a man fresh from Florida might understand, I am up to my ass in alligators! At present my forces are engaged against several thousand of the bloodiest savages who ever raised the war cry on this frontier. The British general staff's schemes are of even more remote interest than the future of that Corsican banditti Bonaparte."

Samuel had encountered this same single-minded fixation all too often in military men to be surprised, especially in those who had come to command through the ranks of their state militias, as had the backwoods politician Jackson.

"The British schemes are a bit more dangerous than you might imagine," he replied, concealing his growing frustration. "They're going to attack New Orleans from their base in Jamaica. Already troops are assembling in the Caribbean. You may not give a tinker's damn about the rest of the country, but before year's end redcoats will be sailing up the Mississippi River if we aren't prepared for it!"

Jackson did pause to consider now, stroking his angular jaw and studying Shelby who did not flinch beneath his unwavering stare. "Ye have this on good authority?"

Samuel pulled an oilskin pouch from beneath his buckskin shirt and opened it. "The best," he replied, grinning. "None other than Britain's best ally in the new world, the Spanish governor of East Florida." He handed the correspondence between the Spanish and the British to Jackson, who could only read what the British officers in Jamaica had written. It was enough.

"Ye'll get yer horse, Colonel, and a dozen men to escort ye—as soon as the battle's over here at Horseshoe Bend."

❧ *Chapter 26* ❧

Andrew Jackson had been a man of his word. Samuel reached Washington and made his reports to Madison and Monroe. After traversing over a thousand miles across the Appalachians Shelby was then given another impossible assignment. Because of an old contact made with a French privateer whom he had met in the Caribbean years earlier, Samuel was selected to find out if the Haitian expatriate's professed loyalty to the United States was genuine.

Now he found himself crawling in the slimy, foul-smelling water of a Louisiana bayou, watching the undulating progress of a cottonmouth moving gracefully in front of him, his pistol trained on it, hoping against hope he need not shoot. He had spent five days making his way from Barataria to New Orleans and was almost out of ammunition.

If the swamp didn't get him, Governor Claiborne might well hang him as an accessory to piracy. In his shirt he carried a set of papers from the British Admiralty addressed to the residents of Barataria, attempting to recruit their services for an invasion of New Orleans. A captain's commission and a thirty thousand dollar stipend had been offered as a bribe to their leader, who had no intention of accepting. Instead, he had given the documents to Shelby. Now all Samuel had to do was convince Claiborne that Jean Laffite was a loyal American.

Grinning, he recalled an old backwoods saying. "This is sort of like winning a lottery and then finding out the prize is a live grizzly."

A heavy fog hung on the marshes at the edge of Lake Borgne adding impaired visibility to the even greater misery of the chill damp December night. The three men standing furtively beneath the thick gray moss clinging to the low-lying limbs of a massive willow tree stamped their feet and clutched their cloaks tightly against the cold.

"You said you would supply us with guides who could show us the back way through these infernal swamps into

New Orleans," the tall imperious officer said in the clipped nasal tones of the British aristocracy.

"Here, take the gold," the second Britain said, thrusting a small pouch into the American's hands. "That's all you'll see until we're in control of the city."

The American laughed softly, an icy hollow sound echoing on the still night air. Contemptuously he tossed the pouch back to the Englishman. "I assure you, gentlemen, I have no need of your paltry bribes. Once your forces take the city, I shall be the official liaison between the British army and the unruly citizenry. Everyone will be in need of my good offices."

"And you will extort a handsome profit from the blood and bones of your countrymen," the first man said acidly.

The American nodded as if accepting a compliment. "Precisely so. My guides will meet you tomorrow night at moonrise at the north promontory of the lake. Do you speak Spanish? Their English is rather deficient, I'm afraid."

"We'll manage," the taller officer said in a condescending tone.

"What is your news from Claiborne's office?" the other Englishman asked. "Has the legislature considered Laffite's offer of help for the American cause yet?"

"As a matter of fact, they've concluded he's a thief and a pirate, not to be trusted at all. They think the British papers are forgeries which Jean Laffite intended to use to get his brother out of jail." There was a hint of dry amusement in his voice.

"What fools those mongrel rabble are," the second British officer sneered. "Laffite has enough artillery and skilled gunners to blow Keane's Highlanders halfway back to Scotland and they turn the man away!"

"Just be grateful they've not accepted the Baratarian's help yet," the American replied darkly.

"What do you mean—yet?"

"The American officer who brought the papers from Laffite to Claiborne is a dangerous man. Samuel Shelby will not not give up easily."

"Then I assume you shall deal with this Shelby before he changes the governor's mind?" the tall Englishman purred.

"I shall deal with him in my own good time. I have something very particular in mind."

With that the American turned and vanished into the fog,

leaving the British officers to climb back into the small pirogue and make the long dangerous trip back to the mouth of the bay.

"Damn redcoats commin', Missey, I feels it in m' bones," the wizened old servant said as she placed a tray filled with freshly baked gingerbread and milk on the parlor table.

"Now, Florine, we've already discussed it. Mr. Darcy assures us we're quite safe. The British forces will most probably head up the Mississippi, if they arrive at all. Edmond Darcy is Governor Claiborne's secretary. If anyone should know, he should." Olivia poured a small glass from the pitcher of cool milk and began to break up a ginger cake into small pieces as she looked across the parlor to where her son sat on the carpet playing intently with his toy soldiers. "Time for some of Angeline's sweet ginger cakes, David," she said.

The sturdy toddler's black curly hair fell in unruly locks across his forehead as he looked at her. Bright blue eyes lit up as he scrambled to his feet and scampered over to her. "Ginger cakes. Mmmm, good," he babbled as he climbed into his mother's lap.

Olivia stroked his hair and held him fast as he wriggled with the usual restlessness of a bright, energetic child. He had become her reason for living over the past two and a half years. His resemblance to Samuel had been a bittersweet pang from the first moment she held him in her arms after his birth and had seen the thick cap of black hair covering his head. Olivia had wanted something of her love's to keep and she had him, but David was at the same time her greatest joy and a tragic reminder of all that she had lost.

In the last three years she had grown to accept the fact that Samuel was dead, killed on some nameless battlefield half a continent away. There had never been a single response to the dozens of letters she had sent. Surely if he were alive he would have received at least some of them and written back to her—or even come to see his son. That was what a naive young woman in love had believed, she thought bitterly.

But then several months ago while visiting her Spanish friends in Pensacola, Louise Freul had learned about a great scandal concerning an American spy they called the Spanish Yankee. A man masquerading as a Spanish court official had infiltrated high-ranking circles of the British military who were encamped with their Spanish allies. He had stolen vital information regarding their prosecution of the war against the Americans. One of the Spanish officer's wives had been quite graphic in describing the spy to Louise. It seemed he had nearly made her swoon with desire, a tall black-haired, blue-eyed devil with the most marvelous scars on his body— scars that could only belong to Samuel and would only be visible if he were naked. Olivia could still imagine the lascivious Señora Garcia entwined in a torrid embrace with him.

Samuel was alive. He had been a scant few hundred miles away and made no effort to come to her. No wonder his sister had never answered any of Olivia's letters. Elise was most probably too embarrassed to reply. Olivia had been wounded to the core of her soul, so shattered by the betrayal that if she had not already spent the past years secluded at her country estate, she would have hidden away now to lick her wounds.

She had gladly given up all the gaiety and social life of the city after the successful hoax of her marriage and widowhood. Retiring to Belle Versailles, Charles Durand's huge plantation, she had awaited the birth of her child with only Louise and Dr. Freul in attendance. As far as the gossipy Creoles in New Orleans knew, the boy was Don Rafael Obregón's son. How tragic that the nobleman had not lived to see his child born, the elderly matrons lamented. How tragic the beautiful and wealthy widow chose to live in isolation and refused to consider remarriage, the young bachelors lamented.

But the "widow" had decided that after Samuel there would be no more marriages, no more lovers, no man to break her heart again. She had given herself over to a quiet life in the country, developing an interest in the management of the huge plantation, content to watch her son grow and live out her days with no further risk to her heart. Louise Freul and her brother, Albert, often came to spend weekends at the plantation, and each summer she took David upriver to visit Micajah, who was thrilled with his grandson. She had a full life with good friends.

But her peace was suddenly shattered when Louise brought word that Samuel had arrived in New Orleans a scant few days ago. His support for the Baratarian pirates was the cause célèbre of the city and his name was on everyone's lips, together with speculations about when the British invaders would land. Given a choice, Olivia would far rather have faced Admiral Cochrane's whole fleet than Samuel Sheridan Shelby.

As she watched her son stuff pieces of gingerbread into his chubby cheeks, grinning adorably at her, a sudden thought occurred. Surely Samuel could not have come for David! He could have no way of knowing about his son. By the time David was born, she had finally given up sending letters. Or did he know? Shelby was a spy, a very good spy. She had seen him in action. But why would he wait three years before returning for the boy?

It's only a coincidence that he's been sent on a mission in the city, she reassured herself. All she need do was to remain secluded here at Belle Versailles until he was assigned elsewhere. That was her principle reason for staying in the country in spite of rumors that the British might cross Lake Borgne and march through Bayou Bienvenue. But Edmond Darcy had offered her assurances that such would not happen. After all, he was privy to the governor's inner circle.

Darcy had briefly been a suitor before she had made it clear that under no circumstances would she ever again marry. Olivia had been grateful when he accepted that and offered her friendship instead. He had become a frequent visitor at the plantation, often bringing David toys and sharing with her the latest news regarding the progress of the war. Edmond had insisted that she remain at Belle Versailles in case the worst indeed did occur and the British occupied the city. Here, she would be safe.

But would she be safe from Samuel if he rode up the long magnolia lined drive to the front porch of the big house? Would he expect her to run out and throw herself at his feet? Or give up David without a fight?

The idea gnawed at her relentlessly. He could easily expose her marriage as a sham, leaving her to face cruel censure from the good people of New Orleans while he nobly claimed paternity. She knew the courts would side with him. Men always won in legal matters.

I'll fight you with everything I have, Samuel Shelby. If need be, I'll take David to Micajah. See if you dare try to steal his grandson from him! But she knew that if Samuel wanted David, he would dare that and much more.

"Mama, you squeeze too tight. Can't eat," David complained, breaking into her troubling thoughts.

She kissed his cheek as she relaxed her hold on the boy, then stared out the front window down the drive with haunted eyes.

If Samuel Shelby had thought Andrew Jackson was gauntly thin back at Horseshoe Bend last spring, the general was positively cadaverous now. Fevers and dysentery had wracked his body for months until his face looked like a death's head. After utterly decimating Britain's Indian allies in Mississippi Territory and chasing the remnants through upper Florida, Jackson had finally deigned to follow the orders given by Secretary of War Monroe to march for New Orleans. The city welcomed the hero of the Red Stick Rebellion with typical Creole delirium, but Jackson remained alternately cantankerous and taciturn. At the moment he was being exceedingly cantankerous.

"By the Eternal! I simply don't believe it! I've never in my life seen a Kentuckian without a pack of cards, a jug of whiskey and his long rifle!" He paced furiously, darting scorching glances at the two militia officers who had just reported to him.

Two-thirds of the Kentucky State Militia had just arrived without weapons or supplies, expecting to have everything provided by the federal government. Their plight was only one more incident in what had been an incredible series of debacles and blunders which had left Jackson with a motley group of twelve hundred militia—Creoles, free men of color, Chocktaw Indians, Baratarian pirates—in conjunction with his own small detachment of regulars. Together they had faced a British landing force of five thousand men on December 23. With Jackson's usual impervious daring, he attacked in the dead of night.

The fighting had been brutal hand-to-hand combat in mud and fog so thick that the British commanders called a retreat, never realizing that the fierce American troops were outnumbered nearly five-to-one. The seemingly impetuous assault had done precisely what Jackson intended for it to do—bought them time for more troops to trickle into the city from upriver. But many of the Tennessee, Mississippi and Kentucky militia came poorly provisioned and, in the case of the Kentuckians, scarcely armed at all.

"Governor Isaac Shelby's sent more militia to fight in this war than any other state, sir. We're plumb out of supplies," John Adair, their commander, said stiffly.

"He's right, General," Samuel added. "My uncle has done all that's humanly possible to supply men and materials, but after sending ten thousand men to the New York border, he had no choice but to rely on the federals at this point."

"A lot of good that does us with a commissary general who doesn't know mortar balls from bowling balls," Jackson snapped.

"If I might make a suggestion, General." Samuel interrupted Jackson's agitated pacing. When he had Jackson's attention, he continued, "I happen to know where I can obtain several hundred crates of rifles, powder and shot."

Jackson raised one shaggy white eyebrow. "And that wouldn't happen to be at the Temple, that accursed banditti Laffite's warehouse for selling pirated goods, now would it?"

"That accursed banditti and his Baratarians have fought right well beside us. Already they've given us ordnance enough to turn the tide of the siege. Why won't you trust Laffite?"

"Ye are regular army, Colonel. Those men are outlaws. The governor of Louisiana placed a five hundred dollar reward on Jean Laffite's head."

Samuel couldn't resist smiling when he replied, "And Jean countered by placing a five thousand dollar reward on Claiborne's head. The governor took it rather well."

"By the Eternal, I do not see the humor in this situation! There is a rule of law in this state and that leaves no room for piracy and smuggling."

"Even if those smuggled guns can arm your troops to fight when our own government can't get so much as a single musket to us?" Shelby's voice was strained with impatience. Jackson was narrow-minded and focused only on what he wished to see. Few dared to challenge him.

The other officers around the table shuffled uneasily as Jackson and Shelby locked stony gazes. Finally Jackson threw up his hands. "Ye've been lobbying for me to meet with the Haitian freebooter. I'm going to the Macarthy plantation to inspect the lines. Bring him to me there and we'll discuss the disposition of his ill-gotten gains."

Shelby nodded grimly, concealing the relief he felt. By God he'd done it! What Claiborne and the rest had failed to do—Jackson would confer with Laffite. Now if only Jean could impress the recalcitrant general sufficiently to allow him genuine influence in the planning and strategy sessions. Samuel saluted smartly, saying, "Yes, sir, General. Monsieur Laffite and I will be there."

As he left Jackson's headquarters on Royale Street, Samuel's thoughts were chaotic. There was so damnably much to do. The city was under siege and he had already been drawn into the thick of battle, fighting with the regular army since his arrival bearing messages from Laffite. Claiborne had been inclined to believe in the Baratarian's loyalty but the legislative leaders had not, nor when he arrived, had Jackson. All that was about to change now.

"But when will I have a moment to myself?" he muttered as he made his way down Royale Street. Since the British had moved within five miles of New Orleans, most of the citizenry had been waiting nervously behind shuttered doors, terrified that the redcoats were coming to burn the Creoles' beloved city just as they had Washington the past August.

Shelby didn't know if the city would remain safe. He was certain the countryside was not and had wanted to see to Olivia's safety, especially after learning that she had been widowed and lived in seclusion at her plantation house. Belle Versailles was isolated at the farthest edge of Bayou Bienvenue, not in the path which Jackson anticipated the British general Pakenham would take. Major Villeré, a Creole planter and Olivia's nearest neighbor, commanded a force of Louisiana militia which held the area secure thus far. But this offered little reassurance to Shelby.

He was still confused about his conflicting emotions when it came to Olivia. A part of him—a very foolish part—would always love her, but he knew she did not love him. Facing her now would still be painful, although he was reconciled to doing so before he left the city once the British had been defeated—if the British could be defeated.

As a hedge against her safety, he had asked Laffite to send several of his trusted men to watch the plantation house and report any possible danger to their leader immediately. If need be, Samuel would go himself and drag her kicking and screaming back into the city.

Truthfully, he was not certain that she was in danger from

the invaders. Her husband had been a Spanish officer stationed in Pensacola, which was now occupied by Spain's English allies. *She's probably safer with the enemy than she would be with me,* he thought bitterly.

After three years, her betrayal still stung. It had gone from a sharp, burning agony to a hollow dull ache now. But he was still not certain how much he'd reveal once he came face-to-face with her. She had ever been a survivor. If wild bears and hostile Osage couldn't harm her, he doubted the British would. At least that was what he kept telling himself as he went through the grueling days and sleepless nights moving from Jackson's Royale Street headquarters to the Hôtel de la Marine where Jean Laffite held court.

Shelby had come to admire the shrewd and witty Creole whose loyalty to his adopted country was unflinching, even after the American navy, under that imbecile Patterson, had burned Laffite's island hideout to the ground, including all its warehouses.

Of course, Commodore Patterson didn't know that Jean had been warned and removed over a million dollars worth of goods from the warehouses before the naval flotilla arrived!

Entering the dark interior of the cafe where the Baratarians congregated, Samuel let his eyes become accustomed to the light, searching the crowded room for Laffite's red hair, an unlikely strawberry shade achieved by dunking his head in potash and gunpowder. Then Shelby saw the tall, imperious-looking man dressed meticulously in fawn-colored breeches and an elegant cutaway coat. Laffite motioned him toward a private room in the rear.

"You look resplendent as always, Jean," he said, shaking the privateer's strong slender hand.

Merry black eyes danced beneath pale reddish blond eyebrows as Jean replied, "What is a gentleman to do—go about in rags just because there is war?" After pouring Samuel a glass of wine from his own private stock, Laffite got down to business. "My men here just learned that Pakenham's massing his troops for an attack only six hundred yards from where Jackson has dug in at Roderick's Canal. He's bringing up twenty big guns, eighteen and twenty-four pounders."

Samuel rubbed his jaw consideringly. "We have only

twelve, most smaller, although there is one thirty-two pounder."

"Ah, but my friend, you have *us* to fire them," a short swarthy man with a hawklike nose and flashing white grin replied. Dominique You was as scarred and ugly as his younger brother, Jean Laffite, was tall and handsome, but they both possessed the same Gallic humor and the same cool courage under fire.

Samuel got down to business at once, explaining Jackson's desire to confer with Laffite over the matter of provisioning his militiamen with rifles and ammunition.

"So at last the old martinet admits he needs us." Laffite's voice held a note of sly satisfaction. "I don't doubt all that British artillery had something to do with it." He issued crisp orders to his brother regarding the disposition of ordnance, then turned back to Shelby. "Let us go talk with the great man," he said dryly.

Laffite was punctiliously polite, Jackson grim and stiff, sensing the well-concealed delight the privateer took in at last being petitioned for assistance.

"My brother and his men have taken their places on the breastworks, General Jackson, bringing enough ammunition to blast the entire British army back into the Gulf."

"Ye think they'll have a New Year's Day surprise for us then?" Jackson asked suspiciously.

"After inspecting their placements, would you not agree?" Laffite asked.

Jackson nodded curtly. "By the Eternal, *I* would attack!"

"Their guns are heavier but ours are better manned. The line will hold," Shelby said.

"It had better!" Jackson replied sourly, running bony fingers through his spiky hair.

On January 1, 1815, the first daylight battle was fought. As the Baratarians predicted, it rapidly became an artillery duel in which the Royal Army's heavier guns were consistently outclassed by the lighter cannons of the Americans under the highly skilled direction of Dominique You. As Samuel had predicted, the American line held. The British retired from the field, their big guns silenced. They did not even attempt to mount a charge. Silently the crusty old general realized that there was some benefit to the decades of target practice the Baratarians had against the Royal Navy on the high seas, but he would never admit it aloud.

In the days that followed, Generals Pakenham and Cochrane continued to mass their forces along the narrow neck of solid ground with the swamp to the north and the river to the south. Behind heavy earthen breastworks, which had held firmly against the pounding of British artillery, the multinational crew of Americans dug in, waiting for the final assault.

Olivia heard the pounding roar of cannon erupt again. The thunderous racket had continued intermittently during the first week of the new year. No one on the plantation had been able to sleep well since news of the British landing had reached them. Many of the servants fled in terror, as well as the overseer, leaving her and David alone with only the elderly cook and two parlor maids in the house. Major Villeré's militia had been captured in a swift night strike at the neighboring plantation house. Belle Versailles was defenseless if the British chose to occupy it. So far they had not.

David made a fretful sound in his sleep. Clad in a heavy velvet wrapper to ward off the night's chill, Olivia walked to his bed to comfort the sleepy toddler. Then she heard the sound of rapid hoofbeats coming up the drive and her heart froze in her chest. She walked quickly to the window and peered out from behind the Battenburg lace curtain. It was Edmond Darcy, accompanied by half a dozen other men whom she did not recognize. Perhaps he had come at last to take her and David to safety since his predictions about where the British would land had been so sadly amiss.

Seizing a branch of candles, she quickly entered the front hallway and pulled open the heavy door. "Edmond, I am so relieved to see you." Any further words of welcome died on her lips as she watched his companions draw their weapons and begin to inspect the darkened grounds with what appeared to be military precision. "Who are those men?" Suddenly Edmond did not look like the smilingly benign young man she had first met in William Claiborne's office. A frisson of fear snaked down her spine.

His smile was mildly amused. He looked her up and down as if studying a half-bright child who had just committed some gaffe which he would tolerantly pass off. "Why, they are British soldiers, my pet. Out of uniform, of course, but still models of British efficiency."

She stepped back, stunned at the transformation in him.

Gone was the mild-mannered, genially charming clerk, replaced by a ruthless jackal stalking its prey. His lips continued smiling but those pale gold eyes were dead. He took the candlestick from her nerveless hand and placed it on a hall table, suddenly seeming taller, stronger, infinitely menacing as he walked toward her.

Backing away from him she asked, "Why would you bring the enemy to Belle Versailles? You promised me we'd be safe here."

"Tut, you are safe . . . from the British. You see, we're on the same side—the winning side. Once they occupy New Orleans, they'll need civilian assistance in organizing a colonial government. And who better suited to act as liaison to General Pakenham than the American governor's personal secretary, a man who has already demonstrated his worth by providing them with all manner of vital information?"

"You're a traitor! You'll hang for treason after General Jackson's forces drive the British back into the sea." Olivia spoke with a confidence she was far from feeling.

Ignoring her outburst, Darcy swept past her into David's bedroom. The child was crying softly, his thumb firmly placed in his mouth, his eyes enormous. Darcy studied the large blue eyes with their thick dark lashes, the thick cap of wavy black hair, the cleanly molded lines of a face beginning to outgrow the chubbiness of infancy.

"Shelby's bastard." Hearing Olivia's horrified gasp as she rushed over to shield David, he laughed. "Don't bother to deny it. I know he's Shelby's get. Did your late husband, I wonder?" He paused as she watched him incredulously. "Or, did Rafael Obregón ever even exist?"

Like a panther poised to strike, he instantly sensed her tensing. Already he knew the truth. She could see it in those cold eyes, glittering now with triumph. But for what? He had once courted her, albeit rather briefly and at a distance. It seemed unlikely that rape was his goal. *It has something to do with Samuel and David,* she thought with rising panic. Forcing herself to remain calm as David cried, she rocked him protectively until he quieted, then asked, "What do you want, Darcy?"

He studied his nails absently after removing expensively tailored kid gloves. "Why, that's exceedingly simple, my dear. I want you to write a letter for me. You will address it to your old flame."

"You're going to kill Samuel." She knew it as certainly as tomorrow's sunrise.

"Ah, but *I* shan't kill him. The British will. You see, there's quite a price on his head in Spanish Florida, not to mention up on the Canadian border. He's gone by any number of names, Sir Roger Gordon, Don Emelio Velasquez . . . a soldier out of uniform, a spy."

Dear God, he was right! Samuel had spent his career out of uniform. Under the laws of any nation—

"The British will insist on placing him before a military tribunal," he said, intuiting her very thoughts. "They're sticklers for following the letter of the law that way. But then they'll hang him. Very legal and quite proper."

"Samuel is supremely indifferent to me. He wouldn't come even if I begged him." *And I already have.*

"I beg to differ, my pet. He'll come."

"I won't do it." She bit off each word, knowing she had to find a way to reach a weapon, but with David in her arms, it was impossible.

He slid a small pistol from inside his waistcoat as smoothly as if he were removing a snuff box. "Ah, yes, you will, my pet. That is . . . unless you want to see harm befall the boy."

"You're mad!" She shielded David with her body, replacing him in his crib bed, where he began to wail loudly now as she stood in front of him.

"Perhaps," he replied noncommittally. "Now, take a seat at that charming little escritoire and begin composing. Of course, I will assist."

Samuel accompanied Jackson on his inspection of the breastworks in the early hours of January 8. They paused at battery thirteen, watching the intrepid Dominique You giving his men final instructions. Thick fog swirled around them, obscuring vision in spite of flickering campfires. The barrel-chested Creole had his own low fire going behind his artillery battery with a kettle of steaming water centered on it, inside which a tin coated iron coffeepot wafted out heavenly perfume.

"That coffee smells a damn sight better than the muddy swill we've been drinking," Jackson said to You, then added slyly, "Maybe ye smuggled it in?"

You shrugged his broad shoulders and grinned. "Mebbee

so, *mon ami.*" He offered Jackson and Shelby each a cup. The other Baratarian artillerymen chuckled when Jackson accepted it and drank with gusto, raising his cup in salute to You.

"If I were ordered to storm hell, by the Eternal, with ye, sir, at my side, I would have no misgivings of the result. Carry on, Captain You."

"Jean is commanding the gunnerymen from the *Carolina*, General. Between him and his brother, they have destroyed half of the British artillery," Samuel said.

Jackson nodded tersely. "This is it, Colonel. The final face down. I confess my gratitude for yer privateer friends. They've not only supplied the artillery shells to blow the British to perdition, they provided rifles for good Kentucky and Tennessee sharpshooters who know how to use them." He snorted. "Dirty Shirts. Did ye know that's what the lobster backed devils call my militia?"

Shelby nodded. "Those ragged frontiersmen have rewritten the tactics of modern warfare in more significant ways than Napoleon ever did. Shoot for the gold braid, and shoot from cover and always hit what you aim for."

Jackson chuckled mirthlessly. "Ye know the rules, Colonel—the new rules. By the Eternal, let's teach them to the British!"

Midway through their inspection tour, a messenger caught up to them, breathlessly saluting as he proffered a sealed envelope for Samuel. "For Colonel Shelby, sir." No sooner had Samuel taken the paper than the youth, dressed in ragged breeches and a homespun shirt, vanished into the fog.

Samuel tore it open, squinting to read in the flickering light from a nearby fire.

"Go closer to the fire so ye can see, man," Jackson said impatiently. Neither man had a good feeling about the mysterious missive. Perceiving the stiffening in Shelby's body, the general said, "Ye look to have seen a ghost, Colonel. What is it?"

"I believe the British are holding prisoners at Belle Versailles, a woman . . . who is very dear to me. And a boy I did not know existed."

"Belle Versailles—that's scarce out of cannon range." Jackson looked at Shelby's dark haunted eyes, almost glazed with shock. "The boy . . . he is yours?"

"So it would seem, sir. I'd heard Olivia had a child by her

Spanish husband. I should've guessed, should've taken more precautions with her in that isolated place. I left two of Jean's men to guard her. Obviously they failed."

Jackson cocked a shaggy eyebrow. "How can ye be certain? The British would hardly want her to alert ye to their presence."

"She's encoded a hidden message in the plea for me to rescue her." Again he scanned the page:

My Dearest Samuel,
Please forgive the untimely arrival of this letter. I realize the situation at the battlefront is grave, but I must see you at once. I am alone at Belle Versailles plantation, defenseless against the British invaders.
I would not beg for myself, but for our son, David. No matter if you care nothing for me, you must recognize your own flesh and blood. Please do not let us part as we did when I left you in St. Louis. You heeded my letter then. Do not fail to heed this one, I implore you.

Olivia

You heeded my letter then. But she had not written that letter. It was Wescott's forgery—and they had not parted voluntarily in St. Louis. Someone, most probably British invaders were holding her hostage. As to her mention of a son . . . his mind simply shut down. Was it possible? Had she found herself pregnant after he left and opted to wed a conveniently gullible nobleman rather than bear an illegitimate child in seclusion while waiting for him to secure an uncertain divorce a thousand miles away?

He had to find the truth. "Permission to go to Belle Versailles, General."

Jackson looked at him with shrewd dark eyes, squinting in the miasmic air, then cackled suddenly. "As if I could stop ye in all the pandemonium, Colonel! Go and don't be gettin' yer tail shot off by those damnable lobsterbacks!"

When he approached the plantation grounds, Samuel reined in his mount and swung from the saddle. No point in riding directly into a bullet. If the British were here using Olivia as a cat's paw, they wanted him badly. During his little adventure in Pensacola he had rubbed the Spanish governor's nose—not to mention the British general staff's—in the dirt, then escaped in spite of heavy guard. The last time he'd heard, the agent known as "Spanish Yankee" had a ten thousand dollar price on his head. Smiling humorlessly, he thought it was twice what Laffite had offered for Claiborne, a prize well worth baiting a trap for.

He found the two Baratarian guards in a shallow creekbed several hundred yards from the big house. Their throats had been cut. Judging from the congealed blood, several hours had elapsed since the murders. He was on his own.

Inside the house, Olivia prepared breakfast. She had sent the old cook Angeline back to bed, saying the slave was too fearful of the British soldiers around their house. She hoped to be able to secret away a weapon while using the cutlery to slice bread and fry ham for the men. So far no opportunity had presented itself.

Down the hall in the study, a pair of her uncle Charles's British dueling pistols lay primed inside a teak case on the desk. If only she had a way to reach them or the trusty old carbine Micajah had given her. It was hidden beneath her bed. If she could but inflict enough damage with a knife here in the kitchen, she could make a run for the weapons, but Darcy had given her no opportunity, yet. At least she had convinced him to leave David in his room. Darcy had agreed, but one of the soldiers was sent to guard him while another kept watch outside the front door.

"You never have explained why you hate Samuel," she said, forking golden slabs of ham and turning them in the sizzling iron skillet, trying to distract him.

"All in good time. Once the colonel arrives, everything will become clear."

The sudden sounds of a scuffle outside caused him to turn and yell for the man with David to hold the boy in his room. When he turned, Olivia used the moment to slip a narrow, sharp paring knife into the pocket of her wrapper. Almost instantly his eyes returned to her. "Come here, my pet." He took hold of her arm roughly, causing her robe to gape open, revealing her breasts.

The lush enticement of golden skin did not hold the slightest interest for him as he dragged her toward the front hall, yelling, "Show yourself, Shelby, or my man will shoot your bastard."

Outside on the porch, Samuel cursed his rotten luck. Just as he reached out to seize the guard and slit his throat, the sentry had sensed his presence. Subduing him had taken only a moment but it was not silent. Now he was discovered.

Shelby could not believe his eyes when he stepped inside the door and confronted the slender blond man holding a gun to Olivia's breast . . .

"Richard Bullock!"

~ *Chapter 27* ~

As Samuel dropped the brace of pistols at Olivia's captor's command, the sharp report of rifle fire erupted down the bayou, followed by the deafening roar of cannon. Jackson's final battle had at last been joined.

Olivia stared hungrily at Samuel, her eyes sweeping up his tall lithe body to his face, to those incredibly mobile lips and the dark blue eyes framed by wavy black hair which still needed barbering. His uniform was wrinkled and muddy and he needed a shave. To her he looked absolutely beautiful. And disbelieving as his eyes narrowed on the man holding the gun between her breasts.

Richard Bullock, Samuel called him! At once the name stirred memories. "But he can't be—this is Edmond Darcy, Governor Claiborne's secretary," she said, dreading what Darcy, or Bullock, was about to reveal. She could feel the aura of madness shrouding him as he began to speak.

"You poor deluded little slut," the man she had known as Darcy said with contempt. "How pathetically simple it was to play you two fools each against the other. Such sadly unrequited love . . . or so you thought when I intercepted and destroyed all your impassioned *billet doux* to one another."

Samuel felt as if Bullock had slammed a booted foot into his guts. Olivia gasped aloud.

"Of course, I enjoyed reading them before I burned them. So tragic, the pregnant lover left behind by her gallant soldier, so desperate that she invented a husband to cover the embarrassment of her bastard. Your letters were more entertaining than a novel." At the poleaxed look on Shelby's face, Bullock gave a sharp bark of laughter. "Of course I failed to mention Don Rafael Obregón was a figment of the imagination when I composed Claiborne's letter to you. Getting him to sign it concealed in a sheaf of boring government documents was rather easy, too."

"You kept us apart for three years," Olivia said, unable to take it in. Samuel had not deserted her! The look of raw anguish on his face spoke volumes.

"You denied my son his father and left Olivia to face the censure of society alone. I know you always hated me but why them? They're innocent, Richard." He fought down the rage boiling deep inside his gut, stalling for time, drawing Bullock out.

"Innocent," he spat contemptuously. "A whore and her bastard." He jerked Olivia's arm, painfully jamming the gun barrel against the soft flesh of her breast.

"It's me you hate, Richard. I was the one you never believed good enough for your beloved Tisha," Samuel reminded him, moving a tiny step closer.

"You killed her. You're responsible—both of you." He glared at Shelby. "You destroyed her dreams of becoming a president's lady. You left her alone, facing the disgrace of a divorce so you could chase after your whore. I found Tisha sobbing, broken and desperate, my proud, beautiful, splendid Tisha, crying because she'd lost you to this foreign nobody. I tried to comfort her. I did everything for her . . ."

"Even trying to kill me to prevent the scandal of the divorce?" Samuel was beginning to make sense of the erratic series of attempts on his life four years earlier.

"He was the one who shot your horse out from under you on the Virginia post road?" Olivia said.

"But he failed. Just like he failed that night in the inn and then in St. Louis. Tish must have been quite vexed. She always was quite the bitch when she didn't get her way," Shelby said softly, inching yet nearer. Bullock suddenly moved the gun away from Olivia's breast and aimed it at Samuel.

A sardonic smile mercurially flashed across his face. The eerie light in his eyes glowed with utter madness now. "Yes, she was a bitch, the most magnificent bitch on earth. In heat all the time."

"You were her lover," Samuel said, damning his own stupidity for never figuring it out before.

"Ever since we were in the schoolroom. You never knew, did you, you pathetic idiot?" His sneer turned to rage then as the memories rolled over him. "She was my first woman . . . my only woman. The only one worthy." He jerked Olivia's arm, glaring at her as he raised the gun to her head. "You actually believed I had a tendresse for you, Shelby's leavings?"

Olivia could feel the paring knife in her pocket, pressed

against her hip but she could not reach it. She struggled to get free of the madman's rough hold.

When Bullock looked down at her, tightening his grip, Samuel again moved closer. Almost near enough to jump him, but only if he could make Richard lose control and point the pistol away from Olivia, at him. "It must've really galled you to have me bed your beloved Tisha," he taunted with an easy arrogance he was far from feeling. "I remember how you looked at me after she had the abortion. I'd done what you never could—planted my seed in her belly. You wanted to kill me all along, didn't you, Richard?"

Bullock's jaw worked, grinding until the veins stood out in his neck. His body reflected the fury of the firing going on a scant mile from them. Then he regained a sudden icy calm, speaking over the boom of the cannonade. "You deserved to die for all you did to her."

"Especially for upsetting her grand schemes, for leaving her. But she didn't give up, did she, Richard? She followed me to St. Louis and decided to try again. If you were such a magnificent lover, why did she do that, hmmm?"

"You left her sobbing, you fucking bastard! You destroyed her pride! Tisha never really cried, not until that morning when you left her."

"And that's when you killed her. It wasn't thieves as Senator Soames believed, was it?"

"I . . . I asked her to come away with me, to forget you." An almost placid expression flashed across his face for an instant, then the dream dissolved into reality once more. "We could've gone abroad."

"But she refused, of course. Knowing Tish, not in the most gracious terms either," Samuel said dryly. "You quarreled over a gun and then you shot her."

"I didn't mean to! God, I didn't mean to kill her! It was an accident. When she died in my arms I thought of joining her. I reloaded the gun. I almost did it, but then I realized who was really at fault . . . the two of you who wrecked her life. And just killing you wasn't good enough. Too quick, too painless.

"You had to suffer for years just as I did. When I followed you to New Orleans and learned that you'd been forced to leave your doxy behind, my plan crystallized. I disposed of Claiborne's secretary, then secured the job for myself so I could intercept your correspondence.

"Oh, how I loved reading those impassioned letters you wrote one another, pouring out your hearts, you asking her if she was carrying your child." He looked down at Olivia. "And you begging him to come and claim it."

"It must have gotten complicated when I showed up in Claiborne's office," Samuel volunteered, breathing tightly as a steel band seemed to squeeze all the air from his lungs. How well Bullock's sadistic plan had worked!

"Once you nearly saw me coming out of a meeting in the Cabildo, but I slipped away. By then I was already prepared for this, the final act."

"He's a traitor, Samuel. He's been passing information from the governor's office to the British," Olivia said, twisting away just enough to reach the knife and close her fingers around the smooth wooden handle.

"And those same obliging British are going to hang you as a spy while your whore and her bastard watch you kick and struggle. Your face will turn black, you know?" he said conversationally, his calm once more restored.

"You're the one who'll hang, Bullock. There won't be a redcoat left in Louisiana after Jackson's men finish with them."

As they spoke the loud crashing of artillery continued to rumble from Roderick's Canal to the west of them.

"Jackson's pathetic Dirty Shirts will be cut to ribbons by British bayonet charges. They'll turn tail and run."

"By the sound of those rifles, they haven't yet. You're gambling everything on a British victory, aren't you?" Shelby replied with equal calm. *One of his men has David. I have to lure him into leaving the boy.* David, his son, whom he might never live to see.

Olivia saw what Samuel was doing, playing on Bullock's obsessions and his ego, all the while moving closer to make a desperate leap. But it was too risky—unless she evened the odds. Just as she clenched the knife and started to inch it from her pocket, a blast of artillery, no doubt wide of its mark, shook the house as it landed in the nearby woods. The windowpanes rattled. Then the front door burst open and a breathless man came running into the foyer.

"Sir, Sergeant Matthews reports that General Keane and General Pakenham are both dead. General Lambert's ordered retreat!"

Bullock emitted the snarl of a cornered animal and jammed the gun into Olivia's breast again. "Take Shelby to Lambert. See that he hangs!"

"No!" Olivia broke free of Bullock's punishing hold, driving the small blade into his thigh. He cursed in surprise, then struck the side of her face with his pistol in an attempt to subdue her. The British soldier started to level his musket on Samuel but the American was too quick for him, knocking it away. It discharged harmlessly into the carpet as it fell to the floor with a thud.

The two men exchanged swift desperate punches, moving together and circling so Bullock could not get a clear shot. Knocked to her knees behind him, Olivia struggled to clear her vision and overcome the buzzing pain in her temple. She still clutched the knife, trying to regain enough steadiness to lash out again at Bullock before he could shoot Samuel. But suddenly he moved away from her, dragging his leg, which oozed a slow trickle of blood.

She wobbled to her feet, her eyes darting between the no-holds-barred fistfight and Bullock. Instantly she knew what he planned. He was headed down the hall to David's room! Holding onto the wall for balance, she started after him. There could be no mistake this time. He was utterly mad. She veered into the study across the hall just as Bullock opened the door at the end of the long passageway.

Bullock motioned for the soldier standing by the child's bed to move aside as he raised his pistol and pointed it at the little boy huddled beneath the covers staring at him with wide blue eyes—Shelby's eyes.

"I want my mama," the boy said boldly, even though his thumb slipped into his mouth afterward.

The Englishman's eyes widened in shock as he realized what the American intended. "No, you can't—"

"Get out there and help Brady, you imbecile," Richard screamed, reaching down to yank the covers away from the boy who now froze, instinctively knowing terror. Somehow, even over the pounding of cannon, Bullock heard the click of a hammer. And that was the last thing he ever heard. The shot hit dead center, smashing through his spinal column and penetrating his heart. He dropped like a stone. Olivia lowered one smoking dueling pistol and raised the other, pointing it at the soldier's chest. "Step away from my son. I don't miss."

His Adam's apple bobbed and his face was ashen. Hands raised, he obeyed. "He was bloody crazy, m'am. I'd never hurt a child."

"The war's over. Your army's been beaten. They're retreating. I suggest you follow them," she said, ignoring David's cries, eager to get everyone out of his room. She pointed to the door with her pistol, motioning the soldier out into the hall where the sounds of fighting continued.

A second man had apparently joined the fray against Samuel, who was trading punches with him over the inert body of the first.

"Tell your friend it's over," Olivia said, prodding him in the back with her pistol after relieving him of his weapons.

Before he could speak, Shelby came in beneath his brawny opponent's swing and landed a sharp powerful punch to his stomach, doubling him over, then smashing his clasped hands across the fellow's neck as he crumpled. He seized the unfired pistols he had been forced to discard earlier and looked frantically toward the man advancing on him.

"Where are they? Where's my family?" he rasped out, not seeing Olivia behind the tall soldier.

"We're safe, Samuel. Bullock is dead. It's over," she said, standing clear of the soldier.

In the distance the cannonade and rifle fire had fallen silent. Down the hall a child's plaintive cry echoed softly. Shelby held his pistol steady on the Englishman while one of his companions stirred on the floor. As they regained consciousness, the American said, "Round up the others who came with you and get the hell out of here if you don't want to end up prisoners of war."

"Bullock's dead," the one by Olivia said to his companions.

"Let's go. Ain't bloody nothin' we can do 'ere," the first big brute Samuel had downed replied. "Give me a 'and with Toomey, mate."

Once Olivia lowered her pistol, her captive hurried over to do as he was bid. They dragged the third man out with them. Samuel and Olivia could hear them calling to the remnants of the detachment as they rode away.

He stood, bloody and battered, staring at his love with disbelief. "I'm afraid if I blink, you'll vanish," he said hoarsely.

"You're hurt," she whispered, hurrying across the distance separating them to touch his bloodied lip gently, affirming that he was real and alive and safe here in her arms. "Oh, Samuel, I can scarce take it in . . ."

He stroked her hair. "Neither can I . . . I have a son—David. Is he—"

"He's unharmed."

Knowing what she had done, he said, "I owe Micajah Johnstone the whole earth for teaching you to shoot."

Olivia nodded. "Come," she said, taking his hand in hers, "meet your son."

He followed her down the hallway like a dream walker, into the small room at the far end. Bullock's body lay sprawled in a pool of red at the foot of the child's small bed. Amazingly, David had fallen asleep now that the noises had at last abated. He lay on his stomach with his head turned facing them.

Swallowing painfully, Samuel looked down at a miniature replica of himself. Slowly, almost shyly, he reached out one large brown hand and stroked the boy's raven hair. "It's curly just like mine was when I was a boy."

"He has blue eyes, too," she said, her voice breaking.

"What must you have thought," he asked, "when I deserted you—all your letters to me unanswered?"

"I believed you had been killed on some dangerous mission," she replied simply.

She had believed in his loss even in the face of such overwhelming circumstances, alone and unwed in a strange city, carrying the child of a married man. "You trusted me and protected our son by faking a marriage to give him a name." He shook his head sadly, letting his hand drop away from David.

Olivia watched as his fists clenched on the wooden railing along the child's bed. She could feel his anguish. "You believed I really was married when the governor's letter came, didn't you?"

Her voice was soft, without accusation, yet it cut him to his very soul. "Yes. I'd spent months waiting for you to answer my letters. Then just after I learned I was free of Tish, I found out you'd supposedly wed a Spanish nobleman." He turned and looked into her fathomless green eyes with a guilt-stricken expression on his face. "I didn't believe in you, Livy. And I can never forgive myself."

Almost of its own volition, his hand touched her face,

stroking the cheek where Richard had left an ugly bruise which was beginning to darken the tender flesh. She pressed his hand against her cheek. "I forgive you, Samuel. I knew who you were and what you were when I fell in love with you. Life had given you little reason to trust anyone. The evidence against me was damning."

He shook his head. "No, it was my damnable pride—I'm only a soldier. You're an aristocrat and an heiress. I believed you'd choose a nobleman over me. Hell, I already had one rich, ambitious wife. I was afraid of another, even though I knew in my heart you were nothing like Tish."

Her chest tightened and she felt her pulse begin to race painfully. *We can't have come so far to lose each other now!* "I could have married a rich, aristocratic man, Samuel. I had offers. I didn't want them, even when I thought you were dead. But then I found out you were alive—last spring." His eyes met hers, startled, as she went on, "I have friends in Pensacola. They passed on the gossip about the 'Spanish Yankee' who outsmarted the British and escaped. I knew it was you and I hated you then for deserting us." Her eyes looked up imploringly then. "But I still couldn't stop loving you. In my heart of hearts I was glad you were alive."

"When I came to New Orleans I wanted to see you but I was afraid. They said you were a widow living in seclusion. I knew you were free . . . but I still couldn't gather the courage to come to you, Livy. Oh, Livy." He reached out and enfolded her in his arms. "I've been a fool, such a fool."

Through her tears she whispered against the scratchy wool of his uniform, "No more than I."

David awakened and looked up at his mother in the arms of a big dark-haired stranger. Although he knew it was not the bad man with yellow hair, he was still afraid, not understanding what had transpired. "Mama?" he said tentatively.

Olivia turned in Samuel's arms and reached out for the boy. "Come here, darling." She picked him up and pressed his head to her shoulder, shielding him from the bloody mess of Bullock's body.

Samuel looked into David's eyes and the primordial shock rocked him again. *His son.* "Let me have him. You're hurt," he said to Olivia as she winced when the child bumped her chin with his head as he wriggled.

She gave him over, saying, "David, this is someone you've waited a long time to meet."

As Samuel carried his son out of the room, the bloodshed and hatred of the past fell away from them all. Outside the fog lifted and clear winter sunshine beamed a benediction through the open front door.

✎ *Chapter 28* ✎

Sounds of jubilation echoed up from Chartre Street as the citizens and soldiers of New Orleans celebrated their incredible victory. The British invaders had been utterly vanquished before the combined firepower of Baratarian artillery and Kentucky long rifles, suffering nearly fifteen hundred casualties to a scant fifty on the American side. Jackson was paraded through the streets as the hero of the hour along with the Laffite brothers and the leaders of the intrepid Tennessee and Kentucky militias. The city was delirious as church bells pealed out the glorious tidings.

But all was quiet upstairs in the Durand city house where Samuel and Olivia had taken refuge after he reported Bullock's treachery and death to the general and an amazed Governor Claiborne. David slept peacefully in the room next door with the maid Florine watching over him.

In the parlor a warm fire crackled on the hearth, taking away the chill of January air. Samuel filled two crystal goblets with Madeira and brought one to Olivia, who stood warming her hands by the flames. The fire reflected on her hair, making it blaze in splendor as it fell down her back. Her slender figure, dressed in softly flowing green muslin, was outlined in the light. His eyes traced the soft swell of breasts, the curve of hips, then moved up to her patrician face, so proud and lovely in profile. He ached with wanting her.

Silently he handed her the glass and she took it. Their gazes locked over the rims. Neither one drank. Finally he said, "I just received a letter from my sister. Claiborne's new clerk brought it to me when I reported to Jackson. The Santa Fe trade is flourishing. Santiago's building another warehouse in St. Louis. He wants me to live there and run the American end of the business."

"What about the army?" she asked hesitantly, half-afraid to dare hope his words indicated what she prayed they did.

"The war's over. I've read the dispatches from Jemmy. It's only a matter of time until the negotiations in Ghent are worked out—if they haven't been already. I'm resigning my commission as soon as I make a final report personally to the president."

She took a sip of wine to fortify her courage, then said, "I didn't tell you how afraid I was when I first learned you were in New Orleans, afraid you'd come to take David away from me."

Her words stung him. "I can understand why you'd feel that way, Livy, but I would never have done that even if I'd known about him."

"Now you do and I know you love him." *Do you love me, Samuel?*

He set down his glass on the Pembroke table and took hers, placing it beside his. "Yes, I love him. Thank you for our son, Livy," he said gravely, then hesitated, combing his fingers through his shaggy hair, searching for the right words. "I've done you grievous wrong, Livy, over and over. You've never done anything but good to me in return. I'm no bargain, just an ex-soldier with a modest income, living in a frontier town that's rough and small compared to all of this. I have no right to ask—"

"Damn you, Samuel Sheridan Shelby! I've had enough of your guilt and your stiff-necked Virginia pride to boot! If you don't love me enough to marry me, then I'll just take David upriver to his Grandpa Micajah to raise. And damn the Durand fortune, too! It can rot for all I care. I've scarce spent a sou of it in the past three years and I don't plan to start now."

She was spitting mad. Her green eyes blazed darkly and that small pink mouth . . . oh lord, that mouth. Smiling tenderly, he cupped her face with his hands and centered his own over it, murmuring against her lips as he brushed them with his, "What I've been trying to work up to, Madam Obregón, is a clumsy proposal of marriage. But you, with your usual fiery temper, have beaten me to it. Yes, I will marry you. Of course, I will! I love you more than life."

Olivia threw her arms around him with a cry of pure joy. "I've waited so many years to hear that! We can go to the cathedral in the morning. Father Dubourg can interrupt his work on the great Te Deum he's planning long enough to perform a simple marriage."

He pulled her closer to his body, holding her tightly as he murmured, "Tomorrow we get married, but tonight . . . I've waited three years for this, Livy."

She held tight as he swung her up into his arms and carried her from the sitting room into the bedroom beyond, placing her on the high tester bed, then sitting down beside her. When she started to slip her gown off, he stopped her with gentle hands.

"Let me be your ladies maid." With that he reached down and slipped her dainty kid shoes from her feet, then peeled her silk stockings from those deliciously long slender legs. Raining soft kisses on her shoulders and throat as he pulled her up, he attacked the gown next. "It's been years since I've worked these accursed things," he murmured, unfastening the stubborn hooks holding together the frothy concoction of dark green muslin.

When he slid it off her and reached for the lacy camisole, her arms came up, covering her breasts. "Samuel . . . I . . . I don't want you to be disappointed," she said softly.

He groaned. "If you want to wait until we're married, I'll understand, Livy." *It damn well may kill me, but I'll understand.*

She shook her head. "No, I don't want to wait. It's just . . ."

"What, love?" He tipped up her chin and gazed into those liquid emerald eyes, dark mysterious gypsy eyes.

"I gained so much weight when I was carrying David. My body isn't the same."

He smiled, letting his fingertips graze along the edge of the lace covering her breasts. "So I can see." Then he cupped the heavy globes as his lips brushed the tops, searching for the hard nubby points of her nipples through the sheer lace. "You're perfect to me, no matter what," he said hoarsely, peeling the camisole down to suckle one breast, then the other.

Olivia moaned and dug her fingers into his heavy black hair, pressing him closer. She accommodated him as he finished stripping her of the rest of her lacy undergarments. When he lay her back and sat up to study her from head to toe, she felt a flush of shyness. Did he find her thicker? Stretched? Less attractive?

"You're even more beautiful than before. I left a girl. I came back to a woman." He worshipped her with his eyes and his hands, caressing and kissing her. Then he reached down to pull off his boots.

"Now you must let me be your valet," she said, sliding to

the edge of the bed and slipping to the floor. When she turned her rounded buttocks to him, straddling his leg to tug off a boot, she could hear his strangled gasp of desire.

"Hurry," was all he could choke out as his hands caressed the smoothness of her bottom and skimmed inside her pale thighs.

Olivia turned to find he'd already pulled his tunic off while she was finishing his boots and hose. When he stood up, she knelt to unbutton his fly. He fisted his hands to hold himself under control when she freed his aching staff and tugged his breeches down his legs.

Kicking them away, he reached for her and brought her up into his arms. "I . . . will . . . try to go slow, Livy . . . to make it good for you . . . but it's been so long . . . I don't know if I can."

Her heart turned over. "How long?"

He looked into her eyes and was lost. "A moonlit night on the Mississippi in December of 1811," he confessed.

She wet her lips. "Samuel, a certain Spaniard's wife described your . . . your body in great detail . . . she said it made her swoon with delight."

Shelby looked puzzled, but then chuckled bitterly. "Swoon, huh. Well, she must have had strange tastes. When the British caught me, they turned me over to the Spanish who decided to have a little sport with me . . . to humiliate me, soften me up. Hell, they stripped me and put me on public display in a cage . . . along with two monkeys. We drew some very large crowds."

Olivia was torn by guilt and horror. "My darling, I'm so very, very sorry. Please forgive . . ."

Samuel interrupted, grinning. "So, my little cat was jealous." He laughed. "I like that . . . very much . . . but you have no cause. In all those accursed three long years, no cause at all. But I must admit after several days in that cage one of the monkeys was beginning to look somewhat attractive."

"Samuel! You wretch!"

"Oh, I've been very, very wretched for a long time."

Olivia laughed in joyous relief. There had been no other woman for him since he left her. "No wonder you were furious to hear about Rafael Obregón," she said with a low wicked chuckle that ended on a sob. "Oh, Samuel, we've lost three years but now we have everything back and all the rest of our lives together."

He pulled her onto the bed beside him, then rolled on top of her. Looking down into her eyes, he slowly slid into the welcoming warmth of her body. "Let's not waste another minute of it," he whispered hoarsely as he struggled to remain still, willing himself not to spill his seed before he had brought her along with him.

Olivia held him buried deep within her, not moving, understanding his struggle, thrilled by how deeply he still desired her, how splendidly they still fit together after so long a separation. When he began to move in long slow strokes, she accommodated his gentle rhythm, tightening her legs around his hips, arching up to meet each thrust. She, too, had been without this since their last night together on the Mississippi.

Gradually as their hands caressed and their mouths tasted of each other and kissed, the pace of their mating began to increase until soon they were in a frenzy, bucking and rolling together. Sweat poured off them in the cool night air. Her choked gasps and sobs of pleasure mixed with his muttered endearments and curses, which were endearments, too. At last when she felt the crest shimmering over her like a crystal cloth, she cried out and arched high, her nails digging into his hard buttocks as he rammed into her fast and furious, crying out exultantly as he joined her in the long denied surfeit.

They trembled in the aftermath as he collapsed on top of her, cradling her in his arms while she clung to him. Then at last, he chuckled, nuzzling her ear. "That just might start another earthquake right here on the delta."

"I thought I felt the earth move, didn't you? Say, did you ever think, maybe we started the quake in 1811?" she murmured, then looked into his eyes and asked, "How long will it take us to travel upriver to St. Louis?"

He shrugged. "A week if we can get a berth on a steamer, a month by keelboat."

"Let's take the keelboat, Samuel," she whispered conspiratorially.

"Then let's pray we don't start another earthquake," Samuel whispered back.

"She sure does cry a lot, Grandpa," David said as Father Louie poured cool baptismal water on the forehead of Elizabeth Louise Shelby.

Micajah Johnstone chuckled at the boy perched on his shoulder. "Wal now," he whispered, "she's jist a leetle mite, not all growed up like yew. Yew'll have ta learn her."

"Like you did me?" the boy asked, receiving an affectionate nod.

They both looked down on the scene around them from the vantage point of Micajah's considerable height. The giant frontiersman towered over David's father as well as the other tall men in the assembly, the baby's godfather, Santiago Quinn, and his dark and mysterious half-caste brother, Joaquim. During the ceremony little Liza Shelby's godmothers, Elise Quinn and Louise Freul had taken turns holding her while Olivia and Samuel beamed their approval.

Father Louie completed the prayers and the group in the small chapel at Fort St. Francoise filed out into the bright autumn sunshine, laughing and talking. Louise Freul reluctantly handed the now quieted baby back to Elise, whose daughter, Orlena, and niece, Aurelia, hovered near, eager for a chance to hold the newest member of their family.

"Never fret, my dear, you'll have plenty of chances to spoil your namesake," Albert Freul said to his sister as she watched little Elizabeth Louise adoringly.

"So many children in your husband's family," Louise said to Olivia, watching as Elise bent down to lace her six-year-old son Samuel's boot, which had come untied while the three tall dark sons of Orlena and Joaquim Quinn talked with their father and Uncle Santiago, who was holding his two-year-old son, Elkhanah.

"I was delighted that Elise and Santiago were able to convince his brother Joaquim's family to come all the way from Santa Fe," Olivia said. "It's so good to have all the cousins together. Samuel and I visited with Joaquim and his family when we were in New Mexico last winter. Then I understood why Elise named her daughter after Orlena—just as I named mine after you and her. It means a great deal to me that you and Albert made the long journey from New Orleans all the way up the Missouri to attend the christening," she said, fondly squeezing the elderly doctor and his sister's hands.

"We would not have missed it for anything," Louise replied, smiling as Micajah Johnstone approached them.

"I see Mr. Johnstone has his handsome grandson in tow," Louise said, admiring Micajah, who had cleaned up remarkably for the occasion, even having his shaggy hair barbered and his beard neatly trimmed.

"Micajah had to explain to David what Father Louie was doing. After all, he is David's godfather as well as his grandpa and he takes both roles very seriously," Olivia replied, noting her older friend's interest in the giant frontiersman. "Have all of you been formally introduced?" she inquired of Dr. Freul and his sister. *What a striking couple they'd make,* she thought as she presented her beloved mentor to Louise Freul.

Micajah startled her by making a courtly bow over Louise's hand as the doctor stood by, amused. David turned up his nose in the manner peculiar to small boys. "Mushy stuff," he said, grimacing at Dr. Freul, who laughed.

"Yew shore are a rare sight, mad'mozel," Johnstone said, looking into Louise's dark eyes. "Hit ain't often a feller my size meets up with a female he kin look in th' eyes without gettin' a crick in his neck. Yore a right handsome lady."

Louise's face pinkened as if she were a schoolgirl, but her Gallic common sense remained in place as she replied, "In Creole society I have always been considered a bit over long, Mr. Johnstone."

"Why, thet's jist 'cause them Cree-ols 'er sech leetle-bitty fellers. Thet heavy air down south plumb stunts thar growth. Yore a Missouri-sized woman, an' from whut my Sparky tells me, yew got a heart as big as all Loosiana."

Olivia and Dr. Freul beamed in approval as the tall couple strolled across the compound, headed for the open gate of the fort.

Samuel approached his wife and whispered, "I couldn't help noticing the, er, interest Micajah and Louise seem to have in each other."

"It looks as if Father Louie might have another marriage

to perform," she replied, her lips bowed into a mischievous smile.

He squeezed her hand affectionately and brought it to his lips. "Micajah will be a lucky man if it works out as well as ours."

"Aw, more mushy stuff," David said with a sigh, looking from his father to his mother.

❦ *Author's Note* ❦

There is something mystical about big rivers. Perhaps I feel this way because I grew up at the confluence of the Missouri and Mississippi in St. Louis. After a twenty-five-year exile, I recently returned home and the idea of setting a story on the rivers caught my imagination.

My associate Carol J. Reynard and I had a great deal of assistance on this book, which became the most sweeping saga of the twenty we've produced to date. We would like to express our appreciation to the Public Libraries of St. Louis City and County for getting us started, and to the Mercantile Library and its tireless reference director, Charles Brown, master of arcane information on old St. Louis and New Orleans. For arming our protagonists and their foes, we are once more indebted to Dr. Carmine V. DelliQuadri, Jr., D. O., weapons expert extraordinaire, and to my husband, Jim, who gave "Sparky" her shooting lessons, as well as devoting countless hours to copyediting the text.

The Trans-Mississippi West at the opening of the nineteenth century was a microcosm for the American mythos. All the players shaping modern American history were in the great river basin in that pregnant year of 1811: dispossessed Native Americans, fighting to retain their culture and their land; intrepid French voyageurs, fearlessly braving the far reaches of the Upper Missouri in search of beaver and riches; Spanish soldiers, manning their isolated outposts against the American deluge; British agents provocateur, promising friendship and providing weapons to the restive tribes along the rivers; and squirrel-tough Appalachian frontiersmen, bringing their families and their plows to new and fertile soil.

Nature itself reflected the cataclysmic winds of change. Eighteen-eleven was the year of the great earthquake at New Madrid, Missouri, the most violent quake in recorded history on the North American continent. The Mississippi's channel was completely redrawn and the topography of half a dozen states significantly altered. Miraculously, little life was lost owing to the sparcity of population. Although there is some disagreement among geologists, diarists at the scene said the river ran backward for a brief period of time as I described in this story. The best single compendium of eyewitness accounts I found was by James Lal Penick, Jr., *The New Madrid Earthquake.*

At the opening of the nineteenth century, the Napoleonic wars eventually embroiled the fledgling American republic in its first genuinely international conflict. Both England and her Spanish allies wanted to halt the steady westward expansion of the United States. They made common cause with Native Americans, supplying them with weapons and recruiting them to serve under European commanders. My secret agents Samuel Shelby and Stuart Pardee are fictitious, but in real life such men did exist on both sides. The Osage, gatekeepers of the Great Plains, were the pivotal tribe in the Trans-Mississippi West. The most numerous and powerful group, they were firmly in the American camp. A successful British bid to undermine this alliance could have materially changed the outcome of the war. Ironically, the men most responsible for holding Osage loyal to the United States were a descendant of New Orleans Creoles, Pierre Chouteau, and a renegade Spaniard, Manual Lisa. Both these early St. Louisans had become American by default when Thomas Jefferson made the greatest real estate deal in history, the Louisiana Purchase.

The real losers in the War of 1812 were not European but Native American. Tecumseh's dream of an independent Indian state free from white encroachment was doomed to failure. In spite of Osage loyalty to the United States, they suffered the same fate as all the other tribes. In researching Native American life and politics during this critical era, I used John Joseph Mathews's, *The Osages;* William T. Hagen's, *The Sac and Fox Indians;* and Patrick Brophy's *Osage Autumn.* The seminal reference work remains *The Imperial Osage* by Gilbert C. Din and Abraham P. Nasatir.

Micajah Johnstone was a joy to create. Although fictional, he epitomized the American trailblazer, a hearty frontiersman who braved everything from grizzlies to geysers in pursuit of his dream. *Wilderness,* a poetic epic about Hugh Glass and John Colter, written by Roger Zelazny and Gerald Hausman, provided the inspiration for his character, as well as some of the improbable but true adventures which Samuel and Olivia experience. Other splendid resources that helped me weave the rich tapestry of frontier life were Thomas James's *Three Years Among the Indians and Mexicans;* Stanley Vestal's *The Missouri;* Hiram Martin Chittenden's *American Fur Trade of the Far West;* and the superb pictorial, *The Trailblazers* in the Time-Life Old West Series, text by Bil Gilbert. As Micajah might have said, "Yew fellers is sharp as a Osage plantin' stick in early spring."

Carol and I thought Samuel Shelby was hero material when I first created him as the heroine's idealistic younger brother in *White Apache's Woman.* Reader mail confirmed our opinion, so we began to brainstorm about how we could give him his own story. We knew he would follow in Elise's footsteps and become a spy. Conveniently, the War of 1812 rolled around just when we needed it. Samuel certainly had his work cut out for him: If the various tribes up and down the Mississippi river basin had united against the Americans, and if Pakenham and Cochrane had planned their invasion of New Orleans with greater care, the Treaty of Ghent might well have opened a British corridor stretching from Canada to the Gulf, ending our westward expansion.

The real life men and women who prevented this from happening are every bit as fascinating as those any writer could imagine. The Madisons and James Monroe are portrayed much as history records them, as are the mysterious and romantic Baratarians. No book set during this era could overlook the Battle of New Orleans and its general. Andrew Jackson can be hero or villain, depending on whose accounts you choose to use or whose shoes you stand in. Jackson was an inspired backwoods militia leader and stump politician—a real man of the people—providing, of course, your people did not happen to be Native Americans. In any interpretation he still remains larger than life.

Since its rescue from obscurity by revisionist historians, the War of 1812 has become a popular subject. *Dolley Madison: Her Life and Times* by Elswyth Thane is a rich and sensitive account of her remarkable life. *The Expansionists of 1812* by Julius W. Pratt, *The United States and the Disruption of the Spanish Empire* by Charles C. Griffin and *The Scorching of Washington* by Alan Lloyd provided excellent background material. *The Battle of New Orleans* by Zachary F. Smith gives a detailed account of the American triumph. Even better is the wry and insightful commentary of John R.

Elting in *Amateurs, to Arms!,* which exposes not only the government's bungling of the war effort, but also Jackson's rather dilatory performance enroute to accidental glory. *The Baratarians and the Battle of New Orleans* by Jane Lucas De Grummond gives excellent evidence supporting the Laffites' contributions.

Many readers may recognize "old friends" from two previous books, *White Apache's Woman* and *Night Wind's Woman.* Carol and I found it difficult to bring the saga to a conclusion in *Deep as the Rivers.* I hope we have provided the Quinns and the Shelbys all the happy endings they deserve. For a copy of our newsletter or to let us know if you enjoyed Samuel and Olivia's story, please send a stamped, self-addressed envelope for replies to:

Shirl Henke
P. O. Box 72
Adrian, MI 49221

Mercedes Alvarado was a half-English, half-Spanish heiress who had survived the desertion of her husband, the scorn of his aristocratic family and the ravages of a civil war. Now she was holding together a magnificent estate until her soldier husband returned to claim it...and her.

Nicholas Fortune was a war-weary mercenary who had been raised in a New Orleans bordello, never belonging to any place or anyone. His only loyalty had been to himself until, amid the flames of revolution, he took another man's identity...and his wife.

The dark and dangerous man who rode home to Mercedes touched her soul with fiery need. But was he her husband...or a stranger with her husband's face?

Bride of Fortune

by bestselling award-winning author
Shirl Henke

"Bride of Fortune is Shirl at her best." —*Romantic Times*

KAT MARTIN

Award-winning author of *Creole Fires*

GYPSY LORD
_____ 92878-5 $5.99 U.S./$6.99 Can.

SWEET VENGEANCE
_____ 95095-0 $6.50 U.S./$8.50 Can.

BOLD ANGEL
_____ 95303-8 $5.99 U.S./$6.99 Can.

DEVIL'S PRIZE
_____ 95478-6 $5.99 U.S./$6.99 Can.

MIDNIGHT RIDER
_____ 95774-2 $5.99 U.S./$6.99 Can.

Against the backdrop of an elegant Cornwall mansion before World War II and a vast continent-spanning canvas during the turbulent war years, Rosamunde Pilcher's most eagerly-awaited novel is the story of an extraordinary young woman's coming of age, coming to grips with love and sadness, and in every sense of the term, coming home...

Rosamunde Pilcher

The #1 *New York Times* Bestselling Author of *The Shell Seekers* and *September*

COMING HOME

"Rosamunde Pilcher's most satisfying story since *The Shell Seekers*."

—*Chicago Tribune*

"Captivating...The best sort of book to come home to...Readers will undoubtedly hope Pilcher comes home to the typewriter again soon."

—*New York Daily News*

COMING HOME
Rosamunde Pilcher
_____ 95812-9 $7.99 U.S./$9.99 CAN.